FREE RANGE PROTOCOL

TALES OF THE TSCHAAA INFESTATION

MARSHALL MILLER

Blue Forge Press

Port Orchard ✿ Washington

Blue Forge Press
7419 Ebbert Drive Southeast
Port Orchard, Washington 98367
360.550.2071 ph.txt

DEDICATION

I dedicate this book to my loving wife and my four-legged family, Benjamin, Cinnamon, Jasmine, and Lancer. Without their support, understanding, and love, this new edition would never have happened.

ACKNOWLEDGEMENTS

I wish to thank all my friends at Kitsap Literary Artists and Writers for their support and assistance finding the correct mix of writing, publishing, and promotions. Without their knowledge and advice, I would still be stumbling in the dark. Also, I must give kudos to my publisher, Blue Forge Press, who—in the form of the DiMarco Family—helped me find and sustain my muse.

Of course my friend Greg Brashear—who not only helps me keep my cardio rate up, so my heart does not explode—but also aided in reading my 'stuff' and letting me know if it rang a bell or two. He also helped with the 'badass marine' characters. Every book needs a 'badass' or two in it to keep the readers from being bored. Semper Fi, Greg.

Also, Darryl Small, actor, writer, businessman, filmmaker and friend, needs a shout out. After all, without him, 'VILE SMUT' would have never happened.

I hope everyone who reads these stories will want more in the Tschaaa Universe.

Muchisimo gracias!

TABLE OF CONTENTS

Free Range Protocol

Tales of the Tschaaa Infestation

Marshall Miller

PROLOGUE

This is the history of the coming of the Tschaaa, the heroes and villains it produced, and the Great Compromise, which has allowed two species of apex predators to exist together in relative harmony.

Records of the coming of the Tschaaa appear in various places and have been touched by many hands. Their appearance was startling, as most unexpected arrivals are. People of the Earth had become accustomed to the usual sources of mutual opposition. In fact, as the 21st century proceeded, a certain inertia had set in. This may explain why some renegade groups rejoiced and aided the Tschaaa when they came. Some even attributed religious connotations to the invading forces. After all, they *did* come from the skies. Still others looked to the new regime of the World Order as a chance to obtain personal power and profit. The best, however, valuing their freedom above all else, escaped to the Unoccupied States and the other areas where the occupation had not extended its tentacles. They could retain the best of what the human race had ever produced and over time mount a counter attack.

Not everyone who acted as surrogate for the Tschaaa was evil. These individuals began to realize that every species has its own particular virtues. As time went on, the Tschaaa appeared to be less alien, and merely different. In fact, the human race began at this period to separate into its component parts, much as a prism separates the beams of light. Some scholars even suggested that, had the Tschaaa not shown up when they did, a final battle amongst us might have extinguished the human race altogether. Not that the beginning was any less horrifying. To all of those who disappeared and had family members who survived, but whose stories will never be told, the invasion was an unparalleled disaster, coming upon us like a thief in the night.

This history is not meant to vindicate the actions of the aliens to my readers, as I myself am a human being. But I ask all of my readers to recognize that although Shakespeare was correct when he wrote "There are more things on heaven and earth..." he was aware of only the ills of the human heart. However, he may have also been prophetic in hinting at what lay beyond in the vast abysses of space.

Royal Princess Akiko
Free Japanese Royal Family
This twenty-fifth day of December, 2053

PHENOMENA

THE FOLLOWING PAPER IS PRESENTED FOR SUBMISSION TO THE AMERICAN SOCIETY OF ASTROPHYSICISTS BY PROF JAMES L. STEVENS, NEW MEXICO ASTROPHYSICAL INSTITUTE.

TITLE: SOME ANOMOLIES IN THE PERTURBATIONS IN THE ORBIT DIFFERENTIALS OF ASTEROID 18666 AS IT ENTERED AND TRAVERSES THE SOLAR SYSTEM.

ABSTRACT:

This paper explores potential causes for the observed behavior of Asteroid 18666 between the dates of January 1st, January 31st, and February 28th, 2026. Strange phenomena were noted that could not be explained by the usual supposition of inaccurate observation or equipment distortions. Inquiries were made as to the possible effects of dark matter fields on the object in question as well. Consideration on the effects of the known planetoids, planets, asteroids, and other space objects were examined.

Simulations were conducted and still yielded negative results. No specific conclusions could be drawn as to the reasons of these unusual observations. Actions and movements are out of sync with current knowledge of the workings of the physics of objects passing through the solar system.

John C. Bodinky, Professor Emeritus, of the New Mexico Astrophysical Institute skipped down to the conclusions of the draft submission once again to insure he had read them correctly. He then cursed.

"What in holy hell is Jim trying to do?" he muttered to himself. He and Jim Stevens went way back in academia. In fact, Jim had married John's baby sister Suzy and they were expecting their first child. Between the two men, John had always been the one more politically astute . He was always better at figuring out which way the academic winds were blowing. He always knew what *not* to say to piss off, first the University and now the Institute Administration, not to mention those with money.

Thus, he was now the Head of the Science Department at the New Mexico Astrophysical Institute, a nice sounding name for a foundation that completed basic research, as well as provided advanced education for emerging young scientists. Under John's apt leadership, both government and private funding had greatly increased. More than one endowment had been received over the last year, because the estate of a local businessman or some self-made millionaire had wanted to feel like they had contributed to the scientific process.

John had become quite adept at dodging controversy and seeking consensus.

Thus, this draft submission of Jim's for the Foundation's journal was immediately unsettling, especially the initial conclusions. John could just hear some large contributor, after reading this article in the journal, or on the Foundation website, questioning if somehow one had lost their mind. Or, maybe asking if they were experimenting with some new type of marijuana on a staff wide basis.

John went to his computer and immediately composed a

terse email to contact him ASAP. He had to nip this in the bud before things became too weird.

It was still surprising when, only two minutes later, John's Administrative Assistant (read: attractive secretary-with-benefits) buzzed him and said that Jim was on the telephone.

"Jim, how are you."

"Just fine John. I…"

"And how is my baby sister? Does she look like she swallowed a basketball yet?" John always tried to make some joke, but half the time they came off weird or out of place. Stand-up comedian material he was not.

"She is doing just fine, John. She's still just as beautiful as the day I married her." John tried to extend the conversation, but Jim cut to the chase.

"I know you want to talk to me about my submission, my paper."

John sighed. He was hoping to slide into it a bit slowly, trying not to become adversarial straight off. No such luck. "You could always read me, my friend. Why don't you come over to my office, and we can discuss it."

"I'll be right over."

John knew this was going to be a pain in the posterior. Jim was a slender, red-headed dynamo who had the energy of any three people. It took just minutes for Jim to hotfoot from his office to John's. Jim came in, plopping himself down into the most comfortable chair in the office.

"So, shoot, John."

"Jim, I read your submission and…"

"Astounding what I found, isn't it?" Jim broke in. "I didn't realize what I had really found until I really crunched the numbers…"

John recognized Jim was in one of his periods of bubbling enthusiasm, like a young boy who had just found a new puppy, telling his mother how great it was and could he keep it?

"I crunched the numbers and *boom*! There it was. Smacking

me right in the old snot locker. Well, I can tell you..."

"Jim..."

"...I checked and rechecked, thinking maybe I had too much coffee, or Susie's pregnancy was distracting me, making me..."

"Jim..."

"But, *boom*, there it was again! Something was happening that was completely out of the ordinary, was new to the extent..."

"Jim..."

"It's going to make everyone sit up and notice..."

"Damnit, *Jim! Stop!* Be quiet for a moment. Let *me* get a word in edgewise."

Jim paused mid-sentence. John was one of the few people who could get Jim to stop and smell the proverbial flowers when he was in the midst of one of his scientific rants.

"Sorry," Jim said a bit sheepish. "It's just that this is so new, and so profound..."

"Okay, okay. I know how excited you are. But we have to take this one step at a time."

"Once I publish this in the Foundation periodical, and put it up on the website, we'll really be on the map, John. You think we get a lot of outside notice now, just wait..."

"No," said John.

"Wha...?"

"I said, No. N. O. *No.*"

"You mean no, as in no to publishing my findings, or..."

"I mean 'no' in *not* publishing your conclusions, which seemed to be a big leap from the observations you claim to have seen, from your calculations. So, let's start from your calculations. Just how many times did you check you figures, calculations, assuming all you observations and measurements were correct?"

Jim flushed a bit. "You're going to question what I have observed in through the telescopes? You *know* my reputation for accurate and precise observations."

"Didn't I just say I was going to assume you saw what you said you saw, Jim? Now, back to my question, how many times did you recheck your calculations?"

"I did three rechecks myself, John. I ran them through the program I designed that everyone here uses. *And*, then I had my best grad student do a manual, line by line, check. The young lady is a wiz catching any erroneous formulations, old fashioned math mistakes and poor calculating. They all checked out again." Jim snorted. "Why all this, this concern, agitation over my work? You know the standards I set for myself and my grad students."

John pursed his lips. How to explain this without having his friend and brother-in-law go storming out of here and doing something stupid.

"To put it bluntly, it's the conclusions you reach based on your observations. Specifically when you state that, on the one hand, there is no standard reason for the anomalies in the perturbations in the movement of this specific celestial object. Then you jump into several what I consider as being wild theories as to why the asteroid is moving and behaving the way it is, as it heads out of the solar system." John pulled out Jim's work. "To wit. Here, I quote, 'One very possible reason behind the movement of Asteroid 18666 outside of the range of standard deviations is the possibility of an unknown outside agency is affecting the course of the Asteroid. This would explain the minute course corrections, similar to those done by a yacht as it nears the harbor berth.' *Then...*" John flipped to another page.

"Then you throw this comment into the mix. Quote: 'There is also the possibility that large or dense objects hidden from our view *behind the asteroid* could also be providing just enough gravitational effects that would cause the object to shift its course, a little at a time.'"

John threw the submission onto his desk.

"What *are* you getting at? Space aliens? Unknown objects

hidden behind the Asteroid so dense as to be a new class of matter? Hidden and moving black holes? What?" Now it was John's turn to have a flushed face. He ran his hand through his thinning brown hair, and heard his paunch gurgle.

Jim paused, looked with concern at his friend, boss and relative.

"You read that stuff into all that, John? All I was doing was brainstorming a bit."

"A bit? Jim, it sounds like you're trying to throw everything but the kitchen sink into the mix."

John paused, began drumming his fingers on the table.

"You observed these, anomalies, using both the conventional, as well as a radio telescope, correct?"

"Of course! You know I always use all the tools available."

John stopped drumming his fingers, then yanked his right hand bottom draw open, and pulled out a very uncharacteristic bottle of bourbon out, with two glasses. He poured a shot in each as Jim looked on, a bit surprised.

"Shut the door, will you Jim." His friend jumped up and complied, then began talking again.

"Look. John. I know this is weird. This asteroid was seen by complete chance as it came into our solar systems orbital plane. An amateur astronomer just happened to see it as it seems headed directly to Earth's orbital sphere, past Mars. All of the analysis of its trajectory points to it coming from the edge of the known solar system, from those random hunks of material way out there that kind of orbit our system."

Jim took a sip of his drink. "Which makes its current trajectory even more fascinating, strange. Did something bump it out from all the other left over planetary stuff? Or is it an object that has a huge orbit that which is only now resulting in it coming in at us? Then, of course, there are the small, mini almost seemingly purposeful course corrections outside the effects of the other planetary bodies."

John held up his hand. "Please, stop right there. We are back to the same problems. Your brainstorming."

John took a substantial swig of his scotch before continuing.

"Now, Jim, let me explain something. First, a little history lesson. Do you remember the Hale-Bopp Comet in the 1990s?"

"Kinda. I was just a kid, but I remember it was bright enough to see during the day, including a long tail. You're not that much older than I am, what do you remember?"

"Okay. Well, remembering may be a bad term. But let me tell you the story. The Hale-Bopp Comet entered our solar system, and it was a big deal. It seemed to have had a very large orbit around our sun, larger than Halley's Comet, and it came in off of the planetary orbital plane like most comets. Because it was bright and going to pass close enough to the Earth to be easily observed, was bright, it immediately got a lot of people's attention."

"Well, some nimrods on talk radio began to spin some stories about it not being a real comet, that there was something hidden in its tail, that a spacecraft was shadowing it, or it was a spacecraft."

Jim smirked. "So? There are always nut jobs on talk radio."

John gave him a hard look. "Well, some people with PhD after their names were dragged into pontificating about it. Later on, it was discovered that a certain cult-like group that who adopted the name Heaven's Gate decided that the comet was their sign of redemption by aliens, the second coming. Hell, it all depends whom you talk to. But what is remembered is that a large group of them, after the males castrated themselves, committed ritual suicide at their basic mini compound in California. They were all discovered in their beds, with almost matching running shoes, in these white almost uniform clothes."

Jim frowned. "What has that got to do with me?"

"Anyone of those PhDs who were dragged into this were remembered along the lines of 'Oh, yeah. You were connected to that comet which all those people killed themselves over.

What did *you* say about it?' See what I'm getting at?"

"Not...really."

"Jim, you can be so dense sometimes. Think about it. You alluding to possible 'unknown agencies' affecting the path of Asteroid 18666. What do you think is going to happen when someone grabs onto that idea. Next will come 'Professor Stevens says unknown agencies, possibly alien in nature, affecting Asteroid's path."

"That's not what I said!"

"Close enough to leave yourself open to allegations and ridicule. And then to add the crap about possible objects hidden behind the asteroid affecting its path? That's what a couple of nut jobs started spreading about Hale-Bopp. That there was something hidden behind it, maybe a starship, in its tail."

"John, you know that's not what I meant."

"Maybe. But *that* is how it comes across."

The two men sat silent, sipping their bourbon, the high end kind, not the cheap stuff.

Finally, Jim spoke. "So, what do I get to publish?"

John sighed a bit. "You publish the basic findings, *after* we tone down the adjectives a bit. But you also publish in some small independent journal. No conclusions. Just facts."

John knew the subdued Jim was signaling that his feelings and ego were hurt. There were times when John wished Jim did not work for him. He was a good friend. Hell, John introduced his baby sister to him. So, having to sometimes step on his head bothered him.

"Look it, Jim. I know you think this is all about the Institute. But it's also about you, your wife and soon your child. Do you want to be the subject of tabloids, or have people who wear caps made out of aluminum foil bugging you all the time? Bugging you and your family?"

"I guess you're right, John. It just that it's so damned interesting."

"That enthusiasm is what makes you a good scientist. A

better one than me. Nope, no protests, you know what I say is true."

John refilled the glasses. "But I am a good administrator. I have to worry about your funding, my funding, everyone's funding. Not to mention the NSA is snooping around in everything, just looking to make some project classified, under their control."

Jim let out a long sigh. "You're right, damnit. Once again, you keep me from hurting myself. But it will be published, what I found, right? We'll just let someone else make the correct connections."

John raised his glass. "A toast, my friend. To the Professor Stevens' paper on the Asteroid 18666 and its odd ride through the solar system."

"I'll drink to that, John. And to your new nephew."

"Nephew? You guys cheated and found out?"

"Yes. And he's going to be named John, after his uncle, his dad's best friend."

"You're going to make me tear up, buddy."

"Pour us another round, John. We might as well make this a real celebration."

A half hour later, John began to try and sober up. If he went home, half in the bag Joanie, his wife, would give him her signature glacier stare. His administrative assistant, Stephanie, knocked on the door, and came in.

"Anything else, Professor?" Stephanie was a knock out blonde with curves in all the right places. She gave him a slight pouting smile that she knew drove him to distraction.

"Yeah, my dear. Shut the door. There. Now, come over here and show me that garter belt, nylons and panties I bought. I want to see how well they fit you." Stephanie giggled, walked over and began to hike her skirt. Nothing like good old office politics, John thought, to get his juices flowing.

A month later, the paper was published, with Professor John

C. Bodinky listed as editor, Professor John L. Stevens as author and researcher. Staff members at the Central Intelligence Agencies and National Security Agency perused it, logged it in, and then filed it away under basic "that's nice" identifiers.

The draft copy sat in the bottom drawer of John C. Bodinky's desk, under the bottle of scotch and a pair of Stephanie's panties.

Then, on September 13th, at 9:13am, Jim's possible conclusions arrived in the form of a large rock.

FIRST STRIKE

The September morning was sunny and clear, as Adam Lloyd sat waiting for his friend in Atlanta, Georgia. He smiled to himself as he again thought how Chief Master Sergeant William "Willie" Hamilton always managed to find these off-the-beaten-track small diners that served excellent breakfasts. As Adam Lloyd glanced through the diner's fairly clean window, he could see his reflection.

Since exiting the U.S. Air Force as a Captain some six months prior, Adam had still remained clean shaven, and kept his brown hair short, as required by military grooming standards. His just under six foot frame was actually in better physical shape than when he had been in the Air Force. He was still looking for a decent job in law enforcement, had limited funds from savings and odd jobs, and no love life. Thus he spent a lot of time at the gym and running the side streets around his extended stay motel room. He was waiting for a possible training academy class at the Federal Law Enforcement Training Center in Brunswick, Georgia. However, once again, the Federal budget was screwed up, so various agencies were unsure as to when they could start their next new hire classes.

Adam sipped his coffee. Hurry up and wait. He had left the

Air Force because people seemed more involved with their own egos than doing the Mission, or even doing their job the way it was supposed to be done. Thus, inertia set in, and no one wanted to make the hard decisions. For someone who believed in working for a higher cause, it was time to leave.

Willie, as his friends called him, was still in. He had managed to be attached to some special operations and programs that kept him active and busy. The Chief had told him on more than one occasion that his idealistic tilting at windmills would just get him more frustrated. But then, Willie had ten years of age on him, was enlisted, and could let the Officer class deal with all the higher level B.S. Willie had enough time in that he could retire, if forced to do something he really didn't believe in.

Adam looked up to the entrance in time to see the red-headed and small-mustached Chief Hamilton walk in. Shorter than Adam, he had retained the muscular build of a much younger man. His eyes shared the same blue color as Adam's. Judging by the way the waitress flashed him a smile, he had been here before. Adam chuckled. Leave it to Willie to make contacts no matter where he went. Willie saw him, smiled, and headed his way.

"Chief," Adam said as he shook hands.

"Boss. Looking good in civvies. Been working out too, I see."

"You're looking good in those civvies you're wearing also, Willie. Wife picked them out?"

Willie grimaced a bit. "Yeah. Get her here to the land of the big BX from Afghanistan and she goes all Western civilization on me. She's running the NCO Wives' Club like she's been in charge for years."

They both laughed and sat down. The smiling, attractive young waitress came over with menus, and Willie waved them away.

"No need, darlin'. Steak and eggs, pancakes on the side, with some o.j. and coffee." The Chief still had an Alabama accent despite all of his travels.

"Will do, Chief. Coming right up."

Adam raised an eyebrow. "Been coming here long?"

"On and off for years. Good place to have an off the record conversation. Nobody of any importance comes here, especially not at nine in the morning."

The waitress came with the coffee, and poured them each a cup. The Chief slurped it in his typical style.

"They do have good coffee here. So, any job nibbles yet?

Adam shrugged. "I'm still waiting on the budget problems to get sorted out. Hiring is paused until they get some more funding. You know the drill."

"Unfortunately, yes I do, Boss. You should have stayed in, so I could've stayed working for you."

"Nah, Willie. I just would have said the wrong thing to some martinet field grade fool. Then I would have been in the shits. It was time for me to leave."

The Chief gave him a firm stare. "Well, if you need some work, let me know. I have some irons in the fire where I could hire a 'civilian contractor' for at least a few months."

Adam smiled. "Thanks, old friend. Give me a few more weeks of pounding the pavement, and I may give you a call."

"Make that two weeks. This window won't stay open forever."

"Okay. It's a deal. Shake." They shook hands. Willie suddenly looked up at the television that had been mounted above the old-fashioned diner counter and frowned. Adam turned and looked also. The regulars seated at the old-fashioned diner the counter were all intent on a bright "Breaking News" logo plastered on the cable news screen. Just then, something in the Chief's diddy bag made an odd beeping and ringing sound. He reached and pulled out a state of the art encrypted satellite phone.

"Hamilton here." Willie listened intently, trying not to draw attention to his unique-looking piece of equipment. He frowned.

"You're bullshitting me, right?" he replied to the person at the other end of the conversation. "Alright, you're not. I'll get my family packed up, report back from leave ASAP. Out."

"Trouble, Chief?"

"You are *not* going to believe this. The breaking news is what appear to be meteor strikes around the world, including four blocks from the White House. They are coming in hot, with some as big as semi-truck trailers."

Adam's eyes widened. "My God! At that size, depending on the speed of impact, it can hit like a small nuke! Was Space Command asleep at the switch?"

"Good question. That large Asteroid they numbered 18666 is nearing Earth and moon orbit. They were supposedly watching it, and said there was no dangerous fragment field around it. But it has to be connected."

He looked intently at Adam. "By the way, consider yourself hired at this moment, Shanghaied if you want to consider it in those terms. We'll go get my wife and kids sent home, then find a Western Union or some other wire transfer place. I can get a down payment on your wages wired to us from a fund I have access to in D.C."

Adam smiled. "Shanghaied? Hell, I volunteer. I think this will all turn to shit in a minute. People are going to throw accusations and missiles around like tennis balls. Conspiracy theories seem to fuel international politics."

"You got that right. By the way, does it bother you that I'm your boss this time?"

"Nope. Now *you* get all the headaches from being in charge, not me."

Willie Hamilton chuckled. "I guess you get your revenge. Now, I'll pay for the meal we didn't eat, we take off, and pick up..."

A rushing, crackling, thunderous sound like a freight train passing nearby shook the diner. Adam stared out the large pane front window, catching a glimpse of a sight he could never forget. A large fireball was streaking towards impact on the next block over.

"Get down! *Bomb!*" Adam figured by yelling that he would get the automatic response from the diner patrons and staff he desired. It worked. Nearly everyone hit the floor. Adam and Willie also dove under their booth table, as the entire front window was shattered by the shock wave of a huge impact.

Adam and the Chief recovered quickly, having experienced similar events before. They made their way out the front door of the diner, stopping to stare at the scene around them for a few moments. The next block was becoming a flaming mess.

"That parking garage is where my car is parked. *Was* parked," Adam stated.

"Ditto, Boss." Willie turned and placed some bills on the counter. As he did, the vehicle gas tanks in the parking garage where the supposed meteorite had hit began to explode.

"We need to get to your wife and kids, Chief. How far out of Atlanta are they?"

"Wingate Hotel near the Six Flags theme park, which is about nine miles west of here on Interstate 20. Azita, my son, and my daughter made a weekend of it while the water park was still open."

"We need some wheels. Let's get looking." The two military comrades left the diner and headed in the opposite direction from the parking garage. Adam's motel room was a bit east of their location, but he made a split second decision that getting to the Chief's family was more important than getting any of his equipment.

Adam glanced down the first alleyway they came to, while the air around them resounded with sirens. Someone had pulled in their dark blue SUV and fled, in an apparent attempt to find cover. The door was open, engine was running.

"The Gods of War are smiling on us, Chief."

"That they are, Boss."

Adam automatically went to the driver's side door, then stopped. He looked at Willie. "I seem to remember something about you being in charge..."

His friend waved him off. "We'll worry about that later. You do what you do best. Make command decisions. Just like old times... Captain."

Adam gave him a grim smile. "Okay. Let's find a way to Interstate 20, and get you to your family."

"Roger that."

Adam drove through the alleyway, then out onto the next street. Traffic was complete chaos as people maneuvered around abandoned vehicles and responding fire trucks, or just stopped, frozen in place. The explosions from vehicle gas tanks had sent people scurrying for cover in any available building, so Adam ran the SUV up on the sidewalks, maneuvering around the remaining traffic.

"Hauling ass in a stolen vehicle," the Chief opined. "Been playing Grand Theft Auto a lot?"

Adam laughed. "You've got a point there, Chief. It just comes naturally, I guess."

The former Air Force Security Police Captain cut down a couple of alleys, then turned toward what looked like a highway onramp. As they neared it, the two military men noticed a large number of figures milling around the roadway. Adam honked the SUV's horn as he tried to maneuver up the ramp.

Two dark-skinned figures suddenly appeared, each with some kind of pistol in their hands. They pointed their weapons at the slow-moving vehicle.

"Get the fuck out of the car, motherfucker!" the one on Willie's side yelled.

"Okay, okay. No problem," Adam replied. "It's not ours anyways. Be advised, it's stolen."

"Like we give a fuck," growled the scruffy looking black male on Adam's side.

As the two men exited the stopped vehicle, the Chief produced a small pistol from some hiding place and, in one smooth motion, shot the man on his side through the right eye.

The carjacker toppled backwards.

The ne'er do well on Adam's side yelled and swung his gun towards Willie. This gave Adam the chance to close the distance with him, grabbing the gun hand with his right hand. He twisted it so the arm's elbow was extended and pointing upward. With his left hand, he smashed the elbow joint in the wrong direction, breaking it.

The man screamed and dropped the handgun. Adam followed with a blow to the throat, then kicked the thug's left kneecap. After the man fell to the ground, Adam stomped on his head. The attempted carjacker laid still.

"Also been doing some hand-to-hand training I see, Boss."

"I started working out with a couple of MMA fighters at the gym. They specialize in teaching attitude adjustments." Adam recovered the dropped pistol, and saw it was a .38 five shot snubby revolver.

"What did you shoot your guy with, Chief?" At the sound of the shot, everyone else had scattered, leaving Adam and Willie alone near the SUV.

"Little Smith and Wesson 22 Passport auto. They stopped making them years ago."

Adam laughed. "Still going the retro route."

"Hell, Boss. The old shit works just fine. Sometimes better than all this twenty-first century crap."

"What was your guy carrying?"

"Cheap thirty two auto. It'll do for now. Let's be sheep and get the flock out of here."

"Roger that, Chief." Old habits came back. They were a deadly team again.

"Ever notice, Chief, that there are always some assholes around making bad situations worse?"

"Well, those two won't be doing that again."

Adam maneuvered the SUV up the ramp and onto Interstate 20 westbound. He drove in any available lane, through any available space, up on the shoulder, down the median. Adam didn't care about breaking any traffic laws. He was focused on getting his friend to his family.

Between the Chief's satellite phone and the car radio—now broadcasting National Emergency Alerts—they pieced together the narrative so far. There were "rock strikes", as some bright eyes had labeled them, all over the world. The term "a natural disaster of biblical proportions" was bandied about.

"Looks like a big one passing over Atlanta broke up, Boss," Willie shared. "Led to a shotgun effect instead of just one good sized smack."

"Why aren't they breaking up, exploding in the air like that one over Russia some years back?" Adam asked, as he passed a car slowing on the shoulder.

"Your guess is as good as mine, Boss. Leave that one to the big brains, along with why no one noticed them incoming until the last moment."

"Yeah, Chief. Someone is gonna have some 'splainin' to do', as Rickie Ricardo once said."

Willie laughed. "Now who is going old and retro?" Just then, all traffic stopped. Adam pulled onto the shoulder. They made a few more car lengths before that avenue was blocked.

"I think I see a stalled tanker truck up ahead, with some flashing cop lights, Boss."

"Still have some type of special ID that might get us through, Chief?"

"Yeah, I think so." Willie grabbed his diddy bag. "Hide your pistol and follow me. We'll see if I have any magic today."

The two men left the SUV with the doors open, still running. A car thief would get nowhere in this traffic jam. They walked forward about fifty yards, weaving their way through the stopped cars and up to a Georgia State Trooper, who was arguing with an older retiree in front of the man's RV.

"No sir, I *cannot* let you through. See that tanker truck? It's sprung a bad leak and is rapidly soaking the area around it with flammable gasoline. A hot muffler, a large spark, *boom!* The fumes go up, then the tanker."

The Chief walked up, interrupted the conversation with a set of credentials. "Homeland Security, officer. Chief Master Sergeant William Hamilton. This here is Special Agent Adam Lloyd. We need to get by to meet up with a group near Six Flags, trying to figure out this mess."

The heavy set older trooper grunted. "Hell, Chief, I figured it out. Hell from the sky made a mess of everything. But I can't let you near that tanker. If it goes up, this part of the Interstate is toast. And an evacuation of Atlanta has started. Just got word."

"That bad, officer?" Adam asked.

"Yes sir. Half a dozen rocks have hit, a bigger one in the southeast corner. Went up like a fuel air bomb in Iraq. Fire and rescue are overwhelmed." The trooper glared at the retiree when he appeared to be about to speak, then thought better of it.

"If you want to climb down off the freeway and walk around, be my guest. Just don't smoke within a hundred yards."

Adam and Willie looked at each other. Adam shrugged. "Well, Chief, nice day for a walk. We're within two clicks, I think."

"Yeah, Boss. Let's secure the vehicle, and take off on foot." Willie turned towards the trooper. Thanks, officer. Good luck, and be careful."

"Yeah, I could use some luck about now," the trooper answered.

Adam and Willie turned around and began walking back to their stolen SUV.

"Special Agent?" Adam asked in a low tone.

"Hey, you're special. You can be my agent. It works. Right?"

Adam smiled. "Still fast on your feet. Good. We need it."

Just then, they heard a loud, un-muffled motorcycle engine nearing the retiree's RV they were passing. The two men watched it rocket by in between cars and turned to see the state trooper yelling at the driver, trying to intercept the cyclist. The man maneuvered his Harley around the now screaming trooper and tossed what Adam thought was a lit road flare toward the disabled tanker truck.As the bearded and long haired blonde biker tossed the flaming object, Adam noticed what seemed to be a logo of some type of octopus in black and red as his club colors. Adam had never seen that in any law enforcement report before.

"Down!" Adam yelled as he yanked the Chief behind the RV. Instantly, everything exploded. The retiree had apparently set his vehicle's hand brake and had it in park. That, plus the vehicle's weight, stopped it from rolling onto the two men as the blast hit.

Adam felt a wash of heat go by, his ears ringing. He slowly began to rise and saw the retiree on the ground, on fire and not moving. He heard what must have been the man's wife screaming from inside the RV. Adam carefully made his way around to the front of the vehicle, as the Chief slowly rose to his feet.

Jammed into the grill of the RV was the now dead trooper. Burnt, and with his head at an odd angle, Adam saw he was clearly dead. He went over, reached down and gingerly removed the 40 Caliber pistol from the dead trooper's holster. It looked like it had been protected by the trooper's body from the blast and heat, and still seemed serviceable. The Chief walked up to his side.

"Yeah. He won't be needing that anymore."

"Willie, *that* was no accident, no Act of God." The heat from the burning tanker was still intense, so they walked back to behind the RV, trying to ignore the woman's screams inside.

"Boss, did you see that? What the fuck was that guy doing?"

Adam paused, staring at the burning carnage. How did this happen? he thought.

In the hardened Battle Staff Room under the White House grounds, a much-abbreviated National Security Staff was attempting to gain as much information about the situation as they could. The near hit by a rock on the White House lawn had been the first of several in the D.C. Area. A large one had hit a secret underground monitoring, command, and control station outside of D.C., in Virginia. Chaos reigned.

Vice President Lisa McAuliffe was in over her head, and she knew it. The President had been on a fundraising, press the flesh trip to California when the first rock struck.

The pretty blonde looked at her notes. Nine fucking thirteen in the morning, she thought. At least four enormous objects had struck worldwide at that exact moment, to be followed by many more.

The ones that had hit in D.C., at first thought to be random, now seemed to have been aimed and timed to disrupt the operations of the Nation's Capital to the maximum extent. They were just big enough to pack the equivalent punch of a World War II "blockbuster" bomb.

However, the psychological effect of flaming balls from the sky seemed to have as much disruptive effect as the actual physical destruction. The Capitol building area had been evacuated, with many of the normal National Security Staff apparently caught in the ensuing panic. After all, at first it was thought to be a natural disaster. Some personnel had stayed in place in such locations as the Pentagon. Now, it looked like no additional staff would make it to the battle staff room.

Lisa cursed under her breath. She had never been in the military, never been a Governor, never run a large organization. She had been chosen by Congress all along to be eye candy and to soften the image of the President with her more progressive stances on the issues. She knew that. So did the majority of the President's staff.

But now they were stuck with her as the authority. The President had been routed to a passenger train when it was deemed too dangerous to fly, thanks to an AWAC's bird being knocked out of the sky by a piece of apparent space junk. The

Vice President, who had been told by the President that she had to step up and hold the fort until the President returned, was reminded she had experienced commanders to help. That had been twelve hours ago. Things were getting progressively worse, the situation was deteriorating hour by hour, as the reports came in.

"Ma'am, we have that Colonel you were looking for on the line," the Assistant National Security Advisor to the President told her. Lisa McAuliffe sighed. They were all the second string in this room. Those with real experience were scattered to hell and gone, with a few reported dead. Now, she had to take charge. And she had no idea what to do.

"Vice President McAuliffe here. Is this Colonel Reed?"

"Yes, Madam Vice President. Colonel John Reed, Russian Affairs desk at the Pentagon."

Lisa took a deep breath to calm herself, as she was afraid of the answers she was about to receive. She stepped in front of the computer with the encrypted real time video feed.

"Colonel, I understand you speak fluent Russian?"

'Yes, Ma'am. I am married to a Russian former embassy staff member, and we have two sons. She made me learn fluent Russian."

"Where is she now?" There was a pregnant pause at the other end of the line. Then, Colonel Reed answered.

"I don't know. She was visiting relatives outside of Moscow when this all blew up... Madam Vice President."

So, Lisa thought. He has a personal stake in this situation.

"What are the Russians saying, Colonel? Who are they blaming for this? Are they blaming us, claiming it's part of some grand conspiracy...?" Lisa tried to catch herself, knowing she was on the verge of rambling.

"Well, Ma'am, to put it bluntly, they are panicked. I have never seen nor heard this before. Russians do *not* have a reputation for panic. They are considered ruthless, but not the panicking type."

Lisa tried to think of what to say next. Panic? That is what she felt like being on the verge of... a good screaming panic.

"Ma'am. They are reporting unknown aircraft in their airspace, just as we reported here a few minutes ago."

Lisa glared at the other battle staff members.

"Why didn't I know about this?" she asked no one in particular.

"We're trying to verify the information, Madam Vice President," a one-star General stated.

"*What*? Where in the hell is all of the special surveillance and military equipment we've been spending money on all these years? Why is everything so confused? What the hell are you people worth if you can't figure out who is attacking us?" Lisa asked shrilly, on the verge of screaming when Colonel Reed broke in.

"Here, I'll send you raw, open broadcast material the Russians are providing to anyone who wants it, no encryption." Within moments, the raw feed was coming over the screens to the battle staff. What they saw was so astounding, a person could think it was all faked with modern computer graphics. Only it wasn't.

Delta-shaped aircraft, somewhat larger than the typical U.S. fighter bomber (such as the older Strike Eagle) came into the film footage at a high rate of speed, sonic booms resonating off the soundtrack of the video feed, sometimes causing the film to shake. Then huge disc shaped craft, larger than a B-2 bomber by a factor, came into view. At first seemingly to maneuver like a conventional aircraft, it suddenly stopped in mid- air and hovered. Then, it took off like a shot straight up.

"My God!" exclaimed Lisa. "That doesn't look like anything I've ever seen." She stopped, realizing what she was saying.

"Here is some more daylight footage of something bigger. Russia has time zones, it's daylight there now, eight hours ahead."

A shape appeared that looked to be longer than a football

field with the characteristic fat body design of an Earthly large military jet transport, only on steroids.

"Russians are calling these huge things arks. They are transports of some kind, protected by the Delta Fighters and those large disc shaped craft," stated Colonel Reed.

"Have any craft like these been seen here, in the U.S., up until now?" Lisa asked, chin quivering.

"It's night here, and confusing as hell thanks to all the rocks hitting us. But we just received reports of the Deltas and those other battle cruiser type discs along the east and west coasts. The numbers are unknown."

"Any occupants?" the Assistant National Security Advisor inquired. He was late middle aged, just starting to go gray. After tonight, if he survived, the Vice President surmised he would be completely gray.

"Some Russian pilot claimed to have seen some fleshy tentacles around the cockpit of a downed Delta. That has not been verified…"

"You mean they can be shot down?" Lisa interjected.

"Yes Ma'am. At least the Russians are doing it. They also report some very tall humanoid shaped soldiers, apparently in armor, around one of those huge disc shaped craft."

"Colonel, why do the Russians seem to have more information that we do?"

"It's daylight there. The Russians can see them better." Colonel Reed paused, then continued.

"We have run into one problem over here in the U.S, which is not being reported much in Russia."

"What is that?" Lisa asked.

"We have guerrilla actions, a form of terrorist activity by some sort of prepositioned Fifth Column. They all seem to be humans, of the more criminal in nature. These…minions are popping up all over the country, attacking our military and police. They are also committing acts of sabotage on our infrastructure, such as our fuel supplies, power stations and transportation routes."

Lisa began to swear like she and her friends did when she was still a cheerleader smoking behind the bleachers after the football games in Massachusetts.

"Does anyone know what the hell is going on? Is anyone doing anything against these... these Bug Eyed Monsters?"

No one on the battle staff responded. Then Colonel Reed spoke. "Local commanders are forming quick reaction forces made up of whatever military resources they can find. Aerial strike packages are being formed, and the Navy is recalling all their Carrier Groups. Once we have the targets identified, we'll hit them. But the idea that this was a natural disaster at first really confused the response."

"Colonel Reed. You seem to be the only person who has any idea what is going on. Since I am acting President—congratulations, you're now in charge. You start organizing any way you want. See if you can get the Russians on board. My red phone to them is not getting answered by the Kremlin."

John Reed frowned. "That is really screwed. It means their command and control is breaking down faster than I thought."

"Any other Generals or Admirals at the Pentagon with you?"

"A couple are floating around, Ma'am."

"Get them on this connection ASAP. I am going to tell them that you are in charge, per my orders."

An Assistant Secretary of Defense, again the second string, started to protest.

"Ma'am that is going to screw up the Chain of..."

"Fuck the Chain of Command. I was never in the military, so guess what? I don't care how things are normally done. This is not normal!"

Everyone shut up. Then Colonel Reed seemed to be listening to a separate earpiece. Even on the computer screen, the fact his face seemed to go ashen was noticeable.

"Madam Vice President, we just lost Cheyenne Mountain. Contact was cut in mid-sentence. I have to assume attackers targeted it, just took it out."

"That would take a large nuke, wouldn't it?"

"Yes, Ma'am. Or the equivalent."

Lisa put her face in her hands and groaned. Slowly, she raised her head.

"We still have some satellite communications, right? Wait a minute, why haven't these, these objects taken out satellites?"

John Reed shrugged. "They may plan on taking them over, using them. Though, if they studied us, like I am sure they did, having your satellites destroyed is a tip off someone is attacking you, that it's not just some large meteors coming in." He paused, then continued.

"They played us, Space Command, even the Russians like old fiddles for twelve hours. We did not even know we were under attack."

"Work your magic, General Reed. Try to raise the President. When the sun comes up, I want some targets, I want some enemy to kill. I'll be *damned* if the acting female President is going down in the history books as being a *wimp*."

Lisa paused for a moment. Damn girl, she thought, I didn't know you had that in you. And judging by the looks on faces in the room, neither did they.

In one unified voice, she heard, "Yes, Madam Vice President."

For the first time, the Vice President, now in charge for the time being, smiled.

"Alright, gentlemen. Shall we?" With that, the second string huddled up, looking for a Hail Mary play.

Fourteen hours after leaving Atlanta, the two men were sitting on the floor of a "Stop and Rob", passing a bottle of malt liquor back and forth. The only light source was the battery operated emergency exit lights required in public commercial businesses. All other power was off.

They had made it to Six Flags and the hotel where Chief

Hamilton's family had been. Or at least they had tried. An hour after the tanker explosion, they had woven their way around burning vehicles and groups of panicked civilians to the Wingate Hotel. It was a mass of flames.

The Six Flags Theme Park itself was on fire in several locations, spreading beyond the confines of the resort. Everyone in the area was fleeing, primarily west, away from Atlanta.

There were no signs of Willie's wife Azita, his son Jacob, or daughter Sarah. Adam and Willie decided to follow the panicked crowds west, on the off chance Aznita and the children had been caught up in the groups of fleeing humans. Hours later, they had not seen a sign of the woman and her children.

As the sun was setting, they came upon the Stop and Rob. It had been locked up by its fleeing owner. That did not stop a group of a half dozen men and women from smashing in the front door glass in an attempt to gain entry. Adam and Willie had approached, and spread out a bit.

Before they could even try to make a friendly contact, a long-haired young male who looked as if he had just taken a hit off a meth pipe grabbed a high end—probably stolen—pump shotgun. As he pointed it in Adam's direction, the former Captain had double tapped two bullets in the guy's chest, then one to the head from the pistol he had taken from the dead trooper. The shotgun wielder collapsed, his comrades frozen in place by the sudden violence.

"Leave, *now!*" Adam called out. One of the females started to approach the dead man.

"Leave him and the shotgun. Go. Death just arrived. You want to stay and say hello?"

"Hey man!" The woman said. "He has the drugs. Give them to us."

Willie strode up, and efficiently rifled the corpse's pockets. He found a bag and a pipe, and tossed both to the woman. She caught the objects, and the five survivors began to run off. If any of them had other firearms, they had apparently decided discretion was the better part of valor. Within a couple of minutes, they disappeared into the fading sunlight.

"So much for the veneer of civilization, Chief."

Adam and Willie recovered the shotgun, stripped the body of all usable ammunition and items, and then propped it up on the gas pumps in front of the store. It would serve as a warning to others to give the store a wide berth.

The two men had not seen a single law enforcement official since the tanker truck. They had heard some military jets in the distance, but had not seen them yet. People in the Atlanta area were on their own.

Now they were sitting on the store floor. Willie had picked the front barred security door lock to get in. Breaking the front door glass had been a futile effort by the departed looters. The power had stayed on long enough for Adam and Willie to microwave some sandwiches and frozen fried chicken, as well as some cups of coffee. The lights had flickered, then went out. The military men had eaten enough, then filled some plastic garbage bags with leftovers, beef sticks, and bottles of water. After a couple cans of beer, they were passing a bottle of malt liquor back and forth.

Adam looked at his friend. "You know, Azita could have…"

"We'll never know, Adam. This area of Georgia is toast. The aliens hit us too hard and fast."

Willie took a long drink and looked at the now empty malt liquor bottle.

"Dead soldier. Give it a proper burial, Boss. Then get us something else from the cooler."

Information from the Chief's satellite phone, plus other info snatched from vehicle radio broadcasts, had confirmed the suspicions that the rocks were part of an attack. Twelve hours in, the alien Delta-shaped fighters and large disc-shaped craft were followed by huge—larger than a football field transport—craft, to be later named harvester arks. It was soon apparent what they were doing. One of Willie's contacts at the Pentagon he had managed to contact on his sat phone told them one of arks had landed on the White House lawn. Some wheeled robots and some large armored humanoids had disembarked, and began to grab every human in sight, killing those who tried to flee.

Adam had managed to get through on his cell phone to a 911 hysterical dispatcher. All she could say was "Stay away from the ocean!" Then the line went dead.

Adam returned with a bottle of higher end wine from the store cooler.

"Here. The relatively good stuff. Cork and all." He took a wine bottle opener from a store rack, used it to pop the cork, and then passed it to Willie. The Chief raised the bottle.

"A toast. To friends and family. Both here and lost."

"Willie…"

"They're gone. I can feel it. I had a good seven years with them, my wife and kids. They were happy. Things could have been worse." He handed the bottle to Adam.

"Kempai, as we used to say in Okinawa," Adam toasted.

"Yeah, Boss. Okinawa. Seems like a million years ago." The older man looked at Adam.

"What now, Boss?"

"A night's rest, start early in the morning. I want to travel when I can see what's going on around me."

"Yes, Adam. The people I was working with were setting up a secret task force to start monitoring the smuggling activity again in Florida. This time, Middle Eastern types through Cuban waters instead of dope. How about us heading there?" He took the wine bottle from Adam, had another drink.

"Some people were already in place at the Key West Naval Air Station. Hopefully, some survived… this." He looked at Adam.

"Adam, what do you think is the long term outlook?"

"Christ, Chief, I have no crystal ball." Then he realized his old friend looked at him as the Commander, not as a friend. He was still in shock from losing his family, though he would never admit it. He needed someone to help shoulder the load, to tell him there was hope. Adam stood up, and squared his shoulders.

"Chief, we save as many of the living as we can. Where there is life, there is hope. *That* will be our Mission. Sound good?"

Chief Master Sergeant William Hamilton stood up, saluted his former—now current—Boss.

"Sir. Come hell or high water. That's what we'll do."

"Now, Chief, sack time."

"Sure, Boss. Sack time."

They woke just before dawn. As they quietly collected their gear and supplies, they heard a whirring, electrical sound. Both men crouched, carefully looked out the Stop and Rob entrance door.

What looked like an oversized six-wheeled ATV was headed straight for the body of the dead looter they had propped up on the gas pumps. Sticking up from the center of the ATV was a large metal ball, with what looked like a large electronic iris in front.

As the machine approached the body, it hit it with a quick flash of blinding light emanating from the iris. Some of the side flash made the two friends see dark spots.

A very flexible cable like structure extended from the ATV's body, latched onto the corpse, and warped around the body. In the blink of an eye, it was pulled to the ATV as the machine turned and headed back the way it came.

"A goddamned robot," the Chief finally said.

"Yeah. A type that seems to be hunting us." Adam looked at Willie.

"Based on what we just saw, your contact at the Pentagon, and the comment that dispatcher made, I think we are no longer the apex predator."

The Chief shivered a bit. "Let's get moving. I don't want to be here if that thing comes back."

"Roger that, Chief." Then Adam paused. "I think saving as

many humans as we can just took on even more ramifications."

The Chief looked hard at Adam.

"We save who we can. We fuck up anybody, or *anything* that tries to stop us."

"Old friend, you just hit it on the head. Now, shall we? It's going to be a long trip."

"Copy that, Boss. Copy that."

PAYBACK

Under the cover of darkness, the two black Special Ops aircraft out of Edwards Air Force Base came in low and fast over the Southern California desert. Both were variations of the C-130 four engine tactical aircraft that had been a workhorse of the U.S. Air Force for over fifty years.

As they neared their destination, the AC-130U Spooky II Gunship prepared to pull back and orbit some ten miles away from the drop off. The MC-130H Combat Talon would continue on to a designated makeshift landing strip within a mile of the All American Irrigation Canal. A straight and flat section of dirt road that the Bureau of Land Management and the U.S. Border Patrol maintained together would serve as the landing strip. Supposedly some U.S. Border Patrol Agents would be there to light a couple of road flares to help the Special Ops pilots line up on the temporary landing zone.

Marine Corps Gunnery Sergeant Torbin Bender had just finished a last minute check of the personnel and equipment jammed into the MC-130H. Three Humvees, two motorcycles, a four wheel ATV, and thirty armed personnel did not leave a lot of room for comfort. But hell, he'd seen and experienced worse. Eight years active duty in the Corps, with five of that as a SEAL and Delta Force member, and more years in the Marine Corps Reserve, meant that he had pretty much seen it all.

All, that is, until tonight.

He was heading in for an assault on a reported alien craft. Not the type of alien as in illegal alien sneaking across for Mexico. Rather, alien as in space alien, little green men. But recent intelligence reports said the aliens were anything but green or little.

As he made his way to a crowded fold down side fuselage seat, he heard his name called. He looked up and saw Lieutenant Jacob Roth weave his way to him around the vehicles and equipment. Roth was Army, just out of Ranger School, having graduated the week before the Tschaaa began throwing rocks. At least that's what the surviving NSA and Military Intelligence assets said the attackers called themselves.

Lieutenant Roth was a small, wiry jet black haired, brown eyed young man, with a somewhat boyish face that made Torbin feel old, even though he had not hit thirty years old yet. The Marine seemed to tower over the Lieutenant, although Torbin was a shade under six feet tall. The fact that the Gunnery Sergeant was a certified physical trainer in civilian life gave him a cut to his physique that made him look larger.

"Lieutenant."

"Gunnery Sergeant Bender."

Torbin smiled a bit. "Sir, may I suggest you just call me Gunny? It's easy shorthand, especially since I'm the only Marine Corps NCO around."

Lt. Roth was a cherry when it came to combat. He had just pinned on his First Louie Bars, but was literally the only company grade officer around when this hodgepodge unit had been thrown together. An assault unit, platoon-sized, needed an officer. Or so the upper Chain of Command had decreed.

The young Lieutenant took in a deep breath, then let it out. "Gunny, I won't insult a combat vet like you by asking if everything and everybody is ready. But I would like to say..."

"Sir, I've got your back."

Lieutenant Roth stuttered a bit, the interruption throwing him off his short prepared speech. "Excuse me, uh, what?"

"Sir, I've got your back. You're the OIC—Officer in Charge. You say jump, a Marine Gunny says how high, Sir. I will keep you from getting yourself killed, tell you when you are about to get me killed. Other than that, no worries, Sir." He smiled at the young officer, knowing that the man had so many things going through his mind right now. One of those thoughts, Torbin knew was—will he screw up, and get people killed.

Lieutenant Roth looked at him, then chuckled.

"Here I had this little speech that would have fit right into some Hollywood action flick, and you beat me to the punch."

"Like I said, Sir. No worries. We have our orders, know what to do. The easy part is when we land. Your training will take over, as will my experience. Those Tschaaa, or whatever they call themselves, won't stand a chance."

The young officer extended his right hand. Torbin took it, felt a firm grip.

"It's an honor to serve with you and these men and women."

Torbin grinned, his blue eyes twinkling a bit. "Hell, Sir, we're about to make history. We are about to kick some outer space alien ass."

Just then, the Aircraft Commander came over the intercom. "Nearing the ten mile mark," the female voice said. "About to crash the party."

With that, the assault troops all went to their assigned places. Torbin felt a sense of confidence, as well as excitement. The fact that thirty men and women, Air Force, Army, Navy and Marine, had come together in just over twenty-four hours to form a cohesive team was saying something about the U.S. Military. Air Force ParaRescue, Army Rangers, an active duty Navy SEAL, and an all-female aircrew had clicked as if they had all known each other for years. That almost never happened. Throw in Torbin as the token Marine, and he knew the big man upstairs must have their backs.

But of course a pessimist would ask why the big man (or woman) had allowed the Tschaaa to get to Earth in the first place. That train of thought was above Torbin's pay grade.

Within moments, the MC-130 went into a bank, as the pilot began to line up for an approach. The border patrol must have shown up as agreed to mark the landing area, as there was no hesitant flying and searching by the aircrew. A couple of quick banks, and the pilot went straight in.

She's good, Torbin thought as the pilot almost greased the four engine transport on the makeshift strip, despite it being only somewhat hardened dirt and sand. Even as she was braking the aircraft, Torbin and the Lieutenant were up, as were all the others. The Air Force loadmasters hit quick release straps on the Humvees and other vehicles, as the Assault Force got ready to disembark. Twenty of the thirty armed personnel would haul ass to the target, sixteen in the Humvees, the other four on the motorbikes and ATV, the four wheeler supporting two riders in tandem.

Within sixty seconds after the load ramp was down, all the vehicles were off, personnel quick to mount their assigned ride. The remaining ten personnel set up a three hundred degree security zone around the MC-130. It had been decided to keep the transport craft on the ground, with the pilot and crew having it lined up and ready to go when the twenty assault team members returned. Of course all twenty would return, the newer people thought. Torbin knew better.

The Lieutenant took the lead vehicle, Torbin, as Second in Command, took the third and rear Humvee. The motorbikes and ATV would skirmish out ahead. Before they mounted their Humvees, a border patrol agent in an SUV with a shot out windshield approached Torbin and Lt. Roth.

"Watch yourselves. There's some pieces of shit humans helping the aliens. And their wheeled robots are nasty."

"That ark craft still by the freeway overpass next to Yuma

and Winterhaven?"

"Yes Gunny, big as day."

Torbin paused for a moment, looking at the border patrol agent. "Former Corps, right?"

"Semper Fi, Mac. We fought them along with the Air Station personnel. But a large rock took out the airfield, and then the Deltas hit." The law enforcement agent ground his teeth. "We Mean Green are tough, but we were never set up to fight a pitched battle, like when I was in the Corps."

"Well, Sir," Lt. Roth replied. "As the Gunny here will attest to, payback's a bitch."

"Give it to them, Lieutenant," the Agent spat out. "Fuck'em up. They killed my buddies. I'm one of the last."

"You have my word." Lt. Roth shook the Agent's hand, turned towards Torbin. "Shall we?"

Torbin flashed a broad grin. "Let's rock, Lieutenant."

As they mounted their respective vehicles, Torbin heard the border patrol agent call out, "Vayan con Dios!" Go with God. Torbin hoped once again that God had their backs.

Sixty seconds later, and they were moving out. Lights out. There was enough ambient light in the clear desert night that the vehicle drivers did not really need the night vision goggles.

Torbin heard the secure radio channel crackle. "Your curfew is set for three hours from now. Late, and your coach turns into a pumpkin." It was the MC-130 female command pilot, Captain White.

"Roger that, Captain. Cinderella will be back with both her glass slippers," replied Lt. Roth.

"Get back here. I owe you a drink at the officer's club." Torbin smiled. Was the Captain flirting with Roth? War seemed to make people horny, in his experience.

Then he was focused on the task at hand. The assault group rode in silence the rest of the way, some twenty miles to where the alien craft had landed. The three Humvees had a 50 Cal and two 40 Mike-Mike auto grenade launchers attached on their respective roof mounts. The twenty men were weapons heavy, with additional grenade launchers on their assault rifles and a 30 Caliber general machine gun backing up three Squad automatic weapons. The also had a Barrett .50 Caliber long range sniper rifle with penetrator rounds, plus two AT-4 shoulder fired anti-tank missiles, and an old M-72 LAW someone had found stashed. These weapons gave them some heavy metal penetrating capability. No one had any idea on about the thickness the skin of the ark spacecraft's skin.

That was what this hurry-up mission was all about. Get up close to the ark, assault it, see what makes it tick, then blow the hell out of it. If they found any humans to rescue, great. But destruction of the ark and its inhabitants or crew was the primary task.

Torbin had a pound of C-4 plastic explosives plus detonators in his combat pack. Four other team members were also carrying various amounts of C-4 also. Two lucky troops had thermite grenades, in addition to their regular grenade and ammunition issue. If the assault personnel could get inside of the craft, they were to set the charges and destroy it. This was a chance to strike back with terminal destruction.

According to fragmentary intelligence reports from what was left of the U.S. command structure, the Russians and the Japanese did not paint a pretty picture. Areas were blasted from above, then the large arks began landing. Reports were that six wheeled ATV Robots were dragging humans into the arks with metallic tentacles, never to be seen again. Seven foot tall armored humanoids—or maybe cyborgs—appeared, impervious to most small arms fire.

Torbin's jaw tightened. Everyone had been caught flat footed. For twelve hours they had thought it was a disaster from space. Then the alien attack craft showed up, followed by the arks. All during this time, there was sabotage and Fifth Column attacks from apparent quislings and human traitors. How these terrorist cells from outer space had existed with only late night radio talk shows sounding the alarm over the years was a complete mystery.

Now, some eighty-four hours after the first rock hit, D.C. lay in ruins. For the space projectiles had been identified as masses of rock with heat shields of some very efficient design to help hold them together. A space ark was sitting on the White House lawn, and the female Vice President who had been running the show was presumed dead. Also believed dead were most of the Pentagon staff, Cheyenne Mountain, and Congress, with the President's status completely unknown. Contact with him was lost within the first twenty-four hours, as he was trying to make it back the White House via train. U.S. Armed Forces reverted to local Tactical Command.

It was a local tactical commander out of Edwards Air Force Base who had identified the target ark. It seemed the majority of the hundreds which had landed so far had come down within twenty miles of an ocean, sea, or a major body of water like the Great Lakes in patterns that provided mutual support. In the United States, however, about a half of dozen of the large arks had come down further into the interior. One had come down next to the Winterhaven Drive Overpass that crossed over Interstate 8 near the California and Arizona border, in between the tiny town of Winterhaven, California and Yuma, Arizona.

That was the target only minutes away from their assault unit.

The vehicles maneuvered around various wrecks, as they drove down a county and state road that paralleled Interstate 8 on the north side of the freeway. Even with the wrecks, the unit still made good time. There had been some concern that the target might be concealed somehow. As the assault personnel neared Winterhaven, they saw there was no reason for concern. The ark was lit up like a Christmas tree.

Lt. Roth signaled for the vehicle to stop, requested Torbin up front.

"Well Gunny, it's not like they are trying to hide or anything."

"No, Sir. I get the impression they're not used to being on the receiving end of creative violence."

Lt. Roth flashed a quick smile, then his face turned serious.

"I'm a cherry for this type of assault. I'm going to demur to your expertise."

"Hard and fast, Sir. We don't have the numbers for a drawn out assault, so good old shock and awe, like Desert Storm. Then beat feet. Yes, Lieutenant, I'll take in the assault in. You cover my ass."

"Roger that, Gunny." The young officer paused for a moment, and removed his helmet. He quickly placed a yarmulke on his head, then re-secured his helmet.

"I wore that at my Bar Mitzvah. Figured my first combat might be like that."

Torbin stuck his hand out. "Sir, say a prayer for me also. I need all the divine help for my soul I can get."

As Lt. Roth shook Torbin's hand. "I thought Marines patrolled the streets of heaven?"

"In my case, I'll be lucky to get past the main gate."

Lt. Roth chuckled. "Well, guess it's time to get this show on the road. Pick your men for the assault squad, I'll take the rest for the cover fire."

"Roger that, Sir."

With practiced ease from numerous operations and combats, Torbin had his assault squad formed, briefed and on the move. The ark was sitting on the main road, Winterhaven Drive, with its "nose" pointed directly at Yuma, Arizona. A large very human looking loading ramp was deployed from the front. As Torbin and his personnel approached the jump off point, a low crackle from secure radio was in his ear.

"In position, Gunny."

"Roger that." Torbin knew the Lieutenant's squad was hunkered down behind cover, locked and loaded. With all the light emanating from the craft, night vision goggles would be useless. As Torbin readied the signal flare to signal the beginning of the initial assault, he saw what looked like a couple of vehicles approaching the ark's loading ramp from across the freeway overpass. He paused, looking at them through his binoculars.

Approaching at speed were two of the six-wheeled ATV robots described in the intelligence reports, carrying something. As they neared, Torbin made out what they were. Bodies—human bodies—which were not moving. Torbin had seen death on enough occasions to recognize it again.

"Unleash the hounds of hell," Torbin murmured as he fired the flare, arcing it towards the approaching vehicles.

The artificial intelligence in the robots saw the approaching flare and fixated on the movement. Motion meant possible prey, to be investigated. The two six wheelers turned towards the flare, as it arced low overhead.

The 50 Caliber from one of the Humvees turned the two harvester robots into flaming wreckage, the gunner knowing, as did Torbin, that the humans aboard them were already dead. Then the two human assault vehicles broke from cover, hell bent for leather towards the arks loading ramp. 50 Caliber rounds and 40mm grenades peppered the side of the ark, as the Humvees screeched to a halt next to the loading ramp.

"Move it, move it, move it!" Torbin yelled as he leapt from his vehicle and went up the ramp. He had a live video feed unit on his helmet, so if there was a good signal, what he saw was being beamed back and would be transmitted to their transport MC-130 and the AC-130 air cover. The AC-130 would try to re-beam the message to Edwards Air Force Base.

Torbin was met by a gray, slender, humanoid shaped being that had something in its hands. He fired a burst from his assault rifle , and was satisfied that the .223 rounds had the desired effect. The "gray" went down, an odd colored bluish blood spurting form from its wounds. Then all hell broke loose.

A brace of the harvester robots boiled out from the confines of the spacecraft. The ball turrets swung towards Torbin, so he automatically dove behind a very human style looking table. Thus his eyesight was spared when the robots unleashed their extremely bright spotlights. Some of the side and back flash from the blinding lights caught the first troops behind Torbin, causing them to yell out as their vision degenerated into blobs and shapes. Torbin felt the heat from the light beams, realizing that at close range they could not only blind human prey, but burn it up also. With practiced ease, he grabbed a handy grenade and lobbed it over the table.

"*Fire in the hole!*" he yelled, warning his personnel to duck down.

The shrapnel grenade landed between the two robots and exploded. Wheels were shredded and sides were punctured. They began to spin around, damaged, but still trying to complete their programmed mission.

Shots rang out from further down the ramp, and the robots turned into sparking and burning toasters. Torbin popped up from behind the table.

"Those who can still see, follow me. Those who can't, stay here until you can."

Everyone, including a couple of newbies, functioned flawlessly. Eight armed men and women followed him up into the bowels of the spacecraft.

Several more "grays" popped up, trying to operate some types of projectile weapons, at which they were not very good. Then, for the first time, humans in the U.S. came into contact with lizards. Bipedal creatures, they looked like the work up some scientists had done years prior as to what a humanoid dinosaur would might look like, if the ancient asteroid had not hit Earth. They were more efficient, and a couple of troops went down. Then the lizards were chopped into lizard meat.

Torbin and five of the effectives left made their way further into the holds of the ship. He found the combination stairs and ramp that seemed to go up to the large cockpit area, which sat (just like human aircraft) right above the large ramp loading area. Torbin hadn't paid much attention to the windows or vision set up for this control area when they busted in, but he knew that he had to make sure anyone in it did not try and launch the ship with them aboard.

"Sergeant Robbins, take the rest of the people and clear this ship's hold. I need to make sure there is nobody up stairs."

"Got it, Gunny." Robbins was one of the combat vet Pararescue troops, so the Marine Gunny knew the job would get done. Torbin clambered up the almost two story tall combination ramp and stairway to the doored off area, where the ships operating controls seemed to be. He knew he was being macho going it alone, but the unit needed to clear the holds of any surviving humans before they set the charges to destroy the ark. Otherwise, they'd have to stand off and use the AT-4s and the LAW to destroy the engines, or punch holes in it large enough in it that so the Ark could not head back up into orbit. Still existing radar sites and some civilian telescopes had told the intelligence types that this was the way the arks operated. Land, take what they needed, then blast off within twelve to twenty four hours.

Besides, Torbin had often worked alone, doing things he could never talk about, and he still had speed and surprise on his side.

Torbin met nothing on the stairs, then he stood at what looked like the cockpit access door. Of course it was locked, the lever type door handle did not move when he yanked on it.

"Time for some creative door breaching," he mumbled to himself. He took a small amount of C-4, placed it next to the door handle and slid an explosive blasting cap into it. Stepping back atop the stairs some seven yards away, Torbin pulled a squeeze type remote detonator from his small butt pack and disengaged the safety. Crouching down, he activated it and was immediately rewarded with a substantial explosion. He was up and moving towards the door before the dust and debris settled. A hard kick and he removed the remains of the door from his path.

Sitting stunned on the floor was what he first thought was a human, even down to the tan jumpsuit he/she was wearing over its slender body. Then Torbin saw the eyes and nose. The spacing just seemed a little off, as it there had been a birth defect that required surgery.

"Show me your hands," he ordered, and the being complied. It then began to speak English, which almost floored Torbin as it sounded like it had learned British English, accent and all.

"Please, I am a man, like you. I did not want to be here. Can you take me with you?"

Torbin looked into the dark eyes set too far back, saw the odd angled sloping head. Then he heard the weirdest combinations of clicks, almost musical notes and grunts emanating from a good sized video screen. Torbin glanced at the screen and almost froze. He saw very large eyes, a large head like structure which looked like an octopus, but with a dome shape to it. He also saw what looked like tentacles moving, shifting, and waving.

"What the..." He never finished the thought as the false human lunged at him, swinging what seemed like a glowing wire at him. As he automatically parried it with his rifle, he saw the wire slice through its handguard and barrel, leaving him holding two pieces.

"Fuck you!" he yelled as he lashed a booted foot into what would be a human's kneecap. He thought he heard and felt a crack, though that might have been his imagination. The being let out a scream and toppled forward, dropping the wire weapon and grabbing at its wrecked knee. Torbin dropped his useless rifle and pulled his Ka-Bar fighting knife in one quick motion. He wrapped his left arm around the neck of the creature and grabbed its chin. A quick pull upwards, a slash of his blade, and red, human-appearing blood of the creature was spurting out on the cockpit floor of the cockpit.

Torbin took a deep breath, then looked up at the large video screen. The tentacled creature seemed to be waving its appendages in an agitated fashion, which meant that the vision screen worked both ways. Torbin stepped forward, gave it the universal one finger salute.

"Sit on this and spin, you slimy fucker!" he yelled just before he picked up the remains of his rifle and used it to smash the screen. With rage fueled speed, Torbin prepared another small C-4 charge with a small timer detonator he had brought, squeezing it in a gap on the side of what had to be the main control board. As he finished, his secure frequency radio crackled.

"Need you here ASAP, Gunny." It was Robbins.

"On my way." Torbin grabbed the magazine from his broken rifle, left the rest of it there. Someone may need his ammunition. He also gingerly pinked picked up the wire weapon, and found a stud that retracted the business end into the handle. Intelligence would *love* this.

Torbin slid and clambered down the ramp/stairs in record time. He went further into the ark, where he had sent the rest of the squad. An ashen-faced Sergeant Robbins met him before he entered a large bay, lit by very subdued light.

"It's a scene from the lower levels of Dante's *Inferno*, Gunny."

"Dante's hell..." Torbin began to say as he strode forward. Sgt. Robbins had not exaggerated.

Even in the dim light Torbin could make out the human shapes hanging from a large ceiling rack, like so many sides of beef. Several were child-sized.

One of the soldiers began to vomit all over the deck of the spacecraft. Torbin pulled out his tactical flashlight, and against his better judgment, illuminated the scene.

"Who has the camera?" Torbin asked, as he slowly played the beam of the flashlight around the large bay. "I hope my helmet cam is broadcasting all this, but I have to make sure we have a record."

"Here, Gunnery Sergeant," another of the combat vets, this one a Ranger, answered. Torbin glanced and saw it was a small digital one. Then he saw another young troop pull out an old disposable type with a built in flash.

"You two with cameras. Record everything. Someone else get a light up here to help with the picture quality." As the personnel complied with his instructions, Torbin walked further into the bowels of what he could now see was a mobile slaughterhouse.

He found a large door that looked suspiciously similar to a door leading into a butcher shop cooler. He figured out the latching mechanism and swung it open. Inside was a shop of horrors.

Torsos, arms, legs, even a couple of heads were either hanging or stored on shelves along the side of the large cooler. He saw it had the size of a railroad refrigerated unit, used to ship perishables across the U.S. This unit would go into space instead of riding on rails.

Torbin cursed and spat. "This doesn't leave here," he said to no one in particular. He turned and walked back to Sgt. Robbins.

"Time to wire this thing for destruction. There's no one here to save."

He then spoke loudly enough for everyone to hear.

"Two minutes. You with the C-4. Stick the charges against the hull. We don't have time to examine the engines on this thing. Those two thermite grenades we put with the remains here, along with anything that looks flammable. If we are lucky, a lot of these... victims will be cremated. We don't have time for decent burials."

Then his anger boiled over. "But I'll be *damned* if I leave anything, anybody for these monsters to chew on."

There were a couple of "*ooraughs*" and then everybody got busy.

"What happened to your rifle, Gunny?" Sgt. Robbins asked.

"It's in two pieces. I'll explain later." Just then, his secure radio crackled to life. It was Lt. Roth.

"Gunny Bender, we have a lot of threats approaching. Time to blow this place."

"Roger that," he answered. He turned and yelled. "No time for anything extra. We have enemy approaching and we need to bug out." As soon as he said that, he heard echoes of weapon fire from where the Lieutenant had the cover force emplaced. He jogged to the front ramp, picking up the two troops whose temporary blindness was finally going away.

"Can you two see to shoot?"

"Yes, Gunny," they both answered together.

"Out to the end of the ramp, man the weapons on the Humvees. Nothing gets in." The two, combat virgins, did not have to be told twice. They beat feet to their new assigned positions. Torbin yelled back into the ark's interior.

"Grab our two wounded and let's go. Time's a-wasting." He pulled out his M-9 pistol. Better than nothing, he thought.

Torbin heard the automatic grenade launcher of the Lieutenant's squad begin thumping rounds, followed by the report of the Barrett 50 Caliber rifle. Then the rifles and machine guns opened up. Things were now hot.

He keyed his radio. "SITREP, Sir. How many, what type?"

Lieutenant Roth radioed right back." At least a dozen wheeled robots, some human shapes. They must have been recalled when you hit the ark."

"Roger." Torbin turned to yell "Hurry up!" when he saw Sgt. Robbins was just yards away.

"Left them a nice surprise, Gunny," the Sergeant said as he strode up. "Got the wounded, ready to blow this joint."

"Sounds good to me. Mount everyone up. I still have a small piece of C-4 to use."

As Sgt. Robbins yelled orders, the Marine went over to what looked like part of the huge ramp's motor mechanism. A quick shaping of the clay like explosive, slap in the detonator, and Torbin was beating feet to the Humvees. The two young troops manning the weapons atop the vehicles began firing across the overpass. Torbin looked up.

It appeared that there were still about a half dozen of the wheeled harvester robots approaching at speed, playing their combination light and heat beams at where the Lieutenant had his people dug in. He could hear the screams, as one troop began to smolder under the effects of a direct hit. They did not have a very long range, but those lights were dangerous.

He then noticed the sounds of angry bees as someone was firing human projectile weapons at both his people and the Lieutenant's squad. He crouched down by the Humvee's front left fender of the Humvee and tried to count muzzle flashes. He thought there were at least four.

"I need a rifle!" Torbin yelled.

"Here, take this one—it's from the wounded," one of the other squad members yelled back. His two casualties had taken projectiles to the legs, the human chest armor stopping the grays' and the lizards' projectiles. Bad and multiple hits, but they would still live.

Torbin caught the tossed rifle, checked the magazine. Then he dashed at an angle from in front of the Humvees. There was a small ditch and a few large rocks on the side of the road that would provide cover. Torbin went prone and began to fire at the human shapes, as the Humvees' heavy weapons began to find the harvester robots and make junk out of them. Torbin could tell the Tschaaa were not used to organized resistance with effective weapons.

He heard human screams from the figures approaching, as he and others hit them. So the stories were definitely true about there being organized cells of traitors and Fifth Columnists fighting with the invaders. The creature who Torbin had killed with his knife was something else. But it had looked human enough to pass in many situations.

Torbin keyed his radio. "Time to leave, Lieutenant. I think you have a date waiting."

"Moving, Gunny. Cover us."

Torbin used his tactical flashlight to get the attention of Sgt. Robbins and pointed towards the cover unit's position, hand signaled signaling him to have the Humvee-mounted weapons to provide cover fire, as the squad moved. Torbin watched, as a couple of the six-wheeled robots continued on despite .223 hits, until rifle grenades and the heavier machine guns took them out. Torbin thought he had better glom onto a 30 Caliber rifle, as the standard assault rifle round could only reliably penetrate the metal and some other substance that made up the body of the harvester robots at about fifty meters.

Torbin dashed back to his squad's vehicles, and made a quick check that they were ready to move at a moment's notice. He used his binocs and saw the Lieutenant's squad vehicles move out, heading to an agreed upon rally point about a mile back.

"Let's *move!*" Torbin bellowed. A couple of troops still under cover jumped aboard the Humvees, as Torbin squeezed his remote detonator. The charge on the ramp mechanism went up with a solid "whumpf", a few pieces of metal flying outside the ark. Good, thought Torbin. They won't be able to leave anytime soon even if none of the other charges fail. But soon he wondered—were there any other "they" out there?

Torbin's group arrived at the rally point near an abandoned convenience store just moments after the Lieutenant and his squad arrived. Everyone who could deployed automatically into a three sixty degree formation to cover the rally point. They were still in enemy controlled territory. Torbin hustled over to Lieutenant Roth. As he did, he noticed what looked like a wrapped body secured on the top of the Humvee.

"I lost one dead, Gunny," Lt. Roth proffered before asked. "Took a human bullet to the head from those goddamned quisling traitors. I have another with third-degree wounds and one blinded... probably permanently."

"My squad has two with leg wounds from alien projectile weapons. A couple were temporarily blinded, but seemed to have recovered."

Torbin looked at the young officer, and saw the sorrow in his eyes.

"Sir, you did good. Soldiers and Marines die. That's part of the job description." He pointed towards the still illuminated ark.

"Any minute now, that thing should start blowing up, thanks to all the C-4 we placed in it on timers. We also have some photos, video, and good intelligence info. We did good, Lieutenant…"

A large bolt of energy came from the desert in the direction away from the ark. It struck the Lieutenant's Humvee, causing it to explode like a giant firework. Torbin was knocked down, stunned for a moment by the explosion. Through his ringing ears, Torbin could still hear the troops on the perimeter firing at whatever had launched the attack. Through sheer will, Torbin stood up, looked into the desert. Illuminated by the bullets whizzing by it, as well as striking it, was an extremely tall figure, moving very fast for a bipedal creature, closing the distance at what could be called warp speed. It had a large object in its arms, and was bringing it to bear again.

Torbin tried to bring his rifle into play, but the Barrett 50 Caliber sniper rifle beat him to the punch. The impact of the half inch round sent the weapon in its arms spinning off into the darkness. Another round slammed into the figure, knocking it over. Then a third round hit the figure as it, against all logic, tried to rise up. Torbin thought he saw an electrical discharge as the third round hit, and the figure finally laid still. Some dry brush and tumble weeds had been set a fire, throwing flickering light into the desert.

"Lieutenant…" Torbin began to say as he turned around. Then he saw Lt. Roth. A piece of the exploding Humvee had impaled him through the back of his neck, sticking out his throat. He was gone.

"Fuck." Torbin paused for a moment. Then years of

experience and training took over.

"Sgt. Robbins!"

"Yes, Gunny!"

"The Lieutenant's down. I've got it. Get the wounded and the dead on the remaining Humvee, head towards the pickup point. I'll meet you there after I make sure that the ark goes up."

"Gunny, how..."

Torbin jerked his thumb to the back, "Back of the ATV. The driver gets to stay with me. Now *move!*"

Everyone snapped to, loaded the dead and wounded on the remaining Humvees, the functional troops hanging on to the vehicles where ever they could. There was were two to a motorbike, people shucking unneeded equipment. Then they were hauling ass, with Torbin watching them the vehicles recede into the darkness.

Torbin glanced at the ATV driver. "You're Moore, right, soldier?"

"Yes Sir... I mean Gunny."

Torbin recognized him as a FNG—fucking new guy—right out of Army Infantry Training.

"Well, Private, any time now..."

"Gunny, look!"

They saw the huge disc shape approaching, began to feel the electricity in the air that accompanied the battle craft that had been named a Falcon by Military Intelligence.

"Jesus Christ on a crutch. Moore, you have a round in your rifle's grenade launcher?"

"Yes, Gunny."

"Can't let that thing find the C-130, or the others. So, get ready for some distraction. We're about to find out just how tough those so-called Falcons are."

Right as Torbin stopped speaking, there were a couple of whumps from the direction of the ark. Then, a huge explosion created a shockwave which shook the two men. A large mushroom cloud rolled up from where the ark sat. All that

Torbin could see then was a large fire and a few fireworks as there were small, secondary explosions. The approaching Falcon craft spun on its axis, then was above the burning and wrecked ark in the blink of an eye.

"Looks like we hit something nasty, Private."

All Moore could do was nod yes with his mouth open.

"Come on. Time to go. By the way, are you good driving this thing?"

Moore seemed to snap back to the task at hand. "Gunny, I used to race these four-wheelers in Eastern Washington State."

Torbin chuckled. "Let's see if you can set a personal best for speed, shall we?"

Moore smiled. "Will do, Gunny. Get on and hang on."

They made it to the MC-130 just as the pilot was revving its engines, the loading ramp already up. Moore accelerated the ATV in front of the aircraft so the pilot could see. Torbin heard a crackle on his radio.

"Can you make it through the side hatch in thirty seconds, Gunny?"

"We'll have to." Moore accelerated to the starboard side, the two men leaping off with the ATV still running. One of the female loadmasters had popped the hatch, and began to pull Torbin and Moore inside, as the MC-130 began to accelerate down the makeshift landing strip. Torbin and Moore made it into large cargo bay. There were some happy cries of greeting as the other survivors saw them. Then the aircraft rotated into the air, and next a warning over the intercom system to hang on. Everyone grabbed a strap or a piece of the aircraft to hang onto, as the pilot put the plane into a hard left bank at about five hundred feet. Then the MC-130 leveled out, heading back the way they had come.

Torbin made his way up to the cockpit, quietly entered and sat on a jump seat. A couple of minutes later, Captain White spoke over her shoulder.

"Lieutenant Roth didn't make it, did he?"

"No Ma'am. All I can say is it was quick."

There was silence for a few moments, then Captain White spoke again.

"I was looking forward to buying him a drink."

"Buy one for him, Ma'am. Toast him. He did his job well."

"Yes, Gunny. I think you all did. Sorry I had to almost leave you. But we picked up a large bogie headed our way on the AC-130's radar."

"Funny you should mention that..." Torbin then began to give her the quick and dirty story about the alien Falcon. When he was done, the Captain whistled.

"Gunny, it looks like we dodged a big bullet."

"Yes Ma'am. That Falcon, or whatever they want to call it, was looking for that large humanoid, or whatever what it was. The ark blowing up distracted it, and let us all get away. Otherwise, it would have been two men against a battle cruiser."

"You've got balls, Gunny. Since you're a guy I can say that. Thanks for the thoughts, but I for one am glad you didn't have to do a last stand at the Alamo."

"Yes, Captain. So am I. Now, if you'll excuse me, I need to be with the troops." He turned to leave the cockpit.

"Gunny."

"Yes Ma'am."

"I'm not a Marine, but, well, Semper Fi."

"Semper Fi, Captain. Consider yourself an honorary Jarhead."

She and her co-pilot were laughing as he went down to the cargo bay.

Twenty-four hours later, Torbin was sitting in an office at Edwards Air Force Base, waiting to be called to a debriefing in a secure room. The room was shielded from all known types of eavesdropping, even some unknown from what Torbin had been told.

He had already done a quick debrief when the aircraft had returned to Edwards. That had been with Military Intelligence. This debrief was with some spook from D.C.

Torbin laughed to himself. There *was* no real D.C. left. So, just like Torbin Bender, the spook was a man without a home. Torbin sipped his coffee, sat, and waited. He had gotten good at waiting in his Military career. Yessiree, hurry up and wait—the mantra of the Corps.

Then he heard steps approaching, and he set down his cup, and stood up.

A tall and wiry man with dark hair and a tan, wearing plain urban camos with no rank, no insignia or name tag of any kind, walked into the waiting room.

"Gunnery Sergeant Torbin Bender?"

"Yes Sir."

"Come with me."

Torbin followed the man down the hallway to a windowless room with an electronic keypad lock to it. The man punched in some codes in, then placed his thumb on an electronic fingerprint pad. The door buzzed, and they went in. Torbin remained standing at parade rest, as the Spook sat at a nondescript wooden table. There was a somewhat padded chair opposite where the man was sitting. The supposed Intelligence Agent looked up at Torbin and frowned.

"Why don't you sit down, Gunny."

"Just waiting for you to say so, Sir."

"Alright. Sit down."

Torbin sat, still stiff. He had been told that at times he was too much of a hardass, too rigid. He didn't care. It was the way he was, and he wasn't about to apologize for it now.

"I'm Agent Leer. Who I'm with doesn't matter. Especially now that all the Headquarters Buildings in D.C. are empty, and many more are rubble. But what does matter is that I have been tasked by the Commander in Chief to verify the information we have received so far on the Battle of the Yuma Overpass, and to obtain anything new you may know."

Torbin frowned. "Excuse me, Sir. But Battle of the Yuma Overpass? Who in the hell came up with *that* name? And why?"

Agent Leer sighed. "Someone up the chain came up with it. Seems we need some victories and heroes right now. We can't have either without a catchy name for what happened."

"Heroes? Victories? And who in hell is the Commander in Chief? Did the President make it?"

"No, Gunny. We are all the way down to the Secretary of Veteran Affairs." Agent Leer chuckled. "Seems ironic, don't you think? I think before this is over, we'll *all* be veterans."

Torbin was a bit stunned. That many losses in the civilian chain of command? How could that happen?

Agent Leer must have noticed the look of concern on Torbin's face, for he began speaking and responded.

"As you know, during the first twelve hours, everyone thought it was a natural disaster. 'Of biblical proportions' was what the talking heads called it. They even started arguing over on the boob tube as to who coined the phrase first. Then the Russians started screaming, the Deltas and what we now call Falcons showed up. Then the arks. harvester arks is what they are, as confirmed by your mission. Which is why we are here."

Agent Leer looked sharply at Torbin. "I saw those video transmissions from your helmet cam, also the digital pictures and those pictures from that disposable camera. But I need to know what *isn't* on the cameras. Some of the feed was interrupted. There are some gaps."

"Ask away," Torbin said. "I'm an open book. Never was a spy, never wanted to be one. I was ordered to do the mission, I did it. Case closed, as far as I'm concerned."

The Agent tossed a file in front of him. "Start by explaining those pictures."

Torbin looked. There was were a couple of cloudy shots of the fake man whose throat he cut, laying on the ark cockpit floor.

"That's all you have of this POS?"

"We have some blurry feed, audio, but until you busted that video screen, the frequency it was transmitting on interfered with your video feed. Which gives us some info on how they communicate.

"So what's the beef, Agent?"

"You killed him. He would have been a wealth of information."

Torbin exploded. "What was I to do? Let *him* kill *me*? What about that weapon I recovered? Was *that* just a piece of crap also?"

Agent Leer leaned back in his chair a bit, steepled his fingers, and said nothing.

"Well? What are *you* supposed to do, Agent Leer, if you don't get the answers you want? Shoot my ass? Care to dance?" Torbin began to stand up. After what he had been through, he was *not* going to put up with some shit from some spook agent.

Agent Leer let out a sigh. "Please, sit down, Gunny. I was told I had to ask these questions by my higher-ups. Like you, I follow orders. There is a high level of frustration as things are not going well."

"No shit, Sherlock." Torbin sat down, still fuming. He was an action person, a doer. Not someone to sit around, sift through Intelligence briefs and navel gaze.

Agent Leer snorted. "We are losing or have lost both the West Coast and the East Coast. That odd creature on the screen feed you thought looked a bit like an octopus? Bingo. These so called Tschaaa are cephalopods, like squids, scuttlefish and octopus, all rolled into one. The head looks a bit more doomed shape, like maybe a crab. And they have appendages and tentacles like our sea creatures."

"You got all that information from my blurry video feed?"

"No. Naval forces around the world have been fighting them, have visual contact, some photos, and a few recovered body parts." Agent Leer stopped, sat still, his eyes seemed to focus on something not in the room.

"To head off your questions, no, the Navy is not doing well. Some small versions of the arks landed in all the major bodies of water, discharging Tschaaa warriors. Yes, they have warriors just as we do, not just robots, cyborgs, gray aliens, and lizards. They also have a very efficient set of what we would call limpet mines and underwater torpedos. Being as they are amphibious ocean-based creatures, we soon had a large number of naval surface vessels with holed hulls."

"What about out our SEALS and combat divers? Weren't they used?"

"We are a land based species. We swim as a secondary function. The Tschaaa, or Squids as many in our limited government have started calling them, are apparently born in the ocean. They easily kick our ass under water."

Torbin paused, thinking. Then he asked, "Our submarines. What about them?"

"Still a few in deep water. They get swarmed in more shallow seas. The Tschaaa seem to see them as a personal affront."

"So the world's navies..."

"Pretty much decimated. Naval aircraft are all land-based now."

Torbin thought back to the Falcon.

"How is our Air Force doing? How are they handling the Delta fighters and those Falcons?"

"They're trying. The Deltas use a form of scramjet engine, and also some type of advanced thruster we're trying to figure out. Zero to almost infinity it seems in the blink of an eye when they get in trouble. But that's an exaggeration. They can accelerate like a bat out of hell. Despite that, they've taken casualties here, in Russia, over Japan for sure. They can't always outrun our missiles and our guns."

"The Falcons, you call them. Like I saw. What about them?"

"Well, the Russians said they took a couple down with tank

gun, tube launched missiles they use. On Day Three one of our fighters took out an ark, then a Delta escort. Then the pilot rammed..." The Agent frowned, then seemed to go pale a bit. He looked at some papers in one of his folders.

"You have a...relative in the Air Force."

"Yes, Agent. My younger Brother, William. He's an Air Force Puke, a Fighter Pilot. I lost track of him the last few days..." Torbin's voice trailed off as the look on the Agent's face sunk in.

"Ah, shit." Agent Leer looked directly at Torbin. "There is no easy way to say this, do this. No one ever thought, put two and two together..." Leer cleared his throat.

"Captain William Bender, while defending the Port Area of Los Angeles from further incursions and landings, intercepted with his wingman a harvester ark. He took that down with a couple of missiles. An escorting Delta fighter attacked him and he took that out also. A couple minutes later, a Falcon battle cruiser showed up, blasted your brother's wingman, and tried to latch onto your brother's fighter with a form of tractor beam and metallic tentacles. I guess they wanted to examine the human who had taken out two of their craft so quickly." Agent Leer paused, then continued.

"Your brother William rammed the Falcon. It bellied in, his fighter still impaled in it. That's the last report we have of him."

Torbin sat frozen. He had always assumed he would have been killed first, being in Delta Force, the SEALS, and constantly in harm's way. Torbin had started at age 18, while William had gone active duty after college, at age twenty-one. William was two years his junior, had stayed on active duty when Torbin had gone reserve, and was up for Major below the zone...

Torbin quickly wiped a tear away. Marines don't cry.

"Gunny, this is a hell of a way to find out..."

"Not your fault. It just happened, what, a day and a half, two days ago? No one saw..."

"Nothing. The limited forces we had there were beaten back. The Falcon did not explode. It was still sitting there when the land forces abandoned Los Angeles. They're all deployed around Edwards now."

Torbin was numb. He had seen his share of death. He'd caused a lot of it. Now it was personal and really hit home.

"You say the West Coast is—overrun, I guess would be a good word—with these fucking Squids and company?"

"They control from ten to twenty miles in from the water. They landed mutual supporting arks, some of the Squids came up from the ocean. While the Tschaaa are amphibious, they can move somewhat on land. With the rock strikes starting fires and spreading panic, everything fell apart fast."

"San Diego...gone?"

"They're all over there, and down into Mexico, especially Baja."

Torbin took a deep breath, let it out. "My parents were in San Diego. Their neighborhood was hit by a good sized rock in the first twelve hours. I was unable to contact them after that. Then I got activated." He paused.

"I guess San Diego is gone."

"It looks that way, Gunny."

Both men sat quietly, both lost in their own thoughts. Then Agent Leer spoke.

"If it's any consolation, the information and video you and your men obtained from Yuma was excellent. It helped confirm our suspicions on how these Tschaaa are operating. One of the men even brought back this harpoon thing that was lodged in his body armor. Those robots seem to be land fishing."

"By the way, Agent, how did we learn what they call themselves?"

"Radio broadcast intercepts. Though it doesn't look like they or their minions know anything about communications security, so it wasn't exactly difficult. Some of their, 'Front Men' we are calling them, beings who have been sitting here watching us for a while, coordinated some of their activities in Earth languages. Referred to the Tschaaa Lords. So, we figured that's what those in charge, what we think of as Squids, call themselves."

Torbin grunted. "That fake man I killed, you think he was one of these front men?"

"Affirmative, Gunny. That's why the higher ups were so pissed you killed it. They really wanted to water board one of them, find out what makes them tick."

"Not in the cards that day, Agent."

Both men sat silent again. Then Agent Leer spoke once more.

"Look, I know it's easy for me to say, but your brother died a hero. And based on your actions, heroics seem to run in your family."

Torbin locked eyes with Agent Leer. "I'll trade all the heroics in the world for having my little brother here, so I could buy him a drink."

Torbin walked back to his temporary quarters in daze. He had never thought in his wildest dreams that he would be the surviving family member, even out living his parents. Hell, he thought they would have attended *his* funeral by now, based on the shit he had been involved in. Now, he didn't even have the ability to have a funeral service for his family. He didn't even have any remains.

A rage began to course through him as he thought about all those families who would never have the chance to say goodbye, have a casket funeral. The fucking Squids *ate* what would be in a casket.

He walked into the hallway of the Temporary Quarters Building and punched a hole in the wall. Then another. Somehow, it just wasn't very satisfying.

"Gunny, you okay?" It was a woman's voice. He looked up and saw dark-haired Captain White, in her flight suit, standing with a couple of bags in her hands.

"Ah, sorry Captain." He gave an embarrassed smile. "I guess this isn't very professional, is it?"

"Gunny, we heard over at the squadron about your brother William. Some of the people knew him, and thought very highly of him..."

"A lot of good that does him now!" Torbin snapped before he could catch himself. "Ah, fuck. I mean, sorry Ma'am. I'm not very good company right now."

"Call me Lori. Forget the rank. Is your room nearby?"

"Yeah. Over there." He grabbed one of the bags from her without thinking, walked over and unlocked, opened his door. They went in and he set the bag on the room's table.

"Can I get you a drink, Captain? I have some beer..."

"Gunny, I came over to share a drink with you. That's what's in the bags."

Torbin looked in the one he had carried. There were bottles of scotch, tequila and bourbon.

"I need to toast Lieutenant Roth, along with everyone else we have lost. Including your brother."

"Captain..."

"If you don't start calling me Lori, I am going to get angry. You don't want to see me angry." She said it in such a serious voice that Torbin suddenly started laughing.

"What? You going to go all she-Hulk on me? Turn green, start punching holes in the walls?"

Lori burst out laughing. She laughed so hard she had to sit down at the table. Torbin joined her. Finally, they both stopped, wiping tears from their eyes. Torbin looked at the Captain.

"Humor. God's way of helping us cope."

"I couldn't agree more... Torbin." She looked into his eyes.

"Church goer?"

"No. But it's true, you know. There are no real atheists in foxholes. Now, Lori, let me get the ice and glasses."

"I brought us some eats. Philly cheesesteak sandwiches, in honor of my home city."

"Good. Suddenly, I'm starving."

The two comrades-in-arms sat, ate, and bullshitted, talking

about missing friends and family. Then Lori raised a glass. "A toast. To Lieutenant Roth, your brother William, our missing families and friends. May they be safe, or at peace."

"I'll drink to that." Torbin clinked his glass with Lori. They each took a large drink, then Torbin refilled the glasses with scotch.

"Trying to get me drunk, Torbin, and take advantage of me?"

"That would be unauthorized fraternization, Lori. We could really get in trouble."

They both chuckled.

"Do you have anyone... special, Torbin?"

"No. Funny thing, William was the one who was engaged to be married. Had a lady friend with Hollywood connections. In the L.A. area. My parents thought once I got off active duty, got my teaching degree, I would be the one to settle down. No such luck. Now look at me. Back in the war."

"You're good at it. We need men like you, Torbin. Especially in the long haul."

"Lori, is there going to be a long haul?"

Lori paused, sipped her drink, and then answered. "Talk at the squadron is that some are moving forces and survivors into the interior. Live to fight another day."

"Yeah. That Agent Leer told me that my unit taking out that cyborg, or whatever the hell it was, with the weapons we had and showed they weren't as tough as everyone was saying. Panic does funny thing to people, makes them exaggerate the threat." Torbin sipped his drink, continued.

"But the energy weapon that thing had can take out an M-1 Tank if close enough, according to Leer."

"And you guys took out that ark. Tell me, Torbin, are the stories—"

"Yes." He cut her off. "Sergeant Robbins called it Dante's Inferno. It fit. Don't ask for any more details right now. Please."

The man and woman sat silent for a moment. Then Torbin looked at Lori.

"Anyone special?"

"Husband. With my parents in Philly. A big fucking rock hit there. Now, nothing." Lori took a drink, set it down, began to cry.

"Ah, hell. I didn't mean to..." He got up walked over and put his arm around her. Lori stood up, grabbed him in a bear hug.

"Torbin... I need some good-old fashioned human loving. I'm not a slut, but I need to know I can still feel. Right now, I feel numb. I don't like that."

Torbin began to gently stroke her hair that she had let down to her shoulders.

"Well, you do have nice hair." He smiled at her.

She looked up at him, though she wasn't that much shorter than he was. There was strength under the curves.

"You know why they don't send donkeys to school, Marine?"

"They don't like smartasses. The story of my life."

"Now kiss me, damnit. That's an order."

"Yes, Ma'am!"

Torbin pretended he was asleep when she got up, put her clothes back on and left. It was better that way. Torbin had seen this before. Near death, fear of death, and then people wanted loving. They needed to feel the hope that human contact causes, the hope created by another warm body next to theirs.

After he was sure she had left, he got up, visited the bathroom. Then he went in the main room and saw the note on the table.

"Torbin Bender," it read. "You are one of the best men I have ever known. Here's my full name, Social Security Number, DOB. Look me up later. Please. I'll need to know you made it. Take care, you crazy Marine. Love, Lori."

Torbin carefully folded the note, put it in his wallet. Then he got dressed, grabbed all his gear. No one had called him for another mission, but hell, there was a war on. He wanted those Tschaaa, those Squid aliens, to know something. Payback's a bitch.

"Yea, though I walk through the valley of death, I shall fear no evil," Torbin muttered to himself. "Because I'm the meanest son of a bitch in the valley."

He left the room unlocked, and the key on the table. He wouldn't be coming back.

INTERRUPTED TOUR

The two tall, tanned, and athletic young ladies were jerked awake as the tour bus they were riding in braked to a sudden stop.

The blonde, Sharon Wagner looked across the aisle at her best friend and beach volleyball partner brunette Susanne Shaw.

"What is *that* all about?" Sharon asked. "Somebody forget how to drive?"

"I'll go up and check," Susanne responded.

The two eighteen year old women were on the last leg of a beach volleyball tour, sponsored by a major beer brewery. They had already set their mark playing on their high school team and then in summer leagues in the sunshine state of Florida. The beer sponsor had seen them play and offered them a job for the summer after high school graduation, and before they attended college on athletic scholarships. They were both that good. The fact that they were hot and sexy in their small bikinis was a plus when it came to selling beer to men.

Then an Olympic games sponsor had also contacted them, while on advertising tour for the beer brand.

"You two are excellent," Mister Grant informed them on the telephone. "Call me after you are done with the tour. I know you two have college scholarships, but I think we can work around that and still get you ready for the next Summer Olympics. Beach volleyball is a *big* draw on television. Even if you don't medal, you can still write your own ticket after you make the team and compete. And ladies, you *will* make the team."

So here they were, on the last legs of a tour through Florida and Georgia. They had just departed Panama City en route to a weekend bash in Savannah, Georgia via Jacksonville, Florida. Then, home to prepare for college and the Olympics.

Susanne walked up to the front of the tricked-out tour bus, past four other nubile young women who were also part of the tour. It would be a definite exaggeration to say that it had always been fun traveling with sometimes bitchy strangers. But Sharon and Susanne's long term friendship, since childhood, made most things a lot easier. They even looked so much alike that most people thought they were siblings.

"Everything okay, Mister Jones?" Susanne asked the driver. Jones had done this tour many times for the beer company. After driving a beer delivery truck, this job was heaven.

"No, young lady," the beefy black man replied. "There was an explosion up ahead. I'm trying to pick up something on the radio and the CB. So far, nothing."

Dave Jones acted gruff, but when it came to the six young women in the bus he was a big teddy bear. The fact he used to be a semi-pro boxer helped them deal with some of the more beer-fueled "fans" at the various beach venues.

Just then, Mrs. Julie Norwood, the bleary-eyed, dark-haired official chaperone walked up. Some of the out-of-sorts look was caused from being on the road since 7:00am. The rest of it was probably due to her sampling the sponsor's wares with many of the older men who came to watch the beach volleyball tournaments late at night, and occasionally the younger studs as well. Julie was beginning to show the miles she had spent on the road, but was still cougar chic to many.

"What's the holdup, Dave? We have a schedule to keep."

"I know that. But look at that big plume of smoke. Something blew up."

"Shit. Stay here, I'll go up and look."

It was 9:20am.

Susanne thought about telling Julie Norwood to stay in the bus, but knew that the woman *hated* to listen to the younger women. So, she held her tongue. Instead she stood and watched Julie walk up the line of stopped vehicles.

"That women has the patience of a starving rat," Dave said.

Susanne laughed. "Yeah, she does seem to want everything to go right *now*, doesn't she?"

Just then, the Goodtime radio broke into the music with a news alert.

"This just in," the announcer began. "There has been a report of an explosion caused by a possible aerial collision on Interstate 10. Drivers are advised to find alternate routes and yield to emergency vehicles. This radio station will keep you advised of further developments..."

"That's just great," fumed Dave. "Now I get to listen to Julie bitch about the schedule for the rest of the trip."

Before Susanne could answer, they heard a loud crackling and whooshing sound. Through the windshield they saw a small fireball come smashing in, striking the line of cars some two hundred yards up. The bus shook from the impact and explosion. Debris fell by the bus.

"What the fuck was *that*?" Sharon was standing next to Susanne and behind Dave. The other four women were now awake in the rear of the bus, one of them screaming in sudden fear.

"Sit down!" Dave called out. "And hold on!"

They had been traveling in the far right hand lane. With

practiced ease, Dave swung the large vehicle to the shoulder. Then, to the surprise of all, he slammed it in reverse and began backing up at speed on the side of the Interstate.

"What *are* you doing?" Sharon demanded.

"Getting the hell out of dodge, youngster. *Sit down.*"

"But Mrs. Norwood...," Susanne began.

"She's flattened. You felt the explosion, saw the fireball. I need to save *you*. Now, *sit down.*" The bus accelerated.

Sharon grabbed her friend and pulled into a nearby seat.

"Seatbelt on, Sue."

As Susanne belted herself in, she asked, "What's happening?"

"Something bad, partner."

Susanne looked at her best friend. "Glad you're here."

Sharon smiled at her. "Hell, we're a team. The two of us together are unbeatable. Always were."

Susanne kissed Sharon on the cheek. "I know."

The tour bus jumped as Dave ran over something.

"Get the fuck out of the way!" he screamed out the driver's window, his head halfway out, looking to the rear.

Sharon looked out the passenger side windows, and saw what he was heading for. While the women had dozed, they apparently just passed a freeway on-ramp. Now Dave was maneuvering at speed to go down the on-ramp. The bulk of the bus made other cars swerve out of the way.

Within minutes, the tour bus was at the bottom. Dave swung it around, took off down the road parallel to Interstate 10, back towards Panama City.

A bleached blonde named Adriana dashed up to the driver's seat and began screaming at Dave.

"Turn around. We have to go back and get Mrs. Norwood!"

"She's beyond getting. My responsibility is to get you all home..."

Adriana was not good at accepting people who refused to do what she told them to do. She began to grab and claw at

Dave, causing the bus to swerve.

"*Turn around!*" she screamed.

Sharon grabbed onto Adriana. The hysterical female made the mistake of clawing at the tall, natural blonde's face. She wound up on the bus floor, Sharon having her in a painful wrist and arm lock.

"*Hey.*" Marjorie, Adriana's statuesque friend came up the aisle with fire in her eye. She went down holding her stomach after she received a well-placed kick from Susanne.

"Stay back," Susanne commanded. "Dave is trying to get us to safety, he does *not* need us screwing with his driving."

"Listen up." Dave had managed to get on the tour buses public address system. "The CB is going nuts with reports of junk, maybe meteors, coming from the sky and smashing into stuff. Atlanta has been hit. Apparently Washington D.C., as well as this Interstate, have taken hits also. We are headed to a rest stop we passed a few miles back. If you don't like that, I'll stop and let you off. Understand?"

All the young women verbalized by grunts or other means that they understood. Sharon let Adriana up, who gave her the stink eye. Sharon smiled.

"Don't like Jeet Kun Do, huh?"

Adrian turned on her heel and stomped to the rear of the bus.

"Thanks, Sharon and Susanne," Dave said.

"Where'd you learn to drive that way, Dave?" Susanne asked.

Dave laughed. "After driving a deuce and half in Iraq, dodging IEDs, then a beer truck, this bus is a piece of cake. Now, help me find that rest stop."

Ten minutes later, Dave drove the bus into the back of the Interstate rest area via a dirt access road they found. The rest area was already filling up when Dave stopped in the truck and RV parking area.

"All right. Bathroom break, then load up on any water and

snacks you can find. I know you have some empty cans and bottles in the back. Fill them up. I don't know when we'll be able to load up again." When the ladies seemed to hesitate, Dave yelled.

"*Move*, goddammit! Or find another ride."

The women went to the restrooms, where there was already a line. Dave hustled around, found a water faucet, and began to fill up a couple half gallon plastic water containers. Susanne came back with a bunch of vending machine snacks.

"Used up my money and change, Dave. Sharon's still out scrounging."

Dave smiled. "You two are quite the team."

"We try. We grew up together, are like sisters in some ways. We *are* a great beach volleyball team."

"Well, this may get nasty. So remember, Susanne. If you have someone watching your back, and you watch theirs, you are one up on a lot of people."

Sharon and the others began returning, the women subdued.

"All right ladies. Please stay here while I go around and talk with some of the other drivers. I need to find out what they know."

The six volleyballers got back on the bus, staking out spaces in which to relax. Susanne, smiling, began throwing a volleyball back and forth with Sharon. The other four ladies were more subdued.

A half hour later, Dave returned, with a serious look on his face. He stood in the aisle and addressed the women.

"The Interstate is closed." He held up his hands when people began to protest, question.

"Look—that's not my call. There are some massive traffic jams and vehicle fires up ahead. The State Police and all the emergency services have their hands full. There are some wrecks and fires behind us. So, we spend the night, hope we can move in the morning. Get your sleeping bags, clothes you are going to need for a comfortable night. Maybe somebody around here will share some hot dogs or something with us."

"Mrs. Norwood put a case of beer in the luggage compartment," somebody called out.

"That will be our emergency rations. I don't need some tipsy underage girls staggering around. So, get some rest. We may have to leave at zero dark thirty." When Dave saw quizzical looks, he added, "That means early in the morning." He went back to the front of the bus and plunked down.

About half an hour later, some dozen adults approached the bus. Dave got off and met them, as the six young ladies watched. The gist of the conversation was that a couple of good ole boys with full truck rifle and shotgun racks said they would help keep watch that night, as everything seemed to be breaking down outside the rest area. Radio stations were beginning to go off the air, and the Emergency Broadcast System had started to broadcast warnings and instructions. In addition, Dave and the adults organized a cook out around a couple of permanent grills on the edge of the rest area. Everyone shook hands, and women from some of the vehicles and RV's began to congregate around the picnic area.

Dave got on the bus again. "Alright. I would like a dollar donation from everyone to help defray the costs of the kind people supplying the hot dogs, hamburgers and other stuff. Also, if you would please dig out a volleyball net and string it up over there on those poles. We'll get some games going for the kids. There are quite a few."

The driver continued, "If you want to, you ladies can show off your skills. Give everyone a little entertainment. Okay?"

Soon close to a hundred men, women and children were organized in a good ole fashioned community picnic. Dave knew that humans had the ability to regroup after times of incredible stress. "Let them play, relax," he said to himself. "That's what we had to do in Iraq and Afghanistan, when we never knew when we were going to get hit. You have to be able to de-stress." A few people stayed at their vehicles, apparently not wanting to socialize with a bunch of strangers. At least not yet. Dave saw a few who were crying and red-eyed, overheard some children asking if they were still going to Disney World.

After a short private discussion, Sharon and Susanne set up a little demonstration they usually did for drunk college kids. After the volleyball net went up, and they had changed into their bikinis (with a last minute beer company t-shirt to cover up some of their skin after they saw the number of children present), then they set up some plastic drink cups up on one side of the net at various distances from the net. They began to pass and hit the ball back and forth. Once they had a small audience, they went into the routine.

They alternated their activities. First Susanne would set the ball up, and Sharon spiked it at a cup at on the other side of the net. Then, Sharon would set it up and Susanne would spike it. That was what made them so dangerous as opponents. Both were equal in defense, offense, serving and spiking. Someone called them the "nasty clones" once, claiming they had been manufactured, not raised as normal children. They had just laughed.

Soon the majority of the children were racing each other to recover the spiked balls and reset the target cups up in new locations, with laughter and yells.

Susanne smiled at Sharon. "I wonder how many of these kids would usually be playing video games?"

"Well, they're having a fun time now. And their parents seemed to be appreciating our show also."

Quite a few of the parents began to watch and applaud the young women's skill. The partners never missed their targets.

Someone whistled loudly, and then a yell of "Come and get it!" The two ball players did not have to be told twice. They had built up an appetite with their ball play. As they walked over to the picnic table and grill area, a woman with two young, red-headed twin girls walked up to them.

"Excuse me, Ladies, but my girls really *love* to watch you play. How did you get so good? Oh, by the way, Karen Andersen. And these two eight year old redheads are Ruth and Belinda." She shook hands with the two tall athletes.

"Were you always this good?" one of the twins asked.

"This is Ruth," Karen interjected.

"Well, Ruth, we had to practice a lot," Sharon said. "We started out about your age."

"Are you sisters too?" Now it was Belinda's turn for a question.

"No, young lady," Susanne said. "We just look a lot alike. Though we feel like sisters, don't we Sharon?"

Her volleyball partner smiled and squeezed her hand. "We've been together since about age eight so yeah—we're family."

"Mind if we sit with you? I like my daughters to see women who work hard, and are successful in what they chose to do."

"Of course," answered Susanne. "If you don't mind me stuffing my face while we talk. I'm hungry."

Within a few minutes the two long term time friends were sitting and talking with their new friends at a picnic table. Someone had access to a bunch of hot dogs and hamburgers, as there seemed to be plenty for everyone. Sharon counted over a hundred men, women and children in the rest area, as well as a few dogs and one cat. For once, a group of strangers met and got along despite the problematic situation swirling around them outside the rest area.

There was some beer and other alcohol, but everyone seemed to police their own. The absence of any uniformed official responders was a subject of occasional worried conversation. One young man who had apparently started partying early had started to stumbled up to the young ladies on the beer tour, but was intercepted by Dave. The man's sober friend came and collected him before his mouth wrote a check his butt could not cash.

Susanne looked around, did not see a man hanging around

Karen and her daughters.

"Don't want to pry, Ma'am, but is there a Mr. Andersen?"

"You're not prying, and call me Karen. Ma'am makes me feel like my mother. I'm not that much older than you two."

Sharon and Susanne smiled. "Okay, Karen. Deal."

"But to answer your question, we are meeting my husband, their father in Key West. We're a Navy family, and he was just transferred there. He's a Naval aviator, going to be assigned to the Sundowners, a Squadron that acts as enemy aircraft for air to air training."

"You sound very proud of him, Karen," Sharon said.

"I am. He's a good Naval pilot *and* a great dad. Just ask the girls."

"Daddy's the best!" the twins answered in perfect unison. The three adults began to laugh.

Then Karen's face looked serious. "This, whatever is happening, has me concerned. If Larry was were here, he'd be able to find out more through his contacts. I feel blind and stupid right now."

"You're definitely not stupid, Karen," said Susanne. "Tell you what. When Dave, our driver and chaperone, gets ready to leave, I'll tell him you're going to follow us. Safety in numbers. Dave is one tough dude, former vet and semi-pro boxer. You can at least stick with us until Jacksonville."

Karen patted Susanne's hand. "Thank you. That would make me feel better. But you two look like you can handle yourselves."

"Yeah. But a big, older guy like him makes people think twice," Sharon said. "Especially young drunk males. We've seen quite a few on this tour." Then she told Karen about the tour, their college plans, and the Olympics.

"After I and the kids make it to Key West, I'd like to stay in touch with you two. I know Larry would like to try and recruit you into the Navy.

The two volleyball players laughed. "Let us get to the

Olympics first," Susanne said. "*Then* we can see about a military career."

The women and girls visited a bit more, then Karen took their leave.

"Time to get these two cleaned up a bit. I made a bed in the minivan for us tonight, as I think we'll be stuck here until tomorrow." She hugged Sharon and Susanne. "Thanks for being nice to me and my daughters. It helped keep me from running around screaming."

"You don't look like the screaming type, Karen," Susanne said. "Come on over to our bus if you want anything. Deal?"

"Deal. Talk to you later."

Susanne and Sharon went and found Dave, who was enjoying a large plate of potato salad.

"Enjoying yourself, Dave?" asked Sharon.

"Learned in the Army. Eat when you get a chance, especially with good food. It may be awhile before you get another good meal."

"Heard anything, Dave?"

He took a drink of his beer, then frowned. "News on the radio is that we, the Earth, were hit by a meteor shower that the government and scientists seemed to have missed completely. Lots of casualties, as well as reports of some dirt bags taking advantage of the situation, stealing and trashing. So, I definitely want to stay here. Safety in numbers."

"We were just thinking the same thing," said Sharon. The two friends then explained to Dave about Karen and her daughters.

"Sounds good to me. Question is, which roads are going to be open?"

As Susanne and Sharon collected their sports equipment, leaving the net up with a ball for kids to play with, Dave went to round up the other four women. As all six of the tour participants moved back to the bus, Adriana was heard making comments about the "fucking showoffs" as she looked in

Sharon and Susanne's direction. Sharon started to turn around but Susanne gently grabbed her arm. "Ignore the ignorant whore."

Sharon's mouth dropped open a bit. "Whore? Hey. I'm the one with the potty mouth, not you."

"Sometimes a word like that just seems to fit someone. So, it's not obscene, it's just being truthful." At that explanation, Sharon began to laugh, and Susanne joined in. They made their way to the bus, staked out a couple of bench seats.

Dave herded the other four females to the bus, despite some grumbles about having to leave a couple of young studs behind. "Let's get this sorted out, ladies. Then you can try to pick up all the man meat you want." Without Mrs. Norwood, there was no one to complain about his bluntness.

Tired, with full stomachs, Sharon and Susanne made themselves beds on the bench seats they had claimed and went to sleep, the other women complaining about the horrible cell phone service in the area.

The two friends woke up as the sun was setting. They roused themselves and made their way to the communal rest area restrooms. Susanne picked up an empty sports drink bottle and took it to the restrooms to wash out and fill it with water. For once, the bathrooms were vacant, so the two volleyballers had their choice of stalls.

After relieving herself, Susanne went to one of the sinks. She washed out the bottle and began to refill it with fresh water. As she topped it off, the flow of water began to sputter.

"Uh oh."

"What's up, Susanne?" Sharon came out of her stall and asked.

"I think the water system is beginning to have problems. I wonder if the pipe system has been damaged."

"Let's let tell Dave know. He might have some ideas."

They found Dave talking with two of the good ole boys with their guns. All three men had concerned looks on their faces as

Sharon and Susanne approached. They smiled at the approaching young ladies, one even touching the bill of his ball cap.

"Ma'am," the young man with a scraggly beard said with a thick Alabama accent. The two men then turned and walked towards the far side of the rest area.

"What's going on, Dave?" Sharon asked.

Dave paused for moment, then shrugged. "Hell, might as well tell you that everything from Atlanta south is a complete mess. Atlanta proper was hit by small chunks of space debris or rocks, which started some big fires downtown. A couple of blocks were completely burned out, tall office buildings and all. This lead to the city being evacuated, all non-emergency workers told to hit the road." Dave paused again, then continued. "Then a big one hit on the outskirts, took out Interstate 85 by Union City. There's a big crater there, from what we can gather."

"This all came from the radio stations?" Susanne asked.

"Mostly from CB traffic. A lot of the radio stations have dropped off the air. Power lines have been knocked out. There are reports of pieces of scum taking advantage of this mess and are running around looting and raising all kinds of problems." He shook his head. "Here we have all of us at this rest area cooperating, helping each other out, as it should be. But then others just have to act like the nasty apes we seem to be descended from, start fighting and fussing. Humans are our own worst enemy."

A small smile formed on Sharon's lips. "Getting philosophical, Dave?"

"Don't need a lot of college degrees to figure things out, pretty ladies. Now, let's get back to the bus."

As they walked, Dave gave some more details. "We have quite a few people on guard tonight. In the morning, we'll see what which roads are open. We may head back to Panama City. We're about an hour's drive from Jacksonville. But from what I have heard, a couple of chunks of space junk come came down on Interstate 10, including the fireball we saw. There is a large bunch of cars still smoldering up ahead, blocking all traffic lanes of traffic, including some more near the intersection of Interstate 75 and 10."

"Think we can find a side road around the problem?"

"We can try in daylight. Right now, get yourselves settled for the night. We leave at sunrise."

The three walked back to the tour bus and saw Adriana flirting with some young stud, who was standing and talking with her through an open bus window. The stud smiled and said goodbye when he saw Dave approaching, the word having gotten around that he did not cotton to people hitting on his female charges right now with all that was going on.

After getting on the bus, Dave made an announcement to the assembled young women.

"Okay, at sunrise, we get up and I try to find us a way out of here. We may have to turn back to Panama City, based on reports of serious road damage and fires ahead. Either way, we find a town or city to hold up in until this all gets sorted out."

Adriana sniffed loudly. "Well, if I could get my father on my cell phone, he'd figure something out. He's a State Representative, you know."

"Well, young lady, unless he has access to some airlift resources, I don't see him doing much more that than what we can do on our own.

"What about all the others, Dave? What are they going to do?" asked Susanne.

"I'm concerned with you young ladies. No, don't argue. I told you I am driving this bus. If you really don't like this, then find another ride." He paused, and sighed. "Look, you think I am being a complete hardass here. But if you need a reason, I'll give you three."

He continued. "First, we are exposed here. We need to find a secure location. I have not seen a single State Trooper, soldier, whatever—in hours. We cannot wait for them to come to us, we need to find them.

"Two, we don't know the extent of this disaster. So far, it is parts of the East Coast. So we have to get some accurate information."

"Third and last, we will soon need food and water. We cannot live on air and good intentions."

The six young ladies were silent. Except for Marjorie.

"How am I going to get back to Colorado Springs?" she asked.

"One step at a time. We'll work on that later. Alright. Lights out, get some rest. I'll monitor the CB radio for a while."

Sharon and Susanne re-staked their claim on their two bench seats, got a few things from their suitcases in the bus luggage compartment. Susanne noticed Sharon had grabbed two small packs they had and was stuffing various items in them.

"Are we going for a little hike in the morning?" she asked.

Sharon looked at her friend with a worried expression on her face. "I have this feeling I just can't shake. That we need to be ready to bug out."

"That the influence of your survivalist uncle?"

"Hey, he may seem paranoid at times, but he has shown me how to be ready if the crap hits the rotating blade. He told me that sometimes your gut and intuition puts together things that your mind hasn't figured out yet. So, when I feel like this, I plan for the unexpected."

Susanne sat on the seat next to Sharon and hugged her.

"We have always made a good team, haven't we?"

Sharon hugged her back. "Yes, we were always there for each other. Even when we got in trouble and got had our butts paddled."

"Remember that time we t.p.'d Old Lady Brown's house on Halloween?"

"Well, if she hadn't been calling and complaining about us kids all the time we never..."

"Sharon, Susanne."

"Yes Dave."

"You are not getting ready for sleep."

"Yes sir."

Five minutes later, the pair were finally settled on their bench seats.

"Good night, Ellen."

"Good night, John Boy."

"You two...," Dave began, then chuckled. Never a dull moment.

It was 9:30 PM.

Sharon and Susanne had just begun to drift to sleep, when loud screams over the CB jerked them wide awake. Then they heard a faraway rumbling. The two women jumped up and stood by Dave in the front as he tried to talk to someone on the CB.

"Say again. What happened?"

"It's *fucking huge!*" the voice said, then stopped. Dave kept trying to raise anyone on the various CB channels, but kept getting yells and screams as people all tried to talk at once.

Sharon opened the bus door and jumped out.

"Oh my God."

"What?" Susanne joined her and looked east, where Sharon was staring.

It looked like a huge light show some two miles or so away in the darkness, as rumblings similar to large aircraft engines shook the bus windows. The lights were accentuated as all the street, roadway and rest area lights were now out.

"Ladies, get back in here. *Now!*" Dave commanded. He grabbed the bus intercom microphone.

"Everyone, up, get clothes, shoes on. We may be moving any minute."

"Where?" a voice called out.

"Anywhere but here," Dave replied.

The rumblings stopped, but there were still some fairly

bright lights emanating from the original location of the noise and light show.

"Stay here," ordered Dave, then he opened the bus door and was out.

Sharon and Susanne heard him talking loudly to a couple of men, probably from the volunteer guard detail. Then they heard a worried sounded woman's voice, then a mixture of some others. The parents and others where trying to figure out what was happening, what they should do next. Sharon and Susanne could only pick up bits and pieces of the conversation, but after some ten minutes, it seemed everyone was returning to their respective vehicles.

A loud gunshot resounded through the darkness. Then another. Then another. Then screams.

Dave burst back onto the tour bus, a large crowbar in his grasp.

"Down. *Everybody down!*" Dave yelled as he tried to start the bus.

There was an extremely bright light off to the left, followed by screams.

Adriana screamed from the rear of the bus.

The bus engine roared into life and Dave yelled, "Hang on!"

Then something slammed into the front of the bus—and the engine died.

Dave grabbed the crowbar as more shots rang out. Something latched onto and yanked the front bus door open. Adriana released a scream an opera critic would have liked on opening night.

Something else tried to yank open the rear emergency door, setting off the buzzer.

A long cable or snake-like shape grabbed at Dave through the front bus door and he smacked at it with the crowbar. The sound of metal on metal resonated, as Dave knocked away whatever was grabbing at him. He let out a war bellow. "*Not tonight, you fu...*"

Dave was slammed into the driver's side window as a long sharp object impaled him. All the girls screamed. Then he was gone, yanked out through the bus front door.

Sharon grabbed Susanne. "*Move.* Follow me." She pulled Susanne down to the bus aisle floor, then began to scramble up until she could peek out the front entrance.

"Now," she yelled, and Susanne scrambled with her out of the bus. As they did, something yanked the rear bus emergency door open as the remaining four occupants screamed, tried to run away.

Sharon and Susanne ran into the darkness as hell continued to unfold. Gunshots resounded, gun flashes lit up parts of the rest area. Odd shapes were seen moving in the darkness, whirring sounds heard as they traversed the parking areas.

The two sports partners moved as fast as they could through the shifting darkness. Then they saw a small figure run screaming in front of them. There was enough light to see it was one of the redheaded twin girls, either Ruth or Belinda. Then the two young women saw why the child was running and screaming.

A six-wheeled monstrosity came with an accompanying whirring noise in pursuit. It looked like an overgrown ATV with an oversized volleyball-shaped turret exuding up from the chassis. It clearly had the young twin targeted.

"No!" screamed Susanne as she saw and picked up a rock. In a series of practiced moves as if was it were a volleyball, she went forward in a vicious spike with her strong right arm. As it hit, it resounded off the side of the ball shaped turret on the mechanical beast, causing the turret to jerk about.

The six-wheeled apparent robot spun into the direction of the threat, just as Sharon tackled her friend to the ground behind a picnic table and grill. An extreme bright light flashed over where Susanne had been standing only a moment before, the after effects causing the two athletes to see some spots in front of their eyes.

A large caliber weapon boomed. Then again. And again.

A male voice yelled over some crackling sounds. "Get up and *run*! I'll hold them as long as I can." The origin of the voice was the scraggly haired ball cap wearer with the thick Alabama accent.

As Sharon and Susanne jumped up, they saw that the left side of Alabama accent's face was covered in blood.

"Mister..." Sharon began to say but was cut off.

"Just go, goddammit! I've got something to finish here."

Now it was Susanne's turn to grab and pull her friend along.

"Come on. We need to find Karen's daughter."

As the two ran, they saw the six-wheeled threat was sitting smoldering and throwing off sparks, the 12 gauge rounds of the Alabama native having permanently rearranged its gear works.

"Come on, you motherfuckers!" He yelled as he loaded more rounds into his weapon's tube magazine. "Come on and get some."

Sharon and Susanne ran in the same direction as the little girl twin had run. But they could not catch sight of her. Two loud shotgun blasts from behind them, then a cut off scream. They ran as fast as they could into the night.

They ran for an hour straight, their excellent physical shape and adrenaline-fueled muscles carrying them along at breakneck speed. They were lucky they did not fall into a ditch, or run into something in the darkness. However, they did not.

They plunked down alongside an abandoned car in a ditch to catch their breath. For the first minute they just sat there and breathed in oxygen. Sharon began to sob.

"Sharon?" Susanne said, as she slid over next to her friend.

"They're dead. Dave, the other volleyball players, even that guy with the Alabama accent who saved us. Fuck, I don't even know his name." Sharon's voice broke at the end of the last sentence, sobs clawing their way out her throat.

"Hey, Sharon. You're the badass one of the two of us, remember? We'll... "

"Half the time it's all a bluff, Susanne. I'm more scared than you are, I just don't let on."

Susanne grabbed and hugged her best friend, tears now running down her cheeks.

"We have each other, partner. We are two of the baddest beach volleyball players in the U.S.—hell, in the world! We're not going to let some assholes from wherever they're from, mess us up. No way."

Sharon stopped sobbing, sniffed, and wiped her nose with her arm.

"Now who is sounding like my survivalist uncle?"

The two women began to laugh, as the fact they were alive began to sink in. They held onto each other as they laughed. Finally, they stopped and stood up.

"We are badasses, Susanne," Sharon said. "At least together."

"And that is the way it will stay. Us together, watching each other's backs. Like Dave said."

With a new found resolve, they both looked around in the night.

"Need to find a place to sleep, safe, tonight, Susanne,"

"Yeah. Let's head down this road, stay on the shoulder. We can dash into the brush if one of those...robot things comes along. Damned things sounded like they ran on electric motors."

"They were definitely quieter than something run on gas," opined Sharon. "Okay. Let's get going. I hope we find something soon. I don't feel like staying up all night."

The young athletes made their way down the road, keeping an eye peeled for anything moving. From what Dave had said, there were some nasty humans out there also causing problems.

A half hour later, they came upon a small, former country store that had been modified into a convenience Stop and Rob. As they approached, slow and careful, they saw that a large RV was parked at the gas pumps in front, with the driver's door open. The only lights on appeared to be small emergency exit lights in the store proper.

"Is that someone sitting in the driver's seat?" Sharon whispered.

"I think so. But nobody is moving," Susanne answered. The two crept closer to the RV.

"Hello," Sharon said in a low voice as she approached. Then she saw why the person was not moving.

The older and rotund male was leaning on the steering wheel, his blank eyes staring at nothing in death.

"Damn, he's dead," Susanne said. "Heart attack?"

"Could be. Looks like he was talking on his cell phone. Maybe what he heard sent him over." Sharon looked at Susanne.

"Looks like everyone else bugged out. Should we..."

"Yes, Sharon. We move him. He's beyond caring and we need to get out of here."

The two athletes lifted him out of the RV, set him down as gently as they could. Sharon tried to start the RV, and it surprised her by starting right up.

"Damn. Gas gauge is almost on 'E'. It looks like the power is off at the pumps."

Susanne patted down the pockets of the dead man, telling herself that the living take precedence over the dead. She pulled a small book of matches out of one pocket, then was surprised what was in another.

"Hey, a gun." She handed it to Sharon.

"Little five shot revolver. My uncle has one."

"You shot one?"

"Yes, once or twice. Point and shoot. Come on, get in. I don't know how much gas this has in it."

"What about food in the store?"

"No time. Besides, there may be a surprise in there. Get in. Time's a-wasting."

Susanne climbed into the passenger seat and Sharon accelerated the large vehicle on to the road way. About a minute later, the little "ding" and low gas symbol came on at the gas gauge.

"Well, we'll run this until it stalls, I guess," said Sharon.

"Let's look for a hiding place first. We're both exhausted, need some rest, and then we can look to see what is in this RV."

"Good idea, Susanne. Start looking."

Five minutes later, they found the remains of a closed gas station. Sharon pulled over behind it.

"We can at least hide here until daylight. Now, let's see what supplies this thing has."

The two women soon made a search of the vehicle. In the small icebox was some lunch meat, bread, part of a cake and two diet colas. The found a few condiment packages and some crackers in the cupboard, along with a hidden unopened bottle of bourbon and a bottle of wine. Back in the separate sleeping area they found some partial bags of chips and a six pack of beer. In the small bathroom was a twelve ounce bottle of water. The women quickly divided the spoils between their two packs, got everything ready for a quick bug out.

Susanne took two beers out of the six pack and handed one to Sharon.

"Nightcap?" Sharon asked.

"Kind of. It'll help us calm down, sleep. And, it's liquid bread, has some food value."

"You were always the smart one, Susanne."

"Oh, yeah. You were so in danger of flunking out, little Miss Straight A's."

"Hey, I flirted with the teachers."

"Sharon D. Wagner, you did not! Oh. You got me again. You are such a smartass!"

They started to laugh and sipped at their beers. Then they began to get sleepy.

"Here, you find some blankets, Sharon. I'll make sure everything is locked up."

Five minutes later and the two were preparing for bed.

"Here, Sharon. Something else you might need." She handed her a long and sharp carving knife. "I've got the butcher knife. They're both very sharp, so watch it. We'll have to make some sheaths to keep from cutting what we don't want to cut."

Sharon looked at the knife, than then at Susanne.

"Do you think our families..."

"I don't want to think about that right now. Let's go to sleep."

"Okay." They laid down next to each other, then hugged.

"I love you, Susanne."

"I love you, too. We'll get through this."

"I know... By the way, you smell all nice and sweaty. You must drive men wild with your funkiness."

"You are so cruising for a bruising."

"Promises, promises. Good night."

"Sleep tight."

Then they were both out like lights.

COASTIE

The young female Coast Guardsman pulled herself up and out of the surf on a stretch of south Miami beach. Both her floatation gear and physical conditioning had helped her swim against a current about a mile after her Coast Guard cutter had sunk.

Heidi Faust squished up from the surf, took a few more steps, and then sat down to catch her breath. She thanked her parents for owning that gym/martial arts dojo in Palm Beach that which kept her in excellent physical shape. Otherwise, she might have been floating outside Miami Bay, dying.

She shook the negative thoughts out of her head. She was the only one who seemed to have survived the massive explosion that had spilt her boat in half. Heidi would mourn her ship mates later. She had tried to question the Chief's idea of trying to make a run for it outside Miami Bay, in an attempt to hook up with any surviving U.S. Navy units a week and a half after the first rock strike. Years later, Heidi knew, the question would be "where were you when the rocks hit?" At that moment, as she sat on the beach, the question was, how was she going to survive and not be eaten by the alien Tschaaa?

She had regained her breath back so she and stripped off her floatation gear. Her issued pistol was still in its holster, as was her armed forces knife. In her front pocket was her personal butterfly knife, a present from her fiancé, also Coast Guard, location and status unknown.

Heidi walked up and off the deserted beach, carrying her floatation gear. She stashed it on a bench on the paved beach road, figuring she would come back and get it later. She had no plans for another swim, as she knew the Tschaaa owned the ocean. Plus she felt, and probably looked like, a drowned rat.

They had barely made it a hundred yards from Government Cut, when their cutter blew in half, throwing her out into the Atlantic Ocean. Stunned, she had floated for a while, the current carrying her from Miami Bay. Based on what little intelligence she and her fellow Coasties had received, anything over fifteen feet was fair game for the cephalopod monstrosity that humans—at least the military—cursed as Squids. They were a true ocean-based lifeform, putting paid to the myth that the Navy ruled the sea. Humans were just rubber duckies out there, floating around until the Tschaaa became irritated by their presence and threw a mine or a torpedo at them.

Heidi took a deep breath, looked, and listened. No sounds other than seagulls. The harvester robots must have swept through already, any survivors either fled or were in hiding. Which she also needed to find, a place to hide. She got her bearings and made her way to the MacArthur Causeway and bridge to cross into Miami city proper. She wanted to be as far from the actual Atlantic Ocean as possible right now.

Heidi shifted her body armor on her five foot six buxom frame. There was a female MMA fighter who had once said that a large chest often got in the way of physical activities. Heidi knew from experience that she had only known the half of it. Trying to get body armor that fit and didn't rub your breasts wrong was always a challenge. She seemed a bit solid because of her excellent shape, but not steroided out. She was strong, capable, a woman not to be trifled with, especially with her martial arts background in Jiu Jitsu. But many men still said she was smoking hot when she dressed up.

She kept a sharp lookout with her hazel eyes, letting her brown hair down so that it would dry. Heidi didn't think anyone would worry about uniform regulations right then.

It took her about an hour of jogging and walking to make it into Miami City. Still, no sign of anything or anyone.

"Biggest ghost town in the U.S.," Heidi said to herself. She knew a couple of harvester arks had landed nearby, which was a reason why the Chief had wanted to get underway, so that he and his personnel were not picked off. Now they were all dead anyway. Heidi worked her way south on the shore front, past apartments, condos, and office buildings not far from the water.

Then she saw him. A slender Cuban boy, medium complexion, about nine or ten years of age, who stepped out from hiding in a building entrance. Heidi knew that she must look like a like a drowned rat, wet uniform and all, as he approached her in a cautious manner.

"Hey, guy. How you're doing?" Heidi called.

"Okay, I guess," Pablo answered. He kept looking her over. "Are you a soldier, lady?"

"Coast Guardsman, my good man. Better than a soldier in my estimation. Why are you looking for a soldier?" Pablo paused for a long time, as Heidi slowly walked along. He finally answered.

"I need some help. My mom left yesterday, but never came back. She said she was going to my uncle's place. The phone doesn't work, so I can't get ahold of anyone." Heidi saw he was trying to hold it all together, not to cry.

"Tell you what. How about you take me to your place so I can at least get out of this soaked uniform? Then, as part of the deal, we go look for your mom. Okay?"

"Okay... Is that a gun?" He pointed at her sidearm that somehow made it through the dunking.

"Yes, it is. I was trained how to use it, so don't worry, it won't go off by accident."

Pablo inched closer, then put out his hand. "Here, take my

hand. I'll lead you."

"Okay. How about my left hand? I need to keep my right free for my pistol. Okay?"

"Okay." He took her hand. Pablo shivered a bit, from fear, Heidi believed. Mother gone, aliens trying to kill and eat everyone, Hell, *she* was scared! They made their way along a street about a block inland from the shoreline. After walking for about fifteen minutes and seeing no one, they arrived at an apartment complex that had seen better days as a hotel, a couple of blocks from the beach.

"This is my home," Pablo said. "We live on the third floor. I can only find Mrs. Melendez and Mrs. Kleinman in their apartments. Every else is gone—even the Super, Mr. Hernandez."

Heidi made a quick glance up and down the street to see if anyone was watching. She did not see a single human, or anything else.

"Let's go in, my man. After I'm a little dried off, we'll see about rustling' up some grub, like the say in the westerns. Okay?"

"Okay." The boy started walking, then stopped. "What's your name?"

It dawned on Heidi that no names had been exchanged.

"Well, since I *know* we will be friends, you can call me Heidi. What's yours?"

"You can call be Pablo. But not late for dinner." He smiled at her for the first time. "That's what my Uncle Manny says."

Heidi chuckled. "I can agree with that. Let's go in, shall we?"

In the apartment, Heidi asked for permission to put on a pair of sweats that were clearly his mother's, with a promise that she would clean them up after she used them.

"Alright. Mi casa es su casa." Pablo had been taught some manners by his mother.

Heidi went into the bathroom, stripped off her wet uniform and underwear, her ballistic vest, placing them on the shower curtain rack to dry. After changing into the sweats, Heidi took her pistol to the front room and asked Pablo if he had any rags and oil of any kind. He quickly produced a bunch of rags and a small container of household lubricant. With practice ease Heidi cleared, then stripped her M-9 pistol, wiped it off, and stripped the ammo from the magazine. She found a pencil and used it to push small pieces of rags she had ripped up to dry out the barrel, then put just a smidgen of oil on a rag and swabbed it again. She lubed the pistol frame rails, then wiped them dry. Heidi dried each and every bullet, then disassembled the magazine, dried and lubed it. She repeated the process with her two spare magazines that she somehow had kept from losing in the Bay. Thank God her floatation equipment was top of the line in the load bearing department. Otherwise, all the stuff she had on would have sunk her.

All the while, Pablo was watching her intently. Heidi smiled at him. "A penny for your thoughts, Pablo—like my mom used to say."

He gave a hint of a smile. "My mom said, 'A centavo for your thoughts.'" Heidi saw that he was hurting.

"Hey, my man! This lady could sure use a hug." Pablo quickly closed the distance and hugged her. He tried not to cry.

"Pablo, I promised we would go look for her—and we will. Petty Officer Heidi Faust never goes back on a deal. Let's eat something first, find me some dry shoes, then we go. Deal?"

Pablo sniffed. "Deal."

Heidi found some fairly fresh bread, lunchmeat, and cheese. Some cans of pop rounded out the lunch. With food in her stomach, Heidi felt more human. Pablo ate a little, but was clearly nervous. He found sandals that fit Heidi, thanks to the leather being all stretched out of shape. Her uniform boots would take some time to dry out. Heidi dried out her holster and spare mag carrier, then slung the equipment belt over her shoulder. She quickly wiped down her service knife as well, blew inside the plastic sheath, and then sheathed it. She then did the same with her butterfly knife, planning to check it for signs of wet and rust when they returned. Southern Florida and its humid salt sea air was horrible for rust and corrosion.

Pablo watched everything she did. "You do that a lot, don't you?" He asked.

"Well, Pablo, all this was beat into me by a couple of training drill instructors. You take care of you equipment and it will take care of you." She walked to the door and listened. Then she turned to Pablo. "Do you have your key?"

"Yes, Heidi."

"Well, it's off to see the Wizard, or at least the yellow brick road. Let's go."

Pablo kept quiet as they walked down the three flights of stairs, seemingly knowing that noise brought danger. They went out a side exit, then slowly down the street, trying to keep in shadows as much as possible. Pablo led them in the direction of his uncle's place, about a mile away. It was still like a ghost town in this area of Miami.

Halfway there, they saw why the area was so quiet. A harvester rob suddenly came trundling down the middle of the street, its electric powered motor being rather quiet. Heidi grabbed Pablo and ducked in a nearby alley. She put him behind her, pushing up against a building wall as she drew her pistol. Fuck, she thought. She did not even know if her pistol was any good against that thing. Suddenly, she was scared to shit.

The six-wheeled overgrown ATV trundled past, not noticing them. Finally, Heidi could breathe again.

Pablo whispered. "I'm scared. I want to go home!"

"If we keep real quiet, we'll be at your uncle's place in no...."

"My mom is dead. So is my uncle."

Heidi froze. "How do you know, Pablo?"

"I just know. That machine tells me they are dead. We see no one else. Just the machine. They killed everyone."

Heidi looked at the young boy, now taking in adult

sensibilities. Heidi crouched down and looked him in the face. "Pablo, I'll keep my word. You want to go on, we will. You want to go back, we will. Your decision."

Pablo took a big breath, letting it out. A tear ran down his face. "Back, home. Please."

"Okay, Pablo. We'll go back. Slow and quiet."

They took a half hour to cover six blocks and waited another ten minutes to make sure no harvester robs would sneak up on them. They made a dash to the side door, and Pablo used his pass key to let them in. They made their way to the relative safety of the third floor apartment. Pablo went straight to his mother's room. Heidi spent a few minutes looking out the apartment windows that faced the main street. Nothing. She then went to check on Pablo.

The young boy, being quickly forced into adulthood, was sitting on his mother's bed. He held a stuffed bear up to his face. "Pablo," Heidi said quietly.

"I gave her this bear on her last birthday. Bought it with my own money. It still smells like her. She always liked bears. My dad left years ago. It's just been mom and I, with my uncles." He began to sob. Heidi went up and hugged him, tears beginning to run down her cheeks. They held each other for about five minutes, as Pablo began the horrible grieving process of losing your mother. But then again, Heidi realized her family was probably gone too. Florida had been hit hard with Squids and harvester robs prowling the waterways and shorelines, of which Florida had a lot. She swallowed the lump in her throat and spoke.

"Pablo, this hurts like hell. I know. I just realized my family is also probably gone. But I know they would want us to do our best to live, to remember them." She kissed his forehead. He hugged her, hard.

"Thank you for helping me, Heidi. I knew a soldier would help me."

Heidi laughed. "Coast Guard. Better than any soldier. Just

remember that." They sat for a few more moments, then both stood up, went to the kitchen area. Heidi noticed the stove used gas, turned it on. It worked.

"Pablo, might as well use the heat as long as we have it. Have any hot chocolate?"

"Yeah. Several boxes. My uncles loved it!"

"Well, my main man. Time's a-wastin'! Hot chocolate always makes me feel good, even on a warm day. Marshmallows too. Ah, here are some. We're in business!" The two humans began to survive.

That night, Heidi started to sleep on the front room sofa, but Pablo demanded she sleep with him in his mother's bed. As she crawled into bed with the ten year old, Pablo finally telling her his age, he said, "Will you be my sister? I always wanted a brother or a sister."

Heidi hugged him, trying not to start bawling. What a kid. He gave her hope.

"Yeah, I'll be your big sister. But you know big, older sisters can be bossy. We do that to keep younger brothers from being hurt."

Pablo seemed to consider that idea, then answered. "Okay. Say my prayers with me?"

"Sure thing, kid. We need all the help we can get."

After Pablo had said his prayers, including asking God to look after his mother and uncles, he snuggled up to Heidi and was out like a light. Quietly, Heidi added a prayer of her own.

"Hey, boss man—or woman—upstairs, at least give us some luck. We need it." Then she was out.

Hours later, Pablo shook her awake.

"Heidi, wake up! It's just a dream. Wake up."

She jerked awake, was disoriented for a moment before she realized she was in Pablo's apartment. She was sweating, shaking. But she knew the reality they were facing was almost as bad as her dream. She hugged Pablo.

"Thank you, my man. That was a *bad* dream."

"You okay now, Heidi?"

She smiled at him. "Hey, my little brother is here to protect me. Of course I'm okay."

Pablo grinned, his first since Heidi had met him. "Go to sleep, Big Sister. Tomorrow is going to be a busy day."

Heidi did an out of character giggle. "Yes, sir," she said, then put her arm around him and was fast asleep.

The next morning, the two new siblings went around and began scrounging things from the vacant apartments. The super had hung himself in the basement because he couldn't take the stress. Heidi managed to wrestle his body outside and into a dumpster down the block, there being no place to bury him. A couple of days later she found some gasoline and had an old funeral pyre for him. He hung himself, so Heidi figured he wouldn't care that he was being cremated. Mrs. Kleinman and Mrs. Melendez, Pablo's neighbors, had disappeared. They had no idea what happened to the two women, who could have been snatched by the harvester rob the two had seen, or maybe they had just fled. Pablo and Heidi would never know. So, it was Heidi and Pablo for about a week, scavenging food, water, candles, batteries and anything else they could use. Then Joseph and James showed up...

Heidi was outside, looking into abandoned vehicles for usable items. Between the apartments and the cars, she had found a good supply of canned and dry goods for food, some booze, beer, water and soft drinks, as well as a .22 rifle and a cheap .38 revolver. She treated Pablo like the younger brother he wanted to be, making sure he did not go out alone. So Heidi was outside, and Pablo was doing look out duty from the apartment window when the two human figures appeared, walking down the street. Heidi was dumbfounded for a minute that they were strolling down the middle of the thoroughfare. Then she noticed the Navy flight suits and M-4 assault carbines.

Heidi called out from behind a parked pickup truck, her pistol in her hand concealed by the truck bed.

"Are those two Swabbies I see, Airedales or what?" She called out in a friendly sounding voice. The two men stopped. Then stared at her.

"Lady, where did you come from?" the one identified as James called out. They were both caucasian, medium build, brown hair, and—she would soon discover—gay. They were also hitched to each other. So, it solved the question of whether she would have to fight them off or not.

"I come from around here. The question is, where are you headed? Or coming from?"

The two former chopper crew members were all that was left of a detached air unit, operating out of Homestead Field. They had tried to keep things together after Miami took a couple of minor rock hits, followed by a major invasion of harvesters and Squids. The Tschaaa liked the area around Miami Bay, the reefs and coves heading down into the Keys, and decided to make it a principal point from which they could expand their operations. A former active duty Air Force Base, the military tried to use Homestead as a place from where the invaders could be counter attacked. It didn't last very long. It was a prime demonstration that any real estate within a few miles of the ocean could be owned by the Tschaaa if they wanted it—within twenty-four hours.

Deltas softened things up, harvester robs went after the fresh meat, young warrior Squids snuck up on humans close to the water, using a color changing camouflage ability to ambush any sentries. They demonstrated a short dash ability, which enabled them to hack or shoot someone, then disappear into the shadows as their skin achieved the color and texture of the surroundings. A few grays and lizards were also seen during the attacks, fielding weapons. John and James had watched their chopper be destroyed on the ground and had to flee for their lives. So they started heading north to Miami proper, trying as much as possible to stay away from the waterways and inlets, which the Tschaaa prowled. Here they were, just shy of four weeks from the first rock hitting.

Joseph saw how Heidi was giving them the once over, calculating their level of threat to her.

"First, Ma'am, we are gay. So no, we won't try and jump your bones. We're a committed couple."

Paused for a minute, then added, "And don't take this the wrong way, but neither of us are into large breasts, either."

Heidi began to laugh. "You may be gay, but you still noticed my chest! Must be a guy thing."

The two men laughed, and the three former military members shook hands and began to discuss plans.

Joseph Bone and James Lawson, after clearing it with Pablo, moved in next to them in a now vacant apartment. Two days later, all four humans were carefully prowling the marinas around the area, looking for something in particular. They found it fairly quickly.

Scrambling into the long Open Fisherman, the three former mariners checked out the boat. They were surprised the batteries still held a charge. Heidi turned on the blowers and let them clear out any gas fumes. Then, glancing around for any signs of Squids, she turned the engines over. They started right up.

"Somebody kept their boat in good order," Heidi exclaimed.

"Lucky for us," James added. "So, if we round up some more fishing gear, I think we can put this plan into motion."

The Plan was to slowly go into the bay, see if there were any actual Squids around. Then, they would try fishing. They needed some fresh food stock, and an early winter seemed to be headed their way. Although southern Florida would be spared the worst effects of the long, or nuke winter, it would still be colder than normal. Viable food stocks would soon be short. Fish, dried, salted, whatever, would be an important food source. Other than the single harvester rob which Pablo and Heidi had seen, everything else appeared to be quiet. The Tschaaa seemed to be spending time in the South, towards the

Keys and Homestead, rather than around Miami, now that they had cleaned out most of the local populace.

The next week, same day the ole Emergency Broadcast System managed to broadcast one last time that the Central Government of the United States had ceased to function, the three adults plus one kid slowly left a dock berth not far from the apartments. They had moved the Open Fisherman from the main marina where they had found it to a small dock not far from the area of the apartments. Some thirty-one days prior, everyone had a fairly normal life, with day to day mundane activities. Then, the Tschaaa arrived, and people were in danger of being eaten.

The group slowly headed out to the Bay opening. They had a gill net, some lobster and crab pots, several lighter weight trout poles, and a couple of heavy duty deep sea rigs. Aft they had a drag line with various types of hooks. At this point, anything remotely edible was fair game. Heidi had more small boat handling skills, so she was at the wheel, with Joseph to port and James on starboard. Pablo sat by the twin outboard engines. If any Squids appeared, Pablo, with somewhat darker skin, was to hide on the deck, out of sight. Word had gotten out that the Squids preferred dark meat, and people with lighter skin tones were being ignored. Unless, of course, you stuck the proverbial thumb in their eye, drawing attention to yourself. Then a robocop might just take you out.

They reached the entrance to Miami Bay before a Tschaaa appeared off the bow, floating and treading water. It had a spear that it pointed straight up. "Shit!" Heidi cursed as she throttled back the engines. Pablo flattened into the bottom of the boat. Joseph had one of the two spear guns ready, the thought was that at first something less noisy than a firearm would be better in any conflict. Heidi let the boat drift, as she made her way to the bow. She looked at the Tschaaa, a young warrior, apparently playing picket duty.

"Well, here it goes," she said to herself. "Avast ye, my

tentacled friend! We just need to get a little fish, to eat. We promise not to take too much, disturb you and yours." She had no idea if the thing could understand her. She hoped they had some type of Star Trek universal translator, but at this point no one knew for sure. Joseph nervously handled the spear gun.

Suddenly, the Tschaaa forcefully blew out its gills, then slipped beneath the water. Everyone held their breath. No other Squid appeared. Everyone started breathing again. Five minutes later, they passed out into open sea.

Later, they would try and figure out what the alien was thinking, and doing when it blew its gills.

"It sounded rude," James opined.

"You mean that Squids gave us a raspberry?" Heidi asked.

"Or maybe that was a laugh," James said.

"A laugh about what? Was there a joke—or something they saw was funny?"

James got a slight wry grin on his face.

"Well, there are those rather large protuberances on your chest. Quite noticeable in that tank top."

Heidi's mouth popped open.

"Keep that up, and I'll slice you up and use you for bait, airedale."

Pablo joined the other two males in laughter.

"All right little brother. What's so funny?"

"I'm just laughing because they are. It's fun."

"Men. Can't live with them, can't live without them." Later they would find out just how close to the truth they were, when they mentioned Heidi's large breasts as being a factor in their survival.

The three adults and Pablo were soon recognized, a going concern the Squids left alone. Heidi saw Squids coming and going from some of the larger reef areas. So, putting two and two together, she figured they had some kind of home base set up under water. When through binoculars she noticed young Squid following adults and adolescents, she figured, rightly so, the reefs were a breeding area. She steered far clear after that. No use pushing their luck.

The first month, they fished and collected a substantial amount for drying, salting. They also ate a lot, with protein being a welcome addition to the canned food they had been eating. They neither saw nor heard any other humans around until the end of the first mouth. Then, as they were heading into the dock, they saw two figures slowly approaching

"Pablo, bottom of the boat," Heidi directed as she pulled out her pistol. James grabbed one of their assault rifles and stood ready. Heidi slowly brought the boat into its berth, Joseph jumping onto the dock to secure it. She casually looked through her binoculars and saw that the figures were a man and a woman, about in their late twenties. She exited the Open Fisherman, slowly walking towards the figures, her pistol still in hand.

"Good afternoon. Can I help you two?" The two stopped, empty hands extended towards Heidi.

"We don't want trouble, lady," the male spoke. "We were just wondering if you would take something in trade for some fish. We're about out of food. Looking through all these empty buildings is nerve racking. Plus, the smell of rotted food got old real quick."

Heidi nodded. They were having the same problem. Also, feral animals of all sorts were beginning to prowl around the smell of garbage.

"So what do you have to trade, mister?" Joseph, who was now standing a bit behind Heidi, asked. The young woman slowly reached in her handbag and pulled out some rings with good sized stone settings in them. Heidi could see they were of good quality.

"I have to ask. Unless you have a sniper covering us, what's to stop us from just taking them, giving you nothing?"

"Nothing," the woman replied. "But we have been watching you fish for the last few days. The way you treat each other tells us you still have some morals."

That comment actually made Heidi feel good. It was nice to know there were people around, and that they noticed humane treatment. She called to Pablo. "Go ahead and come on up, meet the... I need your names, please."

They were Stan and Joan Johnson, a married couple with no children. They were surprised when they saw Pablo, but did not let on that the surprise was from the knowledge that children were sought after by the harvesters.

"Pablo, see if a ring will fit you, one you like. It's an early Christmas present. Then take a bigger one you can grow into."

Pablo grinned and looked through the booty. After choosing two, he then took a third, a gold ring with a stylized shark design in it. "Here, Heidi. A present. Merry Christmas."

Heidi felt a lump in her throat. "Aw, damnit, you shouldn't have!" She took it, found it fit perfectly.

"Unless my partners here have an objection, this is your one and only payment. Joseph, James. Okay?"

"Fine with us," James answered from the boat. "You'll have to find something to carry your fish in. We have a limited amount of carriers."

Stan pulled a large garbage bag from under his loose fitting shirt. James and Joseph helped them select enough of the catch so as not to overburden the bag.

"If you see us go out, when we come in, you can have the extra," Heidi told them. "Where are you staying?"

"We were trapped in the office building a few blocks up. It's where we worked together. We have been living off what we could find in the offices, watching for those god awful harvesters. There are some also not so nice humans floating around... we have been laying low."

Heidi looked at Joseph and James, They must have realized what she was thinking as they both nodded slightly.

"Grab you stuff and come on over to our apartment building. There are plenty of rooms, and we have a couple of small generators for electricity when we need it. We have access to decent water also."

That was the beginning of about a year of relatively benign existence. Stan soon proved to be an excellent scrounger and tinkerer, finding needed items in the area around the apartments, as well as being able to get almost any machine to work. Joan had been taking night classes to be an EMT, to get out of the office work, so she had some decent medical knowledge. And she was one hell of a cook. Bring her the most basic items, she could make a scrumptious meal out of them. She was soon the official cook and food preparer, an expert in salting and preserving fish.

They also brought some religion with them, being transplanted Mormons. They had come to Miami for job opportunities, hoping to return to their family in Utah someday. Heidi had told them *not* to try and convert Pablo, a good Catholic, as it would not be fair to such a young boy. Heidi was a lapsed Methodist, Joseph and James Unitarians. After a discussion, every Sunday morning became a time of rest, with a formal group meal early in the afternoon. They had found a larger dining table with extra leaves and managed to squeeze it into Joseph and James' place. They would all help to prepare the meal. Then one of them would say grace. The human concept of religion gave them a bit of comfort, hope, that things would be different. Stan told them stories of the trial and tribulations of the creation of the Mormon Church, the trek to Utah. Heidi told stories of growing up in a martial arts dojo, learning numerous ways to hurt and maim people. She also began teaching Joan and Stan some of her Jiu-Jitsu techniques, as well as Eskrima knife and stick techniques. Then John and James told stories of being gay.

When Stan and Joan had first realized the men's homosexuality, they had a private conference. Then, Stan had talked to Heidi, Josh and James, while Joan kept Pablo busy. They liked each other, Joan becoming an aunt to Pablo, though he still came to Heidi for major advice and guidance.

Stan took a deep breath, then began. "I was always taught to be honest. So, here it goes. My religion views homosexuality as a sin. But, the Prophets also did not exactly foresee the Squids. I see, Joseph and James, that you two seem to ...love each other. You are also two of the nicest, most morally honest people we, Joan and I, have met in a long time. Pablo seems to love you like older brothers, or uncles."

Stan paused, waiting for a reaction, then continued. "So, it is a case of not liking the sin, but loving the sinner. You are humans who fought the Squids. I think it is safe to say that they are the Ultimate Sin, an abomination. But God allowed them to exist, so they must have a purpose also, though I have no idea what that is. Bottom line, I will not try to judge or convert you. I would appreciate it if you did not try to... convert me. Or Pablo."

Joseph began to laugh, then James. Stan looked at them quizzically until James spoke. "We were gay by birth. Do you think we chose to be different than the majority of people? So no, we do not convert people. We are not goddamn child molesters!"

Stan turned a bit red. "I did not mean..."

"Oh, we know that! It just always comes up. But, since a bunch of straight people seem to like little girls, I guess it is logical to assume we might like little boys."

John broke in. "Look, like you said. We're all humans. Whatever differences we have, I think we can forget them for the foreseeable future. I think to avoid getting eaten by some alien piece of shit is more important than worrying about how we have sex—or with whom. Right?"

"Agreed," Stan answered. He put his hand out. John shook his hand, then hugged him.

"You are a nice man, Stan Johnson. Hopefully, someday you and Joan will have your own family. Right now, I think it's all of us here."

"Damn, you are all making me teary eyed," Heidi broke in.

"Can we stop with this love fest and get ready to eat? I'm starving!"

James looked at her. "The reason they don't send a donkey to school is because they don't like smartasses, Petty Officer Faust. Ow! Quit jabbing me in the ribs!"

Heidi grinned. "Rank doesn't mean anything now, does it? Now, come here James, I need some lovin'..." She grabbed him in a hug and tried to kiss him.

"Damn it! You know I don't swing that way. Damn lady wrestler!"

Joseph was laughing so hard there were tears in his eyes. Stan was laughing also.

"Hey, what's going on in there?" Joan's voice came from the other room.

"Just telling dirty jokes, Joan," Heidi replied.

"Well, when you are all through corrupting my husband, come on in and help me set the table. It's getting time to eat."

After over a year of living together, celebrating birthdays, holidays, Christmas, they were a tight family. Joan broke the news that she was pregnant and everyone celebrated. The weather had been very cold, but they had survived together. A few other survivors appeared, bartering for fish, swapping stories about what was going on. Occasionally, someone would start broadcasting on a local radio transmitter they had managed to set up and passed on what they knew about the world under the Tschaaa.

Humankind was surviving, after a fashion.

Heidi and the others would come back from a fishing trip, take the catch to the apartment to be divided. About another dozen people had moved into the complex, trying to keep a low profile. So far so good. No harvester robs had shown up since almost a year ago. The only Squids seen were around the reefs outside Miami Bay. No lizards or greys were seen either.

Heidi had seen a robocop one day as they were unloading the Open Fisherman. She froze, as did John, James and Pablo.

He was on shore, about a hundred yards away, staring at them.

"Oh fuck!" Heidi exclaimed. She knew the light weapons they had would mean nothing against this armored giant. All she could do was to give a silent prayer. Suddenly, the robocop waved at them. So Heidi waved back. It watched them for a few moments, then turned and strode off. Heidi realized she had been holding her breath. She finally let it out.

One day, about two weeks after waving at the robocop, a Haitian couple suddenly showed up, much the worse for wear. Elsie and Alain Bertrand had been visiting relatives on a tourist visa when the rocks hit. They soon found a basement to hide in when the harvesters showed up. The couple barely had water to survive with, not to mention food. The Haitians had eventually came out at night, scrounging what they could find. They found the remains of a bodega that provided a day's shelter and some food, until feral dogs showed up. Grabbing what they could, they ran to the next block. Barricading themselves in a coffee shop just a mile from the apartment building where Pablo lived, they had stayed put. At least they had a source of water. There were a few snacks left, and they went out to nearby cars to scavenge. Somehow, they survived, dodging a harvester rob or two. Then, they saw the first Church of Kraken.

The ones they saw were literally slaughtering a human being on the street, as if it were the most normal thing to do. They had been in hiding ever since.

Finally, food gone, they had left their hiding place and just happened to see Heidi and company coming back in the boat. After watching them, they had approached them, as they were taking their catch back to the apartment building.

Heidi, Jame, and Joseph, seeing their gaunt condition, took them back to the apartments, found a place for them, and some fish to eat. Two weeks passed.

Pablo had kind of taken them under his wing, feeling a desire to help two people worse off than he was. He was downstairs on the first floor with them as they went through empty apartments to find any additional clothes, bedding and other incidentals for them.

Heidi kept the apartment stairway doors open so that she could hear if they needed any help. She was still very protective of Pablo, even when he was with other adults.

Heidi was sitting on the fire escape stairs at the end of the apartment building, looking at the streets and buildings in the area. Nothing seemed to have changed in the last few weeks.

Then she heard a scream emanating from downstairs, followed by another.

She was up and running before she realized it, her pistol in hand. She took the stairs two, three at a time, risking breaking an ankle. She reached the bottom, the first floor, looking for Pablo. Nothing.

Gun at close-in ready position, she made her way down the hallway. Then she found the blood. There was a large pool and spattering on the walls from an apparent arterial spurt. There were signs of a body being dragged around the corner at the end of the hallway, into the main entrance of the apartment buildings. Heidi did a quick cut the pie around the corner, saw the front double doors swinging shut. She ran as fast as she could, still scanning for threats, and made it to the front doors, moving low through it.

She glanced to the left, in a southern direction. That's when she saw them.

Three Krakens. One had a loose Pablo slung over his shoulder. Another had Elsie thrown over his shoulder, blood dripping from her throat, The last Kraken was dragging Alain on his back by his leg, a large swath of blood being left by the now dead Haitian.

Heidi was screaming and shooting before she even realized it. The head of the Kraken carrying Pablo on his shoulder exploded into a red mist and the now dead man collapsed into a heap. The Kraken dragging Alain spun around, an unnoticed pistol in his hand. Heidi and the man both fired at the same instance, the pistol in Heidi's hand being knock from her grasp by a bullet impact. Her shot struck the Kraken in an unprotected chest, causing the man to stumble, then collapse.

The third Kraken male had dropped Elsie and pulled a razor sharp butcher knife from his belt. His face was one large tattoo of a devilfish octopus, an affection becoming popular with hardcore Church of Kraken members. Seeing a now apparently unarmed foe, a smaller female at that, he sneered. "You just signed your death warrant, bitch!" He rushed to Heidi. He didn't stand a chance.

A balisong butterfly knife appeared in Heidi's left hand as if from nowhere. She sidestepped the Kraken's thrust, then severed the fingers of his knife hand with her balisong. As the man screamed and dropped his butcher knife, Heidi thrust her razor sharp balisong into his lower abdomen. She cut sideways, then jumped back as the Kraken's intestines began to spill out. The man screamed and fell to his knees, as he tried to hold in his guts.

Heidi went to where Pablo had fallen. He was still, unmoving. As Heidi reached down to him, she saw a deep puncture wound at the base of his skull. The blood from the wound had been running down inside of his shirt and his hair, concealing the seriousness of the wound.

"Pablo! *Pablo!*" Heidi cried out, gently shaking him. But she knew he was gone.

By now, the other apartment dwellers were coming into the area, all of them armed in some way. But it was all over. From the time of the screams to the time of Heidi reaching Pablo, only some two minutes had passed.

The Kraken who was still alive was crying, still trying to hold his intestines in. Heidi stepped away from Pablo and towards the Kraken. She reached down and grabbed an exposed piece of intestine and began to pull. The man screamed so loud Heidi thought he would deafen some of those around him.

"Any more of you motherfuckers around?" Heidi asked in a

low voice.

"No!" the Kraken cried out.

Heidi let his guts loose. "Why did you come here?"

"We heard there were some dark meat around to be gotten," the dying man gasped out.

"Just couldn't leave the harvesting to the Squids, you piece of shit!" Heidi kicked him in his exposed intestines and the man fainted. She turned, walked over and gently picked up Pablo. She began to carry him back into the apartments entrance way.

Someone asked, "What do we do with him?"

"Fuck, I don't care. I need to bury my dead."

The family buried its dead. Stan and Joan dressed Pablo in his favorite shirt and pants. They found a couple of his favorite toys and the teddy bear that he had given his mother. Stan crafted a beautiful coffin for him. Then the group went a bit Viking, finding an outboard motor boat they could use. They put Pablo in it, piled some wood around his coffin and soaked it in gasoline. Heidi pulled it out into the Bay with the Open Fisherman, set it adrift. She backed off and set it ablaze with a flare gun. Pablo loved fishing with them. Now he could fish forever.

The family group tried to get back to fishing. But it was not good. Heidi would go along, memories of Pablo would pop up, and she'd start crying. There were too many memories.

So Heidi decided to stay behind, on shore, watching for Krakens. However, the last trip she took with Joseph and James to make sure the Tschaaa were still comfortable with humans fishing, something very strange happened.

They were about a quarter mile out from the Government cut, slowly trawl fishing, when a bunch of small figures popped up, surrounding the Open Fisherman. Heidi immediately cut the engines.

"Shit. Little ones. Young Tschaaa."

She and the two airedales knew how protective the Tschaaa

were to their young. They had seen a couple of strangers in a boat a few months prior that had stumbled into a small group of young, having gotten too close to a reef breeding area. They had panicked, started splashing about. Within seconds an armed Squid appeared and skewered both with their version of a harpoon before the two humans knew what had happened. After the bodies had bled out into the water, a group of young Squid appeared, crawled aboard the small craft and started to feed as best they could at their young age. All this was under the watchful eye of the adult.

Now, they were in danger of the having the same fate.

Joseph slowly raised his assault weapon.

"Hold on, guys. Let's see if my boobs will give us luck again."

Heidi bent over the gunwale.

"Hey, youngsters," she tried to say in a soft and calm voice. "Sorry to bother you. We're just passing..."

Two large eyes of an adult appeared just under the surface, then the head and torso broke into the open air. Heidi weighed grabbing for her military fighting knife, then hesitated. The adult had no observed weapon. And, its two tentacles, the ones with the hand structures, were empty. Heidi looked closer. The tentacles were shorter than usual, the fingers on the hands seemed longer and slender. Then it dawned on her.

The humans had been able to garner some information over the last year or so. One bit was that there were male and female Tschaaa, the female Breeders having shorter social tentacles. This was the first time Heidi had ever seen one.

Heidi's eyes were a bit red as she had been crying, as memories had come up again. The Squid seemed to be looking specifically at her face with the extra-large and sensitive eyes, taking in every pore in her face. Heidi swallowed.

"Hello, young lady. How are you?" She tried to motion to James and Joseph to stay still. Then the strange happened.

Very slow and sure, the Tschaaa female reached up with its right tentacle hand, and touched Heidi's cheek. The fingers felt like soft wisps, feather-like as it explored her face, went up to below her tear stained eyes.

"Yeah. I've been crying. I lost a young one, like family. It hurts." Heidi had no idea why she said that, but then some tears came.

The soft and sensitive fingers touched the tears, rubbed the moisture between opposable thumb and fingers. Heidi then heard a soft and rhythmic tone emanate from the female.

For some reason, Heidi reached out and gently grasped the hand of the female and supposed Breeder. The fingers of the two species touched, held on for several moments. Then, the Tschaaa slowly removed its hand. A slightly lower and louder tone was heard, and the young disappeared below the surface. The female looked at Heidi, its sensitive eyes seemed to take in every part of the human face and body. Then it slid beneath the water and was gone.

The three humans sat silent in the boat for several minutes, as if afraid to disturb what had just happened. Finally, Joseph spoke.

"It now knows you, Heidi. Fantastic as it may seem, but that...first contact beyond them trying to eat us..." He shivered, went quiet.

"It was a female thing," Heidi said. "Two women meeting, having young being a common bond. It knew. *She* knew. I had lost Pablo. Only a female Breeder would notice that. I know that now." She took a breath, let it out.

"Let's not push our luck. We'll trawl on the way back in, maybe pick a few small fish."

On the slow way back in, Heidi thought she saw some young Squids near their trawl lines. When they reached the dock, pulled in the lines—stuck on the hooks were some rather large fish.

"Those are not hooked like normally caught fish," James said.

"That was a present from that female, the Breeder. And as

they say, never look a gift horse in the mouth. Come on. Back home. Joan and the others can dress this fish. And we can have a good meal. In memory of Pablo."

After that, Heidi kept watch for Krakens and other threats from the top of the apartments. They had located a scoped .300 Winchester magnum rifle in the trunk of a car one day. Heidi now claimed it and used a few rounds to make sure it was sighted in. The next time a Kraken or some other threat came by, she'd take them out as far away as she could. After the contact with the female Tschaaa, Heidi knew they were not in any threat of being harvested by the Tschaaa. Slaughtered by asshole humans, Krakens, yes. So, she kept watch.

About ten days after contact with the Breeder, she saw them. Using the high powered scope on the rifle, she could see a dozen well-armed, uniformed and organized group coming up the local main street several blocks away. She grabbed one of the battery operated, short range walkie talkies Stan had gotten to work and sounded the alarm. After losing Pablo and the two newly arrived adults, they had come up with a defensive plan.

Joseph and James had stayed in that day from fishing, so they grabbed their ex-military weapons and took up defensive positions on the street level. Stan had a pistol to cover the main entrance to the apartment building, the other occupants spread out in the building proper. If the approaching personnel were a threat, they were about to run into a hornets' nest.

When the armed formation reached the end of the block, Heidi used their special weapon. Stan had hooked up a kids karaoke machine so that some distant speakers at the end of the block were connected to the microphone. Heidi spoke on the machine, hoping it would sound like the voice of God above.

"You can stop right there and state your business."

The people stopped, several dropping behind abandoned cars for cover, as the others tried to figure out where the voice came from.

"Whoever your boss is, step on up and state your business

so I can hear him or her."

Without hesitation, a stocky older looking man with red hair and a handlebar moustache moved forward. He had some large looking clip fed weapon that Heidi did not immediately recognize. He walked to within fifty yards of the apartment entrance when Heidi told him to stop. She could see through her rifle scope that he had what looked like Chief or Master Sergeant's stripes on his urban camouflage fatigues. The man also had a good voice.

"Chief Master Sergeant William Hamilton, former U.S. Air Force. To whom am I speaking?"

"Petty Officer Heidi Faust, U.S. Coast Guard. Now, state your business."

The man shook his head. "Look—you people probably have me, at least, dead to rights. But since you did not shoot first and ask questions later, you may be the group we are looking for, are trying to find."

"Oh yeah? Who is *we*?" Heidi said over the sound system.

"Look it, I don't want to keep yelling at a disembodied voice. What say I lay down my weapon, your friends keep me covered, and you come down and talk to me face to face—I promise I don't bite."

Heidi laughed, which sounded load over the microphone.

"Yeah? If you do, I bite back. And some people think I have rabies."

She thought the Chief was laughing. "Oh Hell, Coastie. Come on down. See. I'm laying my weapon down."

Heidi watched as he laid that large weapon down. Then, she called over the sound system.

"Okay. I'm coming down."

She made it down from the roof in record time and handed her rifle to Stan at the front entrance.

"Stan, think you can hit something with this?"

"Used to hunt in Utah. Think I can handle it."

"Good. Take that Chief out if they try to take me down."

Stan chuckled. "They won't. You're too tough."

Heidi smiled. "Just remember that."

Heidi had her hand on her pistol as she approached the Chief.

"I'd salute you, Chief, but then I'd have to take my hand off my pistol."

He shrugged. She saw that he had a slab side 45 automatic in a shoulder holster, but he made no movement towards it.

"Always pays to be careful, Petty Officer."

"You Kraken, Chief?"

The older man sneered, then spit on the pavement and his blue eyes seemed to flash when they looked at her.

"Do I look like I slaughter, eat people?"

Heidi paused. "Well, I don't see any of those God-awful tattoos they like to sport. So, who is with you?"

"Director Adam Lloyd. Heard the name before?"

"Is he the guy they talked about on the radio, who according to the rumor mill has some agreement with the Squids not to eat any more people around here?"

"He's the one. And you sound like the fishermen group who has an agreement with the Tschaaa to fish around here, without them sinking you."

Heidi smiled. "Guilty as charged. So I guess you have heard of us."

She paused for a moment, looking at the Chief.

"The wheels in your head are turning," the man said.

"Yeah. They let me be in charge, because I think too much. The two Naval Airedale officers said they were tired of being in charge. So they let the bossy bitch do it."

Chief Hamilton began to laugh. It was a nice, natural laugh, not forced or fake. Heidi realized she could like this man. If he wasn't trying to lie to her.

"Alright, here's the deal young lady. Key West is being set up as a sanctuary of sorts, soon to be the nerve center or capital of those former States and other areas under Tschaaa control. The

Squid Lord who controls all of North America has set up a unique system. No more general harvesting. He has a three state compound now with a breeding stock of us humans. Sorry, they still eat some of our fellow humans. But not us. And not you if you join us."

Heidi was silent. They were still eating humans. But at the same time, some of them were trying to *work* with humans. Bizarre.

"Why?"

"Why what, Petty Officer?"

"Why not eat all of us? Why work with some of us?"

"The Director says His Lordship has decided we could eventually be a client, a helper species. It's a special Protocol they are developing, about our relationship. Like dogs are man's best friend."

Heidi's laugh was like a bark.

"Yeah. Like I eat dogs."

"The Chinese did. They're still considered human."

Heidi stood quiet. Joan was about to give birth. A couple of other women in the group were pregnant. They would, if the Chief was correct, be able to give birth in a protected area. Maybe they had a hospital up and running. That Breeder the other day. *She* could have killed, eaten them all. Plus the robocop had waved at them.

Something was changing.

She looked hard at Chief Hamilton. "I need to discuss this with the group, our family. But I will say one thing. Try and pull something on us, try some Kraken bullshit, you'll wake up with your balls in your mouth."

The Chief had a wry smile when he replied. "Coastie, I have a strange feeling that was just a promise, not an empty threat. I could use someone like you in our Security Forces. The Squids may work with the Krakens, that Church, but we keep them at arm's length. And yes, I have killed a few."

"The Squids don't care?"

He snorted. "Humans killing humans? As long as they get the leftover meat, and it's not veal, they don't care. But humans *eating* humans? Cannibalism is like a blasphemy with them. A species eating their own kind is an aberration to them."

"But they eat us, an intelligent species. Great, Chief."

The Chief sighed. "The universe isn't fair. It is what it is. Right now, the Tschaaa are the top, apex predator. They make the rules. If we were on top, and we ate *them*, they would understand."

"You're kidding, right?"

The Chief gave her a hard, steely-eyed look.

"I've never been so goddamned serious in my life. They have a rigid social order. Follow their basic rules, you survive. Violate them... you're meat."

Heidi could tell he was serious, dead serious.

"So no more Kraken's butchering us at random?"

"Not if we or the Squids find out, no. The official word just went out not too long ago to a certain Most Reverend Kray. Rein in your people, or become number one on the menu. After the dark meat in Cattle Country, that is."

"So that exists. People bred for, and kept as meat."

"The big trade off, Petty Officer Faust. Some die, so others, and the human species, can live."

Heidi was quiet. If the Chief had just come a few weeks earlier, Pablo would still be alive. Now, there was a chance that future children in her group would live.

"Alright. Wait here, please. I need to discuss this with the group."

The Chief smiled. "Take your time. We're not going anywhere."

"If the answer is no?"

"Hasta la vista, Coastie. But you deal with feral humans and Krakens on your own."

"Okay. Be back in a while."

The apartment building dwellers had a meeting down at the

main entrance so they could keep an eye on Chief and company. Stan cut to the heart of the issue.

"My wife is about to give birth. If they can provide secure medical facilities, insure my child isn't going into someone's meat locker, you have my vote to go with them. Things out here are not getting better."

Everyone murmured ascent. They were willing to take a chance. Suddenly, all eyes were on Heidi. She could tell what they wanted to know.

"Yes, I think the Chief is telling the truth. Otherwise, they could have snuck in, started picking us off."

She paused of a moment. "I know, if Pablo were still here, we would've already left with them."

Everyone was packed, ready to move within two hours. The Chief had put the call out for some large deuce and a half's and other large trucks to move people and property. Heidi stood next to him, as they began loading the vehicles.

"So, Heidi Faust. Are you considering my job offer?"

She shrugged. "Yeah, sure. That way I'll know if anyone tries anything against my family."

The Chief turned and faced her. "This is your family, isn't it?"

"Yes Chief. Same as if we grew up together. And you?"

"My family is the Director and any one in his inner circle. We go back a long time, the Director and I."

"Will I meet him?"

"Later. He used to come out on these little forays, but now has to spend a lot of time coordinating with His Lordship."

"Squid royalty, huh?"

The Chief laughed. "Yeah. Crazy asshole has us calling him Lord Neptune, from our mythology. He is quite the student of human culture and history."

Heidi motioned with her chin. "And that robocop cyborg the next street down. He with you also? Or is he just checking all the activity?"

"That is Andrew. Created from a man born of Earth woman,

and assigned to help and protect the Director. Plus, he was the one who found you."

"What? Wait a minute. He's the one who waved at me?"

"The very same. He remembers everything he sees and hears. You can meet him later."

"Yeah. *Much* later, Chief. When I see a robocop, I get that run and hide feeling."

"Suit yourself. Now, you have anything you need to take care of right? We'll be leaving soon."

"Yeah. I'll be back."

Heidi walked down towards the water until she could see the Open Fisherman boat. They were planning on coming back with a boat trailer, once everyone else was secured in Key West.

"See you soon, ol' girl. Pablo, watch over her until we get back."

Heidi looked out towards Miami Bay, her home for the last year and a half.

"And whoever you were, my female Squid friend. I hope I see you someday. I think you and I might just have something in common that the males of our species will never understand."

Heidi stood at attention and saluted the ocean.

"Love you, guys, all my shipmates who didn't make it. I love you too, Pablo. I always will."

She turned and walked back towards the apartment building. Time to go with her family to their new home, never to move again. At least, that was her hope.

Hope can keep one alive. Especially when it is strong.

BUSINESS AS USUAL

Blonde and blue-jeaned Sharon Wagner looked through the battered binoculars at the open for business gentleman's/strip club. It was the only business they had found operating since they had fled the Interstate 10 rest area about fifty miles east a week ago. The sign read "Toys in the Attic," with the obligatory outline of a busty feminine figure. It was on the far west side of Jacksonville, Florida.

"What do you see?" asked Susanne Shaw, Sharon's best friend from childhood and beach volleyball partner. The tall and athletic brunette, also decked out in blue jeans and blouse, brushed her hair back from her face, as she finished speaking. She and Sharon had hoofed it some three miles after overheating the RV they had been using for transportation. A couple of bullet holes in the vehicle's radiator had finally done it in. Now, survivors of one apparent space alien attack, plus a couple of conflicts involving fellow humans, they were short of food, water, and patience.

"Looks like a typical strip or topless club. How in the hell they stay open, with all the crap flying around, people getting killed and taken, I don't know."

"Well, they must have a generator, and a working water supply," said Sharon. She handed the binoculars to Susanne, who resembled her enough that they were often mistaken for sisters. Then again, their near six feet tall, athletic and tanned frames reflected the fact they had been on a beach volleyball tour for a beer company when the rocks came down and everything began to fall apart.

Susanne looked through the binoculars. "There are some guys standing out smoking by the front entrance. I think I see a large man in the shadow of the entrance. Must be the bouncer."

"Makes sense, Susanne. They must have a pretty tough staff to keep this place in one piece. Unless they are considered a pillar of the community."

Susanne set the binoculars they had gotten from a now dead young soldier after the last bit of violence they had experienced. In the past week, most people they came into contact with had the habit of dying.

"So, we just walk up, try and get in?"

"Well, I don't see another way. We're low on food and water, so we don't have a lot of time to wait and see what else happens. And you say all those aircraft flying over aren't ours, so driving on the road anymore seems to be asking to be a target. Even if we *had* a vehicle."

"Like I said before, that background material I received from the Air Force Academy had a ton of nice color photos of all the U.S. aircraft. And I have a good memory for shapes and designs."

Sharon sniffed. "Yeah, I forgot. You were thinking of taking off to the Air Force Academy, leaving me with no volleyball partner."

Susanne's face flushed. "Damnit, how many times do I have to say this? I was *not* getting ready to just take off. I was just getting info on colleges and universities, like you were."

"If they had offered you a scholarship, you would have gone."

Susanne exploded. "After all we have been through, that is one of the most bitchy, nasty things you could say!" Tears of rage began to stream down her face. "I am *not* going to keep defending myself. If you are going to keep this up, you can just go fuck off."

Susanne was so angry, she was beginning to shake. Sharon realized when Susanne had said "Fuck off," she had pushed the wrong button one too many times. Sharon was the one with the aggressive potty mouth, not Susanne.

"Okay. I'm sorry. I'm just on edge..."

"*You're* on edge? What about *me*? We see old man Brassy at the used car dealership get shot and killed. Done in by those biker assholes that seemed to be helping the aliens—'Squids' the soldiers called them. Then Private Jones dies in front of us. You think I have a lot of experience with people getting shot, dying and *things* chasing us? *Do you?*"

Sharon reached out and grabbed Susanne's hand as a tear ran down the blonde's face.

"Please. I just fucked up. I didn't mean to upset you so. Please, forgive me. I can't..." She began to cry.

It had been an extreme week. The two women were lucky to be alive. And now they were lashing out at each other.

Susanne took a deep breath, let it out. She pulled Sharon's head towards her so they were forehead to forehead.

"Okay, Sharon. We need each other. Me blowing up is not doing either of us any good. You are my best friend. I can't stand to lose you. Especially not now." She kissed Sharon on her forehead. Sharon nodded her head, put a hand on Susanne's shoulder and looked into Susanne's eyes.

"Sorry. I just feel insecure sometimes. I know I act like the bad-ass most of the time. But without you being a rock to me, I'd be dead by now."

"You, dead? I will not allow that."

Sharon smiled through damp eyes. "Like I said. You're my rock. Remember that." She gave her volleyball partner a quick peck on the lips, then turned and reached into her pack.

"Here. I still have some of my orange juice..."

"That's your share. I already had mine."

"And I want you to have this. Please don't argue." Sharon handed the half full bottle to Susanne. The brunette took it, unscrewed the top and took a swig. Then she pushed it back at the blonde.

"Here, your turn."

"You're stubborn, you know that?"

"I know. That is why I stay with you, and you with me. We're both stubborn mules."

The two young women laughed, their conflict forgotten. They turned their attention back to Toys in the Attic.

"Well, Susanne, I guess sitting here won't solve anything. You still have that revolver we got from Brassy?"

"Yeah, with just the one round left. You still have your five shot?"

"Yep. Keep the gun handy out of sight, along with your carving knife. I'll do the same with the snubby and the butcher knife."

The two looked at the strip club. Then they both stood up and began to walk towards it.

"Think they'll ask for ID, Sharon? We haven't even reached nineteen yet."

The blonde laughed. "Yeah. The liquor control board or vice squad is waiting around the corner. They're going to take one look—then try to take advantage of us. We're hot looking. Men often get horny in dangerous situations. Fucking us would make them forget how fucked they actually are."

"I wish you were wrong," said Susanne. "But I know you're right. Alright. Like the late Dave the tour bus driver told us, we have each other's backs. That gives us an advantage."

"That it does, my friend, that it does."

Once the group of males noticed the two very attractive females approaching them, they forgot the tobacco and marijuana cigarettes they were passing around, all eyes now on the beautiful women approaching, dusty appearance and all.

One medium-sized man with a wry smile and tied back long hair separated from the group and approached the athletes.

"Well hello, ladies. Out for a walk?"

Sharon snorted. She knew the guy thought this was the ultimate example of wit and a good pickup line. Before she could make some nasty comment, Susanne broke in. "So, is this place open to the public?"

"Why yes, pretty lady. They have an active bar and stage. You two applying for jobs...I hope." This elicited a round of laughter from the group of young men.

"Right now, we're looking for a place to wash up and something cold to drink."

Long Hair snickered and stepped closer to the two young women.

"I can get you a shower if you let me watch, or we could save water and shower together."

Once again the group laughed. Before Sharon could snap something back, Susanne gave a half smile and replied.

"Right now we'd kind of just like to be alone. We've had a rough week."

"You two aren't into men at all, are you?" It was apparent that Long Hair had never really learned how to talk with women much past asking "how much" or "Here, have another drink."

"Hey, buddy," Sharon butted in. "Act like a shepherd and get the flock out of here. We'll call you if we want you."

Long Haired frowned. "That's not very nice," he said, as he grabbed a hold of Sharon's tanned arm... And was on the ground, crying in pain as Sharon put the hurt on him, using a combination wrist lock, arm twist, and a foot on the side of his neck.

"Didn't your momma tell you it is rude to grab things?"

Sharon asked with a bit of a feral grin.

"Hey!" someone yelled as the group of men began to advance. Susanne had the revolver out in a heartbeat and pointing it in the faces of the advancing men.

"Stop, Now! We just want a cold drink and wash up a bit. Got it?"

The men backed up slowly, grumbling. But no one wanted to take a bullet, no matter how horny they were.

Sharon let loose of Long Hair's arm. "Stay there until we're inside," she ordered.

"Bitch," the man said, rubbing his hurt arm. Sharon choose to ignore him, as she walked into Toys in the Attic, with Susanne keeping an eye on the others. The entrance was dark, their eyes trying to adjust from the sunny outside, when they heard a deep voice from the shadows.

"Leave me the gun. Then you can go in." The owner of the voice was the largest man they had ever seen close up. Tall, caucasian looking with braided blonde hair, his seven foot frame bespoke of a Viking warrior of old.

"You going to give us a receipt, Mister...?" Sharon asked.

"I'm John. I'll remember who it belongs to. Not too many pretty women been around here lately." He said all that with a straight face, but not with a stern demeanor.

"Here," Susanne said as she handed over the revolver. "I'd appreciate it back in the same condition I gave it to you, John."

"Of course, ladies."

"To whom do we need to talk about washing up, getting a drink?"

"Talk to Hernando at the main bar. He runs the place."

"Thanks, John." Susanne smiled, then gently led Sharon into the establishment.

Like all such businesses, its lighting was very subdued, except for two stages in the center of the main floor, where additional lights helped illuminate the local talent. As the two friends walked towards the bar area, they saw a less than enthusiastic woman on one of the stages, going through slow attempts at bumps and grinds to some rock and roll music.

"If that's the best they have," Sharon said in low tones. "No wonder so many guys are smoking outside."

Both of the athletes noticed that there were about a dozen figures lounging around the stages and bar areas, nursing various beverages. They continued on to the bar and saw a young, rather small dark haired man behind it.

"Excuse me," Susanne asked. "Hernando?"

The man looked up, his eyes focused, then flashed a large smile.

"No, sorry to say, if you two are looking for him. I'm Mike, the assistant bartender and bar back. Can I help you two young ladies?"

"How about something cold to drink?" Sharon asked.

"How about draft beer in a frosted mug?"

Sharon grinned. "I'd almost die for that."

"Hey, no need to die, pretty lady. Two beers coming up."

With practiced hands, Mike drew the two beers, flipped coasters onto the bar top and placed the beers on the coasters."

"What do you take as payment, Mike?" Susanne asked.

He laughed. "Not plastic! Machines have been down for a week. Cash, although that's inflated. Precious metals, jewelry, ammunition, food, firearms..."

Sharon pulled two 5.56 millimeter rounds out of a pocket, from a small stash provided by a dead Private First Class they had watched die.

"Will this do?"

As if by magic, the shells disappeared.

"Any more where those came from?"

"Maybe. If you give me the going rate."

"Two rounds per beer. How's that?"

"One and a half, plus a little of that inflated cash you mentioned."

"Done."

Sharon pulled out another couple of rounds, plus some wadded dollar bills.

"Here. One bullet for your tip. You figure out the dollars. Just keep the cold beer coming."

"Will do, ladies."

"You have a restroom?" Susanne asked.

"Yeah. See the sign? Plumbing still works, too. All the comforts of home."

Susanne smiled. "Thanks. Mike. Sharon—be right back."

As Susanne walked away, Sharon asked Mike, "Home near here?"

Mike snorted. "*This* is home now. Whatever those things are the military is fighting out there, my neighborhood in Jacksonville is trashed. I just moved up here from the Keys, so what condition my family is in, I don't know. How about you?"

"Pensacola, Florida. No idea either—we were on a working tour." Sharon then gave him a quick and dirty explanation as to how the two friends had come to be at Toys in the Attic.

"Beach volleyball players. No wonder you two look so fit."

Susanne returned at that moment, so Sharon went to the use the facilities.

"Heard Sharon telling you our story, Mike."

"Yeah. We have one now, that's for sure."

Susanne drank her beer. "Man, that's *cold*. You guys have a generator to keep the refrigerator going?"

"Yes Ma'am. And once the word gets around that we are one of the few places with power, we may start having problems controlling the riff-raff."

"John looks huge enough to take care of just about anything."

"Yeah, but enough bullets can take down anyone."

"Mike, is Hernando coming back anytime soon?"

"Yeah. He's in the back, checking on things. By the way, you know my name, I don't know yours."

"I'm Susanne. " She shook hands with Mike.

Just then, a large bearded, middle aged man who—judging by the smell of alcohol on him—had apparently been in the business location for quite some time, came up to Susanne.

"Can I buy you a drink, young lady?"

"Well Sir, we have already bought some..."

"Mike, set them up again. With a whiskey chaser. With all the shit going on outside, everyone needs a good stiff drink."

"I don't suppose, Sir, I could have a glass of cold water instead of the whisky?"

"Mike, give her both."

"Okay, Big Jake."

Sharon returned from the ladies room at that moment, sliding into the seat between Big Jake and Susanne, saying "Excuse me," with a smile.

"My God. There's two of you pretty ladies. Mike, a round for her also."

The two had dealt with so many beer addled older men on the tour that it had become second nature. The overall majority were harmless, just wanted to flirt a bit with younger ladies to feel young again. Those who were "real" problems, there had been Dave and Jeet Kun Do if necessary.

"This is Big Jake, Sharon."

"Good to meet you—I understand you want to buy us drinks. That is very nice of you. You're not trying to get us drunk, take advantage of us, are you?"

Big Jake sputtered a bit, then said "Hell no—I have daughters not much younger than you..." He stopped, realizing he was talking as if it were weeks ago, when things were normal. His look turned serious.

"Sorry, ladies. I'm a truck driver, on the road, can't reach my home. I'm stuck here until they get this... mess worked out."

Sharon's voice softened. "Can I ask your daughters names?"

Before Big Jake could answer, a hard-looking, bleached blonde woman who had seen better days stomped up.

"What the hell do you two bitches think you're doing,

muscling in on my action?"

"Now, Cindy," Mike began, but was cut off.

"Mike, you son of a bitch, you forget about our arrangement?"

Susanne and Sharon knew then that Cindy had been "working" the bar, probably an older "pro", who had found a place to stay until the problems blew over.

"Cindy, Ma'am, excuse me, we didn't..."

The bar girl cut Sharon off. "Fuck you. You want trouble, I'll give you trouble." She tried to claw at Sharon's face.

Susanne grabbed her by the hair before Sharon could get a hold of her, spun her around away from her friend and slammed her face into the bar top. She slid to the floor, out, when Susanne let go of her hair. Someone yelled "Catfight!" Then chairs were pushed back and hollers began.

"Damnit, Susanne, I had her," protested Sharon.

"No old whore is going to lay a hand on my..."

Just then a new loud voice was heard. "What the chinga is going on?"

"Who wants to know?" Sharon snapped.

A tall man with permanent, medium skin tan and a sculpted bodybuilder physique stepped up and eyed the two athletes. Before he could say anything else, the other strip club patrons became even louder. This was the most fun they had seen in hours—if not days.

"Quiet!" a voice used to being listened to boomed out. "Or do I have to use Mister Hand Cannon again?" The comment had the desired effect. The decibel level dropped to a murmur.

He fixed the two friends with a stern gaze. "You two, come with me. We need to have a little discussion."

"And just who the hell are you?" Sharon responded in a pissed off tone of voice.

"I am Hernando. I now run this place. This," from under a loose fitting tropical shirt he pulled the largest revolver anybody in the strip club had ever seen, "is Mister Hand Cannon. If you *piss me off*, you may hear it roar. Now, *move*." The huge bore was now pointed in the general direction of the two women. They both weighed their chances of disarming the man and decided that, for now, discretion was the better part of valor. They moved in the direction his non-gun hand was pointing, through the club to a rather large office near the bar. They entered in front of Hernando and headed towards the two chairs in front of a large, padded desk. Nothing cheap existed in this business room, there being an air of opulence.

After the two women put down their small packs and sat in the padded chairs, Sharon said, "Nice office. You the owner of this place?"

"I am now. And before you two try to take control of this conversation with your good looks and big egos, let's set some ground rules." Hernando set the hand cannon in front of him on the desk, the bore pointing over to Sharon's right side.

"*You* have come into my establishment and have disrupted its peace. It started when you took that guy down outside. And yes, along with Mister Hand Cannon, I have Mister Camera System. I can see almost everything in this club."

"Including the ladies room?" Sharon spat out.

Hernando sighed and looked at Susanne. "Let me guess. She's the pushy, mean appearing one of your duo. You come off as the more reasonable one. Good cop, bad cop. Right?"

"If you say so... Hernando," Susanne replied.

Hernando laughed. "Now, want a cold ice tea? I don't drink much alcohol these days—need to keep my wits about me."

"Who's paying?" Susanne asked.

Hernando laughed again. "Man, you two are something. Now I know how two hot chicks have survived this last week, on the road, with outlaw bikers, possible space aliens, the military, not to mention associated scum running up and down what's left of our roadways. You are tough and smart." Hernando paused. "But I am tougher and smarter. I've been at this game for a while. You two were running around beaches, judging by your tan. I was running a business as the managing bartender, especially after the owner disappeared in the rock strikes in Atlanta." He shook his head. "Damn fool just *had* to go there to recruit new talent. I told him there was plenty in Florida, local talent, not run by the mob or dope smugglers. Now he's dead. So, this is mine now."

Hernando turned around and grabbed some ice teas from a small refrigerator behind his desk, ignoring the fact his huge revolver was still sitting on the desk. Was it a test of the two ladies? Sharon and Susanne looked at each other. Sharon slowly checked her concealed snubby, made sure it was within easy reach.

Hernando turned back around with three bottles of iced tea, smiled at the two athletes.

"I know. You two were sizing up Mister Hand Cannon. Thinking about grabbing it and making a run for it. But where would you go? Huh?"

Sharon looked into Hernando's eyes. "Yeah, you're right. We were sizing things up."

"So—now what, ladies?"

"Hey, buddy, you told us to come back here, with that large revolver stuck in our faces. You tell *us* what's up."

Hernando turned and looked at Susanne. "She's the badass, right? You're the more reasonable one. So, good cop, bad cop."

"Don't get us wrong, Hernando," Susanne said. "We're a team that goes way back. No games. You see what you get."

"Which is?"

Susanne pointed to her best friend.

"She's Sharon, I'm Susanne. We just spent a week on the road. We are looking for a place to stay, get some food, hot water, a secure place to sleep. But we are *not* going to be somebody's bitch."

"Bit of an edge on the good cop, I see," Hernando mused.

"So what are you looking for? Why drag us back here?" Sharon interjected.

Hernando leaned back in his chair, sipping his bottle of iced tea. "Tea's still cold, but it will warm up."

With that invitation, both women began drinking their tea, as there was a lull in the conversation. The three sat, and each side sized up the other. Then Hernando broke the silence.

"Okay. As you probably figured out, Cindy gave us a cut of whatever she earned. I don't think her face is going to be up to earning much for a few days. So, there is that. And you two want a place to stay for a while."

Hernando leaned forward. "So other than some more rounds of .223 ammunition, what do have to offer?"

Sharon and Susanne looked at each other. Susanne nodded at Sharon.

"Alright, Hernando," Sharon began. "My partner here wants me to negotiate—so here goes." She took a breath, let it out, and continued.

"Your...talent on the stage out there is getting rather lazy and is not exactly very exciting. But being as this has turned into an oasis with power and hot water, not to mention the booze, people put up with it. Am I right?"

"Go on," Hernando said.

"We can put on a show that will definitely take your patrons' minds off what is happening in the rest of Florida. Hopefully, the military comes back, helps get things organized and running again. Until then, we become—well, contractual employees." She looked at Susanne.

"Those bikinis we wore playing beach volleyball did not leave much to the imagination. So, being nude part of the time won't explode our heads. Especially if it means a safe place to stay, hot food, and cold drinks."

Hernando tented his fingers and leaned back again, a bit of a smile on his face.

"But just like my best friend here said. We are not someone's bitch. No touchee, no pokee. If someone does, they get their testicles handed to them. Even if we have to do it when they are asleep. Got it?"

Hernando shifted and with a quick motion opened a drawer in his desk. Out came a bottle of high end imported rum. Then he produced three highball glasses, which he filled with ice from some hidden container. He placed one glass in front of each of the women.

"A toast to seal the deal. But first, since I have come to respect the hell out of you young ladies in this short time, let me tell you the real situation out there." Hernando made a slight sweeping motion with his hand.

"I have a CB in the back with a bigass antenna. So far, what I have heard is chaos. The on again, off again radio transmissions are all bad news. Basically, it's fend for yourself, we'll get back to you." Hernando paused, seemed to be looking at something in the distance.

"I'm Cuban—still have family in Havana. The last info was an email they snuck past the government four days ago. These creatures, whatever they are, whereever the hell they came from, I have no idea. Anyways, they are taking or harvesting people."

Time seemed to freeze for the two young women. They had heard that from the soldiers they had run into. But everyone seemed to hesitate—to admit it was true.

"They seem to really like the darker skinned Cubans. I look like I have a permanent tan, so if I stay in the subdued lights here, I look like most other people."

He stared intently at Sharon and Susanne. "Miami is being overrun. Everything within about twenty miles of the ocean seems to have been targeted. Spacecraft, wheeled robots, some tall walking armored... fighters and those damned creatures are sinking all of our ships, are hitting our military bases, our major communication centers and roads. Not to mention they have some culeros working for them, traitors to the human race." He paused, then continued.

"Washington D.C. and the President is no more."

The three humans sat quietly, as they contemplated the apparent New World Order.

Hernando broke the silence.

"Well, ladies, we do what me must to survive, maybe prosper. So. A toast to a new business agreement. Maybe a bit of a partnership, as I think you two have the guts and the smarts to help *me* survive. So, a toast, ladies?"

Sharon and Susanne both displayed a small smile before knocking back the rum. Their eyes widened a bit as they realized it was 151 Plus Rum, probably from some smuggled Cuban stash.

"Man, that'll put hair on your chest," exclaimed Sharon.

"I hope not,' said Hernando. 'It will destroy the effect of Los Dos."

Susanne frowned a bit. "Los Dos?"

"Sure. Every good act needs a catchy name. Los Dos—The Pair, or The Two. You're definitely two parts of a very special whole. So, does it work?"

Sharon looked at Susanne, then shrugged. "Okay—why not? Mind if I ask a few detail questions?"

"Go ahead."

"Living arrangements. Where do we sleep?"

"We can put you up at a local motel we have 'occupied', I guess you'd call it. I've got a small team of good ole boy regulars trying to fix up the place, find a generator or two for power."

"Well, Hernando, think these good ole boys could help us tow an RV with a busted radiator we abandoned about three miles back?"

"So that's how you two were traveling. I didn't think you had walked all the way here from... wherever. Good shape other than the radiator?"

"We think so. Stopped after it started to boil over, so I don't think we warped anything. May need the septic tank pumped. Everything else works when it has gas."

Hernando paused for a minute, thinking. "Yeah. That might be the start of a good idea. Find some more decent RVs, park them out back, and hook them up to our generators. Yes, we have more than one. Safety in numbers for everyone who is connected to this place. Then we can scavenge from here."

"Scavenge?" Susanne asked. "You act like business owners, residents of the area won't be back. Ever."

"Pretty lady, I've already had my guys clean out a couple of convenience stores that were abandoned, left wide open. Or the owners and managers were taken against their will. Either way, Big Jake's reefer truck out back is now chock full of perishables. That's one reason why he is still here. I give him a purpose, other than thinking about his family back in Texas."

"I take it's bad all over."

"You hit it on the head. Now, we'll get you two set up. Find some clothes for you to wear on and off the stage, okay? And we'll figure out some type of currency besides room and board for you, if this works out the way it should. If you are committed, that is."

"Hell, yes," said Sharon. "Until we find a way to get back home to Pensacola, we plan to stay here as long as it's safe. Right, Susanne?"

"That's right."

Hernando clapped his hands together and grinned.

"One more question… Boss."

"Shoot, Sharon. But not with that snubby pistol you have hidden."

"How'd you know?"

"Years of dealing with the wrong people. Now, what's the question."

"You were a competitive bodybuilder, weren't you?"

"Yes. And was just beginning to dabble into MMA, though I didn't want to mess up my good looks. Now, one question for you two. Gay or straight?"

"Straight," they both answered in unison, then laughed.

"Does it matter?" asked Susanne.

"Just helps prevent any misunderstandings. We are getting a

tight knit group here."

"And you?"

"Straight. But no, I do not fish around in the office pool. That leads to problems, as the late owner found out more than once. Now, vamonos. Time to get this show on the road."

Things went fast after that. Sharon and Susanne scrounged up some "costumes" for their stage acts. If they were going to perform – it would be an organized act, not just them showing off naked booty.

They started out literally playing volleyball on stage, knocking a ball they had located over an abbreviated net. Surprise, surprise, to the appreciation of the audience, their bikinis magically disappeared off their lotion rubbed bodies. Their toned and tanned bodies with nice sized curves made more than one man *and* woman drool as they bounced balls off their behinds, twisted and turned, did the splits on the stage.

They had one bit of trouble the second night, when a very drunk transient male jumped on stage with his fly zipped down and his hand trying to pull out a very important part of his anatomy. A perfect front snap kick from Susanne to his face sent him toppling off the stage into the arms of his friends, which kept him from a broken skull. After that, everyone kept their distance. Hernando and John never had to get involved, the regular patrons adopting Los Dos as their special ladies. The fact the large hole from Hernando's one and only use of the 500 Smith and Wesson Hand Cannon had a bull's-eye drawn around it on the wall helped people remember their manners also. Toys in the Attic became a neutral zone, a place where anyone could meet, iron out differences, swap items for survival—while having a cold drink. Hernando obtained more firearms and a small security force, in case any Squids and company showed up. They never did. Neither did any authorities or military. Everyone was on their own.

Thirty-one days from when the first rocks hit, the word was

broadcast that all organized governmental resistance was at an end. Fleeing to the interior and Midwest states was suggested, as the aliens no longer bothered those areas, once the military was taken out.

Sharon and Susanne had worked on new acts by then. They dressed as schoolgirls, pigtails and all, then started acting nasty, a fetish fantasy to many. Next, as an extension of their pure athleticism, they began some choreographed "catfights", nude wrestling that seemed to float everyone's boat. References and hints to lesbian action drew in other clientele. It did not matter to Los Dos. It was an act, a performance, pure and simple. They even added basic plotlines of jilted lovers, historical situations, fight over sexual partners, or fights over possessions. Those were performances, meant to entertain, and to provide Los Dos with a living until things got back to some kind of normal. At least that was the fantasy many were living, not just Sharon and Susanne.

A couple of days after the "we quit" broadcast, Sharon and Susanne returned to their dressing room in the RV. Both were sweaty, nude, and holding torn and shredded underwear. Their bodies even sported a few scratch marks, because they had gotten a little carried away with the action.

They entered the RV, grinning like Cheshire cats as they grabbed ice cold bottles of water and sat down together on the RV's sofa.

"Damn, Susanne. We are running out of those full school girl panties. You keep tearing them up."

"And you don't? We'll ask Hernando to take us a little closer to Jacksonville, see if can find some local stores that haven't been picked over. Maybe we can find some women's fashion stores that were shuttered up when people fled."

"Yeah. Except the closer we get to Jacksonville and the water inlets, the Bay—the greater chances are someone getting snatched by the Squids. And somebody mentioned something about a Church of Kraken."

"I know. But if we're very careful..." Susanne stopped in mid comment, the smile gone away.

"Sharon, is this the right thing? Do we still have some basic moral standards? Or are we just whores, selling our bodies for gold?"

Sharon frowned a bit. "Why, is this bothering you? Because we are definitely *not* whores. We are selling fantasy, not our sex. We don't let people touch us..."

"But we are showing everything. Some of our regulars could become gynecology assistants, because they have seen so many close ups." A side effect of this was the appearance of other "talent", copying some of the things Los Dos were doing. Of course none were as good as the originals.

Sharon took her best friend's hand in hers. "Hey, I know this is not what we would have chosen, but we are free, healthy, with food, drink and shelter. Hernando even has a doctor on staff. Hundreds of thousands of people out there don't have all that, are now on the run to the midwest. I say we still have a form of good moral standards. We don't hurt anybody, don't allow anyone to be hurt in our presence—unless they try to hurt someone else."

Susanne was looking down and away from her friend.

"Hey, Suze, there's something else bothering you, isn't there?"

Both women were silent for a few moments, then Susanne finally spoke.

"I'm beginning to enjoy this too much. You and I, rolling around in front of a bunch of strangers...like tonight. I am getting excited every time we do this." She looked up, her eyes now a bit moist.

"Sex and passion are supposed to be private, not for show. They are supposed to be reserved for your lover."

Sharon, a concerned look on her face, gently touched her partner's cheek.

"Hey, I don't want you to hurt. You tell me what you want. I admit it, I get all hot and bothered too. But hell, that's better than getting pissed off every night. Or getting abused every night."

Susanne looked intently into the Sharon's blue eyes, a trait they both shared.

"You're feeling it too?"

"Yes, I am."

Something clicked in a way that had not happened before. The two women stared into each other's eyes for a few moments. Susanne leaned forward and kissed Sharon on the lips.

It started slowly, then both women began to show more enthusiasm and passion. For a good five minutes there was no conversation, no words exchanged as they regaled in each other's touch.

Then they were laying side by side, their fingers caressing each other's bodies. They put their foreheads together, breathing hard, almost panting.

"I didn't expect this..." Susanne began.

"Must you get analytical at a time like this?" Sharon interrupted. "Goddammit, I love you. I have for a long time. I just did not realize to what extent. Now I know. Now *we* know."

"I love *you* too, Sharon Wagner. It's been there simmering. Now, it's boiled over."

"Remember the sleep overs, our game of pinch and tickle?"

"Yes." Sharon's voice was low and sultry.

"Time to take it to the next level, my love. My special love..."

A half hour later, Sharon and Susanne were squeezed together in the RV's shower stall. They washed each other bodies, giggling like the schoolgirls they portrayed on stage. They kissed often, their hands would start to roam again and had to resist.

They still had one more show to do.

They finished, stepped out and toweled each other off.

Again they had to restrain themselves with the touching, the caressing. Someone knocked on the RV door.

"Los Dos. It's Maria. The show, it is about to start."

"Be right there, Maria," Sharon answered. Maria and her husband Pablo, plus a young son and daughter, had showed up some three weeks ago with a large mobile grill and taco truck. Now, they were the kitchen for the operation. And they were good.

Sharon gave Susanne a dreamy smile. "Can we do this?"

Susanne caressed her now lover.

"Yes. Negligée, black support hose. We give them a show without taking *anything* off."

"Watching us reach under..." Sharon began.

"Touching for real this time. But they can't see. Our love is kept... private."

Sharon's face became serious. "I love you. But I'm still attracted to men."

"Ditto. Pact from today on. If you must, we share... everything."

This caused both to break into large grins.

Hernando pounded on the door, yelling.

"Ladies. For the last time, you're going to be late."

"Boss," Sharon yelled back. "You take off your clothes until we get there. The gay guys and the women will just *love* you."

Hernando laughed. "Never a dull moment with you two, is there?"

"No. Sir. Never will be either."

Things went well, as the months turned into almost a year since The Night. As well as it could be expected when the idea and reality of civilization had been greatly reduced. It had become apparent from first person accounts and official reports that an alien species resembling Earth cephalopods, squids and octopus, were the ones behind the Invasion, the rock strikes. These aliens, derogatorily called "Squids" by the survivors, were in control of the coastal areas worldwide, as well as areas around large bodies of water such as the Great Lakes. They had been seen moving on land, and their locomotion seemed to suggest they were amphibious. Bottom line, many humans had fled to the interior areas of the various continents. Those that hadn't, existed in a feral condition in areas the Squids seemed to ignore. At least for right now.

Sharon and Susanne loved and worked at Toys in the Attic. The business became well known as their Oasis in Chaos. It also became a source for information about what was going on in the surrounding former U.S. States. The people who passed through gave definite information that Mississippi, Alabama and Georgia were being fenced and walled off by the Squids. Large numbers of s people of color were forced into the area, which soon became known as Cattle Country. Part of this roundup was being aided by the new Church of Kraken that had sprung up. These renegade Churchers—or Krakens as they were called— seemed to enjoy helping the Squids, as well as playing at *being* Squids. Attempts to don outfits that made them look cephalopodan and garish tattoos of stylized squids and octopus on all parts of their bodies were commonplace. Then there were the rumors of cannibalism.

"Fucking ghetto and concentration camp," Sharon had spat out upon hearing the news of the round ups. "I have some Jewish relatives on my mom's side. A few of an older generation lived through World War II. Never Forget."

Hernando had looked at her after this outburst. "Well, truth is there is *nothing* we can do about it. At least they have left us alone."

"Yes, Hernando," Susanne responded. "But that still doesn't make us very happy about it."

"True, ladies. Very true. Can you two join me in my office for a moment? I have something for you."

A couple of minutes later, the two athletes were staring dumb-founded, as Hernando stacked some treasure in front of them on the desk.

"There. Stack of gold coins. Stack of silver coins. Some gold and silver jewelry. A bag of regular coin with some paper money thrown in, value on today's market about as clear as mud. And Susanne's revolver, fully loaded."

"Why Boss? Why this now?" Sharon asked.

Hernando took a deep breath, then let it out.

"Just so you know you can, and you have the resources, to leave at any time."

The team of Los Dos looked at each other. Then Susanne spoke.

"Are you firing us?"

"Oh, hell no! You can't fire family." Hernando pulled out a bottle of rum and took a swig straight from the bottle.

"To be blunt, I am beginning to feel like a bit of a pimp and a slave master. You and some of the other young women are way too nice to be in this establishment. You can leave if you want to."

Before he realized it, he had two tall and attractive young ladies with tears in their eyes, hugging the crap out of him.

"You're like a big brother to us, you big jerk," Susanne said with a lump in her throat.

"Well, just so you know. I don't want people to think I own them or something. Just because I've had some criminal associations, doesn't mean I'm an asshole."

He gave each of the women a brotherly kiss on the cheek.

"By the way, Big John wants to say something,"

For such a huge man, he could move quietly. So they had not realized he was standing behind them. He rarely said much to them, but Sharon and Susanne were always quick with a hug and a kiss for the giant.

"Here. I knitted these for you." He handed them each a matching sweater.

"You... knit?" Sharon was incredulous.

The huge blonde man shrugged. "Why not? I get bored

sometimes. And this long winter we are having is hard on you young women."

The tears then flowed, as the two women hugged and kissed on him, causing Big John to blush for the first time they could remember.

They came three weeks later in the night.

Sharon and Susanne were cuddled up together, the night being a bit cold and damp. They slept in the nude under a bunch of bed clothes, wanting the feel of the other's skin when they slept together.

Loud shots, shouts, and screams came all at once. The two women were jerked awake by the commotion. Sharon grabbed for her snubby .38—just as the RV door was ripped off its hinges. Yelling figures were on top of them before they knew it. The pistol was knocked from Sharon's hands, and the two athletes fought back with their Jeet Kun Do. The tall blonde grabbed a hold of one male figure's testicles and crushed them with a hammer strike to her hand as she held them. The man shrieked so loud it hurt their ears.

Then the women were tazed into semi-consciousness, with plastic slip ties used to secure their hands. Bags were placed over their heads, as they were manhandled to the back of a furniture van. They found each other in the van by calling out and crawling to each other.

"Who are they?" Sharon asked.

"Sounds like Church of Kraken," Susanne answered. "No one knew they were in the area."

"Everyone in there, shut the fuck up," a male voice yelled.

The young women heard Maria and her children being thrown into the back of the van, as they cried out. They heard female voices, which they recognized as a couple of the other dancers. Then the van roll down door was slammed shut. They lay in darkness as the vehicle began to move.

Sharon and Susanne managed to remove the bags over their heads, since the coverings had not been secured well. They could tell the supposed Church of Kraken members were used to bullying and abusing people who rarely resisted. Thus, the lackadaisical attitude towards the captives. After all, who could call for help? The police, the military? There had not seen hide nor hair of them for months. The two women were on their own.

Thanks to their athleticism, even in the dark they were able to roll around until Susanne could try to chew on the plastic tie on Sharon's wrists. The van motored on in the night, anybody who saw it oblivious to its contents, even if they cared.

Susanne took a break in trying to gnaw on Sharon's restraints. "I think we are heading south. I've always had a good sense of direction."

"Well, I hope the trip is long. Give us more of a chance to get out of these plasticuffs," Sharon said.

"They're hard on my teeth. I'm trying not to break a tooth, but according to my tongue I think I'm wearing a grove in one."

"Here, take a break. Let me feel around with my toes for a nail or something sharp. Vans like these are rarely kept clean."

Sharon was rewarded about ten minutes later with a discarded metal can lid someone had been lax in disposing.

"We're in business", Susanne said. The other occupants of the van had been pretty silent, other than Maria. She had been praying and calming her two children when they occasionally whimpered.

Susanne was careful and managed to secure the sharp lid in her teeth without slicing her mouth. Sharon then began to slide her bonds back and forth on the sharp edge, careful not to push so hard as to dislodge the lid from Susanne's teeth, a slow process. But after about twenty minutes, Sharon moved away from Susanne's face and flexed her arm muscles, trying to move her wrists at the same time. An almost silent snap—and she was free.

"God just smiled on us, lover," she said to Susanne. Rubbing more feeling in her hands, she then went to work on Susanne's bonds, which parted quicker.

"Need to thank Hernando for those weights he got for our workouts," Susanne said in a low tone.

"Free the others?" she asked.

"Let me check the roll up door first. See it it's locked," Sharon replied. It was locked.

"Shit. So, do we free the others, risk them creating a fuss?"

"At least Maria and the kids. I think we can keep them in control."

It took the two about an hour to free Maria and her children, as the can lid was becoming dull and bent. They explained to Maria the importance of being quiet and acting like they were still tied up if anyone opened the roll up door. The other two former dancers began to talk loudly, asking what was going on. Sharon tried to quiet them, just as the moving van braked and began to pull over.

"Alright," Sharon hissed. "Act like you're tied up." She then moved towards the front with Susanne, and they began to play act like tied up prisoners.

Someone unlocked and threw open the back roll up door.

"What's all the talking?" an indistinct male barked out.

"We gotta go. Use a toilet," Susanne yelled back.

The unknown Kraken follower grunted, then turned and yelled.

"Lee, bring the buckets."

About a minute later, two large plastic storage buckets were unceremoniously thrown into the back of the moving van.

"Hey, how are we..." Sharon began to protest, but was cut off by the one called Lee.

"Your problem, bitch, not mine." Then the roll up door slammed back down.

"Well," whispered Susanne. "At least they didn't notice our hands were free."

"Yeah. Let me have the can lid. I'll go have a little talk with the two other dancers."

An hour later, Sharon had already explained to Wendy and Charlene the importance of remaining quiet and waiting for the right moment, as she managed to cut their plasticuffs. She then went and sat back down next to Susanne.

"Think they understand?" Susanne asked.

Sharon shrugged. "Don't know, really. I hope they do. I suggest we get to our feet the next time we stop, get ready to move—while still acting like we are tied up. If we get close, we can kick the shit out of those two Krakens, or whatever those assholes call themselves."

The van trundled down the highway in the night with no other stops. Susanne found that someone had put water bottles in the waste buckets, apparently to be used to clean up any messes. She passed one around and everyone sipped at it. Some six hours after the trip had begun, the van slowed down and changed the angle of travel. Then, it began to make a series of turns.

"We just left the highway," Susanne said. "We're near the ocean, I can feel and smell the salt air."

About thirty minutes later the vehicle jerked to a stop. Then the engine was shut off.

"Get ready," Sharon hissed. "Wait until Susanne and I move before you all do." She stood up and stretched. If given the chance, she would make these so called people pay.

Susanne stood up next to her. "Love you. Always will."

"I love you, Susanne. We'll get through this, together. We're the bad-ass beach volleyballers."

The roll up door was shoved up hard, slamming at the end of its travel and rebounding backwards. Charlene chose that moment to panic and run screaming towards the perceived escape. She was almost cut in half by a shotgun blast.

"Fucking *stop!*" a new male voice yelled. "You think we are stupid or something? Turn around. Walk *backwards* towards this door. I have more shotgun shells to use if you want them."

"Fuck," Sharon whispered.

"Hang in there. We'll make it," Susanne whispered back. As the two athletes reached the back of the truck, they were tazed once more, collapsing into rough arms as they fell out of the vehicle.

"Not taking any chances with you two nasty bitches," the same male voice growled.

Susanne and Sharon were groggy, as they were frog walked past a combination marina office and small motel. At large berth was a long yacht that had seen better days, but was still afloat. Within minutes they were shoved into a cabin at water level that was now a holding cell. Wendy was marched down to a cabin towards the yachts bow. Maria and her children were seen taken into the Marina office and motel area.

With guns to their heads, Sharon and Susanne had thick leather dog collars placed around their throats and secured with small hasp locks. The dog collars were also connected by hasp locks to double loop dog tie out chains that had been secured by large screws in the deck.

"That ought to hold you," said a large and ugly man with a full face tattoo of some form of tentacle beast on his face. He seemed to be the one in charge, as all the other men, around a dozen, demurred to his decisions and opinions.

Sharon managed to stand and looked around. She saw some partially filled water bottles and a waste bucket that looked like it had just been dumped out.

"What do we do for food and water? Not to mention clothes and blankets."

Tattoo Face sneered. "Be nice to our clients, customers, you get food, water, blankets."

Sharon's face flushed with anger. "Look. You may look like Jabba the Hut, but we're not Princess Leia in slave girl attire..."

Tattoo Face jammed a shotgun barrel into her stomach, making her stumble back.

"Bitch, your smart mouth means *nothing* here. No negotiations. We own you. Now, shut up and sit down until we say different." With that, the Krakens left and shut the cabin door. A lock clicked closed on the door.

Susanne sat next to Sharon on a crude bench, touched her hurt stomach.

"Hang tough, lover. We'll wait and get the drop on them later."

Sharon began to cry. "I want my mom. I want my dad. I want to go home. This last year has been a bad dream. I want to *wake up*."

Susanne hugged her best friend and partner. "You have me," she whispered.

"You're the reason I'm still sane, Susanne. Like I said before, you are a rock to me."

The two women sat quietly for a few minutes and just listened as they held each other, when they heard an argument.

"What do you mean, we're low on ammo?" Tattoo Face's voice rang out.

"Brad, you told us to hit quick, grab people, new meat and stuff we could find and get out. There were a lot more people running around than we thought."

"So, fucknuts, what did you get? I know you got these women, a couple of guys and some booze. What else?"

"We only had time to find two pistols. A bunch of people came in cars and trucks from down the road. Locals. I guess, friends of the club."

"So you ran." Tattoo Face began to curse.

"Alright, Tom. Put the word out. We have new talent. Guns and ammo *only* for payment. Well, get a move on! Put the word out. And next time I *lead* the raid." Tattoo Face walked down the gangway from the yacht, grumbling, "Can't get decent help at all these days."

Sharon and Susanne managed to adjust their chains and looked out the cabin porthole.

"Look," said Susanne. "I saw them put Maria and the kids in the motel area." She began checking the size of the porthole.

"We may be able to squeeze out…"

"Yeah, after we've been starved a bit," Sharon answered. "Not before. And not in broad daylight." She began to look at and test the chains.

"Cheap bastards are using pet store dog chains. Cheap dog chains at that. We look for a weak link, start bending on it. Then we are loose next time they unlock the door."

Susanne smiled at her friend. "Bad cop is back."

"She never left. You just help me remember what is needed. Like I said, you're the rock."

As the two began to examine their prison more closely, they heard a voice shout out.

"Hey, Boss. Visitors."

The two women looked out the porthole and finally caught sight of two figures walking towards the yacht gangway. Tattoo Face Brad came from another nearby dock to intercept the two apparent strangers. He met them at the end of the yacht gangway.

"Can I help you two?"

The older looking one of the two, a beefy red-headed, late middle aged man with a red handlebar mustache, shifted his hands under a well-used dark plastic rain poncho.

"Understand you have some new talent."

Brad's face broke into a broad grin, his tattoo being stretched in an odd manner.

"Man, word travels fast. Just got three new pieces of meat today. But we're only taking weapons and ammo as scratch. You have any extra?"

The companion of the red headed man, a younger, clean shaven man with Hollywood style good looks, tight physique, and short brown hair under a baseball hat, looked at Brad. Then he nodded to Redhead.

"Yeah. Boss here seems to think we —"

Before the older man could finish his statement, the younger man produced a sharp bayonet from under the back of his battered Air Force flight jacket and shoved it into the stomach of Brad. He did it in such a smooth and quick motion—it was as if he had only meant to shake hands, and the blade had appeared by magic. The younger man moved the razor sharp blade sideways and up, then yanked it out and stepped back.

Things happened so fast that Brad watched his intestines begin to fall out before the pain registered. He then shrieked as he fell over, trying to hold his guts it.

"My God," Susanne exclaimed at the porthole. "What the hell just happened?"

The two strangers began to clamber up the gangway to the yacht, the red headed man producing a double barreled sawed off shotgun from under his rain poncho.

Sharon pulled on Susanne's arm. "Come on. We'll see if we can pull your chain loose from the deck if we do it together." Their combined strength and Sharon's accurate assessment of the dog chain's cheapness resulted in a bending, then a snapping, as Susanne's chain was freed from the deck. They started on Sharon's when someone pounded on the door.

"Who's in there?" It was a new voice, from the younger stranger. He did not look through the porthole.

"Two pissed off women, buddy," Sharon yelled back as she motioned Susanne to position herself by the door. The brunette began to make a garrote from her free dog chain.

"Know where the keys are at?" The younger man asked.

"If we did, would we be in here?" Sharon shot back. The man grunted.

"That was kind of a dumb-ass question, wasn't it?"

"Hey, Boss," came from the red-headed man. "The others noticed you gutted their boss and are starting to make plans to get us. I thought we were going to wait until the Admiral showed up with his people."

"Chief, that tattooed piece of shit had fresh blood on his boots. Bet you it was human. So it seemed the right thing to do."

The one identified as Chief chuckled. "Adam, you always did have trouble with being patient. Well, I'm going to need some help when the buddies of the guy you killed get their nerve up."

"We'll help if you get us out," Sharon said in a loud voice.

"How's that?" Adam aka Boss asked.

"Just cut us loose. I promise you we are not shrinking violets."

There was a pause. Then Adam spoke. "Alright. Chief, keep an eye out while I try to locate some keys or a good crowbar."

"Roger that, Boss."

Adam found a crowbar and smashed the cheap padlock off the cabin room door. He then yanked it opened and stepped back, with a semi-auto pistol in his right hand. Susanne stepped through the doorway.

"Excuse me. Can I borrow that crowbar so I can free Sharon?"

Adam gave the nude, attractive and dirty young lady a once over, then handed her the crowbar.

"Thank you, sir." As Susanne turned to re-enter the cabin, Adam asked a question.

"You were ready to choke me with that length of chain, weren't you?"

"If necessary, yes."

Adam grunted. "Yeah, I can see you might be of help. Get your friend, any others free, then look for weapons. Got it?"

"Got it... Boss."

It took less than a minute for Sharon to be free of being attached to the deck. She wrapped the left-over chain around her right fist.

"That's going to hurt your hand if you hit someone," observed Susanne.

"It's going to hurt whom I hit more," Sharon replied.

Adam walked up and handed the two nude women some blankets and a small knife.

"Here, ladies. Slice a hole in the center for your head and

instant poncho."

"Thanks," said Sharon. 'By the way, I'm Sharon Wagner, this is Susanne Shaw…"

"Adam Lloyd, the Director. No time for niceties, look for weapons, anyone else who needs to be freed." Adam turned and walked stern, where the Chief was watching the gangway.

"Well, Boss, I think we're in for it now," the Chief said as Adam walked up next to him. The Chief was using part of the access hatch to the center cabin walkway as cover.

Adam looked out, made a quick survey, and then ducked back in.

"Yeah, I count twelve nasty looking Krakens milling around by the Marina office, trying to get organized. I thought the Admiral would have been here by now."

Chief William Hamilton snorted. "Have we really ever been able to figure out his schedule since we met him? Isn't there some comment about a drummer…"

"He marches to the cadence of a different drummer, that he does. But he's been honest with us so far."

"Honest according to his reality. I think he's a can or two short of a six pack."

"Well, hopefully he'll still show up as planned. What do you have in your little diddy bag, Chief?"

"Spare shells for the twelve gauge, my Desert Eagle, and spare loaded mags for your M-9."

"Let me have the spare mags. I'll climb up on the next deck before they start shooting at us, help cover the gangway, and watch for anyone trying to come in from the water on the port side."

"Gotcha. Head and ass down, Boss."

"Head and ass down, Chief."

As Adam left to go top side, Sharon and Susanne showed up with a very scared Wendy. She had just been tied up with rope, so it had been easier to free her. Now she stood in a makeshift poncho, shivering with fear.

"Three of you young ladies, I see," the Chief said.

"That we know of... Chief, I guess that's what the Boss calls you."

"Chief Master Sergeant William Hamilton at your service. Formerly of the United States Air Force, when there was one." He looked out the yacht hatchway to see what was going on with the Krakens. They still seemed to be milling around in the Marina office area, like ants in a disturbed nest.

He glanced at the three women. "Any weapons?"

"I recovered Hernando's hand cannon, with four rounds in it,' Sharon replied.

The Chief glanced at the huge revolver. "Jesus H. Christ, what is that thing?"

"Hernando said it was a 500 Smith and Wesson Magnum. He inherited it from the owner of Toys in the Attic in Jacksonville." Sharon paused. "Now I guess we inherited it."

"The Director and I heard someone had a going community around a former gentlemen's club up there. Had been planning on paying you a visit."

"Don't bother," Susanne interjected. "Everyone there is either dead or scattered."

The Chief grunted. "Yes, Ma'am, these a-hole Krakens have that effect on just about everyone they meet." He glanced at Sharon again. "Can you handle that pistol?"

"One way or another, I *will* handle this pistol."

The Chief displayed a wry smile. "You ladies have spunk."

"We wouldn't be here, honey, if we were wusses."

The Chief chuckling. "I'll give you that much. Now, see if you can find something to prop on that cannon and help me cover the gangway."

"The porthole out of our former cabin should do. Yell if you want something, Chief."

Chief Hamilton laughed. "Like I said. Spunk. I like that."

A couple of minutes later the now half-assed organized Krakens began to fan out around the dock area, trying to approach the yacht using whatever cover they could find, which was not much. The Krakens were not used to armed resistance. They were used to bullying and having their way with scared people. Two tried to make a dash up the gangway, and the Chief let them have it with both barrels of his sawed off shotgun. The spread hit them from head to toe and they went down, one falling into the water, not to surface.

"Come and get it, you sons of bitches!" The Chief yelled out as he reloaded the scattergun, then laid it down and took the large 44 Caliber Desert Eagle automatic from his bag. The magnum loads from the long barreled pistol had better accuracy and range than the buckshot and dime loads for the 12 gauge.

The Krakens returned fire with an eclectic batch of guns, some shots hitting the yacht, some not. As the Chief ducked down, Adam Lloyd began firing from the upper deck with his 9mm, taking down an advancing Kraken, but making himself a target. He ducked behind the leeboards for cover as rounds whizzed by.

The Chief let loose with the Desert Eagle, the loud reports resounding around the Marina area. A Kraken was nearly decapitated, as one of the magnum loads took him in his head, killing him instantly.

During this exchange of fire, two Krakens made it behind a cement wall that was part of a box structure, used to contain large trash bins. They peaked over the rim, then tried to light a Molotov cocktail they had constructed using a whiskey bottle.

There was a huge booming sound, even when compared to the Chief's Forty Four Magnum. One complete cinder block of the trash bin structure seemed to disintegrate, the two Krakens yelping as they dropped their gas bomb, which broke and splashed them with the contents. They were also unfortunate when they dropped the lit Zippo lighter, with which they had planned to ignite the Molotov cocktail. Instead, the Zippo ignited them. They panicked, began to run around and beat at their legs that were now on fire.

"Burn in hell, you sorry fuckers!" Sharon screamed out the porthole, resulting in an answering bullet crashing into the bulkhead—inches from her head. Adam Lloyd answered the attempt at shooting Sharon by shooting one of the burning Krakens in the leg. The man fell over, screaming. His companion finally remembered they were near water and jumped in near the stern of the yacht.

The Chief's Desert Eagle began to boom again, and another Kraken took his last breath. With this, the surviving Krakens began to call back and forth, trying to figure out a way to assault the yacht.

"You still in one piece, ladies?" the Chief yelled out.

"Hell, yeah!" Susanne yelled back.

The Chief chortled. "Spunk. Pure spunk."

Three Krakens rushed to the gangway, expending much of their limited ammunition supply. As they tried to dash up the ramp, Sharon's Hand Cannon roared again, the bullet completely penetrating one Kraken and hitting the rope handrail, severing it. The dead Kraken plopped into the water below, one of his fellows slipping and almost falling into water with his deceased companion. The third one of the group screamed in rage and headed up the gangway, to be met with a blast of buckshot. He died, his blood soon covering the gangway with a dark red pool. The last surviving Kraken in the assault group decided discretion was the better part of valor and rolled off the ramp into the water below.

"We've got two in the water, people," The Chief called out.

"I've got them," growled Susanne. She slid out of the cabin and went up an interior stairwell to the upper deck. Adam looked up as she slid by him and, staying as low as possible, peered over the port side, opposite the dock. She saw the burnt Kraken trying to climb up a small water level ladder, and the Kraken who had exited the gangway surfacing near him.

To say that the last year had built up a feral quality in Susanne that she had not realized was possible would have been an understatement. And now, it was all boiling over. She had wrapped the remaining length of the restraining dog chain around her waist to keep it out of her way. Now, she unwrapped it, letting an end hang loose. Holding it in her mouth to free her hands, she used a gymnast dismount to drop to the deck below, just as the burnt and in pain Kraken climbed on board.

While she and Sharon had learned Jeet Kun Do, they had also studied the use of various Chinese and Japanese martial art weapons. One was the chain whip. Although the dog chain was not as substantial as the chain whip, it was better than nothing.

Susanne did a quick side spin, then whipped it around the throat of the Kraken. As he clawed to free it from around his neck, Susanne stepped in, had a hold of two sections and twisted the chain tight. The athlete stuck her hip into opponent, used her legs and lifted him by the chain garrote she had fashioned onto her side and back, as if to perform a hip throw. She stopped half way through, strangling him as he was partially suspended.

"You killed my friends and family, you shit,' Susanne growled. "Now die." She crushed his adam's apple as she twisted the chain, then dropped him onto the deck. The Kraken spasmed as he died.

She had misjudged the location of the other Kraken, who was suddenly on board and coming at her. Susanne had no time to free the chain from her first victim's throat and tried to step away. The chain still attached the collar at her throat, she had no time to remove it, jerking her up short. The Kraken saw her plight and lunged with a double bladed knife.

Speed borne of panic enabled her to block the thrust with her arms, but she sustained a nasty cut on her left forearm. She yelped as she tried to use a wrist lock on the knife hand and was shoved into the bulkhead, as the large Kraken tried to free his weapon hand. She sank her teeth into the wrist of the hand holding the knife and began to worry it like a Terrier with a rat. The Kraken screamed as he dropped his weapon, then slammed

Susanne into the bulkhead. She kept biting as she tried to hang on, the Kraken punched at her with his free left hand, and she soon saw stars. Her bite was shaken loose, and her feet slipped out from under her, her butt winding up on the deck. The Kraken raised his free fist to punch her straight in the face, as she tried to see it through the stars in her vision.

From what seemed like nowhere, a boot struck the Kraken in the back of the head, knocking him into the bulkhead above Susanne. Adam Lloyd had come to Susanne's aid, swinging down from the railing above. He clambered over the railing onto the lower deck as the Kraken tried to stand up, pushing off from the bulkhead. This despicable excuse of human species was an experienced rough and tumble fighter, who did not want to go down. He grappled with Adam, tried to force him back over the deck railing.

Some automatic function caused Susanne to notice and grab the dropped knife. In one motion she slammed it point first into the inner left thigh of the Kraken. Blood began to spurt from the wound, a sure sign she had slit the femoral artery. He screamed and tried to grab the knife sticking in his leg as he bled out. Adam slammed the web of his right hand into the Kraken's throat, striking the adam's apple and shoving the Kraken backwards. Susanne suddenly had two bodies falling on top of her, as they were tripped by her body. She screamed out in rage and pain, managed to pull the blade from the enemy's thigh. On automatic, she began to stab the Kraken over and over again. She did not notice the body go limp, or that she was covered in blood.

"Susanne. *Stop.* He's dead!" Adam yelled and finally got her attention. She slumped to the blood covered deck, turned her head sideways and began to vomit up what little still remained in her stomach. Adam bent over and brushed her long brown hair from her face and held it back out of the way.

"Hey, Boss. You still there?" Chief yelled loud, trying to figure what had happened.

"We're coming Chief. Give us a moment." Just then, Sharon's hand cannon boomed again.

"Come on, young lady. You have to get up, no time to be sick." He helped her to her feet, and she somehow formed a smile.

"I think I owe you my life," Susanne said.

"Pass it on later to someone else. Come on, the others need us."

Adam produced a multi-tool and used the pliers to free the dog chain from Susanne's collar. The two allies managed to enter the yacht through a bow hatch and went up through the passageway. As they did, Adam produced a small flask and dumped alcohol on Susanne's knife wound. She hissed in pain, and Adam explained

"Infection. I don't know what that asshole had, and you're covered with his blood."

"Thanks again."

"De nada."

As they passed the cabin where Sharon was, she looked and cried when she saw all the blood.

"Susanne!" She started to move towards her partner.

"It's okay Sharon—it's not mine."

Adam had Susanne sit in the cabin and went forward to Chief's location. As he moved up to his side, shots rang out. But they were not from the Krakens. Rather, someone else was shooting at them.

"I think the Admiral just showed up." Just after the Chief spoke, there were several bursts of automatic fire, followed by screams from the Kraken positions. One figure tried to run away and was cut down. Then, silence.

Chief let out a loud and shrill whistle.

"Hey, Admiral. Over here."

Walking towards the gangway came a tall and gangly man, spouting a well-trimmed van dyke beard and mustache. His facial hair and well-groomed head hair were partially gray, but his tanned skin had a healthy and younger tone to it. However, it was his dress that was the most eye grabbing.

The one called the Admiral was decked out in what could have been called an example of Third World military dictator potentate uniform. There were more braidings, epaulets, cordage, and fourragere than on any three senior military officer's uniforms. His naval officer's style dress hat was festooned with braiding, bullion, and leaves on the brim and body. All in all, he looked like an Admiral of Starfleet in some space opera. To top off the image, he was carrying a gold plated 45 automatic pistol.

The Admiral strode up the gangway as if he owned the place, ignoring the blood and guts around him. He stepped down onto the deck and nodded to the Chief and Adam.

"Chief Williams, Director Lloyd. Sorry I am a bit late. I and my personnel were detained by some other scum a few miles back."

"No problem, Admiral," Adam replied. "You always have a way at arriving just at the right moment, with just the right flourish."

This prompted a wide grin from the Admiral. "I do so enjoy our combined operations. I'm glad Lord Neptune arranged for you to set up the new idea of a Key West based country. I'll handle my Conch Republic. I have no desire to be responsible for anything else."

Sharon and Susanne walked out on deck at that moment, Susanne looking a bit pale having had the blood washed off of her. Behind them, shaking, was the dancer Wendy.

The Admiral saw them, his eyes widened a bit. He bowed, taking his military hat off and sweeping it with a flourish towards the ground, like a bit player in some Three Musketeer Hollywood Epic.

"Gentle ladies," said the Admiral. "The Director and Chief did not tell me they had rescued three comely young women. I am the Admiral, leader of the Conch Republic, at your service."

The Chief and Adam tried not to laugh. The Admiral had

become a good friend and ally, despite all of his eccentricities. So they did not want to offend him by laughing at his sometimes over the top behavior.

Sharon stepped forward and put her right hand out to shake, still having her left hand on Susanne to steady her a bit. "Pleased to meet you Admiral..."

"Just Admiral. Everyone knows who I am, I need no other names." He took Sharon's hand and kissed it with a flourish. She could not help but smile.

"No one ever kissed my hand like that before. You have quite the way with the ladies—I can see."

The Admiral gave the three women a once over and frowned. He looked at Adam.

"That is the best you can do, Director, for vestments, clothing? Blanket ponchos?"

"We were kind of busy trying not to get killed, Admiral—had to make do."

"Well, the Admiral will fix that." He turned towards the dock, put two fingers to his teeth and produced a very loud whistle. His personnel all looked at him, as the Admiral made a few gestures they seemed to understand at once, because two of them slung their weapons and began running back from whence they came.

"My people will be here momentarily with clothing suitable for young ladies, as well as food and drink. The area is now secure, the Kraken savages vanquished. We have one prisoner with a leg wound and burns whom we will question."

"Thank you, Admiral, for coming when you did," Susanne said shakily. "And the Director and the Chief here. I don't know how you found us, but if you hadn't..." She started to waver a bit on her feet, and Sharon grabbed a hold of her.

"Chairs! Chief, Adam, deck chairs for the young ladies. Come, be quick about it. They have had an ordeal, watching men die..."

"We killed some of them," Susanne interjected. "We did not want to, but did what we had to."

The Admiral looked at Sharon and Susanne with a piercing gaze.

"You are friends, companions, correct?"

"Yes, Admiral." Sharon put her arm around Susanne. "We're beach volleyball players. We were on our way to the Olympics. Then the... Squids showed up. Then these Kraken sacks of shit."

There was pause in conversation, as the Chief and Adam took the deck chairs from the upper deck and placed them around the stern deck area. The three women sank down into the comfortable chairs, the horrible chain of events catching up with them. Then Sharon started to jump up from her chair.

"Maria! And her two kids. They were up by that crappy motel." She looked at the Admiral.

He paused for a minute, then replied.

"We will look, young lady. I have not heard of any report of my people finding anyone else imprisoned." He gave Adam a quick look——then turned back to Sharon.

"You young ladies seem to have special skills and abilities, yes?"

Sharon sank back into her chair. "Right now, all I have is a headache".

An SUV drove up near the gangway and honked its horn.

"Ladies, if you are up to it, there is food and drink in the vehicle, as well as clothing. May I escort you to peruse the contents, find something you would like?"

Sharon managed to rise out of the chair, then helped Susanne from hers. Wendy sat in hers, shaking.

"Wendy," Susanne said as she looked at the dancer. Wendy began to cry.

"I want to go home. I want my family. I want my dog..." She began to sob.

The Admiral glided over to Wendy. He bent on his knee in front of the crying woman, took her hands in his.

"Milady, I know this is not where you wished to be. I know, like everyone here, you have lost friends, family, even pets. But, we are here. So, here we make the best of it. I would be flattered if you would join me and my people in the Florida Keys. We need all the survivors we can find. Which is why Chief Williams and Director Lloyd have been on a series of quests." The Admiral paused, gently rubbing her hands and fingers with his. Then he produced a silk handkerchief and handed it to Wendy.

"Here, you are ruining your makeup, lovely lady."

"It was already ruined."

"Well then, all the more reason to come to the Conch Republic. We have hairdressers, cosmetologists who can aid you in repairing your makeup. Though, truth be told, your natural beauty needs no enhancements."

Wendy stopped crying and sniffed. "That was nice to say."

"It is the truth, Wendy, which is your name, right? Now, please. Come with me and my people. I promise there are no hidden catches. I, the Admiral, so do swear." He took her hand and gently helped her up. She latched on to him, using him as support as they walked down the gangway.

Within minutes, the three women had located decent clothes and underwear to cover their nudity, dressing behind a privacy screen the Admiral had erected. There even was a little makeup and some cosmetics. Adam and the Chief helped remove the remaining collars and chains from the three survivors. Then some food was produced, including thermoses of soup and coffee.

Susanne, steadier on her feet now that she was comfortably clothed and fed, walked up to the Admiral as he was talking with the Chief and Adam.

"Yes, Susanne. You have a re...."

The Admiral was tall—so tall even Susanne had to stretch a bit to kiss him on the cheek as she hugged him.

"You, sir, are a nice man. That talk you had with Wendy was one of the nicest conversations I have heard in a long time."

She then turned to Adam and Chief Hamilton.

"Sharon and I owe you our lives. Though to be truthful, I am still worried that we have jumped from the frying pan into the fire."

"Well," replied Adam, "sounds as if it's time to explain just what I and the Chief represent. Want to call Sharon and Wendy over?"

They moved some deck chairs from the yacht to around the SUV where the food and clothes were. For the next half hour, Adam Lloyd explained what he was trying to accomplish as the Director in the Florida Keys, and eventually in the Occupied Areas of the former United States. After he finished, they all sat there, drinking Irish coffee, as the three women considered their next move.

Wendy jumped in with both feet. "If the Admiral can find me a job, a place to stay, says I won't get eaten, I'm in."

"Yes, Wendy. I have influence in many business establishments. And there has been no harvesting since I began running the Conch Republic.

Sharon looked hard at Adam before she spoke. "So let me get this straight. We come and work for you, with you. We don't get eaten because you have an agreement with this... Squid Lord Rock Star that we don't get eaten, just all the poor people of darker skin color in this so called Cattle Country we heard about while in Jacksonville."

"Basically, yes," Adam answered.

She looked at Susanne. "I don't know. Sounds as if you are sacrificing Peter to save Paul."

"She has a point, Director," Susanne said. "I owe you my life. That Kraken probably would have killed me if you hadn't jumped in. So, I owe you big time. But this sounds..." Susanne let it hang as she could not find the right word to finish her thought.

Adam looked at the two intelligent and tough women.

"Yes, for the foreseeable future, as the Protocol states, we *are* sacrificing one group to save another, albeit a small group for a bigger one. Eventually, hopefully, the Protocol of Selective

Survival will be adopted worldwide."

He paused, then continued.

"Look. Is it a sucky deal for some? Yes. Am I condemning some people to death, or at least their children to death? For the next five to ten years, yes. Does it mean the human race as a species survives? I think that is a yes also. Because under this system, we obtain, like the lizards and the grays, not to mention those robocop characters, a worth as a client species, as workers and junior partners. Not *just* food, meat on the hoof. We become like dogs. Right now, a dog's life is better than no life at all."

"For how long?" Sharon asked.

"I have been guaranteed an alternate food source is in the works. Maybe even a cleaned up version of their original primate meat source, with a virus immunity, raised here or maybe in Africa. Though many of the younger generation of Squids, the Tschaaa, have apparently already developed a taste for our sea life. The amount of dark meat needed would be greatly reduced."

Sharon looked at Susanne. "Director, we can leave now, if we want to. And go kill Krakens, you don't care."

"Krakens are a home grown problem that may soon disappear, if they don't stop eating their own species. Eating your own species is an abomination to the Squids. I've whacked a bunch of them for that reason. And the Squids did not care."

Sharon stood up. "Susanne, I just cannot sign on, knowing that this new 'world order,' I guess you call it, wants me to help create a national system that helps the Squids eat one group of humans. So, I've gotta go."

Susanne stood up. "We're a team, Director. Sorry, but it sounds too much like we're helping, in a roundabout way, the Squids to eat a bunch of humans who just happened to be born with dark skin."

Adam sighed. "Well, I keep my word. So, the Chief and I will get you some equipment, supplies..."

"I adopt you," the Admiral butted in with no warning.

"Come again?" Susanne asked.

"You join my other daughters, I have many under my protection as family. And, as the good Director can tell you, I am my own man."

"That's true. He was here before Lord Neptune found me and the Chief. They have an agreement. The Squids leave the Admiral and his Conch Republic alone, he leaves them alone. Hell, he was even granted limited fishing in the ocean, something No One has been allowed."

Sharon looked at the Admiral. "Is that true? How did you get such an arrangement?"

"His Lordship liked my sense of humor. I think he likes my eccentricities."

Susanne laughed. "So, we have no connection with him? What if Sharon and I decide to go hunting for his kind?"

The Director shrugged. "That's your problem, not mine. I don't go around playing Secret Policeman, tracking down people who try to kill Squids. I may stop you from killing his Lordship, but it would be for the selfish reason that we have this arrangement, of which you don't want to be a part. The Tschaaa can take care of themselves for now."

"This is bizarre," Sharon said.

"Then it is settled," the Admiral said as he stood up.

"Wait a minute! What job would we have?"

"Why, you can be my bodyguards. My body needs guarding. It is always getting me in trouble."

The two women laughed along with Wendy.

"Or, you could be my book ends, my special assistants, my eye candy..."

"Admiral, Sharon and I are *not* eye candy."

"Sorry. See—I'm in trouble already."

Sharon and Susanne looked at each other, then laughed again. "Well, Admiral, I guess you have a couple of more daughters," Susanne said.

"Now, my dears, we will head back to the Conch Republic. I will leave some of my people here to help clean up this Kraken mess."

"And look for Maria and the kids."

"Yes, they will help look."

Susanne walked over and hugged Adam.

"Thank you again. If not for you two, we would be trying to squeeze out that cabin porthole."

Sharon walked over and hugged the Chief, kissed him.

"You two are tough," the Chief said. "Don't think of us as strangers."

"Never," replied Sharon.

The two young women were soon escorting the Admiral, with Wendy in tow, to another vehicle.

Adam turned to Chief Hamilton. "They already found Maria and the kids."

"Yes. That was some of the blood you saw on that asshole's shoes."

They stood quietly for a few moments.

"Chief, we do what we have to, don't we? To keep as many people alive as we can."

"You got it. And we sure as hell aren't Krakens."

The Admiral was driving the large SUV, as they headed south to the Keys and ultimately Key West. When Sharon asked him why he did not have a driver, he replied. "The Admiral prefers to pilot his own course."

As they drove, Susanne began to question their apparent new employer and minor savior.

"So, Admiral, where will we live? I know we may be your bodyguards or some type of assistants, but I don't see us living in the same room with you. To put it bluntly, we are no one's bitches."

"Perish the thought! The Admiral does not have bitches." The man seemed a bit peeved, for real.

"So then, where will we stay?"

"You will have either a hotel suite, or a couple of large rooms near my suite. I will only need your assistance when I go out of the hotel."

"You control some functional hotels?" Susanne asked.

"I have three now. I controlled one before the Tschaaa showed up, now I have three since the former owners no longer have use for them."

"Where are the former owners?" Sharon interjected.

The Admiral shrugged. "Either dead or they departed, ran. I stayed, survived. So, as possession is nine tenths of the law, I am now in charge."

"And the Squids let you?" Asked Sharon.

"As the Director said, the one in control who wants us to refer to him as Lord Neptune, liked me and my sense of humor. Said once it reminded him of his own."

"You *talk* directly with him?" Susanne asked a bit incredulous.

"They actually speak to us through some excellent translation machines they have. Captain Kirk and Mister Spock had nothing over His Lordship when it comes to such equipment."

"So we have been dropped into some Hollywood science fiction epic," said Sharon. "Great."

The Admiral paused for a minute in the conversation, then suddenly pulled the SUV over to the highway shoulder.

"Excuse me," Sharon said as she produced the Hand Cannon she had hung onto. It still had one remaining round in it. "You are *not* going to try something funny, are you?"

"No young lady. Please exit the vehicle with me so that I may show you something."

The former Los Dos and Wendy stepped out of the SUV and looked around.

"Ladies, you are on the straight stretch on the overseas highway between Homestead, Florida and the former Florida Keys, now my Conch Republic." The Admiral swept his arm towards the north.

"Up yonder is Miami. Not secure at this time."

The Admiral pointed down the highway to the South.

"About a mile further is a checkpoint. From there on is the Independent State of the Conch Republic. We threatened to secede in the 1980s, when the Federal Government became too onerous on our activities. Then, the alien Tschaaa came and we seceded."

He looked hard at the three young women.

"We take care of our own. I have adopted many daughters to insure their safety from the likes of those Krakens and other scum. The most recent one is Jolene, who sports a scar from an attempt by a Kraken to butcher her. The Director stepped in, and now she is here. You may meet her if you wish."

Susanne could tell that this gentleman took his role as Admiral, leader and surrogate father in a very serious manner.

"Admiral, we..."

"You may find other living arrangement if you like, if you do not trust me. As they say, it is no skin off my nose." The Admiral stood still, assuming a regal attitude in his stance.

The three women looked at each other. Wendy stepped over and bear hugged the Admiral, who put a hand on her back.

"Thank you, Admiral," Wendy said as she squeezed him tight.

"There, there, my dear. No need to try and crush me. I may look a bit thin, but I am strong in a wiry sense. I'm not going anywhere."

"Oh hell," Sharon began. "Susanne and I are sorry. We're just a bit paranoid. Damn. I'll admit it, *scared* is the word. Over the last year, our world has been yanked from us. Now, the two of us are just trying to survive."

In just a moment, the Admiral's demeanor softened.

"You know what they say about paranoia?"

"What, Admiral?" Asked Susanne.

"Just because you're paranoid, doesn't mean that someone

is not after you. Paranoia is God's way of saying look out."

The man called the Admiral then stepped back and once again did a grand sweep with his arm towards the SUV.

"Would my ladies please re-enter my chariot. We still have a ways to go. Then you will have the pick of the remaining living quarters. Later, I will treat you at one of the fine restaurants I have helped to reopen."

"There is no need..." Sharon began and the Admiral held up his hand to stop her.

"No more argument, daughter. Your Admiral has spoken."

In unison, the two former athletes said "Yes sir", and re-entered the SUV.

The armed men at the checkpoint waved the SUV through, a couple of them even saluting as he gave them the royal wave.

Susanne reached over in the back seat and took Sharon's hand in hers. They smiled at each other.

"We'll make it, won't we lover?" Sharon said.

"We're a team," answered Susanne. "The best and toughest beach volleyball team around. Of course we'll make it." With that she leaned over and kissed Sharon, who returned it.

The Admiral who was apparently watching them in the rear view mirror, then asked. "Are you two willing to share some of your affectionate activities with the Admiral?"

"You're not going to turn into a dirty old man are you, Admiral?" asked Sharon.

"Dirty?" replied the Admiral. "Never. The Admiral bathes regularly. *And* he changes his underwear every single day... when he wears underwear."

The former Los Dos tried not to laugh, as he seemed so serious.

"But," he continued. "When I do bathe, I would enjoy it if someone washed my back. I would even share my rubber ducky with you two... especially if you washed my front also."

"*Admiral!*" The two survivors cried out in unison before they began to laugh, with Wendy in the front seat joining in. The

Admiral suppressed a chuckle.

As it had often been said before, it was the beginning of a long and fruitful relationship.

RUNNERS 1

She did not think she could run any faster until she heard the bay of the hounds behind her. Somehow, she managed to make her eight year old legs move a little faster.

She was running away blindly. Her momma had always told her, "Honey, when you hear the hounds, run, honey. Get away, any way you can."

It was the last thing she had heard her momma scream before they split up. She turned away from momma and ran, just like momma said. She ran through the brush and the woods, oblivious of the scratches on her arms and the tears in shorts and blouse caused by the tree branches, thorns and the other vegetation that made up forests in the Deep South.

Her breath came in rasping gulps as she ran. She felt a pounding in her head from the long period of exertion. But she kept running, just like her momma had said.

She rounded the trunk of one of the largest trees she had ever seen and skidded to a stop, falling down. She laid there looking up the stars, enjoying the feeling that she was safe at last.

She knew she could not remain there forever, as she needed to find her momma. She got up, started walking and stopped dead still.

Almost a dozen feet in front of her was the largest dog she had ever seen. It was not the hound behind her as she could still hear its distant baying. This dog was a large Mastiff. It growled at her with its teeth bared, but stood at bay as still as a statue. Frozen, she stayed where she had stopped. Then she heard the voice.

"Got you, you little bitch. I told Joe Bob you'd run this way. Can't out smart Ol' Red! Now hurry up and come here. I'm tired of foolin' with you."

She started to scramble in the other direction, the man's voice having unfrozen her.

"Heel, Bruno. No you don't, missy." The large man moved fast for his size, and grabbed her. She did something else her mommy had always told her to do in such a situation. She planted a well-aimed kick to Red's crotch.

Red yelped in pain, but managed to keep hold of her arm. She tried to kick him again, hitting his thigh.

"You fuckin' little bitch." There was a clicking sound, and then she felt a sharp pain in her neck, like that time she had cut herself. Suddenly, the front of her dress was being stained by some warm red stuff. She tried to pull away from Red, felt suddenly weak, and fell.

Red looked at the limp figure he held and the widening pool of blood at his feet. He held the limp body out at arm's length so the pumping of the cut jugular wouldn't spray him with blood.

It was then the two other hunters came up.

"Goddammit, Red. *What the fuck have you done?!*" Joe Bob screamed at him as he broke through the bush.

"Oh shit. We're in for it now." That was Johnny who spoke, the third member of the pursuit. He held the baying coonhound back so that it wouldn't get into it with Red's Bull Mastiff.

"No little bitch kicks me in the balls and gets away with it," Red began to explain.

Joe Bob cut him off. "The Tschaaa said *alive* not *dead*, you fucking moron." He started to advance on Red in his rage, but Bruno's warning growl told him to stop. Whatever Red's failings, he raised and trained some damn fine Bull Mastiffs, which nobody without a 12 gauge dared screw with.

"You think that kick in the balls hurt? What do you think *they* will do when we take her back dead?"

"Who said we take her back? Do you see anyone else around here? Huh?" Red answered. "We leave her here, say she got away, fell into the canyon river, whatever. No one's the wiser."

The three felt it before they heard the humming. Seemingly out of nowhere, the large oval shaped alien craft appeared overhead. The three men stood frozen in place. The two dogs lay down and tried to cover their heads with their paws. A dark blue concentrated light played on the three humans, going from one to the other, stopping on Red. He still had the open switchblade in one hand, and the girl's limp arm in the other.

"It was an accident," Joe Bob began talking towards the craft. "Just a stupid accident. We'll make it up do you. I promise...!"

A sharp flash of dark blue light and there was a smoldering hole where Red's genitals used to be. Red screamed once and fell.

A long flexible tentacle appeared and lifted the body of the girl, then retracted to the craft in the blink of an eye. Only the pool of blood remained behind. The humming stopped as the craft disappeared.

Johnny and Joe Bob were shaking with relief, while the dogs began sniffing at the pool of blood and Red's scorched inert body.

"I told him, Johnny. I told him to be careful. They're real picky about their meat, especially veal. They want it fresh and alive until they're ready to serve it. Would he listen? Hell no!"

"Well, Joe Bob, I guess we need to find an ATV or four-wheeler to move him. I sure don't want to carry his big ass out of here on my back. His wife is sure going to be *pissed.*"

RUNNERS 2

The dark-skinned mother and her fifteen year old daughter moved as fast and as quietly as they could through the underbrush—the brambles, berry vines, stickers and bushes that inhabit the former Deep South—catching their clothes and scratching through their jeans. The mother kept them moving, as they could still hear hounds baying in the background.

"Keep moving, Alesha. I think the dogs are still on our scent."

The fifteen year old, with teenage model looks and bearing, did as her mother, Glenda Taylor, requested. They had just separated from a larger group of what was once called people of color, as they all tried to flee from Cattle Country.

Cattle Country. The euphemism created by the tentacle alien Tschaaa Lord and its human Director to identify the three-state-area being walled in and fenced off, creating a huge ghetto, a concentration camp. Mississippi, Alabama, and Georgia were being used to contain all humans with darker pigmentation, who were designated to be "dark meat".

This last attempt of escape from the round up before the barriers were complete and in place had started with one hundred humans. People from East Indian, African, Southeast

Pacific areas bound together because of one common trait—their skin color. They would never be classified as white, and as a result they were considered tastier to the Tschaaa.

Now, Glenda Taylor only had contact with her daughter, everyone else had scattered when the hounds closed in. Using the hounds were humans, doing the aliens' bidding in order to survive and *not* be eaten. So Glenda pushed Alesha to stay ahead of the pursuit.

Glenda had heard her sister Gloria yell at her daughter Donna, Alesha's cousin, to "Run! Run away!" Both of their respective husbands already had been killed and slaughtered. They knew they had to escape. The dirty little secret was that human females were now being saved to be bred for a delicacy the Tschaaa enjoyed—human veal.

"How do we know we are going in the right direction, momma?" Alesha asked, as they paused to catch their breaths.

"Anywhere northwest is the right direction," she answered. She gave a wry laugh. "Never thought we'd be reliving every runaway slave Hollywood epic in real life. But northwest should take us to the Unoccupied Area we heard about."

"Think people are actually trying to set up safe areas?"

"Doesn't matter, Alesha. It was get out—or be breeding stock for the Squids' tables. This may be our last chance."

The sound of a dog baying was uncomfortably close.

"Follow me," Glenda commanded and began running through the brush again. They came into a partially logged out area, a clearing with fallen trees that had never been picked up for the sawmill. With the Tschaaa on Earth, large commercial operations had come to an end.

Mother and daughter began to scramble over the downed trees, walking along some of them as they created trailways through the brush.

Then Alesha fell into a hidden hole when she jumped off a log. She cried out as a sharp stick jabbed into her leg. Glenda scrambled over to her, and began pulling her out of the hidden danger. Alesha started to cry.

"Hush, honey. Let me look at that..." Protruding from her daughter's left calf was a sharp stick that could have passed for an arrow.

"Shit. Okay. This is going to hurt." Glenda grabbed and yanked back on the stick. It slid out smoothly, but it had gone in at least a couple of inches. Glenda pulled out a piece of cloth from her down jacket pocket. The nuclear winter caused by all the large rock strikes from space had put a premium on warm clothes, even in the formally warm and humid South.

"We'll clean it later. I'll wrap it up for now,"Alesha began to sob.

"Come on, honey. We'll make it. Now, let's stand up. We'll find a branch to use as a cane..."

The sound of dog nails on wood told them a hound was coming down the log they had just left. Glenda yanked Alesha to her feet, pushed her towards the northwest.

"Run, honey. I'll delay the dog."

"No, momma. No. I won't leave you."

"Dammit, child..."

A Black Mask Cur hunting dog jumped from the log, snarling. Glenda pulled a carving knife from under her jacket and met the dog head on. Tall and slender like her daughter, she had a wiry strength that few noticed right off. She fed her left arm to the Cur's teeth, as she struck with the knife again and again. She kept doing it even after the knife blade broke off in the canine. She extracted her arm from the dog's jaws, as it finally died.

"Momma, you're hurt."

Glenda fell over to her knees.

"Damn. Just let me catch my breath."

"Don't move."

A young sounding male voice came from atop the log.

"Fuck you!" Glenda spat. She looked up at him from her knees and glared, as Alesha was surprised by her mother's uncharacteristically vehement language. "Go ahead and shoot us with that rifle. Then you get to carry us back as dead meat. Because we are *not* going peacefully."

"Mister, please," Alesha pleaded. " Just let us go. We're not hurting anyone. Just let us go."

The figure jumped down off the log. Now closer, Alesha saw it was a teenage male, no older than she was. Then it happened.

"Alesha? Alesha Taylor, is that you?"

Recognition flooded over the young lady's face.

"My God, Bobby Parsons. Momma, he sat behind me in math class. He also went to that church camp in Atlanta. Remember?"

Her mother stood up slowly, cradling her bitten arm. The young man reached around to his back and pulled out a small package, which had been attached to his belt.

"Here," Bobby said as he tossed it. "First aid kit. I'll tell them I lost it in the brush."

He looked around nervously. "You need to leave here, Alesha. When Dogman gets here, and sees your mother killed his hound...well, getting taken back will be the least of your worries."

"Bobby..."

"Just go! I used to play sports with dark mea..." Bobby stopped when he realized what he was about to call them. Then he continued. "I went to school, played sports with you and yours. So, just take this as a favor, one fellow student to another. Go."

"All right, Squid lover," Glenda sneered. "We're going."

"*Mother*," Alesha looked at her former classmate. "Bobby, what happened? Why are you doing this?"

"Because I have to." He glanced away. "I have a mom, and a younger sister. Now, please, just leave."

Before anyone realized it, Alesha stepped forward and kissed Bobby, her injured leg forgotten for a moment. She turned, grabbed a sling from the first aid kit and threw a bandage around her mother's bitten arm. Bobby continued to look around anxiously, as she secured her mother's arm in the sling. She stuck a wad of gauze down her jeans, pushing it over her leg puncture wound. She grabbed her mother's good arm, then turned her head towards Bobby.

"We..."

"Just go, dammit."

As the two women turned to leave, Glenda glanced at the young man.

"Thanks...Bobby." Then she and Alesha began making their way through the brush once again.

The young hunter stood for a few minutes, as his former prey disappeared into the underbrush and trees. Then he turned around and looked at the dead dog. He shivered, but not from the cold.

"I always loved you a bit, Alesha," Bobby said to himself. "From afar, like in Shakespeare. Then *they* came." He looked up, as he thought he heard someone moving through the brush towards him.

"Now, it's all fucked up." He clambered onto the log and then whistled. An answering whistle came from far away.

"Godspeed, Alesha," he whispered. "Hope you make it."

He squared his shoulders, and accepted his fate. A man and his family had to live.

"They killed your hound, Dogman," he said to the approaching figure. "Sorry."

SURVIVING

Mary Lou Spencer stood in the shadows at the bottom of the basement stairs outside the old warehouse. She had been standing there for about half an hour, waiting for Guadalupe to return from her scavenging run. Every adult of the dozen members of Mary Lou's group took turns sneaking out looking for food, medicine, and anything else they could use. Some sixteen months had passed since the Tschaaa aliens had announced their presence—first by launching projectiles from space, and then by harvesting humans as prey.

Since that time, humans in the Occupied Area—the aquatic and amphibian Tschaaa controlled areas along all the ocean coasts and large bodies of water—had been living on borrowed time. Initially, every human was subject to harvesting. Then, within weeks, the Tschaaa realized that some groups of humans had a darker pigmentation than others. Due to a complete trick of fate, on the Tschaaa homeworld, lighter skinned "white meat" was a signifier of prey that had been infected by a deadly disease.

The virus-based disease, brought from another world by accident, had not only made the infected primates—the primary meat source of their world—inedible, it also made it potentially poisonous. This had been especially true with the Tschaaa young, the most important segment of Tschaaa society. So, hundreds of years of space travel later, they were knocking on Earth's door with large rocks in order to obtain a replacement meat source for their civilization.

Now, most humans hid from contact with the Tschaaa and their minions, both alien and human. In addition, mixed in with the surviving humans were the dregs of society who would sell out their own species, or enslave and abuse them for their own selfish desires.

Mary Lou heard footsteps approaching. She readied the pistol in her hand, preparing to shoot if the person was a stranger. Then Guadalupe Estrada appeared, wearing jeans and jacket, a small tote sack in her hand. She scrambled to the bottom of the stairwell where Mary Lou waited. As she reached the last step, the hispanic woman began a coughing fit.

Mary Lou instinctually reached out to her, but Guadalupe waved her off. She had a spasm and coughed up blood into a rag she held at her mouth.

"Stay back, Mary. I'm pretty sure this is TB I have, and I have no idea how infectious it is. Goddamn Doc just had to get himself killed." Guadalupe was referring to Matt, the medical student who had been a member of the group until last month. During a scavenger run, he had run afoul of a random harvester robot. Being that he was a dark-skinned African exchange student, he became dark meat. Matt had been a wealth of information, which was now gone.

The coffee-skinned woman finally regained control of her breathing and leaned against the cement wall of the stairwell. "I found cans of food, and a bottle of water in some of those cars in the parking garage. Not all of them have been burnt out, as I guess previous people thought. Then I had a loud coughing fit and had to cut it short."

Mary smiled, then rubbed her back, ignoring Guadalupe's warnings.

"Let's get inside, and let you rest. I can go out later to hit the rest of the cars."

"Mary, you've been out twice as much as the rest of us. That's not fair."

Mary laughed. "I am also the only certifiable pale skin in the group. So far, harvester robs and our friendly cyborg robocops seem to ignore me. Right now, being ignored in San Diego is a plus."

Mary Lou helped Guadalupe carry the recovered items into the warehouse basement and then barred the basement door. A year of living in the basement had shown it to be safe, compared to the other locations the group members had tried. As safe a place as it could be in the post-Invasion world. Plus the natural San Diego warmer weather had helped offset some of the effects of the Long Winter, caused by all the crap thrown into the air by the rock strikes, not to mention about a dozen nukes and a few exploding volcanoes.

The two women made their way into the large central living area they had set up. Guadalupe collapsed on a sofa in another coughing fit. Mary Lou set down the bag of recovered goods, helping her out of her jacket.

"Mommy!" A voice turned into a five year old little girl, grabbing Mary Lou in a bear hug.

"Hey, Susie. How's my little girl?"

The little dark-skinned girl looked up at her mother, a large grin plastered on her face. "Daddy and I have been reading to each other. He says I'm way head of the curve."

Mary Lou laughed. Kamal Sharma, her East Indian husband, still forgot he was no longer working with a bunch of engineers and scientists in the computer tech industry, so he still tried to talk to children as if he were in a planning meeting for some new project.

"How did it go, my love?" Kamal walked up with their seven year old son, Johnathan. She and Kamal had agreed on western names when their children were born, even though both had inherited the darker pigmentation of their father's people. Of course, as they both had basically black hair, so did their children. Mary Lou had kept her maiden name, due to her established business connections. She smiled at her husband, then hugged him and her son.

"Guadalupe found a few items in the parked cars around that parking garage. I plan on going back there today."

"Mom, why you?" Johnathan asked. "You go out twice as often as anyone else."

Mary Lou kissed her son's forehead. "We all to do what we can to help. The aliens and their helpers seem to ignore me. So, I go out more often."

The seven surviving women and children then came and clustered around to see what the others had found.

"I grabbed what I could, but then this damned coughing got the best of me," apologized Guadalupe.

"You made it back," said Grandma Jackson, the oldest of the survivors. "That's what is important."

"Well, I see Bettie made it back in one piece." The comment came from Tyrone Jackson, Grandma Jackson's grandson. The young black man had a tendency of making sarcastic remarks to everyone. He had been able to save his grandma, then found this group. But he seemed to have a permanent chip on his shoulder, as if bad things that happened were a personal affront to him.

Mary Lou looked at him, and sighed. "For the umpteenth time, that's not my name."

"Well, Grandma said you are a spitting image of that pin-up model, Bettie Page. Then I found the magazine with those photos, and damned if you don't... Bettie."

The magazine in question had been from Bettie Page's days with photographer Irving Klaw and featured bondage, catfights and nudity. Not exactly what a mother of two and former software engineer wanted to be compared to, as time passed.

Mary Lou began to get angry. "Look—I can't help you have

some weird fantasies that float your boat. Just leave me out of them."

"Hey, Bettie, I was just paying you a compliment."

Kamal then jumped in. "Do you have to work at being an obnoxious pain in the ass, or does it come naturally?"

"Hey *chief*, you want something? If not, stay out of this for your own good."

"Still can't understand the difference between misguided Columbus and real Indians, can you? Must be due to your limited mental capacity."

"Listen, fucker..." an angered Tyrone began, as he stepped forward.

"Stop it!" It was Grandma Jackson. As probably one of the oldest surviving humans, she had a gravitas others did not. "Grandson, quit being such a pain in the butt. We have to live and work together. Now let's just all see what Guadalupe found, and see what plans we have to make."

An angry Tyrone turned and walked off without a word.

"Ma'am, I'm sorry," Kamal said. "But..."

"No need to explain, Kamal. My grandson has a whole lot of anger and frustration bottled up inside. Some of it was there before the Squids came. But now, it's worse." Grandma Jackson sighed. "Now, let's look at what we have..."

An hour later, after a small lunch, Mary Lou prepared to go out again.

"I really wished you wouldn't, love," Kamal protested.

"It has to be done, and I'm the best candidate. Besides, harvester rob activity seems to have decreased over the last month or so. They might be moving on to greener pastures."

"Or, those radio transmissions on the AM and FM dial about some guy called the Director having made a deal with the Squids may have some truth to them. That 'Cattle Country' is going to be their source of fresh meat, leaving the rest of us alone."

Mary Lou snorted. "What's that old saying? 'Hi, we're from the Government. We're here to help you, trust us. Now give us your money!' I'll believe that we are no longer meat on the hoof when I see a pig fly by."

She shook her head. "How anyone could make a deal with someone's nightmare version of a combination octopus and squid, with a little crab thrown in, is beyond my belief. They didn't even try to talk to us before they started raining hell on us. Why talk or make deals now?"

It was Kamal's turn to shrug. "Who knows? Maybe the Squid Lord in charge of North America found religion." That produced a wry laugh from Mary Lou. Then she kissed her husband.

"When I get back, let's see if we can arrange some quality time together, no kids."

Kamal smiled, then nibbled her neck, causing her to giggle and push him back.

"I said later, my love. Now, who's playing stair guard?"

"The Rodriguez family are up for it, I think. I don't know which one will watch the three kids while the other..."

"I've got it." The voice was Tyrone. "I volunteered. Nothing better to do but sit around and get more pissed."

Mary Lou and Kamal looked at him.

"No funny business...," Kamal began.

"Hey, survival *is* business. I don't fuck with that."

Mary Lou sighed. "Alright. Then let's get the show on the road. I want as much daylight as possible." She kissed Kamal again. "Watch the kids."

"What else is there to do? Visit the local topless bar?"

She slapped him on the arm. "You are such a creep sometime. Okay, love. I'm off."

"Be careful, Mary Lou."

"Always." She and Kamal made their way to the outside door and stairwell. As quietly as possible they removed bar from the door, then stepped out into the stairwell. Mary Lou looked at Tyrone.

"Hey..."

"Just go. I know my job, I have a pistol. I may piss you off, but I won't let some Squid get you."

"Thanks, Tyrone."

"Look for some weapons and ammunition while you're at it. We don't exactly have a lot. Maybe some gangbanger left their ride double parked."

Mary Lou smiled. "Will do. I'll be back soon."

"You'd better."

With practiced ease Mary Lou snuck out of the basement stairwell and onto the street. She stopped behind the large dumpster a few yards away and looked around. Nothing. So far, so good.

The parking garage and lot was a few blocks down, by a former mid-range hotel. When all hell broke loose, some people had managed to make a run for it in their cars. Many did not, as a few rocks had hit in and around San Diego. The resulting fires caused many to stay in place until the roads were cleared, or until they were able to try and catch mass transit, or maybe hitch a ride with someone else after leaving the damaged areas on foot. Stories about the sudden appearance of small gangs of vandals and saboteurs had made others stay at work, or at the local bar.

Then about twelve hours in, during darkness, the Delta fighters and Falcon aerial battle cruisers hit. Within minutes, the first bigger than a football field harvester arks began to land. A half hour later and people were screaming, running every which way in the dark, as the power grid began to fail. The harvester robots, six-wheeled oversized ATVs, blinded victims with extremely bright searchlights, contained in the ball shaped turret that extended from the vehicles chassis. Metal tentacles grabbed the victims, and the harvester robs dragged or carried the victims back to the harvester arks. Later the reason for these abductions were discovered.

The harvester arks were huge mobile butchering and process plants for the human meat they were collecting.

Mary Lou and her family had been on vacation from Silicon

Valley, visiting friends to enjoy the ocean-based marine parks, as well as limited visits to Juarez, Mexico. They had managed to hunker down in their friends' residence in the suburbs of San Diego for the first twenty-four hours. The power grid in the outer areas seemed to hold up better, as initially the Tschaaa and their minions had concentrated on downtown and port areas.

Then a harvester ark had plunked down a quarter mile from their friends' home. Mary Lou and Kamal had run in their SUV, after failing to convince their friends to leave with them. The family of five was never heard from again.

Mary Lou moved slowly and cautiously towards the parking garage. On the street were a couple of burned out vehicles. One block of small businesses had been wiped out by fire and apparent combat. Bullet holes pockmarked some of the remaining concrete and brick walls. The cyborg robocops had been a huge shock. Fast, powerful with some energy and projectile weapons, they took on the points of resistance, allowing the harvester robots to do their horrific tasks. The fact that the cyborgs looked like they had stepped from a Hollywood backlot during the filming of a popular movie series also had a large psychological effect on the human populace.

Later, intermittent radio broadcasts reported that some fifty percent of the population within twenty miles of the ocean coast was harvested within the first thirty days. By then, everything had fallen apart. Much later, after a lot of moving and hiding, she and Kamal had found the warehouse with a few survivors. That was almost a year prior.

Mary Lou paused and listened about a block from her destination. She had gone hunting as a child with her now dead father in Eastern Washington State, and she knew how to move and listen so as not to spook the prey. Now, she and her friends and family were the prey.

She heard and saw nothing. No robocops, no harvester robs, nor any human sounds. She moved towards the ground floor of the parking garage, then carefully up the sloping down exit ramp. Mary Lou figured the lower levels would already be picked clean, and she did not have time to waste.

On the fourth and top level of the parking garage, she started walking from car to car. Over the last few months, she and the others had become adept at picking car locks, using some homemade lock picks they had fashioned. Some of the previous group members had come from very eclectic backgrounds. Mary Lou found nothing in the first two cars, but in the third trunk she had found a mother lode. Someone had gone shopping just before the first rock had hit. Mary Lou did not bother to look into the small cooler as she did not want to deal with the smell of bad dairy and ancient rotted meat. But in two boxes were cans of soup, vegetables, chili, beans and boxes of crackers and cereal. Add some bottles of water and a six pack of soda pop, and all she could do was say, "Bingo!" to herself.

She had a small child's backpack and a doubled garbage bag, both of which she quickly filled. She grabbed the lighter stuff first, deciding that she would have to risk coming back here with another group member. Single humans were often ignored, but pairs and more seemed to draw the attention of robocops and harvesters. She shouldered her load and turned to leave when she heard the voice from behind one of the other vehicles.

"Hey, beautiful." Then, stars and blackness.

Mary Lou did not know how long she had been unconscious, when some cold liquid to the face shocked her awake. She sputtered, then managed to open her eyes. The base of her skull ached, so she decided that was where she had been struck. She noticed she had just her panties on and was tied to a chair.

"Wake up. Time's a-wasting."

Mary Lou managed to focus her eyes on the source of the comment. She saw a scruffy male a few inches taller than her five and a half foot frame, with long greasy-looking dark hair and beard. The man looked about her age, in his early thirties. He smiled, showing surprisingly decent teeth.

"You are definitely good looking. You remind me of someone I saw once. I just can't place you." He paused, then grunted. "Hell, it doesn't matter. You look healthy enough. Must have been eating pretty regularly. You'll be a good replacement for the other two girls."

At the mention of other people she looked up and noticed two young girls, cowering and whimpering in the opposite corner of the room. Under the dirt and sweat she could see they were literally just girls, probably no older than fifteen or sixteen. They were nude, so Mary Lou could imagine what the men had been doing to them. She angrily spat on the floor.

"Keep spitting. You're the one who's going to live in it."

"You know, the others will come looking for me," Mary Lou said. The man laughed.

"Yeah, right. You think we're all fucking stupid? When you disappear from your group, *no one* comes looking. They all assume the robs got you. There's still a few around, backed up by a few robocops. And sometimes…us." With that, the greasy man opened up his dirty shirt and showed off his apparent pride and joy. He did not have a lot of hair on his chest, so Mary Lou had no trouble making out the octopus-shaped tattoo.

A Kraken—sign of the relatively new Church of Kraken and its supporters. Mary Lou had heard of them, but never seen a tattooed Kraken.

"So you're a Squid lover," Mary Lou stated matter of factly.

"Oh, a smart one, I see. Well, neither the aliens nor I give a shit what you call us. In fact, once they saw pictures of the deep sea giant squids, then found them, they think being a Squid is a badge of honor."

Mary Lou stared at him a bit. "You sound well educated. How did you start doing this?" She knew from books she had read once that if a hostage gets the hostage takers talking to you like an individual person, they might think twice about killing you.

The man laughed. "Yeah, sure. I was a car mechanic. The Squids came, and I saw the writing on the wall. Then I found out I had a taste for long pig." He flashed an evil grin at her.

"Long..." It sank in. He was one of the sick bastards who thought being a cannibal, eating human flesh made them like their rulers, the Tschaaa.

Just then, five more people came in, all male, talking and carrying bags.

"Well, looky here. She's awake." The speaker was an older, grey haired and bearded man, with somewhat cleaner clothes and body. He set the bag down and walked over to Mary Lou. He grabbed her chin and lifted her head up.

"Yeah, you'll clean up real nice. Our local customers are looking for some new ass. You'll definitely do." He looked at the man who had talked to Mary Lou.

"Richie. Take her in back. Get her cleaned up. Let her see what happens if she gives us trouble."

"Sure, Dad. Will do."

Mary Lou looked at the older man. "Richie is your..."

A hard slap stopped her comment.

"Shut up. Talk when we, when I say. Now, if you haven't figured this out yet, you are to be our new entertainment. As long as our customers like you, you stay alive, well fed, and get a shower once in a while. Cause me problems, you get turned into meat. Got it?"

The angry Mary Lou nodded her head. She looked at a nearby pile of clothes, and saw her jeans, blouse, and jacket were on top. Dad saw her look and grinned.

"You won't need any clothes for today. If it gets colder, I'll make sure you're taken care of, as long as *you* take care of *us.* Now, Richie. Untie her, handcuff her, and take her in back. Use the shower. I want her clean...for me."

The rest of the men started laughing.

"Hey, Cap'n," a balding man with bad teeth called out. "How about take her panties off, let us get a good look at *all* of her."

Dad turned on him and snarled. "You leave her alone, Baldy. She's mine. Then we put the word out we have new talent. You can pay for it like regulars can." The rest of the men began to snicker.

"Richie. Get a move on. The rest of you, get this scavenged stuff put away. The other group will be back later, hopefully with more stuff." He snorted. "As long as Shorty doesn't piss off the local harvesters and robocops like he did last time. Asshole cost us two good men."

The leader looked at Mary Lou again. "See, the robos around here know us. We find them fresh dark meat to feed the local Squids out in the bay. Word is, they're breeding out there, although no one has gotten close enough to check—and lived."

"Now, Richie. Get her cleaned up."

"Yeah Dad. Clean meat coming right up." Everyone laughed. Everyone but Mary Lou.

Ten minutes later she was having an actual hot shower. They had set up a propane gas water heater in the corner of the large back room. She thought she was in some former office building, but couldn't really tell from the inside. Things had been changed too much.

Her thoughts returned to her clothes in the other room. Mixed in somewhere was the little five shot .38 she always carried when out scavenging. If only she hadn't been caught so flat-footed.

"You have another five minutes. Clean yourself good. Dad is picky."

Mary Lou grunted an affirmative. Her mind was now working a mile a minute. She knew she *had* to get away as soon as possible. Despite the hot water, she shivered. In the far corner from the shower was proof that the threat of turning her into meat was not idle. The torso of a woman, sans the head and arms, hung upside down like a side of beef. Mary Lou assumed the two young girls were next.

She finished her shower, stepped out, and used some towels

provided to dry off, all under Richie's watchful gaze. As she finished, he tossed her a silk kimono.

"Here. Put that on. It's clean. And if I do say so myself, you'll fill it out nicely."

Mary Lou forced herself to say, "Thanks." She knew her survival may depend on how "happy" she kept certain people. Then again, she had been in survival mode for the last sixteen months.

Richie escorted her out to the main room. Dad smiled as he saw her.

"Now I know who you look like! You're the spitting image of that 1950s pin-up Bettie Page. Others have told you that, haven't they?"

"Yes, they have."

The smile turned into a grin. "Well, the gods are smiling on me today. Nice, young, and clean piece of ass that looks like a model. Not many like you around anymore. We'll make a lot of scratch off you, once the word gets out to our regulars."

Dad stepped forward, took her by the arm. "Now, let's go in the side bedroom with the clean mattress. Time for a little initiation…"

Suddenly, the front double access doors exploded open, one door flying off its hinges to the center of the room. Everyone jumped—then stared awestruck as a huge armored humanoid shape stepped in.

A robocop. Mary Lou had never seen one this close before. She thought it must be close to seven feet tall. Then its voice boomed, "In the name of the Director, Adam Lloyd, cease and desist. Stand to and be inspected."

Richie grabbed an assault rifle and began to fire. The rounds ricocheted off the huge cyborg, causing more danger to the humans than to it.

Then a human figure stepped in beside the robocop, carrying a Browning Automatic Rifle, circa World War II. A burst of 30 Caliber bullets tore Richie to pieces, demonstrating that despite its age, the weapon was still highly effective.

Dad bellowed, grabbed Mary Lou, and started to put a knife against her throat.

"Stop!" Dad yelled. Before he could continue, another human stepped in on the left side of the cyborg and shot Dad through his right eye with a silenced submachine gun. By now, the other four Krakens were trying to run for the exits. Mary Lou stood frozen, as Dad collapsed to the floor, dead. The one with the sub gun was a tall, handsome man who seemed to glide to Mary Lou.

"Are you okay?" The man with what Mary Lou noticed were steely blue gray eyes asked.

"I guess." Mary Lou stared at the robocop as it strode forward, moving with a grace that belied its size.

"Director, I want you and Chief Hamilton to stay behind me, until I clear out the miscreants."

"What, and let a bunch of ricochets fly around?" That came from the older, stockier man with the BAR.

"I assure you, Chief, I had the path of ricochets calculated. No one of any consequence would have been hit."

"So you say, Tin Man."

Mary Lou looked at the one called the Director. "You're him. The guy they mentioned on the radio. You exist."

"Director Adam Lloyd, Occupied States. And you are?"

Mary Lou shoved him hard and ran out the broken entrance. The cyborg robocop started to grab her, but the one called Director yelled, "No Andrew! I'll get her."

Somewhere in her mind, the fact that the man machine had a human name registered for future examination. But right now, Mary Lou just ran.

She heard the voices of the Director and the one called the Chief behind her, calling her to stop. But she kept running.

Despite her bare feet, it took her about ten minutes to figure out where she was and then beelined to where her group's hideout was. Some part of her brain heard the two men behind her, knew her bare feet were being cut and banged up, but she did not care.

As she neared the block where the basement hideout was located, she heard an unfortunate, but well-recognized sound. She glanced to her right and saw the harvester robot bearing down on her, all six wheels humming. She screamed and tried to make it down to the access stairs to the basement—then saw a metal tentacle reaching towards her.

Mary Lou heard the silenced submachine gun fire with its clacking of the bolt. The harvester turned toward the Director as the rounds struck, its metal body and ball turret resisting the 9mm rounds. It pointed the iris of the blinding capture light at the Director.

Then she heard the loud bark of a 30 Caliber automatic rifle, coming from the man called the Chief. The heavy rounds sliced through the robot's chassis and turret. Within seconds, the six wheels of the mechanical threat froze up, as it exploded in a shower of sparks and smoky electrical guts.

Mary Lou made it to the basement stairs and began to clamber down. As she neared the bottom, she screamed. A large darkening pool of blood extended from the bottom of the stairs and through the open, broken door. She slid in the blood and almost fell, but continued into what had been her hidden home for months.

"Kamal! Susie! Johnathan!" Her yells began to take on a piercing quality, as she dashed through the living areas.

No one. Nothing, except for more pools of blood.

Mary Lou slid to a stop on her blood slickened feet. "Anybody? It's Mary Lou! Come out!" Silence. A loud wailing came from her mouth, as she heard the voices of her two pursuers behind her.

"Mary Lou. Is that your name? Look, we'll help..." Adam Lloyd got only partly through his comments when he was hit full force by a screaming, crying, whirling dervish.

"You fuckers! You and those robots killed them!" She hit,

kicked, clawed, and bit at the Director, slamming into him so hard that she pushed him back almost to the basement entrance.

She felt strong arms pinning her arms and hands from behind. The man known as the Chief had slung his weapon and had grabbed her, as she tried to kick and head butt herself free.

"Damnit, lady. We had *nothing* to do with this," the Chief tried to explain.

Strong hands grabbed her naked thigh, and before she could try and kick them loose felt a sharp prick on her left butt cheek. A spreading warmth told her that the Director had injected her with something.

"No!" Mary Lou yelled, until she became weak and a bit numb. Then everything began to blur.

"Come on, Chief. Let's get her back to transport, and get the hell out of here." Everything went dark.

Mary Lou came out of the fog an unknown time later. At first, it felt like she had just woken from a bad dream. Reality soon sunk in, and she began to sob. Only then did she realize a large robocop was sitting nearby, watching her. She must have shown that she was startled, as the cyborg spoke.

"I am not a threat, Mary Lou, contrary to your previous experience with my kind. My name is Andrew."

She saw that it/he had a human mouth, chin, lips, lower cheeks. The upper part of his face was covered by an armored visor with some type of built in vision device, or devices. His skin looked light colored, probably of caucasian descent. It dawned on her for the first time that he was part human, homo sapien, modern type. She tried to sit up from the bench she was on and only succeeded in making herself nauseous. She began to throw up the contents of her stomach on the metal floor of the transport vehicle, and would have fallen over into her own vomit, if Andrew had not caught her. She felt very strong, but padded hands on her—as the cyborg gently wiped her face. He laid her back down and produced a bottle with some liquid in it.

"Here. My own formula. Call it a super sports drink with all the required electrolytes. My comrades and I ingest this all the time." Mary Lou sipped it with no protest, figuring it would be too late to poison her now.

She sat quietly, then realized someone had put on her panties, blouse and jeans. Her feet were bare, but had been bandaged. She looked at the being calling himself Andrew.

"You?" she asked.

The huge robocop lightly shook his head.

"Director Lloyd did the honors, with the aid of Chief Hamilton. I did help with the medical examination. My sensor array is quite precise."

Mary Lou stared at him for a moment, then spoke. "Am I going to die?"

"Why, no. You were not that injured... Oh, I see. You think you are going to be harvested."

"That's what you mechanical monsters do, isn't it?" She spit out the comment with more bile than she thought she still had in her.

Andrew sighed as any human would. Then his upper visor retracted from his eyes and forehead. She saw he had very human, hazel eyes. "I am still forty five percent human organic matter, give or take a few ounces of skin and organs. Some two hundred fifty of my comrades and I are from recent Earth born stock, modified to be cyborgs, what you and I call robocops. We joined over a thousand cyborgs created from pre-homo sapien genetic stock. But my brothers—as I call them—and I were all born of women."

"But you were constructed and now work for the Squids."

"Actually, I have been assigned to the Director. I follow his orders, unless his actions are about to get him killed, or maybe His Lordship killed. Or some young Tschaaa injured or killed. Then I decide what to do."

"You take humans..."

"I *took* humans," Andrew interrupted. "I have been taking humans to Key West, where the Director is setting up his headquarters, and the new capital of the areas and former states controlled by the Tschaaa. Not to Cattle Country. Not to be slaughtered for meat, but so that the Director can rebuild some resemblance of pre-Invasion society. The Protocol demands it."

Mary Lou stuttered, "B-but why? We're just *meat*. The Squids eat us."

Andrew smiled. "Not anymore. That's what Cattle Country is for. To provide fresh meat upon request or need. A Protocol of Selective Survival."

Mary Lou felt a bit dizzy. Then she realized she was on a very smoothly piloted airplane. Andrew must have read her expression.

"We are on a rebuilt DC-3 from a Key West based local airline that survived the rocks. Actually, Tschaaa warriors from the ocean easily took out the resistance in Key West Naval Base, with few aerial strikes being needed. They left most of the local humans unmolested, per his Lordship's instructions. He already had big plans for Florida Keys and its humans, even days after defeating the local military forces."

The huge man-creature then stood up slowly, staying crouched to keep from hitting his head on the roof of the aircraft.

"You can rest now. Adam Lloyd will be back later to finish the conversation."

"Uh, Andrew... My family..."

"They were not harvested. They were taken by other humans. Feral, maybe Krakens. We lacked the local resources to do an intensive search. This was one of the first attempts to bring order to the Occupied Areas. Soon, there will be Human Community Councils, overseen by my brothers, comrades. Then, amenities will return. But I will let the Director explain all of that. For now, rest. Do not be afraid, for you are under the protection of the Director."

As the man-machine moved forward in the aircraft, Mary Lou was surprised that she believed him. And she was not afraid.

Mary Lou dozed, waking up still a bit groggy from the drugs and the depression of her loss. She knew the injection she had been given took a little of the edge off her emotional pain, but that it could all come crashing down on her at any moment.

She looked up from her self-introspection to see the men called the Director and the Chief walking to the back of the airplane to her temporary bed. Mary Lou did not know how she should, or would, react to him. So she just laid still.

"Mary Lou, I believe your name is," the Director said. "May I ask your last name?"

"Spencer. And you are Adam Lloyd. Some of the radio broadcasts made you seem like some savior."

This comment elicited a smile from Adam. "I guess an attempt at p.r. by some of my people." He paused, his smile fading. Then he began again.

"I know you feel like you were kidnapped, abducted..."

"I was. Twice. Once by those assholes you killed. Then again by you." Tears began to flow.

"Why didn't you just leave me there with my grief? I could have looked for survivors of my family, friends. Or I could have gotten revenge..."

"You would be dead." Adam Lloyd stared into her eyes. "As for revenge—the four individuals who ran out the back, as we were coming in to your location, were crucified. By my security detail and myself. As an example that there is, as the saying goes, a new sheriff in town."

Mary Lou sat up on her bed, looked at her hands. "I guess I should say thank you. But then again you are working for beings not much better than they were. Who could eat me at any..."

"No." The Director's voice was loud and demanding. "Whether you and any other people believe me does not matter. What does matter is that I *do* have an agreement with the Tschaaa Lord who has control of North America. So, intermittent general harvesting in the field is coming to an end. Period."

Mary Lou looked deep into his eyes. Surprisingly, she believed him.

"Okay. But the Squids will still eat other humans in what we hear is called Cattle Country. True?"

"Yes. I do what I can, save who I can. Eventually, we may achieve the status of a client or service species with the Tschaaa, much like dogs are with us. Until then..."Adam took a deep breath, then released it slowly. "Until then, I try to set up a form of order in the areas actively controlled by the Tschaaa, Squids if you like. That is what I can do today. Tomorrow is another day."

"And me, Director? How do I fit in?"

"Any way you can. You are a tough survivor. I can use people like you in Key West. Care to join? Believe me, it's voluntary. Check it out. If you don't like it, a free trip to the destination of your choosing." Adam chuckled. "I just sounded like a game show host or a timeshare salesman."

Mary Lou suddenly stuck out her right hand. "Shake. It seals the deal."

Adam smiled, as he shook her hand. He also felt a strength in her grip, a strength of someone used to dealing in a tough world.

"What was your career before..."

"Internet web and software design. Still primarily a man's world when everything fell apart."

Adam nodded. "Explains the firm handshake. You're used to dealing with macho men."

Now Mary Lou finally smiled. "*Immature* macho men. Yes."

"Pardon my manners. May I present Chief Master Sergeant William Hamilton. My best friend and right hand."

The Chief stepped forward. "Ma'am. Welcome aboard."

"Who says I'm staying?"

The Chief grinned. "You will. I'm a good judge of character."

This made Mary Lou laugh. She should be angry, or at least scared. But oddly enough she wasn't. For the first time in ages, she felt *safe*.

"Now, Mary Lou, if I may call you that. You can call me Adam in return—I don't stand on ceremony. Please get some more rest. We will stop to refuel in a while at a field where we pre-positioned supplies. You can get out and stretch there."

Mary Lou looked at both of the men. "I guess I should say thank you, for getting me away from those Krakens. Thank Andrew also."

"No thanks required," answered Adam. "Although Andrew may like to hear that. He may not look it, but he has a big human heart under all that hardware. Now, Chief, let's leave the young lady to her rest." The two men got up and walked back to the front compartment of the aircraft. Mary Lou laid down her head and was asleep within seconds.

Up in the front compartment, the Chief turned to his friend.

"Boss, are you going to tell her?"

"What? That we found the remains of her friends and family, being readied for butchering by the rest of that group of Krakens and Feral assholes we saved her from? That I personally gutted them, left them with their intestines hanging out for the rats?"

"Damn, Adam. Not that graphic. But, you know..."

"Let her keep the fantasy that some of her friends and family may have survived. At least until she gets settled. Then, I promise. The whole bloody story."

Andrew approached the two men. "Gentlemen. Again, I must protest. That wheeled harvester was the third one you have shot up and destroyed this week. As the old expression goes, they do not grow on trees."

The Chief grinned. "Did the Tschaaa have trees on their home world?"

"The record banks I have access to say yes. The land areas had trees, bushes, and a form of flowers. But you are deflecting the discussion at hand."

"Oh, all right Andrew," Adam said. "I'll apologize to our Lord Neptune. Although I have to bite my tongue to keep from laughing whenever I refer to him in that name. A Greek and Roman mythical god name? Why?"

"Because he has a developed sense of humor when it comes to humans. Now, Director. I will insure that all of our harvesters and other resources are programmed and informed about the change in the Protocol, especially when you are in the area. That should help you and the Chief restrain your destructive urges."

"Bitch and moan, Andrew," the Chief commented. "You complain like an old woman."

"Ah, but a very large and capable old woman. Which brings me to the point of you two allowing me to protect you..."

"There you go again! Damn, you're good at nagging."

A hint of a smile appeared on the Cyborg's mouth. "I always strive to be the best that I can be."

With that, the Chief threw up his hands. "I need a drink."

The two friends began to laugh, as Andrew looked on and smiled.

Humor was often the best medicine.

AVENGING ANGEL

Abigail Young sat with her back straight, as she waited to be called into the Prophet's oval office. Michael Smith, Prophet and President of the Nation State of Deseret had the equivalent of both a governmental and a religious office, combined into one.

The Prophet had the office added onto the edge of the large Tabernacle complex in Salt Lake City, soon after taking control as Prophet of the Church of Latter Day Saints. Not long after that, he had become President of the new Nation State of Deseret, since the United States as everyone had known it no longer existed. Michael Smith could have easily ruled over the survivors in the area formerly known as Utah—just by being the selected Church Prophet, since the overwhelming majority of the State had been Mormon. But, he had demanded a secular election, stating he did not want to be seen as a theocratic dictator to other surviving states and countries. Actions such as that had made him beloved by the majority of the electorate.

Abigail Young looked up to him as a surrogate father, ever since her Uncle Buck had taken her to the Tabernacle in Salt Lake City. He had brought her there shortly after her parents had died from radiation poisoning in the large area of contamination, caused by the Hanford nuclear reservation explosion. Something, possibly the Tschaaa, had started a chain reaction amongst all of the stored fuel rods and other nuclear waste material. Most of eastern Washington, much of Idaho, and the upper end of the Columbia River were soon awash with radioactive fallout and contamination. Safety experts claimed an explosion was impossible, but they had been proven drastically wrong.

Nearly two years later, and her eyes still teared up thinking about that time. She was not even able to hug her parents goodbye, they were so contaminated from being caught outside and unprotected when the fallout came. Despite her uncle's distaste of organized religion, he had been of the survivalist ilk and knew of the one group that often prepared for the worst: the Mormons.

Now, just over fourteen years of age, she was part of a group of nuclear orphans, brought by people to the one possible sanctuary they could reach. Some had been Mormons, some not, but it did not matter. The Church of Latter Day Saints had accepted them all. One caveat that had developed over the years was fear that the children's and teens' exposure to radiation would make them unable, or unfit to bear children. Of course, such was the age of fear and paranoia, since the coming of the monsters now called the Squids—all possible threats were greatly exaggerated in the minds of many. Thus, out of twenty-four orphans, only four of the youngest were adopted out, all by people past child bearing age. The word "unclean" was bandied regarding those young people who had possibly been exposed.

Hearing this, Prophet Smith had accepted them all as his children. The ones not adopted, soon to be known as The Twenty, were housed in a former hotel under the direct control of the Prophet. After settling in, he had called them all together, the children ranging from twelve years of age—as was Abigail—to fifteen.

"My Children, we are all called by God, Our Lord, to do

certain things, and perform certain missions in life. After much prayer and consultation with God, and due to the demons that have been visiting on us in form of the aliens, it has been illuminated to me the need for a special group of people. This group is to help combat these demons and other evil in the world. They will be special, will undergo much training, and will have to endure hardships, which others in Deseret will not have to endure. For they will be a force of good, used to smite the Evil Ones, and protect the faithful here in Deseret. In the tradition of early days of the Mormon Church, a force of new Avenging Angels will be created. You here, will be the nucleus for this, the first group of Avenging Angels. You, who have become known as The Twenty, will not be seen as outcasts, or unclean. You will be honored to the end of your days, and beyond. All I ask of you is your devotion, faith, and belief in this sacred mission. Now, let us pray for divine guidance and aid in the coming days. For we will need both."

The Twenty became devoted to the Prophet. In turn, he took care of them, even as he demanded much of them. They became child soldiers in an army of God. There was criticism by some that creating child soldiers was a form of abuse. But when the Prophet pointed out that no one seemed to want to adopt them as he had, and that this was the result of divine guidance, criticism soon disappeared. Life in the hotel turned barracks may not have been as easy as compared to normal life in a family, but they were well fed, received excellent medical care, and attended education classes. They also learned the skills of warfare and killing, as they were necessary to fight the Evil Ones.

Now Abigail had been called before the Prophet. She looked at her bruised knuckles of her right hand, covering them with her left. Once again, she had been fighting. Now, it had reached the attention of the Prophet.

A well-dressed woman, in a skirted business suit and coiffured brown hair, came into the waiting room.

"The Prophet will see you now, Abigail Young." The woman flashed a friendly smile, which did little to alleviate the fear in Abigail's guts. She stood up, made sure her natural blonde hair was still in its tightly braided bun, smoothed her pressed combat fatigues, and walked into the Prophet's Oval Office.

Prophet Michael Smith stood up from behind his desk. Six feet in height, well-muscled but not huge, short and immaculate brown hair with just a hint of gray, Prophet Smith had the good looks of a Hollywood movie star. He grinned at Abigail as he greeted her.

"Abigail Young…"

"Sir, Avenging Angel Young reporting as ordered." She stood at attention, straight and firm as a metal rod.

"Oh, come now! Relax. Not so stiff. You are one of my children. Please, come closer."

Abigail tried to relax, tried to smile. She failed.

Prophet Smith put his hands on her strong, yet feminine shoulders. "Let me look at you, Abigail. I must admit I have been remiss lately, not spending much time with members of The Twenty. I have been an absent father, and I must beg your forgiveness."

Abigail tried to say something cordial or friendly in response, but her mouth and voice did not seem to work.

The Prophet, still smiling, let go of her shoulders and reached for her right hand. He raised it to near eye level, and Abigail began to shake nervously.

"Hm. I guess you did injure yourself a bit in that little—shall we say—spat you had with those three young lads."

Abigail cast her eyes downward, her chin quivering. Her voice wavered as she tried to speak. "Prophet, I must beg forgiveness. I have brought dishonor with my inability to control my temper. I am…"

Prophet Smith raised her chin with his hand, looked into her eyes, which were becoming damp. "Abigail, you are afraid. You are afraid of me and my displeasure. Please, you are my daughter. I am far from being displeased or angry with you. Believe that."

"But, Prophet, I..."

"Here, please. Relax." With that direction Michael Smith walked behind Abigail and pulled up a padded chair to the side of his large desk. The Prophet then leaned over to his office intercom and buzzed his female assistant.

"Alice, bring us some cold drinks, please. Abigail, sit down. Please, now."

Abigail sat down and tried to control her emotions. She felt like she had let the Prophet down, and that she had been so *bad*, that she felt as if she would burst.

Alice brought in some ice cold lemonade. The Prophet cancelled the prohibitions against drinking caffeine and alcohol in the early days of attaining his position, after one of many Revelations, stating that anything in moderation which did not harm you was to be used by the Children of God, especially in these times of scarcity and trouble. "It is your bad acts that become a sin, not some substance which the Lord produces or gives us the ability to produce, if the substance had some intrinsic worth. If we misuse it—*that* is the sin."

However, he still preferred lemonade when he wanted something cold. And of course, many people followed his lead.

Abigail sipped at the lemonade, her stomach still in knots. The Prophet smiled. "Since you will not relax until we deal with what you feel is the problem at hand, let's look at this report I have."

Prophet Smith opened a manila folder and began perusing the contents. "So, it seems three young men were bullying a youth much younger and smaller than them, yes?"

"Yes, Prophet Smith."

"And you came to the young boy's aid, correct?"

"Yes, Prophet."

He looked at some photos and his eyebrows raised. He then scanned another document. "Seems to me that—according to these reports—you did quite a number on them. As we sometimes said in the Marine Corps, you 'cleaned their clocks'."

Abigail averted her eyes. "I am sorry…" she began, but the Prophet cut her off.

"Sorry? Why? Because you protected a young innocent, using the unique talents you possess, along with the skills you have been taught? Please explain, my daughter."

"I broke bones and caused severe pain. I hurt fellow followers of God." Abigail hung her head. "And I enjoyed it. I enjoyed punishing them for their evil. Only the Lord should pass judgment like that. Jesus preached forgiveness."

The Prophet looked at the photographs. "A broken arm, a fractured jaw, several ribs. They also attacked you, did they not?"

"Yes, Prophet," Abigail mumbled.

"Abigail. Look at me, *now*."

Her eyes snapped to the Prophet's face, for she was trained to obey.

"Listen well, my favored daughter. You acted out of righteousness. Not *false* righteousness, but *true* righteousness. You saw harm, a wrong being done to a young innocent. You stepped in with a feeling of what was right and confronted those who were doing wrong. They then attacked *you*, an Avenging Angel, whose purpose is to protect the faithful. By attacking you, *they* brought on the punishment they received. Punishment provided by an instrument of God, and your Prophet. As Jesus Christ Our Lord did to the money changers in the temple. The enjoyment you said you felt was actual the feel of righteousness, imbued from the Holy Spirit unto you. So, you have nothing to be ashamed of. Understand, daughter? *Nothing*."

Abigail sat still, not knowing how to respond. She could feel his emotions, his certainty. She began to feel more certain that what she had done was not selfish, but had been what was necessary.

"Do you understand, my dear?"

"Prophet, when you explain it, everything becomes clear. Thank you. I feel better about what I did."

Prophet Smith stood. "Come here my child."

Abigail stood and he hugged her. When he did, she felt warm, safe and loved. She hugged him back, and began to weep a bit.

"There, there, my dear. No reason to cry. The Lord gave me, your Prophet, the ability to explain things so that you may learn about the Holy Spirit, and God's Love. I receive the Holy Spirit, then can pass the teachings and goodness on to you. Though in this instance, God communicated directly to you through Jesus Christ and the Holy Spirit."

Abigail looked up to him. "Really? You mean, the Holy Spirit... touched me that day?"

Prophet Smith smiled. "All things are possible to God, through Jesus and the Holy Spirit. As the Prophet, I am infused with the Holy Spirit. So, why cannot God chose to touch you directly? All things are possible to the faithful."

She hugged him again before she knew what she was doing.

"Oof! I was told you are becoming strong. Here. Step back, please."

He looked Abigail up and down.

"You are keeping your scheduled doctors' appointments, aren't you?"

"Yes sir. The doctors have helped a lot. They have especially helped me understand, as I have become... more of a woman."

The Prophet chuckled. "Ah yes, puberty. All young men and women must deal with the onrush of feelings, hormones, and bodily changes. Even Prophets must deal with such changes, such manifestations from when we were banished from the garden."

"Prophet, may I ask you a question?"

"But of course. You are my daughter. Ask away."

"Is there a chance, despite me being... contaminated,

exposed to radiation, that I may someday bear children?"

Prophet Smith paused for a moment, then sighed.

"Through God, Jesus Christ, and the Holy Spirit, anything is possible to the faithful. But remember that you have been given a special mission. You as an Avenging Angel have been chosen to protect the faithful, especially the children. So, God may decide that it takes precedence over you having children. If that is so, please do not be angry with God."

"Angry with God? Never!" Abigail blurted back. "Thank you again, Prophet Smith. You have lifted a burden from my heart."

"That comment will keep me satisfied and content for the rest of the day, Abigail. For I know I have completed a primary function of being a Prophet... unburdening people's hearts. Oh, and Abigail. I have something for you." He reached in and pulled out a lapel insignia of a cross and stripes.

"Congratulations, Avenging Angel First Class."

"Prophet, I am junior to many others. Why am I being promoted?"

"Because you demonstrate superior characteristics and abilities. You are willing to confront evil, and injustice to the innocent at any time, any place. You understand your mission as an Avenging Angel. I have heard reports that you are more than willing to take the lead in any endeavor, as well as lead by example."

"But I am barely fourteen, Prophet Smith."

"You are wise beyond your years. I have need of that wisdom, ability, and loyalty."

Abigail looked at the insignia. "I swear I will not let you down, Prophet Smith."

The Prophet grinned. "I know you won't. I've heard you are also superior in all of your studies—especially in languages."

Abigail blushed, then had a slight faraway look in her eyes. "My mother was a Romanian linguist. I think I inherited my abilities from her. She was already teaching me Russian, Romanian, and my father's Norwegian, when... the explosion happened, after the rocks began to fall."

"Your parents would be proud of you. They *are* proud of you, because I know they are watching over you, even as we speak."

Abigail's mouth formed in a wistful smile. "I'd like to think that, Prophet. They loved me, as I loved them. I get many of my looks from my father's Norwegian heritage, which may explain my strength. I know I am stronger than most people my age, and some who are older."

"No one has heard from your Uncle Buck, since he brought you to us."

"Yes Sir. But if he is still alive, I know he loves me too. His love for me is why he brought me to Deseret. He knew you would take care of me, ensure I was well and healthy. The fact that Deseret was been spared from many of the attacks by the Evil Ones and their demons shows me that he was right. Most of this safety is due to you, Prophet Smith, I know."

Prophet Michael Smith than hugged Abigail once more, and then kissed her on her forehead.

"I try my best. Abigail. With our faith in God's protection, the Tschaaa are held at bay. Now, I must take my leave, for a Prophet's work is never really done. Feel free to stop by again if you wish to speak with me. My door is always open to you, daughter."

"Thank you, Prophet Smith. Please pass my best wishes to your wife."

"I will. Ester will be glad to know you are thinking of her."

Abigail left the Prophet's office with a smile on her face.

After she left, the Prophet's face became impassive. He called Alice into his office.

"Please get Doctor Shaw on the line. And send for Agent Hall."

"Yes, Prophet Smith."

The most powerful man in Deseret sat at his desk, his fingers steepled.

"Prophet, Doctor Jones is on line one."

"Hello, Doctor. I just had a most productive meeting with Abigail Young... Yes, I did notice how strong she is, and that she is growing and filling out so nicely. I take it most of this development is due to your treatments and tweaks?... Splendid. Out of all the Twenty, she seems to be responding the best to your care... Yes I agree, her genetic stock was excellent, superior... Good, I will be waiting for the full report... Please realize just how pleased I am at what you have accomplished, and that you will be personally rewarded....Yes, this is truly God's work. Now if you will excuse me, I have someone coming in for an appointment. God be with you, Doctor." He hung up the telephone and looked at the nondescript man in dark glasses who had just entered his office.

Agent Hall was not too big and not too small. He was a fit average man, which meant that he could easily lose himself in any given group of humanity. He was also one of the best trained and most efficient killers in Deseret. He worked for Prophet Smith—and no one else.

"Agent Hall, in this file are three names. They had the misfortune of attacking Abigail Young, after she called them out for being bullies. Once they have healed sufficiently, you need to bring them for a private meeting to my office, just you, me, and them. Understood?"

"Yes sir, Prophet Smith."

"There are certain people who are to understand that molesting the Chosen of the Prophet has dire consequences. If these three appear to be unable to grasp this concept, they need to disappear into the Unoccupied States. Never to be seen again."

Agent Hall's mouth showed a slight smile. "Of course, Prophet Smith. It would be my pleasure."

"Oh, while I have you here, on the subject of the Unoccupied States, is it true they have formalized in having a female President?"

"Yes Sir. I am finishing up a full report from my sources on her and the supposed plans being formulated for the reconstituted government in the former Central States of America, plus Alaska."

"Good. That is what I like about you, Agent. You always are a step ahead."

"I aim to please, as they say, Prophet Smith."

Prophet Smith leaned back in his padded chair. "Keeping an eye on the border we will share with these States may be a worthy mission for The Twenty. Especially if the States are a source of malcontents. I have worked too hard to secure Deseret and its people, and to make sure our Squid acquaintances leave us alone and live up to their side of the bargain."

"Yes sir."

"Now, you have a nice day, Agent Hall. I will be awaiting your reports."

"Yes. Prophet Smith. May God shine on you."

"And on you, Agent Hall."

The Prophet sat staring out his window. It was surprising how simple, yet sometimes hard it was to do the Lord's work. He buzzed Alice over the intercom.

"Alice, please call my wife, let her know I will be home shortly. Then make reservations at our restaurant. I think we deserve a night out."

"Yes, Prophet Smith."

Michael Smith, Prophet and President of Deseret, sat calmly for a few moments, savoring what he had accomplished. Truth be told, he had always felt a rush from doing the Lord's work. He looked out his window once again.

Everything was coming together so nicely, he thought. Woe to anyone who fucked it up.

⊓EⱲ SⱯMUⱤⱯI

Ichiro Yamamoto crouched behind a couple of driftwood logs on an expanse of beach near Tokyo Bay. A descendant of a long line of Samurai warriors, this night he was dressed like a ninja assassin, all in black, with just his eyes showing. In his left hand he held a Masamune katana sword, one of the finest of blades that had been passed down through generations of the Yamamoto family and clan. Like many before him, he was an expert in the use of the blade.

In fact, there were those who said he could be recognized as the best swordsman in all of Free Japan, if he put his mind and body to the task. For it had been said that he had the fastest reflexes in all of the Japanese Armed Forces. However, not always had he been so respected among his fellow countrymen.

As he crouched and calmly waited, his mind went back to what had been the beginning of his development as a warrior, a path that had led him to this beach on this night...

Almost twenty years prior, he had stood with his head and eyes downcast, as his father Akira Yamamoto berated him once again. This had become an all too often occurrence in his household.

"Again, Ichiro, you are sent home for fighting," his father said, in the deep voice and sharp and clipped language Japanese fathers had used for centuries to scold wayward sons, and military officers had used to chew out subordinates for unworthy acts. In the past, traditional Japan, the scolding and chewing had often involved physical blows from the superior to the subordinate. In modern, post-World War II Japan, that form of correction had fallen out of favor with many. But, this was before the stones began to fall from the sky.

Thus Ichiro's post-war Japanese father did not beat or slap him. However, in Ichiro's mind, it might have been better. For his father was making him feel that he was unworthy, and should be cast out from the family he loved and revered.

"You fight with your classmates on an almost daily basis. Your teachers say you will not—or cannot—sit still, concentrate, or pay attention to lessons. You seem to have boundless energy that is *completely* unfocused, which disrupts everything about you."

The elder Yamamoto clenched his jaw. "Maybe it is partly my fault. Because of my past work, we were all exposed to deprivations of the Fukashima reactor failure, as well as other radiation sources. Maybe you were made… unclean. Unstable."

Ichiro began to sink lower in despair, into his shame. He heard a familiar voice from the entrance way into their home.

"Akira-San. It is Takeo, your younger brother, come at your request."

"Back, here, brother. Back here with Ichiro."

Uncle Takeo came in wearing a traditional style kimono, often seen on Japanese television shows, but rarely worn by the average modern Japanese. In some ways, he was very retro.

He stood ramrod straight in front of Ichiro, fixing him with a steely gaze.

"So, the miscreant stands before us, brother. What should we do?"

"That is why I called you. I am at wit's end. But I know you are adept at, shall we say, forming rough iron into excellent steel."

Ichiro's father turned and bowed to his younger brother. "I humbly ask for your help, brother. I am unable..."

Uncle Takeo cut him off. "Akira-san, we are family! You are my elder brother. There is no reason to be so formal. I know what you want. And what is needed."

Uncle Takeo looked back at Ichiro. "For we have excellent iron here. He just needs the right touch of the forge and hammer. Then polished to a bright sheen. Like a great katana sword."

He looked at Akira. "With your permission, he will come and stay with me and my wife. Our older twins are away at school, so we will have plenty of time and space to deal with his needs."

His older brother attempted to bow again and Takeo instead grabbed his right hand in a firm handshake. "As the Americans say, we have a deal." Uncle Takeo looked at Ichiro.

"Nephew, gather your school books, study materials ,and sufficient clothes for a week. That includes your school uniforms. Understand?"

"Yes, uncle."

"Well, jump to it. I do not have all night."

That was the beginning of weeks stretching first into months and then into years of extensive training. Uncle Takeo had gone a different route than Ichiro's father. Rather than leaving the Japanese self-defense to become a nuclear technician and engineer, Uncle Takeo had made the military his career. He was well respected by both subordinates and superiors, having received the nickname of Katana: a sharp and dangerous weapon that may be able to bend a bit—but *never* to break, and with a deadly edge to him. Uncle Takeo had opened up a martial arts dojo, which catered primarily to young military members and cadets who wanted harder and tougher training than in the official self-defense courses.

Uncle Takeo did not believe in such catch phrases as

Attention Deficit Disorder. He just knew boys will be boys. He knew that many boys and young men just needed form, structure, and hard physical work to help control any inner demons. All young men had the tendency for inner demons, as their hormones began to rage during their growth.

At the same time, Uncle Takeo soon saw that he had a special student. His nephew had the speed and energy of three boys his age, along with the passion and anger as well. Ichiro was lucky that he had his uncle to guide him and help him reach his full potential. If not, Ichiro may have wound up in jail, then recruited by the Yakuza, who oft times recognized boys who could be turned to the darker side of Japanese culture.

Ichiro was soon taught to curb his basic instincts, his anger and passion. Many times in the dojo he wound up on his back, with his uncle looking down at him when he failed to execute a move just so, or became too impatient.

"Ichiro-san. Again, listen. You have fire in your belly, here." He struck Ichiro in the stomach that was already rock hard. "You have passion in your heart, here." He slapped Ichiro's ribs just below his heart.

"But you still lack reason and control, here." He slapped Ichiro painfully on the side of his head.

"A true Samurai was smarter than most, craftier than most. Others may have had great skill with weapons, but a true Samurai also used his intellect to overcome any obstacle or enemy. Understand?"

"Hai, uncle."

Uncle Takeo slapped him on the head again. "Then why do I have to keep reminding you?"

Before he could answer, his uncle grabbed his hand and boosted him up from the tatami matted dojo floor.

"Now, again. Then again and again and again. Then maybe my words will sink into that overly hard head of yours, nephew."

Ichiro grew fast, and was soon taller than boys in his age group. His size may have been the reason why a couple of military school cadets, who trained with his uncle, felt a need to take the young boy down a peg. After suffering jibes and insults about his supposed exposure to Fukashima radiation, saying he would someday look like Gojira, one made the mistake of pushing him. Ichiro had managed to follow his uncle's admonitions about staying calm, cool, and collected up until that point. Then he exploded.

Both cadets were soon on their backs, moaning and holding various parts of their anatomy. But before he could gloat, a Shinai bamboo practice sword slammed painfully across his back.

"Did I give you leave to fight, nephew? Did I tell you that you had to have *my* permission before any fighting? Did I? *Did I?*"

"Hai, Uncle..." His uncle aimed the Shinai at his head, shifting it at the last moment so that it struck his shoulder instead. Ichiro went to his knees, bowing low.

"This unworthy one asks for forgiveness, Sensei. I have failed to heed your instructions once again."

The two military school cadets stood up at this time, one smirking and whispering in what could only be a satisfied gloat at seeing Ichiro be punished. Uncle Takeo was on them in a flash.

Ichiro dared to sneak a look from the corner of his eye, as his uncle rounded on the two cadets. The Shinai was a blur, going from one cadet to the other—then back again. Their cries of pain became blurred into one long yelping as Uncle Takeo seemed to strike every body part imaginable.

"You *dare* to *insult* one of my *blood*?" Uncle Takeo's voice roared. "You dared to gloat and smirk, after this boy here put you both on the ground?" He now had them both on the ground, crying as they tried to assume protective fetal positions.

"Hear me. In old Japan I would call you out. Or maybe your fathers, uncles, brothers. Two of you attack a younger person, then dare to question his worth, his *manhood*? His honor?" Ichiro's mouth dropped open as he looked straight at his

Uncle. He had never seen him so angry.

"Get out of my dojo! Be glad this is modern Japan. Be glad your intestines are not hanging out of your stomach, as you cry for your mothers."

"Colonel Takeo...," one of the cadets began and was rewarded by a Shinai on his fingers. He screamed like a little child.

"*Get up! Leave!*" The two were up and gone before it registered to Ichiro.

Uncle Takeo looked at his nephew. Ichiro bowed his head again, sure he was to be struck for peeking at the display of controlled violence.

"Get up, Ichiro," his Uncle commanded in a rather calm voice. Ichiro stood, eyes still averted. "Look at me, young man." Ichiro looked at his uncle. His uncle broke into a broad grin.

"I should be angry at you for losing your temper and fighting. But sometimes – and I emphasize only *sometimes*, honor demands it. I know what they were saying about you. Did they then lay hands on you?"

"Yes, uncle."

"And you bested both, unarmed in say, five seconds?"

"Yes, uncle. Maybe closer to four."

His uncle had slapped him on his back. "Well done! Now, it is dinner time. Wash up and meet me at the house."

It was not just in martial arts that his uncle had trained him. One day early on, Uncle Takeo had shown up with some colored sheets of rice paper. He had sat cross legged in front of his nephew and began to fashion intricate origami figures as Ichiro watched, fascinated.

"Those are fantastic, uncle."

"Here." He handed Ichiro some of the paper and a couple of instruction sheets.

"Uncle, I cannot..."

"Yes, you can. It is quite calming, and helps you to forget the problems of the day, as well as concentrate your thoughts. Now, read the instructions, remember what I did, and begin. I will be back later."

Ichiro soon found that his uncle had been correct. His uncle was surprised at the speed in which his nephew picked up skill in this art form. One day he presented his uncle with a twelve inch tall origami figure of the Sensei, which broke down into twelve smaller versions, each representing Uncle Takeo in some activity in the dojo.

"How did you do this, Ichiro-san?"

He had shrugged. "I just did, uncle. It seemed to just come to me, I saw a pattern in my head and followed it."

Uncle Takeo realized, and not for the first time, the uniqueness of this special student.

Ichiro was then schooled in the string musical instrument, the shamisen, with which he became quite good. Then poetry, calligraphy, and painting were added to his studies.

"The classical Samurai was an educated and cultured man, not just some brute with a blade. As I have said before, my nephew, he used his brain more than his sword."

Ichiro grew and was taller than most Japanese, some five foot ten, around one hundred eighty-two centimeters tall. He was wiry, with great strength in his frame. As Uncle Takeo began to allow Ichiro compete in martial arts competitions, he saw abilities he had not originally believed existed. Ichiro was faster, more agile than everyone. He also seemed to be able to wrap himself around an opponent, when grappling like a constrictor snake. He was soon called "anaconda" behind his back.

After one competition, when Ichiro defeated a very experienced older black belt, Uncle Takeo sat—contemplating the match. Ichiro had also competed against some older kendo practitioners and had beat them all in very straight order. He called his nephew over.

"Yes, uncle."

"Nephew, I have been watching with specific intensity your

matches this day. Tell me, while you are fighting, what do you see?"

"Well, uncle. I see my opponents, of course, as they ready themselves. Then..." He paused for a minute and closed his eyes. Uncle Takeo sat patiently, as his nephew examined his matches in his mind's eye. Then he opened his eyes.

"I see patterns, uncle. I can often see what my opponent will do several moves ahead, as they seem to move...slow."

Uncle Takeo face split into a broad grin. "I thought so. You are using your mind, your intellect to determine your opponent's possible moves, as well as weaknesses. Then you create a counter set of patterns. All this is done in microseconds. Then your fantastic speed and reflexes take over."

His face now took on a serious look.

"Nephew, you have been given skills and abilities that could easily be misused. You could be a very dangerous man, should you turn these abilities to the darker side of Japanese culture. You could be a Yakuza, a killer."

Ichiro had a puzzled look on his face. "Why would I do that, uncle? I would bring dishonor on our family. I have no desire to kill anyone or anything."

"Remember those feelings and beliefs, my nephew. They will guide you, even if you go into the military. Only psychotics look forward to killing."

Into the military he did go, following in his father's and uncle's footsteps. While they had been in the infantry, Ichiro's excellent abilities were seen best used as a fighter pilot. He went through officer's training in the Japanese Defense Force first, then to pilot training. A fear of Chinese and North Korean expanding capabilities and aggressiveness had prompted new funding for Japanese Air Defense.

The Japanese instructor pilots soon discovered that Ichiro seemed to pull more Gs and still function as well as most pilots. But even more importantly, his reflexes were so quick that even onboard aircraft computers could not keep up with his motions.

Whether fact or fiction, he was soon out maneuvering the most experienced instructor pilots.

As completion of his initial pilot training was nearing, it happened.

The rocks fell.

American military bases on the main Japanese islands were all hit, as were the bases on Okinawa. Only smaller rocks were used, however, none of the larger, tractor trailer sized ones. But they were enough to limit the combined air forces to react when twelve hours later, the first enemy alien craft showed up.

Many air assets were caught on the ground, partly due to the fact everyone believed at the initial outset that the rocks were a natural disaster. Then the Deltas, Falcons, and harvester arks showed up. Ichiro and his classmates, not being completely trained and certified combat pilots, were assigned combat support roles, to include response to reports of harvester ark landings.

An odd and unique pattern, almost limited to Japan, emerged. After the first seventy-two hours, the harvester arks stopped coming. Even before that time, there were verified reports of arks landing, then taking off within the hour after limited activities. Of course, it did not take the Japanese people long to realize what those activities had involved. A small, tracked Type 60 106mm recoilless rifle anti-tank vehicle was able to respond within minutes of a harvester landing in a remote area of Kyushu Island and shot the craft down, as it was starting to rise again. After it crashed on its side, Japanese combat troops arrived and swarmed it, destroying the harvester robots and a handful of creatures later identified as the alien grays. Intelligence personnel arrived and started going over the craft with a fine tooth comb. They soon discovered that the areas which looked like meat processing or butchering stations were just that. And the preferred meat was Homo sapiens.

On day five, Ichiro was at forward field operations station, which consisted of a bunch of large tents and portable generators. As he and some of his fellows were reviewing aerial recon photos of the area in one of the tents, someone called the area to attention. In walked Uncle Takeo, in full combat uniform.

"Colonel Yamamoto," the senior Major in the area addressed him. "Is there some assistance I may provide you?"

"I need to speak with my nephew, Lieutenant Yamamoto, immediately."

"Hai! Yes, Sir. Lieutenant…"

Ichiro was already standing there, having seen his Uncle Takeo walk in with a stoic look on his face.

"Colonel. Lieutenant Yamamoto reporting…"

"Come with me, nephew. Excuse us, Major." Ichiro followed his uncle out of the tent. They walked in silence away from the tents for a few moments. Then, Uncle Takeo stopped and turned to his nephew. His face looked ashen in the subdued lighting of the camp.

"Ichiro, my beloved nephew, there is no way to do this in an easy manner." For the first time in his life, he heard his uncle's voice crack with emotion.

"Your father—my brother—and your mother are dead. They were killed by a harvester ark. We just confirmed it today. My heart breaks with sorrow, but remember I am here for you."

Ichiro's body filled with ice. He felt numb, in a surreal world. He stood silent, unable to move. Then came the rage. Before his uncle could say anything, Ichiro walked over to a sapling tree nearby and tore it from the ground. He threw it like a javelin into the darkness outside the camp. He screamed in rage and sorrow, his voice echoing around the camp like the wounded beast he was at that moment in time.

The senior Major and some of Ichiro's fellow officers approached, and Uncle Takeo motioned them away. Ichiro gained control of his emotions, and turned to his uncle.

"Sir, I am sorry for that lack of control I just displayed."

"Ichiro, I am here as your uncle, your blood. Not as a senior officer."

The older man took a deep breath, then let it out. "I have already let out my hot rage. Now, I am filled with cold, icy rage. I know you will feel the same. So I bring you something that may help focus that rage into an instrument of revenge." With that, Uncle Takeo handed him the katana he had been carrying.

"This is a Masamune blade, from our ancestor, Admiral Isoroku Yamamoto's private collection. It is now yours. Carry it with you in the hope that you may use it personally against the Tako invaders. May it bite and rend the flesh of these monsters, in fitting memory of your parents."

Ichiro took it from his uncle and bowed low, touching the sword in respect to his forehead. "I will strive to be worthy of this, my uncle."

"You are already worthy, my nephew. Remember that."

In the weeks and months to come, Ichiro did not have the chance to exact revenge with the katana. He did finally become fully certified as a combat fighter pilot, sufficient aircraft and fuel being located to finish training Ichiro and his fellows. It was almost a year after the first rock strike.

A former U.S. Air Force veteran fighter pilot was brought by Ichiro's squadron commander Koji Chiba to brief them just prior to the young warrior's first air mission. Colonel Mike Lynch was one of the just over two thousand former U.S. military personnel and dependents who had stayed behind in Japan, as things began to fall apart. The rest of the American survivors had obtained as many transport aircraft and sea craft as possible for attempts at reaching Alaska, which had received only minimal attention from the raiding aliens. Some of the fleeing Americans were successful in reaching Alaska, many were not. The only other American officials and personnel who had stayed behind were the ambassador and staff at the U.S. Embassy, including the Marine protection detail.

At the former Misawa Air Base, in addition to helping the Free Japan Armed Forces to operate the large radar and satellite tracking facilities, Colonel Lynch was trying to assemble two former U.S. jet fighters from the wreckage of several aircraft, plus spare parts. Free Japan provided a few aircraft technicians and engineers to help, but that was it. They were having enough problems keeping their own resources operational, since all outside imported assistance was gone.

Background information on the Colonel provided by Major Chiba indicated that he was an experienced air combat veteran, with two aerial kills from the various Persian Gulf conflicts. Colonel Lynch had also survived two separate interceptions of Delta fighters and scored two missile strikes on a Falcon aerial battle cruiser. He had survived the encounters and even watched the damaged Falcon flee the area, which made him one of the more successful fighter pilots still alive.

"Afternoon, Gentlemen. I appreciate Major Chiba inviting me here, as I think I may have some information that could help in your efforts to intercept and shoot down the Deltas. Since the remaining former American forces in Japan have very limited capabilities, we spend time collecting as much usable intelligence information as we can find. Including some information about one of the first recorded successful interceptions of Squid, what you call Tako, aerial craft during the initial Invasion."

The Colonel continued. "I'll keep this as short and sweet as possible, because I know you have lots of preparations to complete. So, let's go over what we know about the enemy."

For the next half hour, using a few photos and a bunch of diagrams, the Colonel detailed the enemy's capabilities.

"As you know from your intercepts, the Delta's electromagnetic cannons are still deadly out to some two kilometers, due to their extreme velocity and their thirty two millimeter size. The shells' ability to make inflight course corrections—thanks to a small artificial intelligence, A.I., as part of the warhead—adds to their deadliness. Then, of course, there are their three inch missiles, also with A.I. capability. Because the Deltas usually only carry one of these, it limits their combat capability. The energy pulse weapon the Delta carries in the front can punch holes into a main battle tank at about two thousand meters and fry electronics at twice that range in our atmosphere—although only once or twice per fight. Indications are that all weapons work better in outer space, outside our atmosphere. The Falcons carry heavier energy weapons and more missiles, not to mention their size and toughness are a class above our interceptors."

The Colonel paused for a minute, then continued.

"We have a copy of an intelligence report, which is supported by a news video that we have been unable to obtain. Two U.S. Air Force F-22s intercepted a harvester ark east of San Diego, California. Here is a still photo of the downed ark." The photo showed the huge vessel embedded in the ground on its right side, with smoke all around.

"A young Captain William Bender hit that thing with two missiles, as it was coming in for a landing. As he and his wingman started to circle back, a Delta fighter hit them. Captain Bender's wingman was hit by one of the cannon shells, which damaged his fighter's rudders. As the Delta turned around, apparently looking for the other aircraft, Captain Bender was able to perform a modified hammerhead maneuver and come down on top of the Delta. His wingman saw him score a missile hit on the Delta just behind the cockpit area, causing it to dive into the ground at high speed. Captain Bender contacted his wingman and told him he would escort him back to Base. About five seconds later, the Falcon showed up."

The Colonel displayed a fuzzy photo of a Falcon that had bellied in, with pieces of something protruding from its body.

"This is the only other photograph we have from the area. Like I said, somewhere a video is still floating around, as some people reported to have seen it on a local television broadcast. Then it disappeared. But the wingman made it back to the base and reported the Falcon tried to latch onto Captain Bender's F-

22 with some kind of tractor beam, and one of those mechanical tentacles the Squids like to use. The wingman said Captain Bender rammed the Falcon, causing it to belly in. That is the last we heard of Captain Bender. He was the closest thing to an 'ace' that we had from those thirty one days, before all control went to hell."

Everyone was silent for a few moments. Then Ichiro stood up.

"So, Colonel, what can you suggest from this incident you have described? How should we fight the Takos—Squids, as you call them—in the air?"

Colonel Lynch chuckled. "Knife fight in a telephone booth."

When he was met with confused looks, the Colonel explained.

"The Deltas, piloted by the Squids, or Tschaaa as they call themselves, can pull some fifteen Gs in a turn. So they have the advantage at high speed horizontal combat. And of course, they have the high ground, as they can attack from low orbit, at Mach five or so. Those huge eyes they have in their heads we call Eagle Eyes, because like an eagle, they can see objects way off in the distance, especially if you are a fast mover."

"So what do we do? We do not fight their fight."

Like thousands of fighter pilots before him, he used his hands as two opposing aircraft to illustrate as he explained. "The Squid comes in fast from above, you get in the weeds down low and go into lower speed tight turns. Because even if you can pull more Gs, the aerodynamics of an aircraft limits just how tight an aircraft can turn before it stalls, especially a high speed stall. Even with the two injector scramjets being able to shift a few degrees to help with maneuvering, their delta wings do not supply the same lift capability as our airfoils and flap systems do. Most importantly, they have not developed the aerial tactics of mutual support like we have. Many of their attacks are single ship attacks. If you have four on one, you will almost certainly lose one aircraft to knock down the Delta, unless you can hit them with a high velocity missile before they catch on to what you are doing. So you suck them into a knife fight in a telephone booth, where their lessor speed capabilities and rather poor all around cockpit visibility, compared to our bubble canopies, negates some of their advantages."

Colonel Lynch looked at the assembled young and aggressive pilots.

"Look, gentlemen. I'm not going to blow smoke up your rears. The odds are not all that great. If a Falcon shows up, hide and hope your ground batteries can hit it. I was able to get one to flee. Had it stuck around, even damaged, it would have cleaned my clock."

"But," the Colonel continued. "Our job is to fight. So we fight. If you ever find a spare fighter, give me a call. I'd love to get another shot at them."

Colonel Lynch left with many thanks from the Free Japanese Air Force. Major Chiba turned and addressed his pilots.

"You have heard what the good Colonel had to say. Use it if we meet any Deltas tomorrow on our first combat mission in some time. I know some will question if one pilot took out all those three dissimilar craft as stated. But no matter. They fought, they tried. So we owe them respect."

The Major paused for a moment. "The Takos' attacks on us seem more in form of war games, or desires for individual achievement, rather than organized warfare. We in Japan are lucky that we were not damaged more, and have for the most part been left alone. But if they want a fight, we will give it. Now, I have posted the roster on the flights tomorrow. Get some rest, be prepared. Dismissed!"

The drive back in the jeep from being picked up after parachuting to the ground was the longest ride he ever had. Ichiro kept playing back the events in his mind.

Two Deltas, unusual for flights over Japan, had come in at just under Mach three, clearly looking for a fight. Major Chiba led Ichiro's four man flight, with Ichiro being his wingman.

"Lieutenant Yamamoto," he had said to Ichiro before they took off. "You are one of the finest pilots I have seen, and can do things in a fighter that many can only dream of. Do not get overconfident. The Takos are deadly. Hai?"

"Hai, Major. It is an honor to be your wingman."

"Honor has nothing to do with it. Skill does. Remember that."

One hour after take-off—and it was over. Ichiro had done seemingly impossible maneuvers in his F-35J, and had come down on top of a Delta, as Colonel Lynch said Captain Bender had done. Ichiro let the Delta have it with his missile array, saw it explode and break up.

Five seconds later, the Delta's wingman hit Ichiro, forcing him to bail out. His ejector seat worked fine, and he was in the silk at some two thousand feet above the ground. Then the Delta came at him, helpless in his parachute, seeking further revenge.

It happened in a matter of seconds. Major Chiba rammed his F-35J into the Delta in mid-air, both craft tumbling to the earth below. Ichiro began to scream his rage and sorrow, as he floated to the ground below.

Ichiro was in a daze when he walked into his squadron's day room. He sat down, did not notice his Uncle Takeo standing nearby.

"Nephew. I heard and came immediately. I am very glad you are alive."

"He died for me. Major Chiba died for me. *For me.*" Before he realized what he was doing, Ichiro smashed an end table into kindling. Then his uncle was holding him.

"Young Samurai, Major Chiba died because that was his choice. He died saving you and killing the enemy. He died with honor. Remember that."

Ichiro stood apart, looked at his uncle.

"I owe him, uncle. I owe his memory, his family, his ancestors."

"We will discuss what you owe later. I have arranged that, after an abbreviated debriefing, you will be given a forty-eight hour pass. Now, get some rest. We will talk more later."

"Yes, Colonel. Thank you also uncle, for coming."

Uncle Takeo smiled. "That is what family does. We are there for you."

Now Ichiro's thoughts came back to the mission at hand. For he had decided that ten of the enemy—the Takos, aka the Squids— must die for Major Chiba's sacrifice. Rather than rest on his pass, he was here, on this reported deserted stretch of beach. It was a simple matter to find the intelligence reports as to where the small groups of Takos had been coming ashore, looking for trouble as they rarely seemed to harvest any human meat. It was about individual combat, like in the old days of the Samurai.

Ichiro watched the bay waters intently, because he knew the Takos had the ability—similar to their Earth cousins of color – to camouflage by changing the color and hue of their flesh. It would not bode well to be caught unaware, to let an enemy sneak by him. He wondered where the security patrols were that were supposedly guarding the beaches and coastlines. He would have to talk to his uncle, since his infantry unit was assigned to this area.

The young Lieutenant heard movement behind him and crouched in the darkness behind the driftwood logs. How could one of the aliens have snuck by? But wait, that sounded like human movements, human steps. Ichiro moved back near a bush on the edge of the sand.

"Nephew, you cannot hide from night vision goggles, no matter how much of a ninja you are."

Ichiro stood up, as his Uncle Takeo approached with nary a further sound than slight steps on the sand. He did not know what to say, as he had been caught in what some would think was a childish act of revenge.

"Colonel, uncle, I..."

"Quiet, nephew. Back behind the logs. You picked an excellent spot."

In a minute he was sitting dumbfounded, when he saw his uncle in the same ninja like clothes as he, with an identical katana.

"How..."

"I know your heart and the fire in your belly, Ichiro. On a rare occasion, it is right for a Samurai to ignore his intellect and, as the Americans would say, go with their gut. So, I had you followed, and I had the security patrols pulled back from this area. Though, if a ten limbed monster gets by us, they will be meat from modern firepower, not steel blades."

"You...see this as right, uncle? Violating orders, sneaking here?"

"What orders? A man can do what he wishes on pass, as long as he returns fit for duty, abuses no civilian laws. And since this is my area of responsibility, I have decided this mission is right. Now, hush. I'll use the night vision to keep watch, you keep your ears open. If the pattern is the same, with this tide they should come tonight."

The two man sat, watched, listened, and waited. Having his Uncle Takeo there filled Ichiro with a calm resolve. He knew that nothing would get by him or his uncle.

An hour into their silent vigil, Uncle Takeo patted his arm and pointed out to the bay waters. There was enough of a moon out that night to illuminate motion on the water. Night vision gave Uncle Takeo the ability to pinpoint the cause.

"They come, nephew. Three it appears. Be ready."

Ichiro was filled with an icy resolve, his hand on the hilt of his katana. The figures were then close enough that Ichiro could make out three Tschaaa, the Takos. His uncle shed the night vision goggles and went into a crouch, Ichiro matching his stance.

"Banzai," Uncle Takeo whispered.

"Banzai," Ichiro replied. Then they were moving in short running steps—seen in many a Samurai epic.

The three creatures were just moving out of the surf, rising up on their partial cartilage based interior structures that functioned like a pliable skeleton. They began the scuttling motion of their species, when surprised out of the dark by two bipedal mammals. The Tschaaa young warriors carried long pole weapons with sharp obsidian blades at the end, which they held by their two long social tentacles. Upon seeing the two approaching humans, the young warriors raised their weapons, confident of their superiority against the monkeys, even on land. For similar in the tradition of other warrior groups, to include the Samurai, they had come to test their metal—and the metal of their enemy.

For Ichiro, the cephalopods' motion seemed to slow down. He knew this was due to the fight or flight response that affected humans by changing their sense of time and motion. Then Ichiro began to see the pattern, as the Tschaaa warriors started to attack. He became a wraith in his response.

Uncle Takeo parried the thrust of one pole weapon, tried to strike back with a textbook katana response—which was in turn parried. The longer social tentacles gave the Tschaaa an advantage, enabled them to stay out of range of the katana blades. Despite being sea creatures, they moved well on land, at least for short distances.

From the corner of his vision, Uncle Takeo thought he noticed a blur of action. But he had to concentrate on the enemy at hand.

A severed Tschaaa five-fingered hand landed in front of him and his opponent, just as a horrible screeching reverberated along the sandy beach. Seeing the severed appendage had a deleterious effect on Uncle Takeo's opponent, as it scuttled backwards. Even in the dark, its overly large eyes seemed wide and registered shock. Uncle Takeo saw his opening and advanced in a fast moving crouch, a growl coming from his chest. Slash, parry, slash—and then chop. The sharp end of the pole weapon lay on the sand near the surf. He leapt forward and severed the forward grasping hand of the Tschaaa, and was rewarded by the same horrible screeching. He leapt forward again, past the blunted weapon, and slashed at one of the creatures eight thick arms it used for locomotion, then slashed at another just before back-peddling out of range.

The land octopus let out another reverberating screech and raised its severed tentacle, along with its still intact one, dropping the remains of its weapon. Was it surrendering?

Uncle Takeo had no time to ponder when a blur from his right turned into his nephew, who closed and thrust with his katana through one of the oversized eyes and into the creature's brain.

The Tschaaa shuddered, then collapsed. Ichiro withdrew his blade and was beside his uncle before the older man realized it.

"Are you okay, uncle?"

Uncle Takeo stood dumbfounded for a few minutes. Finally, he managed to speak. "You killed those other two, then came to help me?"

"Why yes, uncle. As you taught me. See the pattern, then strike. They have rather simple patterns."

Takeo Yamamoto knew that his nephew was a very special type of warrior. Now, he had an inkling of just how special.

"Nephew, you are as the Samurai were in our legends. Come, we will contact my personnel to secure the area. Our Intelligence Officers will want to examine this scene."

He threw his arm around his beloved nephew. "Your parents, and all our ancestors are watching, aware of what you did here today. This will be written in the family history, and remembered for generations."

"It is the first of my debt to Major Chiba, uncle. I swore I would kill ten of the enemy for his sacrifice. Then, maybe, the debt will be paid, and I may stop killing."

Uncle Takeo's face turned sad in the dark. "In war, we never know when we can stop killing, unless the enemy is defeated. I fear that will not be for some time."

Hours later, the two were in Commanding General Koji Sakae's office, who was not entirely happy. "A Colonel and his nephew should *not* be running around in the dark, being ninjas. Colonel, what if you had been killed? What would that have done to your command, your units?"

"I am not indispensable, General. There would be another to take your place."

"With your experience and abilities? Think of that next time, Colonel, before you go rushing into the night. We need all the senior trained personnel we can find."

General Sakae then pulled out a bottle of Suntory Scotch and produced three glasses.

"We need to drink a toast to the Emperor and Japan. He called after seeing the report on this incident. Apparently Princess Akiko is taking on the mantel of a soldier to replace her dead Brother, killed in the early fighting. The Emperor informed me you have a 'fan' is the word he used, in the Royal Family. And he asked for a toast in his name for future successes."

The General poured the three glasses, then stood up—raising his glass.

"In honor of older times, banzai! May Free Japan and the Emperor live for ten thousand years!"

The three officers threw back their drinks.

"General. May this lowly Lieutenant ask a question?"

"Anyone who can slay the Takos with a katana can ask almost anything."

"Are we still alone? Is Free Japan still standing alone in this fight?"

The General paused before answering. "We have reports that the remaining United States are electing or appointing a new President, a woman who is said to have steel in her spine. I hope that is so. We are also talking with Free Russia, which is

Siberia. So, we will see."

Ichiro stood straight. "You will always have my sword, sir. You, and the Emperor."

The General looked at Uncle Takeo. "He is of the old breed of Samurai, isn't he?"

"Actually, General, he is a new Samurai. Trust me, he and his fellows will put our ancestors to shame."

"I hope you are right, Colonel. A toast to that then. To the new Samurai. May they live for a thousand years!"

Ichiro and his Uncle left the Generals' office and walked into the parking lot.

"Nephew, I will contact your unit and tell them you will be dining with me tonight. I think I have enough influence to make this happen."

"Yes sir."

The two Yamamoto family members walked towards Uncle Takeo's vehicle, a Japanese Jeep. He drove himself, said only people who spent most of their time in offices needed drivers.

"Uncle, what is next? I mean, we killed three of the Invaders. I feel a sense of personal satisfaction, but I also know that it is a drop in Tokyo Bay."

"We do what Japanese warriors always do. We fight to defend our homeland, our people. Our deaths matter little. Our success matters all." Uncle Takeo looked at his nephew.

"Ichiro, you have a special part to play. I can sense it. Remember that as time passes, when things seem strange. It will all come together. I see a long and fruitful life, with a loving wife and children. And not just any wife, but an equal to yourself, a warrior."

"How do you know that, uncle?"

His uncle shrugged. "I just do. Now, a good meal, good company, and some good sake. Then you can stay at my house with me and your aunt. Our twins—your cousins—should be home tonight from their studies at University. They will also be part of the future of Free Japan. We just have to keep the enemy Tschaaa from our shores."

After an excellent meal and visit with his uncle, aunt, and cousins, a very tired Ichiro went to his bed.

During the night, he had a dream. His parents appeared, smiling at him, and pointing to a woman standing nearby. Ichiro tried to make out her features, but they were hazy. He did know that she was a gaijin, non-Japanese of caucasian heritage. He woke, the image still in his mind. He had the feeling that his parents were happy with the woman and seemed to want Ichiro to meet her. Ichiro smiled, as he went back to sleep. If his deceased parents were happy, he would be happy. Now the only question was, when would he meet the mystery woman. He would think about that later. Right now, he needed his sleep. He would meet his future soon enough. Ichiro knew his ancestors would be watching over him, no matter what happened. The new Samurai slumbered on, as future events began a rush to meet him.

STORM WARNING

George Williams IV stood looking out the window of the temporary office space they were using. He had to admit that Alaskan landscape was beautiful with its trees and mountains. But the damnable cold! As a Georgia native he grew up around warmth and no snow. But then again Georgia—as a part of the United States—was no more.

George was a very large man, whose skin was close to being actually black, not just some vague brownness that was lumped under the racial title of black. A former Chief Master Sergeant of the U.S. Air Force, former because the USAF in reality did not exist anymore, he still had the strong muscular build of an Air Force Judo team member. Nearing forty years old, he realized he should be counting his lucky stars. Or down on his knees, thanking God. Then again, maybe he should do both.

He was one of the lucky ones, doubly lucky because he had his family with him. Had they still been in Georgia, his African-American wife Meagan and their fraternal twins, George V and Ellen would either be harvested dark meat, or waiting to be such, especially his children.

Not for the first time did he consider the grand cosmic joke. After his family lineage had survived slavery, Klu Klux Klan nightriders, and Jim Crow laws, they were endangered by a bunch of multi-armed and tentacle things from another world.

"Wool gathering again, George?"

He turned to the source of the female voice—Sandra Paul, Madam President of the newly christened Unoccupied States of America.

A very fit 5'6" woman, with a firm chin, straight yet feminine nose, and nice lips, she was noted for her attractiveness. But she had not allowed her curves to get in her way when she played sports, including Judo. Her full head of shoulder length brown hair now had small streaks of gray, yet she still had a young, vibrant demeanor. If she weren't Madam President, she would have been classified as a very desirable cougar.

Her pre-Squid political critics had written her off as a conservative bimbo because of her good looks, Midwest demeanor and her uncompromising politics when it came to a strong, moral America.

She had weathered many a political caricature of herself, her family, her background, her residence in Alaska. Now she had the last laugh. Ninety-nine percent of her critics were dead, many eaten.

The joke she made was, "They were right. I was too tough. Yes, too tough to eat."

George smiled at the author of that comment. "Sorry, Ma'am. Still getting used to the tall mountains and all this cold snow. There's not much of it around Georgia."

Madam President chuckled. "Well, that cold and snow helps to keep the Tschaaa—the Squids—away from Alaska and the other Unoccupied States."

She added, "Plus the fact that Montana, Wyoming, the Dakotas, Colorado, Nebraska and Kansas are well away from the ocean and other large bodies of water, like the Great Lakes. Our opponents seem to hesitate on penetrating farther than about twenty miles in from the coast, except for harvester ark raids in the early days of the Invasion."

"Anything else from Deseret, formerly Utah?"

"No, George. They're very polite, but vague—won't commit to anything."

Sandra Paul sighed. "I can't really blame them. Their Nation State had few harvester ark visits and other incursions. The Mormons were always prepared for some kind of apocalyptic disaster, so they had a lot of stored supplies to fall back on. By keeping to themselves, using their own resources for their people, they had much fewer losses."

George grunted. "It would have been nice if they had shared."

"Why would they? Everything fell apart. There was no central authority—or organization. How would they know their limited aid would reach the right people?"

"As usual, Madam President, you have a very relevant point."

She smiled. "You know, George, it still feels funny when people, even you, address me as President. I keep wanting to look around, see if there is anyone else in the room or standing behind me."

George gave her a serious look. "Madam President, you are the right person for the job. Not to mention you are the only one who seems to want the job."

"Well, old friend, you may be a bit prejudice concerning the first point, but the second you are spot on. I am one of the few surviving Congressional Representatives that I know of. The remaining state officials decided if I wanted the job, I could have it. Besides, I feel a responsibility to see Old Glory fly above the complete United States once again. Sounds kind of hokey, doesn't it?"

"Hell no, Ma'am. That's what I liked about you from the very beginning. You were a good, old-fashioned patriot, putting the country and its people first—rather than politics and party."

Her eyes widened a bit. "You saw that in our first meeting,

way back when?"

"Of course," George said. Then he laughed. "I still remember you with that congressional delegation reviewing security on our nuclear weapons bases and installations. You were the Junior Congressperson, marched right by all the brass and went straight to me. Remember what you said, Sal?" The name Sal was a nickname her closest friends used, its origins lost in the passage of time.

"Yes, I do George. I said, 'Chief, my daddy always said that if you *really* wanted to know what's going on in a Military Unit, ask the Senior NCO's. You're a Chief Master Sergeant, so tell me— what's the real story and status around here?' I remember that because I saw the looks on the General's and Colonel's faces, not to mention my fellow most senior Congressmen and women. You thought I had pointed out a turd in the punch bowl."

George broke into laughter. "That's the gal I know. Not afraid to use a little salty language to make the point, or to thumb your nose at convention." He stopped laughing, looking serious again.

"Madam President, it has always been a pleasure to serve you. People thought I was nuts when I was bluntly honest with you. They thought I had sealed a permanent assignment to Nome, Alaska. Then, suddenly everyone was bending over backwards to make sure I was taken care of. You know—you never did tell me the whole story behind all those backroom politics."

"Well, since I didn't give a damn if I were re-elected, I told the General Staff and my fellow Members of Congress that if they did anything to you for telling me the truth, I'd make sure every blogger on the internet would be streaming about the poor shape of our security. Most politicians had trouble with the light of day."

"Yes Ma'am. Now, most of those politicians are dead, and many were eaten."

George's comment brought them back to the present. They both knew the odds of this attempt at a U.S. President succeeding over a crumbled system of surviving States. Many looked at Deseret as a more viable model, one of separate Nation States, operating under the Tschaaa radar. But not Madam President. She meant it when she said she wanted Old Glory to fly over the U.S.A. once again, all fifty states, not just eight.

Sandra chuckled. "You know, sticking with me *did* get you to Nome, Alaska after all. Anchorage and Fairbanks as well." They both laughed, and without warning she stepped over and hugged George.

"I know this is outside normal decorum, but damn, I've always been a hugger. And you are my closest, dearest friend, not just my very Special Assistant."

They hugged for a minute, the warmth of another human being who cared about them giving them both a sense of calm and security.

"Okay George, back to work. This Cattle Country. It exists just like we were told by those who fled to Montana?"

"Yes Ma'am. They now have a complete electronic and physical fence around the former states of Georgia, Alabama, and Mississippi. Trapped in this super concentration camp is every African-American, dark-skinned Latino, Filipino, East Indian, and anyone with much of a tan who could be rounded up and forced into the area. People who resisted too much were harvested. And yes, Madam President, they're going to be used as a breeding population."

The woman's eyes flashed in anger, as she smashed her fist down onto the desk. "*That* will *not* stand! We will start today finding a way to stop these... these *monsters* from treating us as just meat. We are all Americans, human beings, no matter the color of our skin."

"Steel spine," George said.

"Excuse me? Steel spine? What does that mean?"

"That, Madam President, is what people are saying about you. You have a steel spine, and you are the spine of steel for the Unoccupied States."

The new President stood silent, processing what she had just heard. She knew she had trouble backing down from a fight if she felt she was right, or that someone was being misused and abused. But a steel spine? Margaret Thatcher had been the known as the Iron Lady. Did the surviving humans in North America need a symbol like a spine of steel to help them stand together?

"Well, I've been called worse things and been accused of having some less than desirable physical characteristics. Often it had to do with me having my head up a certain fundamental orifice. Or that I resembled a jackass, braying and all. So, having a spine of steel as an identifier? Not bad. Not bad at all."

"Alright, next subject, George. General Reed. Is he in place at Malmstrom Air Base?"

"Yes Ma'am. Lots of people—especially survivors from various military units—have made it there, as well as the bases in North Dakota. He and his people are getting things organized, checking to see what ICBMs can be brought online—plus any other weapons of mass destruction."

The President frowned. "Last resort, George. We start throwing nukes around, not only do we extend this Long Winter, but the Squids may just decide to rain rocks down on us again. Then, a fast trip to the Stone Age—if we survive."

"Well ma'am, our invaders seem to become attached to our oceans and seas. So, they may hesitate on massive worldwide destruction. But they could decide to wipe out as many of us as they can, then start widespread harvesting again."

"Hm. Yes, my large friend. They seemed to have really slowed down. One theory is that they have a billion or two frozen corpses in their starships to take on the long voyage home, with some breeding pairs also. The information about their original primary food source being wiped out by a plague seems to be checking out."

George nodded his head. "Yes, Madam President. I just wish they would have found some other planet to harvest. Or at least waited another hundred years, so we would have a version of the USS Enterprise in orbit to protect us."

The President smiled. "Nice fantasy. But that only happens in movies, it seems. But what about this Director Lloyd? How real is he?"

"Looks like he's as real as we are. He's doing in Key West and the Tschaaa controlled areas what we are trying to do here—create a sanctuary for humans to live, unmolested."

"But under Squid control and cooperation, right?"

"Yes, Ma'am. And with full knowledge of what is going on in what is now Cattle Country. Lloyd is using it as a propaganda selling point to recruit people he needs—that there is no harvesting in the areas controlled by Lloyd and his people. Which seems to work, if for no other reason than that many people have no viable alternative. Move into an area occupied by the Squids and their robocops, lizards, and grays, as well as supported or controlled by the Director, and you are promised you and your kids will not be eaten."

Sandra snorted. "Yeah. Give them better food to eat, a little entertainment, maybe a little self-rule and bingo—Vichy France all over again."

She looked at George. "The problem with being a student of human history is that it keeps repeating itself. You'd think we learned something, especially when they start rounding up people for the rail cars."

George sighed. "Yes, and racism, division based on color and slavery keep coming up. Only this time, a damned alien race is involved."

The woman President stood, looking out the window.

"This scenery is fantastic. But we can't keep hiding here. Eventually, the Squids will come for us. Or those psychotic Krakens and their sick religion. The clock is ticking."

"Speaking of the clock, Ma'am, I'm supposed to remind you that you have dinner tonight with your daughter."

"Thank you, George. Please, talk to your wife, and arrange a time when we can all get together." She looked into his eyes. "You're part of my family now. Families will be made by choice—not just by bloodline."

"Sal, it's an honor to be considered family. I always enjoyed the time we all spent together. Your late husband and son, well, they were special to Meagan and me also."

There was silence for a few moments, then the President spoke again.

"They're with the man upstairs, George, watching over my daughter and me. I feel their presence sometimes."

She seemed to straighten up a bit, pulling her attention back to the present.

"Okay—I'm off. See you back here at zero dark thirty tomorrow George. Time to start cracking the whip."

"Yes, Ma'am."

George Williams walked the new President out to the Humvee and its two military armed personnel. Presidential limos were a thing of the past. He got her seated, waved goodbye and walked over to the beat up but serviceable SUV he used. No guards for him. He was expendable.

There was still some snow on the ground, and he trudged through it. Funny how an old Georgia boy like himself could adapt to snow around most of the time. What was that saying, he thought? That which does not kill you makes you stronger. Yeah, that fit.

As he got ready to drive away he stopped, then said a small prayer.

"Lord, this sometimes lapsed Southern Baptist is thanking you for saving my wife and kids. I know there are storm clouds gathering, that many more good people will die. I just ask you to give me the strength to see this out. Give me the strength to see the day when man and woman kind are no longer reduced to an item on something's dinner menu. In Jesus' name, Amen."

He started the SUV.

"Nietzsche. That's who it was," George mumbled to himself. "That what does not kill you makes you stronger."

As he drove out of the parking lot towards home, he chuckled.

"Yeah. Those Squids should have read Nietzsche, then killed us all. They won't get a second chance."

VILE SMUT

Darryl Biggs unlocked the front door of the shop as he had done so many times before. For once, he actually thought how many years had passed since a specific fateful day when he had opened early in the morning. Was it 6:00am, going on 7:00am? Well, everything was about to change if the rumors were true.

He opened the glass-paned door, then flipped the switch for the neon sign (was this the last operating neon sign in North America, he mused). It flickered into life and then radiated the red and blue lights which proclaimed the business name: VILE SMUT .

Underneath the lit sign was a smaller artistically lettered sign which spelled out Adult Books and Items. Darryl had the faded letters repainted just a year prior by one of the local residents of First Avenue, Seattle, Washington. He had to scrounge for parts for the old neon sign continually. He thought once again that he should replace it with newer LED lights.

"Good morning, Godfather Darryl." The young female voice startled him for a moment before he placed the owner. He turned and frowned at the comely seventeen-year-old redhead, Angie, as he spoke.

"You just have to call me that, don't you?"

"Because that is who you are to us. You're the Godfather of downtown Seattle."

Darryl snorted in response. Not for the first time did he question his fate or karma which had led him to this situation.

"What can I do you for, Angie?" he asked.

"So is it true? Is the War over? How about the Infestation? Are the Squids leaving?" Angie asked all the questions rapid-fire, like a machine gun.

"Whoa. That's a lot of questions for, let me see, 7:00am in the morning," answered Darryl.

Darryl smiled and then paused before he replied. He had known Angie Smyth since she was all of nine years old. He was like an uncle or stepfather to her and her mother, Joanne. If there hadn't been such an age difference... he tamped down that thought.

"Well. Angie, those news reports over Free States Radio and Television are interesting. Maybe hopeful."

"Just hopeful?" asked the young redhead. Darryl shrugged.

"All we have are the news reports. I have not been in contact with any of our so-called Squid friends from what was the Seattle Aquarium for almost two months."

From a very early point in the first year of the Infestation, Tschaaa aliens had noticed him at his business and near the waterfront. He had looked for seafood for the increasing numbers of survivors who attached themselves to him and 'his block.' So the natural result was that one day a cyborg robocop contacted him to let him know that occasional fishing for food was allowed. However, should he or any other humans stray near the former Seattle Aquarium, they would become fish food. It seems the Tschaaa cephalopods had set up a breeding and child-rearing area near there.

"That's all I know, Angie. Sorry."

The young teen pouted. Darryl knew the Infestation had been extremely hard on the young ones. One minute, they were growing up with toys and boys. The next minute, space rocks were crashing down, then Squids and their minions running and wheeling around, harvesting them all like free-range chickens. Darryl had not been a spring chicken when the Infestation began, so had he been killed, hell, at least he had a life. To be killed not out of childhood yet...

Angie perked up. Like many of the younger generation, they had learned not to dwell on things.

"Hey, Godfather. You want some breakfast? Our chickens have been laying really well."

"You know I'll never turn down a free meal." He answered. With that, she flashed a sweet, healthy smile.

"I'll see if Mom can throw in some pancakes and some rabbit meat. They're overproducing again."

"That's what rabbits do. They f--- I mean, you know, they..."

"Make more rabbits by humping," Angie said with a sly look in her eye. "I know the drill."

The young beauty turned and began to run south down the block.

"I'll be right back," she called over her shoulder.

Darryl smiled as he watched her run to the last storefront on the block, then take a left. Up the incline to Second Avenue was a former taco fast food restaurant, something about taco from the sea or a similar sounding name. He had helped Joanne to get the small kitchen up and running again during that first year. Now, it was a well known surviving eating establishment. In a small office space above on the second floor that had once held a small accounting firm was now an oversized hutch for rabbits and chickens. That was the secret source of the fresh meat and eggs the eatery now known as Joanne's Hot Stuff was noted for. Darryl smiled, then went into his business.

Instead of leaving the door open he shut it. He placed the "Be Back in Fifteen" sign up in the window. People would think he was in the John and would come back later. Everyone knew not to disturb the Godfather.

"Damn. How did I get into this mess?" he asked himself. He

walked around the main counter where the cash register was and sat down. Everything was happening too fast and all at once. He looked at all the remaining well worn and oft dusty porno DVDs, magazines, and adult toys. The memories began to come.

That September morning began like so many others. The Early Shift man had called in sick (read that doped up) just before his Night Man, Jimmy, had closed up at 4:00am. Darryl years before had decided to close his shop between the hours of four and seven. Jimmy stayed until 5:00am, cleaning up semen stains in the back booths, any vomit and related smells from the occasional junkie and drunk. The Day Man, now Doug, was supposed to show up at 7:00am to open up. The two-hour break gave the place a chance to "air out" a bit from the smell and residue of human bodies, usually male, some washed, others semi-washed, others just nasty. Adult establishments like his First Avenue Adult Revue and DVD always attracted the transients and sometimes downright homeless who, for some change, rented one of the few remaining video booths to sit down and sleep for almost an hour in a dark and dry room. Sometimes, they pissed and crapped themselves.

Darryl usually arrived around 9:00 AM to check the overnight proceeds, peruse the stock of pornography-related material and see to the regular clientele. He had local office workers who dashed in during breaks to return the rentals, regular retirees who spent hours deciding just what they wanted to masturbate to, and then the occasional newbie who had always wanted to scope out one of the last adult erotica establishments in the Northwest. Internet porn, Amazon Delivers, satellite TV with subscription services to fit every person's fetish, and freelance underground film producers has killed the traditional retail market. Darryl knew he was one of the last places that had the private video booths in the back for the whack-off artists who had a thing about an orgasm in a semi-public place. To each his own.

Thus, every day a beefy Darryl showed up, made sure no one was stealing from him and that all the nasty human and otherwise fluids were cleaned up. Seattle Police Department Vice Squad all knew him, so the only people who used to get picky with him was the Health Department. They *hated* sticky floors and a locker room smell of dirty gym socks. Thus, Darryl went through a can of air freshener almost daily. Seven days a week, even Sundays, he was open. He also owned stock in Jiffy Mop.

With the day man AWOL, Darryl was there at 6:00am to let Jimmy go home. The young and slender black college student did not look like someone who would want to spend time in a porn shop. But he told Darryl he needed the money, and the clientele helped him with his Psychology studies. "Perfect for field studies," he had told Darryl.

"How ya doing, young man,"Darryl greeted the college student.

"Fine, Boss. Now that you are here. Doug's trashed again."

"You talked to him also?" The shop owner asked. Jimmy snorted before he answered.

"He stopped by. I think he's on meth again, all agitated."

Darryl shook his head. Why the guy couldn't stay sober was beyond him.

"I hired him when he was on smack. At least the worst thing heroin does to him is he would nod off. I'm usually around in the daytime to wake him up. Meth makes him too aggressive towards the customers." He looked at his other employee.

"Know anybody who needs a job, Jimmy?"

"I'll check around, Boss, Right now, I need a shower before I go to class. See you tonight, I guess."

"Yeah. A double shift for me again. Ask your friends about a job."

"Will do, Boss. Gotta go." Jimmy took off on his ten speed

bike he kept locked in the shop.

Darryl sighed. He had been covering the gap between 4:00pm until Jimmy came in at 8:00pm for he could not remember how long. Good employees were hard to find. That helped cost him his second marriage a year ago. Now, child support for four kids, two exes, and another house to an ex-wife told him he never would be out of this business. Of course, this store's merchandise was just part of his job. This First Avenue establishment was one of the last Mafia-owned pornography shops on the West Coast. Darryl thought maybe one of the remaining outlets in the entire United States. The once proud Italian/Sicilian Mafia was a shadow of itself. The weakness of the organization helped to keep Darryl in business as he was one of the last "drop spots" for the "family". Selling smut was a cover, and paid the utility bills. The building was owned by a proxy. So, in additional to laundering a bit of currency through a cash business (can't let your wife see that credit charge), there were other items. The money from illegal card games, loan sharking, and some sports betting on the 'big' days like the Super Bowl, in addition to whenever the few Wiseguys needed a place to drop something, no matter what it was, it all came through this place. Darryl locked it all up in an oversized hidden safe in the back. None of his employees knew about the fake paneling which concealed the Fort Knox brand vault. Darryl had been playing this role for some twenty years.

Darryl turned on the small flat screen TV suspended above a sign that proclaimed Catfight/Bondage DVDs. He had a DVD player connected to it and another television if he wanted to show some new film. This morning, he wanted the news. It was nearing 6:30am, west coast time.

Breaking News flashed across the screen as it lit into life. Darryl adjusted the sound volume and stepped closer.

"The verified reports are that meteorites have struck downtown Atlanta and the surrounding area. All emergency units and first responders in the state of Georgia have been activated." The talking head was clearly agitated. Darryl frowned as he watched. Meteors from space? What the hell was going on?

"This just in," the talking head continued. "There are now reports of meteorite strikes across the United States and Canada. We are also trying to verify reports of these... space rocks are hitting locations in Europe and Asia. This is becoming a disaster..."

There was a rumbling sound permeating the entire shop. As the shop's merchandise began to vibrate on the shelves and metal display racks, Darryl swore and stepped to the front door. As he opened it, there was a flash, explosion, and shockwave from the South. Darryl scrambled back into his shop as garbage and debris were blown by his shop front window. The television flickered, then stayed on as a small automatic emergency generator he had installed years ago to help support the vault security kicked in.

As Darryl stood, frozen near the door, he heard the talking head on the boob tube exclaim "It's reported that the Smith Tower in Seattle, Washington, was just struck by a large meteorite. The upper floors are collapsing onto the downtown streets. Please everyone in the area, stay under cover. Do not go to..."

Darryl stopped listening. This could not be happening. The Smith Tower was just a few blocks south. He was fifty years old. He should be relaxing in his old age.

Jimmy, covered in dust and dirt, burst through the front door.

"It's hell out there! The top of the Smith Tower is gone. It's all over the street. And I just saw what I think was a meteor flash by, heading across the Sound."

Jimmy's words finally woke Darryl to action.

"You want to stay here, Jimmy? At least until we know for sure what's going on."

"No!" Jimmy replied. "I need to find my girl, Eve."

"You sure…"

"I'll bring her back here if I can. It might be safer."

Darryl nodded, then answered.

"You're both welcome. Be careful."

Jimmy nodded, then was back out the door.

Darryl locked and bolted the door. He then strode to the back storage room. Glancing around out of habit to ensure no one was looking, Darryl next swung the concealing wood panel away from the vault door. He spun the combination lock dial, then with practiced ease worked the combination. Darryl had the heavy door open in record time. He flicked the small interior light on and examined the interior. There was a couple of bank bags filled with cash, some ledger books, and a long hardwood gun case. Darryl grabbed the gun case, then shut and secured the door. One of the "Wise Guys" had asked him to hold onto the high-end over-under twelve gauge shotgun for him. He never asked why Darryl just stored it. He took the gun case to the front counter and opened it up. The twelve gauge, ornate gold inlay design and all, had a small cloth bag containing a handful of shells tied to the stock. Darryl took two shells, broke open the action of the gun, and loaded it. He placed it and the case behind the counter.

Darryl realized he did not know why he needed to get and load the shotgun. It just felt- right. He reached under the front counter and pulled out his Luger. A guy who owed him a gambling debt years ago had given the pistol to him as payment. Darryl had never been arrested for anything serious, other than a few misdemeanors in his misspent youth back East. Thus, he could legally possess firearms, which was another reason his employers liked him.

The guy who gave him the pistol had said it was a collector's item. Darryl had checked, and it was pretty rare, being an early Swiss military pistol in thirty caliber Luger, not the standard nine millimeters. He test fired it late one night in the alley behind the street shops, killed a beer bottle, then put it away. Darryl cleaned it at times when he was alone in the shop, so it was there if ever needed. So far, he had been lucky.

Darryl ignored the blathering people on the boob tube, as he knew they had no real information. The Mafia employee had good instincts, knew it was best he stayed put. There was no one waiting for him at his downtown apartment, not even a cat. He had a case of bottled water in the back, with some chips and snacks. In his small desk at the end of the front counter, he had a fifth of scotch. Darryl would shut down the generator in a few minutes if the power did not come back on. There was limited fuel in its tanks.

He stuck his Lugar under his loose fitting shirt, laid the twelve gauge on the floor out of sight. He went to his desk, fumbled in one of the drawers and found an old transistor radio. He turned it on and found there was still some juice in the batteries. Once he had a news station with someone ranting about what was happening, he went and shut off the generator. He never knew when he would be able to refuel the tank. Despite the dust and soot from the Smith Tower hit, there was still enough ambient light from the Sun shining through his front display window to illuminate to his store a bit. He poured himself a double shot of scotch from the bottle in his desk into a plastic cup he had and drank it down. He knew it was going to be a long day.

The long day turned into three long weeks. The radio's batteries lasted long enough for Darryl to hear that all the space rocks were not some natural disaster. Instead, there were launched at Earth from a brand new enemy. Of course, the fact that there appeared these six-wheeled overgrown ATVs with metal tentacles emphasized the fact this was not Kansas anymore, Toto. Then the oversized metal men thought to be robots at first but later seen as a form of cyborg appeared. They took out anyone who messed with the wheeled robots. These soon named robocops operated large circular shaped spacecraft which looked suspiciously like some starships from a well-known film series. These Falcons were joined by the Deltas (named after their shape) fighters which liked to blow holes in tall buildings. Darryl turned on the generator just once when he opened the safe and removed the bags of cash. He had a sneaking suspicion that any power used would attract the wheeled harvesters, the new given name of the six-wheeled robots. For they grabbed screaming humans and dragged them away. Someone soon discovered those humans taken were slaughtered for meat.

Rumbling and eruptions from Mount Rainier and Mount Saint Helens did not help. Before the radio shut down, Darryl heard that the Hanford Nuclear Storage area had gone critical and exploded. The three events were mitigated due to the prevailing easterly winds. Darryl knew that it would still be harder to survive in Seattle.

Darryl quietly checked his water supply. He had filled the sinks in the two restrooms with water from his hot water tank, then turned it off and disconnected it from the outside line. He had read somewhere that when the public plumbing system went offline, backflow pressure could rob your tank of its water. The former Mafia worker did not want to die of thirst. Nor was he in any hurry to wander outside and get harvested while looking for supplies.

The porn shop operator sat down quietly in the near dark of the store. He had learned some patience during his three years in the Army. His former employers liked to have their employees use military service to learn some specialized skills. Such as, how to use weapons to kill people who interfered with 'business.' Darryl had also been instructed in how to make an expedient field stove, a solar still to get water back from his piss, and explosives from household products. Darryl chuckled how after more than twenty years, that stuff suddenly became important.

Jimmy never came back. Darryl figured he was dead, a piece of meat in some Alien's larder. As for druggee Doug, he chuckled when he thought how nasty *that* piece of meat would be for the aliens. So Darryl played numerous hands of solitaire, looked at some of the old porno magazines on the discount table, and recounted the money in the bank bags. He had some two hundred fifty thousand dollars in currency. Darryl thought the bills might now be useful as toilet paper or kleenex, nothing more. There were no open shopping malls to buy expensive items even if he could go out without getting eaten. However, old habits die hard, so he kept the money for his employers.

Darryl's stomach grumbled. His breakfast had been a stale cracker he found in the desk with an antacid tablet for dessert. That reminded him that he would have to go out and locate some food soon, whether he wanted to or not. This forced diet helped his waistline, but not his alertness or strength. He started another hand of solitaire to take his mind off of his stomach.

"Come on, Ole Sol," he said to himself. "I'll beat you this time."

Even inside the shop, he heard the shot. The police and military were long gone so Darryl knew the firearm discharge was probably not by anyone he would want to meet. He moved towards the shop front door, with his Lugar in hand. Slowly Darryl peeked through the covering window blinds. He saw nothing moving outside.

Two bodies suddenly slid into the shop's entranceway, bumping his front door. He automatically stepped back from his perch, pointed his pistol in the direction of the interlopers. They began to whisper to each other.

"Honey, keep quiet. They'll hear." The voice was an adult woman.

"It's the puppy, Mom. He's scared!" The speaker was a young girl.

Darryl stood frozen. Two people. Alive. At his doorstep. Were they being chased by aliens?

He heard a loud shout which echoed down the empty streets. That sounded like a man's voice to him. The former mafioso quickly put two and two together. Men are chasing women and children, shooting at them. Not good in his book.

Darryl unbolted and opened the shop door so quickly that the mother and daughter pressed up against the door stumbled into the shop and almost fell. He saw they were both Gingers.

"On the floor," ordered Darryl. "If you want to live."

The mother saw the pistol and glanced out the door. A quick calculation and she was pulling her daughter to the floor behind a rack of DVDs.

" And keep the puppy quiet." The woman nodded at the whispered order.

Darryl shut and tried to bolt the door as quietly as possible. He then crouched down to listen. In about a minute he heard the rough voices of three males. They were arguing much too loudly in Darryl's estimation.

"That was a lousy shot, Bud."

"Shut up, Frank. They're hiding around somewhere."

"Look over here. Footprints in the dust and dirt." That comment was from an unnamed third male.

"What ya got. Sy?"

Darryl heard scruffled footsteps. He made sure he was in the dusty shadows of the shop as the men approached. Then someone pounded on the door.

"Hey, lady. We know you went in there. Can't hide your footprints." The man known as Bud seemed to be in charge. Bud pounded on the door again.

"Look it. We won't hurt you. Scouts Honor." Bud's comment elicited muffled laughter from Sy and Frank.

Darryl knew how to handle punk assholes. And that was who these three seemed to be. He stood up and put his free hand on the bolt.

"What do I get for opening this door?" he said in a loud voice. He heard one man curse in surprise. Darryl slowly began to turn the bolt lock.

"We could shoot you," opined Frank, which elicited a

muffled "shut up" from Bud.

"My stupid friend meant was we can share, be friends. Not a lot of us humans left here with all those harvester robs around."

Using the conversation to cover the sound of the well-oiled door bolt being opened, Darryl next moved his free left hand to the door handle.

"That's it? No added goods, like maybe some weed? Smack?" Darryl had his hand on the handle and thumb on the release latch.

"Hey, buddy, I thought we... "

In a smooth motion, Darryl yanked open the door before Bud could finish his comment. He shot the scrawny bearded malcontent between the eyes. Bud had a silver and gold plated .45 Automatic in his hand, only half raised. The man toppled over backward as the adult merchandise shop manager shot the man known as Frank in his gun hand. The cheap .38 caliber revolver clattered to the street as Frank screamed in pain. Darryl shot past his head at the dirty blond hair Sy. The bullet took off the man's right ear. Sy yelped, grabbed the side of his head where his ear had been, and took off running south down First Avenue. Frank followed him, howling like a banshee.

Darryl knew the shots and screams would draw the wheeled harvesters. He grabbed Bud's .45 off the sidewalk, then stepped over the body to retrieve Frank's dropped revolver. He jammed the two handguns in his Docker pants pockets. Darryl then grabbed dead Bud and moved the body out into the street. He started to go through the deceased pockets when he heard a familiar electric motor sound. In a flash, Darryl was back into his shop, shut and locked the door. He crouched and peaked out through the blinds. The hand holding the Lugar began to shake.

A six-wheeled harvester whirled into view. As Darryl had surmised, the alien robot was attracted by the gunshots and screams. It stopped by dead Bud, examined the body with a metal tentacle which zipped out from some hidden compartment in the robot's body. Its oversized basketball shaped dome 'head,' a combination of exceptionally bright and hot spotlight and some visual sensors for sighting blinded prey (meaning Humans), turned towards the shop front door. Darryl crouched down below the front windows and prayed. He shivered as he heard the scrape of the metal tentacle as it examined the door. The Mafia employee did not know if his bullets would have any effect on the metal monstrosity, but he would not be eaten without a fight.

Then it was over. The harvester used its tentacle to grab the recently dead Bud and zipped north on First Avenue. A couple of minutes later, the puppy gave out a little whimper.

"Hush him, Angie," whispered her mother.

"He's just hungry, Mom."

Darryl looked at the two females. He had not expected to have two visitors in his shop. Three counting the puppy. For the first time, he noticed the packs on their backs.

"You have food?" He asked.

"You gonna take it?" Angie asked defiantly.

"Angie!" Her mother scolded. " He just saved us." She looked at Darryl.

"Sorry about my daughter, she's just... "

"Scared. And rightly so,"Darryl said. "But do you have food? I'm about all out."

The two ladies began to empty their packs, and the puppy started to whimper. Darryl saw a box from Angie's backpack was powdered milk. He stuck his hand out.

" If you let me have that, I'll fix something for the pup."

Angie paused for a minute, then handed it to him. Staying low, he went to the back storage room. Darryl came out with one of his remaining water bottles. He then went to a display rack along the rear wall of the store and searched the packages of adult sex toys. Darryl found what he wanted. Using a box cutter, he opened the package labeled Baby Boys Booby. Below the title was 'Just Like Mommy's.' He soon had a realistic breast with an equally realistic nipple out. He had a supplied squeeze bulb and tube connected in record time.

"If you would mix some of that powdered milk in that water bottle, Missus…"

"Joanne. Call me Joanne, please, Mister—"

"Darryl will do."

In a couple of minutes, the milk was mixed, and the puppy was introduced to the faux but realistic human nipple. The pup soon got the message as Angie slowly squeezed the bulb and supplied the excellent tasting liquid. Angie giggled.

"Look, Mom. He has his own boobie!"

"Angie!" Joanne started to scold her daughter, then saw Darryl had a small smile on his face. She smiled back.

"We owe you, Darryl. Big time as my husband would say." At the mention of her husband, her face seemed to darken. Darryl reached over to one of the cans from the packs and picked it up.

"Hmmm. Green beans. Can I share this with you? My last meal was a cracker and an antacid tablet?"

"Oh, of course! Angies, hand me the P-38 can opener."

"I have one of those on my keychain," Darryl said. "Military?"

"My husband. Submariner." The cloud on her face came back.

"I still have some scotch left. Want a drink before dinner?"

"I could use one. Thanks." Joanne sniffed, wiped a tear from her cheek. In the background, Angie giggled as the puppy sucked vigorously.

Darryl supplied the libations and Joanne, with the help of Darryl's expedient field stove, served up some warm green beans, lightly toasted bread with butter, and a couple ounces of powdered milk. The scotch seemed to help relax Joanne. Darryl told the women they should keep the rest of the milk for the pup until they found some more supplies. Angie readily agreed and made another feeding for the puppy, now christened King.

Angie took King out near the back alley door to 'do his business' on some old papers Darryl had saved. He also showed the women the toilet facilities and explained the situation.

"No water in the system, so we put a trash bag in the toilet and, well, you know."

"I have a couple large trash bags in the bottom of my pack," volunteered Joanne.

"Good. I still have a couple rolls of t.p. With you here, we should be able to do a little scrounging. Angie can be the lookout."

Angie beamed at the situation. Darryl could tell she wanted to do something, anything, that made her useful and in control.

"Today we rest. This has been stressful. I have a couple of jackets and a coat to use for bedding. I've been sleeping on the smelly sofa in the back. Sorry I can't offer more."

"Mom, I have to go the bathroom."

"Okay, Angie. I'll watch King."

When Angie was out of earshot, Loanne asked a hard question.

"Was that the first man you... killed?"

Darryl paused and thought for a moment before answering.

"I shot at a couple of Hadjis in the Mid East as an Army grunt. I think I hit one, may have killed him. Now I did shoot somebody once, here in the States. For my Bosses." He looked ar Joanne intently.

"You know who runs places like this, right?"

" I have heard, Darryl. So, tv and the movies have some truth to them."

"Yeah, so, a guy owed a debt. My boss told me to make it past due. Gave me a twenty- two with a silencer."

Joanne's eyes widened a bit as she spoke.

"So, you—"

"I shot him in the shin. A dead man can't pay you anything. I told him the next shot would be in the family jewels." Darryl grinned. Then continued.

"Funny how he somehow found the money to pay up."

"So, Darryl. He lived."

"For a month," Darryl Answered. "Then his wife caught him in bed with the neighbor. Stabbed him right where it hurt. He bled to death."

Joannes' mouth dropped open. Then, she tried not to laugh, but couldn't help herself.

"God, I'm horrible!" she finally said. "That poor man."

"Yeah. If I shot that guy in the balls, he wouldn't have been able to screw the neighbor. Might have lived another ten years."

Joanne had trouble holding King she was laughing so hard. Angie walked out and asked,

"What's so funny?"

"I was just telling your Mom a story about playing ball games."

Joanne lost it. Darryle had to take King from her as she laughed so hard, she plopped down onto the floor.

Angie and Joanne were soon asleep with a semi-full stomach. Some more scotch for Joanne helped her relax. The Sun had not set when the two women were sound asleep. King snuggled up close to the two warm human bodies. Darryl sat in his desk chair and watched the innocent sleep. To keep busy, he first cleaned the Lugar, then checked the two recovered pistols. Darryl counted just five remaining rounds for his Lugar. The beat-up .38 revolver had three live shells. Now the .45 Colt automatic, that was a different matter. Judging by the gold and silver inlays, the pistol had been owned by someone with money. It still had seven rounds in it. Darryl just knew that dead Bud had a spare magazine or two, but the arrival of the harvester rob prevented him from doing a good body search. Well, it looked basically brand new. Darryl cleaned and reloaded both of the pistols. Then he sat. The man was just not tired. All the events of this day had wired him up as if he had drunk a full pot of coffee or took a hit from crystal meth. Thus Darryl sat and thought.

He had been putting off scrounging for food and water. Now Darryl was being forced into it. The supplies that Joanne and Angie had brought would last maybe three days if they were careful. Thus, he and Joanne would have to go out and scrounge. As he came to grips with this fact, the 'soldato' in the Mafia realized he had been scared for the last three weeks. The Squid aliens, as they were called, were this terrifying boogyman that had frightened him into inaction. Darryl chuckled to himself. All these years being around the violent sociopaths that populated Organized Crime, and NOW he was afraid. One of his former bosses had pulled him aside one day to discuss his future. Darryl's birth name had been Largo from Italy. He had anglicized it to Biggs years ago as it drew less attention from certain Federal Agencies. Thus, he could have some upward mobility.

"Well, Darryl, whaddya ya want to do?" The Minor Boss talked just like a character out of a bad Mafia Movie. In fact, he looked a lot like a character from a certain popular Cable Network Show about "Our Thing." Of course, Darryl never mentioned either item.

"What do you mean, Boss?" he replied.

"Look it. You have always been a good 'soldato'—a soldier, worker. But you're not dumb. So we know you want something more."

Darryl paused for a moment. He had known this conversation was coming. He knew that people who claimed they were not aggressively trying to better their lot in the Organization, made the Bosses nervous. Just like those people who were too pushy made them worry that they wanted to take someone's place. Things that did not fit in their prearranged pigeon holes disturbed them. Thus, Darryl's answer had to be careful.

"Boss, don't take this the wrong way, but I like where I'm at. I have a new wife, she has a bun in the oven, and you pay me well. You even let me earn a bit on the side, which you get your share of just as soon as I earn it."

The minor boss had held up his hand to stop Darryl.

"Hey, my man, no one is questioning your honesty. Hell, all these years, never short, never late, you never complain. So, you know, people worry. You're not like everyone else. So people worry about people who are different. Especially in this business."

"So. Boss, please," replied Darryl. "Don't worry. You have always been fair to me. Thus I am loyal. I don't have any hidden skeletons in my closet. I don't want to be a, a, supervisor. I am a worker bee. I like that. Fewer headaches."

The minor boss had stared at him for a few moments. Darryl knew he was processing all that had been said, according to the Mafia way of doing things. Which could be dangerous. The Boss spoke.

"Nothing gets to you, does it, Darryl. You're not scared, worried, are you?"

"Should I be?"

With that answer, the Minor Boss laughed, threw his arm around Darryl as he spoke.

"Ole Darryl. Solid as a rock. Nah, no worries, my man. You want to stay working outlets for us, so be it."

"One question, Boss."

"Shoot."

"These young guy coming up..." Again the Boss held up his hand.

"Say no more. You're protected by me and mine. I'll tell those young punks to leave you and yours alone. Or else."

No one ever wanted to learn what 'Or else' meant.

A whine from the pup King jerked Darryl back to the present. As quietly a possible he padded over to where the two redheads were sleeping and removed King from between them. He carried the puppy to the back door area and let him do his business on the newspaper. Then the Mafia Soldier returned the puppy to a spot between the two women. King snuggled up next to Angie and was fast asleep. Darryl tiptoed back to his chair and sat back down. He looked at the sleeping innocents and thought about what could have been. If things had been different, maybe he would still be with one of his two ex-wives. Perhaps the Mafia would have let him go to the straight life. He snorted to himself.

"Yeah, right," he whispered. "And I could have been a movie star. Or a stockbroker. Sure, with all my training." No, Darryl knew his experience had made who he was. A soldier, Bag Man for the Mafia. Nothing more, nothing less.

Darryl took another slug from his bottle of scotch. It was getting low. He had a bottle of champagne some wiseguy had left, and a tallboy malt liquor took off of some drunk patron. No other hard stuff was in the store. Another item for scrounging in the coming days. With that thought, Darryl made his way to the old stained sofa in the back storage area. He plopped down and tried to fall asleep. Finally, he dozed off.

Darryl Biggs awoke to the sounds of Angie and her mother talking. They were trying not to wake him, so he laid and listened.

"So, Mom. Are we going to stay here?"

"Where else is there, Angie? Darryl saved us, could have given us up. He seems honest enough."

"But, is he really... safe," Angie asked. "Those men at the church seemed safe. Then they tried to... touch me."

Darryl opened his eyes at that comment. He thought he had two sons and two daughters somewhere. Maybe. If someone had tried to grope them...

"I know, honey," answered Joanne. "The harvesters came and took them. Karma."

"And they almost got us, Mom. I'm scared."

Darryl rose and walked out to where the two women were talking.

"Morning. Depending on what happens, I may add the

'good' later."

Joanne smiled at him as Angie went over and picked up King.

"You have plans, Darryl?" asked the mother.

"A quick attempt on scrounging from a delivery truck in the alley. See how that goes. But first, some breakfast." Darryl mixed a bunch of catsup packets with a can of tomato soup to make them three mugs of hot liquid that passed as an attempt at some tomato concoction. That and a few saltines gave them a hot breakfast.

"Not bad, if I say so myself," opined Darryl.

"Thanks, Mister..." said Angie.

"Largo. My real Italian name. Not the anglesized Biggs. Back to who I really am." He looked at Angie and then Joanne.

" And your last names?"

"Smyth," replied Joanne. Darryl stepped forward with a proffered hand.

"Please to meet you, young ladies."

He shook hands with both of them, which elicited a giggle from Angie. Darryl scratched King's ears, and the pup licked his hand.

"Well, now that we are all formally introduce, shall we compare notes?"

The next half hour they shared their story and their knowledge of what happened and was happening. While Darryl had been able to hide out in his adult sex store, Joanne and Angie (short for Angela) had to leave their neighborhood after some rocks hit. They tried to make it across Puget Sound to the Bangor Submarine Base where her husband's boat was, but things were chaotic. Then they heard that a couple of rocks had hit the Base. Joanne knew that they would have to find a place to hide while things were sorted out. They tried a church on the outskirts of Seattle, but that almost turned into a disaster, Sick bastards tried to molest Angie, then the harvester robs showed up. Joanne and Angie made it out the back of the church as the harvesters came in the front.

"So why then downtown?" Darryl asked.

"I thought maybe we could find a Navy or Coast Guard vessel who might help some military dependents," Joanne replied. "But it was too late. We didn't need the radio to tell us the Squids own Puget Sound now."

Before the batteries died, Darryl had heard on his transistor radio that everyone was headed towards the interior of the U.S., away from the Coast. The Alien Tschaaa, their formal name, was advanced cephalopods, "Squids." Naval vessels only pissed them off.

"Did you hear about who they preferred to eat?" Darryl asked.

"They started to prefer people of color. The darker skin, the better," said Joanne. She shivered. "Those racists Krakens they call themselves, followers of the Squids, fit right in."

"Those three at my door weren't Krakens," said Darryl. "They were just feral ass- I mean, miscreants."

"Well Darryl, whatever they were, thanks again."

"De nada, like they used to say on the Mexican border. Now, we need to plan our scrounging and scavenging."

An hour later, Darryl and Joanne were exiting the rear alley door of the shop. Some twenty yards away in the alley was a former national delivery service truck. Angie performed lookout duties after Darryl had shown her the workings of the Luger.

"I've shot a gun before," Angie said.

"Well, here. You work the slide this way. It's loaded now. Point and shoot center mass, then run like hell."

"What if a harvester rob comes?"

"Don't shoot," replied Darryl. "Shut this back door and hide. Let your mother, and I handle it."

Darryl had checked out Joanne in the operation of the .38 revolver, and he had the .45 automatic. He had no idea what effect they would have on the harvesters, nor any alien.

And with that, the two adults dashed to the delivery truck.

The doors were unlocked, yet no one had ransacked it yet. They grabbed boxes and large delivery envelopes, stuffed them in two large garbage bags as Darryl counted to one hundred silently. When Darryl's count neared one hundred, he motioned to Joanne, and they scrambled back to the rear shop door. He grabbed an unopened water bottle from near the driver's seat as they exited. Then they were at and into the rear of the shop. Darryle closed the rear door and locked it as quietly as he could. Angie went to the box bed they had made for King and kept him quiet as the two adults went through the loot.

Darryl looked up, held his finger to his lips in the near-universal signal for silence. He tiptoed to the rear door and pressed his ear up against it to listen. The man heard a familiar electric whirring as a harvester rob went through the alley. He waited a couple of minutes until he was sure it was gone, then went back to the two ladies.

"Damned things are still scoping things out," Darryl said. "They must have some type of motion sensors or something in the streets and alleys."

"So what do we do?" asked Joanne.

"First, we inspect our loot. Then, I check our water supply. I need to figure out when we have to go out again."

The raid on the delivery truck had netted pharmaceuticals, some clothes, a couple of promotional fleece blankets, some food samples and various packages of batteries. Their big score was a couple dozen packets of a chocolate protein drink.

"Milkshakes!" Angie had squealed with pleasure.

"We'll mix water with them," said Darryl. "Which brings us to the next task. How much water do we have?"

Darryl soon had them helping him drain the last bit of water out of his hot water heater. Using the pans and containers he had, Darryl opened the drain on the tank. They recovered about a gallon of water before the water turned into a trickle.

"I knew I was low, but..."

"What now?" Angie asked.

"Well, I have a couple of water bottles in the back. Here, share this one I took from the truck."

Thy passed the water bottle around, with Angie sharing a bit with the puppy. Darryl sat for a few minutes in thought.

"Well, there was a Stop and Rob two doors down on the street corner," he said. "I guess we wait a few minutes, Angie plays lookout again, and we go on another raid."

"What about that harvester?" Joanne asked.

"I think it didn't stick around. We hit the store for water, and anything else we can find that is easy to carry. It may have been looted some, but…"

"You think the Squids hit the downtown, so fast and hard that people took off?" Said Joanne.

"Yes, I do. After the first day, when the rocks hit, I did not hear any activity on the street. The owners of that store, some Koreans, did not like me much, so they did not share much. But, they would not leave it wide open. They also have a couple of other locations, so they probably lit out for them."

Joanne pause in thought for a few moments. Then she answered.

"Okay. Let's get to it before that harvester swings around again."

The set up was as before. Angie performed as lookout, and the two adults were the scavengers Darryl looked at Angie.

"Remember, young lady, you…"

"Shoot, then run, then hide," Angie answered. Darryl nodded yes.

"Okay, let's move."

The adults moved down the alleyway until they reached the back door of the corner market. Darryl produced a small leather case. From it, he took some small thin metal blades and rods. Joanne gave him a quizzical look.

"Lock rakes and picks, Joanne. To open doors. From my misspent youth."

Darryl was soon at work on the large rear door lock. Within a minute, he worked the door latch and opened the door. He smiled at Joanne.

"Still have the touch," Darryl said. The two adults slid into the store, with Darryl using a small chunk of cement block to keep the door ajar just a bit.

Inside the business, it was dark and musty. Darryl used his cellphone as a small flashlight to locate the parts of the store he wanted.

"Joanne," he whispered. "Get water and cold drinks from this cooler. No dairy products, they have long since gone bad."

He moved to another wall cooler, began to load some wine bottles and Tall Boy malt liquors into a rucksack he had. Next, he went to the counter with the cash register. He was not there for the money but what may have been left behind. A short search and he had a half a pint of cheap vodka and an Asian version of a Bowie knife.

"Store security," he mumbled to himself. He took the knife out of the sheath and tested its edge with his thumb. It was sharp. He laid the Asian Bowie back under the counter and continued his search. He found a small flashlight with working batteries, a working cigarette lighter, and an unopened package of beef sticks. Those small objects all went into his pants cargo pocket, along with the pint

"Hands up, assholes!" The loud voice cut through the dark interior of the store. From the shadows came a dark clothed figure.

"Hey, man. Cool. There is enough for everyone," said Darryl as he raised his hands above the counter. He saw Joanne was crouched in the shadows behind the endcap of one of the aisles.

"Tell your bitch to show herself," the man snapped. Suddenly, a lightstick sprang to life as the unknown male bent it then shook it. The phosphorescent chemical in the lightstick cast a green illumination around the store's interior. It provided enough light for Darryl to see the man had military fatigues and body armor on. In his hands was a standard issued assault rifle.

"Hey, guy. I'm a vet too…"

"Shut up! Now tell your woman to come out where I can see her."

"Joanne, come on out. Bring your stuff."

"I saw you two, sneaking around,' the military man said. "Ole Private Reed here ain't stupid. That Lieutenant thought I was. Now he's dead, just so much dark meat."

"Dark meat?" queried Darryl.

"Ain't ya heard? Those Squids seem to think the darkest people taste the best. If they see you and someone dark in the street, they grab the darker person first."

There was now enough light from the lightstick for Darryl to see young Private Reed needed a shave, shower, and clean clothes.

"Hey, Private. We're all in this together,' Darryl tried to explain. "We're just passing through. You look like you've had it a bit… rough."

Reed let out a high pitched laugh that told Darryl the man may be several cans short of a six-pack.

"Rough? That Lieutenant tried to get us killed being all gung-ho and shit. So when he got zapped, I went one way, and everyone else went the other. Been on my own ever since."

"Well, then you know that harvesters have been snooping around, could hear all this talk."

"That robot wheels through here in the morning then comes back at sunset. I've been watching it for a week. As I said, ole Private Reed ain't dumb. Hell, I should be in charge, not some nigger."

He pointed his rifle at Darryl's face.

"Now, get the bitch out here, and show me what she has. Quit stalling."

Joanne stepped out from one of the display aisles, holding her pack in front of her.

"About time, bitch. Hey, you ain't bad looking."

"Here," Joanne said. "Take a look at what I have." She

shoved, half slung the pack at Private Reed. The result was that the quasi-deserter swung his weapon and attention toward her goods.

"Hey!" Redd called out.

Any further comments were drowned out by the report of the .38 in Joannes' hand, once hidden behind the pack. Darryl grabbed and threw the Asian Bowie at Reed in one smooth action. He ducked behind the counter as Reed screamed in pain. Then a three round burst from the assault rifle demolished the cash register

"You motherfucker! You slashed my face." Reed's cry seemed to come from a mouth that did not work well. Darryl assumed the pistol round had hit the body armor, and his knife throw had been partially successful. Darryl pulled the .45 from under his shirt as he worked his way to the end of the counter for a peek. He hoped Joanne was hidden behind the store display rows.

Further cursing was cut off as something yanked the back door open, and Darryl heard the whirring of a powerful electric engine. The harvester had returned early. He knew what would happen next, having seen harvesters in operation on the streets of Seattle.

"Joanne, shut your eyes" the former Mafia soldier called out. Darryl squeezed his eyes shut as what reminded him of an oversized camera flash cube from his young days exploded light in the interior of the corner store. Private Reed screamed, blinded. Then a whiff of burning human hair invaded Darryl's nostrils. The alien capture light and heat weapon had partially set Reed afire. Darryl head the clunk of the rifle as it hit the floor. The sounds of a human being yanked kicking and screaming from the store followed. Three quick shots from the alley told Darryl that the Army Soldier had brought a handgun into play. A scream was cut off in mid-vocalization. Darryl stayed behind the counter, his gun hand shaking.

Darryl recognized the sound of the harvester's metal tentacle retracting, Reed no doubt a piece of meat secured on the structure of the machine. Then, the loud electric engine sound as the harvester accelerated away. The adult shop manager stayed hidden for close to five minutes, wondering why the robot had not come looking for more prey. Had it been damaged by the pistol shots?

"Darryl, are you there?" Joannes' voice roused him to action.

"Yeah. Just scared shitless. Nice move with the pack and pistol."

Darryl slowly rose from behind the counter, tiptoed to the back door and looked out. Reed had lost his helmet and his pistol in the alley. Darryl snatched both up, then went back into the store. Joanne met him, holding the assault rifle.

"A bit warm, but still looks like it works," she said.

"Take it. And your pack. Head back to the shop," ordered Darryl.

"What about..."

"Damn it, woman, just go. Angie heard those shots, will be scared out of her mind. I got things to check here."

The mention of her daughter made Joanne respond with no further argument.

"See you in five minutes. Or I come looking." With that comment, she left the store.

Darryl controlled his shaking and went to recover his scrounged goods. He found a box of trash basket sized plastic bags and proceeded to fill them up with boxes of cereal, dog biscuits, canned sardines, potted meats, and powdered soup packets. The former store manager topped the bags off with some candy bars, snack cakes, and a couple small bottles of soda pop. Darryl doubled bagged the items so as not to lose them in the alley, He put Reed's helmet on his head, recovered his rucksack, stuck the asian Bowie in his belt, and hot-footed it back to his porn shop while balancing everything. Joanne met him at the back door of his shop.

"About time," she said. Then, Angie had her arms wrapped about him.

"I heard the screams, thought they were you." She began to cry.

"Now, young lady. No harm, no foul. Now, grab King. I found some dog treats he may be able to eat if we soak them in water."

"Where did you learn to throw knives?" Joanne asked him.

"Used to play darts using knives with some wiseguys. Never thought that skill would come in handy." He unwrapped Angie from him.

"Okay. Let's secure the doors and do an inventory. I don't plan on going out there again for a long time."

For the next three days, the three survivors laid low in the in the porn shop. Joanne had grabbed some toys from a rack, which included miniature chess and checkers set, plus a new deck of cards. A couple cheap dolls rounded off that booty, which took Angie's mind off of more adult subjects. Darryl 'modified' an adult toy with his Bowie knife, so King had something to teeth on. Darryl shared the Vodka with Joanne, which helped them both to calm down a bit. If they bounced around too much, they would upset Angie. She had enough stress as it was.

The harvester never came back, and Darryl wondered to himself if Reed had somehow damaged it, so it had to go in for repair. If he had, then at least he had been good for something. They managed to use the scrounged batteries to have Darryl's ancient transistor radio working again. Thus, on the third day after the raid on the corner store, the heard the news.

Organized resistance from a central government was over. Survivors were to head to the interior States of the U.S., the Midwest. There humans would try to rebuild. The Tschaaa, the Squids, owned the coastal cares. Like Seattle and Puget Sound.

"I wished they would have said all that sooner," fumed Darryl. "Like three weeks ago. Then everyone would know where we all stood."

"I guess they thought they could still fight back, the government that is," opined Joanne.

"Then they were idiots. Rocks hit Fort Lewis/McChord Joint Operations Base, then Bangor. What did they expect?"

At the mention of the submarine base, Joannes' face had clouded.

"Ah, hell, Joanne. I didn't mean..."

"Darryl, between us chickens John is not coming back." She looked at her daughter Angie, playing with King. "I have to raise her without her dad." The conversation stopped as both adults looked at the young girl. Joanne turned and looked back at Darryl.

"Could—"

Darryl cut her off.

"You can stay here as long as you want. I'll help you make sure that Angie can grow up. She will not be a piece of veal for some Squid asshole."

Joannes' eyes teared up. She leaned over and kissed him. There was some heat in the kiss, so Darryl gently but firmly pushed her back.

"Not to be a jerk but I am old enough to be your father. So, well... let's just leave it at that."

They both watched Angie some more, as they worked through their emotions. Suddenly, Joanne spoke.

"You can be our Godfather. Hell, you even have Mafia history."

"Now wait just a minute..."

"Godfather Largo. Or Darryl. First or last name, what is correct?"

"This is not funny, Joanne. If a 'made man' came along..."

"He'd be Squid meat. Your organization is kaput. Time to start a new one."

Darryl started to sputter. He knew how to run a drop spot for the old mob. What did he know about running anything more complicated?

Joanne called to Angie.

"Hey, darling. Come over and meet the new Godfather of First Avenue."

Darryl's Godfather position became more formal when 'refugees' began to show up about a week later. First, it was a family of four. He was out dumping the large garbage bag from their "toilet" when he heard voices out by the other bags. Darryl had moved them out to the South end of the alley as their numbers increased.

"These bags look recent," a male adult voice said.

"Someone is living here, Jim?" The question was from an adult female.

"Nearby, Jane. But they may not be friendly."

"But they may be and may have medicine for Mary."

As if cued by her name, Darryl heard a hacking cough from a young girl. He decided to take a chance. The newly appointed 'Godfather' stepped out from the shadows of the alley.

"Afternoon, folks," greeted Darryl.

The tall man named Jim pointed a semi-auto pistol at Darryl's approach.

"Stop right there, mister. Or be shot."

"Now that, sir, would ruin my day. But it would also ruin yours. Joanne!" Darryl called out over his shoulder.

"I got him," Joanne loudly replied.

She was covering Darryl from the shadows with the assault rifle. The dead Reed had been so kind as to leave it with an almost full magazine. Darryl watched as Jim tried to decide what to do. Stress and indecision were written all over the man's face.

"Jim," interjected Jane. "they could have just shot us down, no warning."

"Yeah, Dad," this from a young boy. Darryl now saw a what looked like a ten-year-old brown haired boy step from behind an abandoned car on the street.

"Son and a daughter, ah Jane is it?" Darryl tried to get a conversation going. Shooting would hurt someone and may draw the attention of the absent harvesters.

"Fraternal twins, Mary and Joseph. You have medicine, Mister..."

"Darryl will do. Now, can you ask your husband to lower his gun? The bullet end makes me nervous."

At that comment, Jim lowered his pistol.

"Can't be too careful," said the husband and father.

"Ain't that the truth. Now, shall we get off the street? Its been a while but a harvester could come along and any minute. They cue on human voices."

The couple looked and nodded at each other. Jim kept the pistol in his hand but pointed at the ground. Jane helped a very sick and blanket wrapped toe headed young girl across the street.

"To answer your question, Jane, we have some supplies. But I'm no doctor."

"I'm a pharmacist," replied Jim. "Well, was one until now."

"Well, hell Pilgrims," Darryl said in his best John Wayne voice. "We are a match made in Heaven. I have some packages of stuff with names I can't even pronounce. You can sort them out, I hope."

An hour later the adults had the sick Jane resting in one of the former video booths, now cleaned out. Just the day before Darryl and Joanne had raided a nearby import store of a bunch of rugs, curtains, pillows, and throws for use as bedding. There was plenty of extras. Joanne used Darryl's field expedient stove to warm some soup up for the survivors. The four made quick work of it which told Darryl they had been on the road for a while. The packages from the delivery van had some antibiotics for a nearby drug store that never received them. Thanks to the Tschaaa.

"Those are heavy duty meds," said Jim. "You were lucky to

find them." Darryl shrugged.

"Well, there was no one else around," he said. "So it wasn't hard. Except for the harvester robs."

A tearful Jane took that moment to grab Darryl, hug and kiss him.

"You are a Saint," Jane sobbed out.

"He's a Godfather," piped in Angie, overjoyed at suddenly having friends her age appear.

"Godfather?" asked Jim, as he looked around at the interior of the porn shop. There was just so much concealment of the stock Darryl could do. He saw no use in just dumping everything.

"Well, you know..." began Darryl. Joanne cut him off.

" Yes, he is the Godfather of First Avenue, Seattle. He saved us, he helped you. Things keep going, he may be the Godfather of the whole city. Got a problem with that?" Joanne glared defiantly at Jim as she finished speaking. Jim held his hands up in surrender.

"Hey, far be it from me to complain. You two just saved my daughter from a kick-ass infection." And the end of his statement, he proffered his hand to Darryl.

"I owe you, Godfather."

"Ah, shit," Darryl replied as he shook Jim's hand.

"If you want to help me, Jim, tomorrow we can go scrounging. That way the young ladies can stay with the children, Jane can rest up some more.'

"You have room, Darryl?"

"We'll *make* room, Doc."

"Doc? I'm just a Pharmacist... "

"Now who is the Godfather here? Huh?"

Darryl was told the whole story of how the family arrived in downtown Seattle as he and Jim were out scrounging. The Brown family had come from Kansas on a visit/vacation with relatives on the Kitsap Peninsula. Jim and Jane Brown and their two children had been heading to SEATAC Airport for their return fight when the Smith Tower was hit. They were stuck in a hotel as the airport was shut down. Then the real aliens appeared.

The two parents with their children Joseph and Mary left the hotel when the energy grid collapsed, and people began to go Feral. Evangelical Christians, they thought their Faith and their God would see them through. That all ended when Jim killed a man trying to steal ten-year-old Mary. His military training had come back in a rush. He crushed the miscreant's throat, took the dead man's pistol, and began thinking them or us. It took the family three weeks of hiding in many a God forsaken place to make it to downtown Seattle.

"Why'd you come downtown?" asked Darryl.

"We thought we could find some kind of boat to make it across to Kitsap County."

"With the Squids in the water?"

"We were not exactly thinking well," Jim replied. "We had not realized that those Tschaaa had taken over the oceans. Then, of course, we were here, with Mary sick."

"Yeah. I stuck it out as I had nowhere to go. And to be honest, the thought of being grabbed and eaten scares the wholly hell out of me. It was easier to hide in my shop."

They had decided to explore the area near the Smith Tower where one of the first Rocks had hit.

"Bet you everyone ran, left crap behind,' Darryl reasoned.

"Sounds good to me," Jim replied.

Jim brought his pistol, Darryl had the Over Under 12 gauge and the dead Reed's service automatic. He had the Asian Bowie stuck in his belt.

As they traveled the few blocks to the Smith Tower, they saw no new tracks of the harvester robs in the dust and dirt. Something shifted in one of the nearby damaged buildings and a hunk of the floor came crashing down to street level.

"Well, bet you the Squids decided no one would hide with

buildings crashing down," said Jim.

"Yeah," agreed Darryl. " I don't think creatures who traveled millions of miles would not figure things out."

"Think we'll find any guns and ammo in any of the stores, Godfather?"

"Unfortunately, no. The Seattle city fathers and mothers, in all their wisdom, chased out any store or pawnshop that carried such items. Said it made people safer," Darryl grunted. "Yeah, real safe. Until the Squids showed up."

They came across an SUV parked on the street with a piece of building edifice buried in its front windshield.

"Bet you the driver ran," Darryl said.

He used the Asian Bowie to pop the driver's side window and unlocked the doors. Jim looked in the rear cargo area and exclaimed "Bingo" Darryl went back and saw the reason for the comment. There was a full case of bottled water and canned dog food. Darryl pulled a large paper bag from the area and looked in.

"Bottle of scotch. You drink, Jim?"

"Not anymore. It almost destroyed my life. Jane and Jesus saved me, got me to become a pharmacist on the G.I. bill."

"Well," said Darryl. "It's not for everyone. It can help relax people when they are in danger of being eaten."

Darryl and Jim split the water between their packs. As they tried to decide about the dog food, Jim looked up.

"We have company, Godfather."

Darryl looked up and saw some half dozen dogs slowly advancing. One off to the right of the others was a massive shepard and mastiff mix.

"Damn, that dog is big," stated Darryl. "And she looks very pregnant."

"Want to chase them off?" Asked Jim.

"Hmmm. Not the big one. Dogs make great watch animals. I have an idea."

Darryl broke down the case of canned dog food and began

opening several. The ring top lids made this easy. He pulled a ballpoint pen from his pocket and used it to lever chunks of the food from the cans, then toss them around the street. He next threw the open cans towards the strays. He saved a full one for the massive dog. The dog grabbed the can with its jaws, walked back a few yards and crushed the can in its mouth. The crushing squished out much of the soft food. Darryl opened the second can and slowly approached the mastiff mix. He used the ballpoint pen to break up chunks from the dog food can and flipped them towards the massive dog. Eventually, the pregnant bitch moved to within a yard of Darryl.

"How is ya doing, girl? Want some more?" He dropped the open can in front of him and took a half step back. The dog confidently stepped forward and ate the offered food. Darryl slowly stretched his hand out an brushed the dogs head. She turned her head and licked his hand.

"I think you just made a friend, Darryl," said Jim.

"We'll see if she follows us. Let's check out that coffee shop on the corner."

The two men moved to the coffee shop. The front door had been smashed open. Darryl entered first, with the twelve gauge up on his shoulder. There was a bunch of dried blood on the floor and one broken display case. However, little else seemed disturbed. After making sure the back rooms and bathrooms were clear, they began to scavenge. They ignored the moldy sandwiches in the display cases and concentrated on packages of crackers, cookies, chips and snack cakes. Darryl also grabbed some two pounds of coffee along with some non-dairy creamer.

"We'll make some cowboy coffee, grounds in boiling water," he said.

Their packs now bulging, they exited the coffee shop.

"Think a harvester interrupted the people who smashed in the door?" Asked Jim.

"Yep. That's why the goods were still so intact, but there was a bunch of blood on the floor."

Darryl paused and looked at the business next door.

"Huh. A lawyers office. Hold up while I check that."

The door was shut but unlatched. With shotgun up, Darryl went in with Jim covering the rear. Everything was in order until the two men reached the back office. In the desk chair was a semi-mummified body, the dried brains of the individual splattered on the ceiling. Darryl went around to the back of the deck and found the pistol used to redecorate the ceiling.

"Glock 40 Caliber. Ten rounds left."

Darryl removed the round in the chamber, fed it back into the magazine. He pulled the trigger of the empty weapon, put the Glock into his pack.

"Locked door," advised Jim.

Darryl looked and saw it was secured with a large deadbolt. Out came his lock pick tools, and in five minutes he had the door open.

"Well, I'll be..." said Darryl.

Inside the security closet was a wrapped bundle of long guns. A quick perusal resulted in a count of one pump shotgun, a Mini-Fourteen rifle, two scoped bolt action rifles, a single shot shotgun and a twenty-two semi-auto rifle. Sealed ammo can revealed a mishmash of ammunition that seemed to match the mini-arsenal.

"Why is all this here?" Jim asked.

"Well, it's either held instead of payment or for one of his clients under indictment who could not have firearms. Either way, the gods are smiling on us."

The two men soon had the long gun loaded in a wheeled golf bag they found in the same closet, sans clubs. Darryl also found a lid of marijuana in the lawyer's desk along with a small baggie of heroin.

"Good for medicinal purposes," Darryl stated.

"Wonder why he shot himself?" Jim asked.

"Don't know. Maybe the guy knew his world as a scum sucking lawyer was at an end. What else was he good for?"

The two men laughed and exited the office. The oversized Mastiff mix was waiting for them, wagged her tail.

"She likes you, Godfather."

"Good, Jim. We need all the help—"

Before Darryl finished his statement, the pregnant female dog turned and growled. The two men stopped, listened. Finally. Darryl thought he heard an electric engine.

"Shit!" exclaimed the Godfather. "Take cover behind the wrecked SUV."

Darryl and Jim scrambled to the cover of the vehicle. Jim yanked open the ammo box. He grabbed and tossed a twelve gauge slug round to Darryl, dug out several nine-millimeter rounds for their pistols. Darryl replaced the buckshot round in the shotgun with the slug, then fed a couple of more shells into his handgun. The dog barked.

"Come here, girl. Come here," Darryl called out. The dog stood and growled at the advancing threat.

"I thought harvesters only took humans," Jim said.

"Maybe. And maybe a barking, growling dog will piss it off." He pointed across the street.

"Jim, head over there, by the building wreckage. Here, take the Glock. We'll try a crossfire. Remember to cover your eyes if that thing points its light weapon at you."

"Will do." Jim then sprinted to where Darryl had indicated. No sooner had Jim taken cover than the harvester appeared, whirring down the side street. As usual, the sight of the alien machine made him shake. He did not want to to be eaten.

The Mastiff mix began to trot around, barking and growling. The harvester ignored the canine, seemed to know there was human prey about. As it passed Jim, the trained military man shot two nine-millimeter rounds into the back of the large light beam weapon carrying ball-shaped turret. Darryl thought he saw one jacketed bullet penetrate the metal of the turret. The harvester Rob turned its dome front towards Jim. Darryl popped up from behind the SUV and controlled his shaking enough to fire a shotgun slug in the same area as the nine-millimeter bullets had hit. The slug round definitely penetrated. The shock of the slug caused the harvester to spin its entire mechanical body around to face a new threat. Jim stood up and emptied the forty caliber Glock into the back of the metal beast. The robot turned again, and Darryl fired his second slug next to the penetration hole of the first. Sparks began to emanate from the hole. The harvester started to spin around on its axis as smoke, and more sparks came from the dome. There was an internal explosion, and dark smoke gushed out from the machine. It froze in mid-spin as the smell of burning electrical wiring filled the air. The Mastiff ran up to the harvester and bit at one of its rubber covered wheels. Sparks flew from the bullet holes, and the dog jumped back. Then, silence.

Darryl clambered from behind the SUV, grabbed his pack and the golf cart.

"Let's act like sheep and get the flock out of here," he called out to Jim. The other man did not have to be told twice. He ran and grabbed one side of the wheeled golf bag as Darryl pulled on the other. To say they probably beat some land speed record with a golf bag was an understatement. The Mastiff mix trotted behind.

An hour later, Darryl had his third shot from the recovered bottle of scotch to steady his nerves. Why the thought of being eaten after he was dead was so terrifying to Darryl over all the other threats he had dealt with in his life was beyond Darryl's comprehension.

"I guess I need a shrink," he mumbled to himself. Angie walked up to him.

"So what is the big dog's name, Godfather?" The young girl asked.

"Hell, honey, I don't know. Go ask her."

"You know dogs don't really talk, don't you?"

"Well, Angie, there is always the first time for everything."

An exasperated Angie walked back to the Mastiff mix, who was getting to know King. The growing puppy was wriggling with joy at having another dog around. The pregnant bitch flipped him over and sniffed him all over. Then she lay down and began to give him a good tongue bath.

"I guess we didn't keep him clean enough," Darryl said to himself.

"You okay?" Joanne was the questioner.

"As okay as I'll ever be after coming close to being butchered and eaten by some bug-eyed monsters." The Godfather started to pour another shot, then stopped himself.

"I guess my Good Catholic upbringing is working against me. I can't be buried in a decent cemetery if I'm in some Squid's stomach."

Joanne stepped up and hugged him. "You're too tough and ornery to eat, Godfather," she said.

"Glad you think so, my dear. How's Mary?"

"Better. Jane's feeding her some of that powdered soup you two brought back. You did good in the scrounging department." Joanne frowned, then continued. "Except for this big ass dog that will eat us out of house and home."

"She and her pups will help keep us and all the others who come here safe. They'll warn us when there are Squids and such around. I'll go out and find some dog food tomorrow."

"No, you won't, Godfather. Jim and I will. You've done enough."

Darryl looked at Joanne and saw that look that women get that tells a man not to argue. He patted her arm. "Okay. You win," said Darryl.

Angie dashed up. "Her name is Diana!" she blurted out.

"And how do you know that?" Darryl asked.

"She told me, silly. You said she would."

"Diana, as in Princess Diana, of Wonder Woman fame?"

"Why yes, Godfather. How did you know?"

He smiled, then hugged Angie. His family was getting bigger.

Time to make some plans.

"Joanne. When you get a chance, we need to expand into that Import Store next door. Then scope out some other locations for survivors who show up."

"Won't that attract harvesters, Squids?" asked Joanne.

"We have more firepower now. And I know the harvesters are not as tough as they look after today."

He surveyed the scene of humans and canines.

"Dogs and humans conquered their world once before. We'll do it again, now."

It was a little over a year later, and Darryl was the Godfather of First Avenue for some four city blocks. Plus he was expanding up to Second Avenue. Darryl had to in order to find room for the survivors and refugees. About a week after he and Jim had killed the harvester, some dozen disparent people showed up. One was even an African American little girl named Emily, all of six years old.

"Where are your parents?" Jim had asked her. She began to sob.

"Goddamn Squids. I guess they are focusing on people of color," stated Darryl. He walked over, picked Emily up and hugged her. "I'm your Godfather now. We'll take care of you."

More people began to come in dribs and drabs. All had similar stories. The harvesters were becoming more selective on their prey, and preferred people with darker skins.

"Great. Racist aliens," Darryl grumbled. But the horrors were not ending. For some of the survivors brought stories of humans who were helping the Squids.

"They're called Krakens?" Darryl asked Juan Pena, a dark-skinned Mexican who had just arrived with his family

"Si, Patron. I mean, yes, Godfather. They have tatuajes, tattoos of their masters on their faces and bodies."

"You mean they have tattoos of squids and octopus on them?"

"Yes, Godfather. They are marks of pride to them."

Darryl began to curse long and hard. He even combined words no one there had heard before. Then he stopped.

"I understand another species eating us," said Darryl. "But humans helping them? That is Evil."

"They also have the robocops, Godfather. The big half man, half machine," added Juan.

"Have not seen those yet. Hope we don't."

Darryl called over to Mary and Joanne, his housing coordinators.

"Ladies. Another family to place, if you please."

Jim walked up to the Godfather. The tall human had become the right hand man for Darryl. His steadiness and honesty helped Darryl keep everything together.

"We need more food, Godfather."

"You cleaned out the Federal Building and surrounding offices?" Darryl asked.

"Yes. I think it's time to head towards the Ferry Terminal. I know it's close to the water, but—"

"We may finally run into those Squids we heard were snooping around. Well, time to see if it is true, that they have stopped harvesting us around here." Darryl sighed. Then he called out.

"Angie. Can you get me that fishing gear you found?"

Jim stared at him.

"Isn't that like poking the bear?" asked Jim.

"Nothing ventured, nothing gained. We have seen neither hide nor hair of harvesters for months."

Jim shrugged at Darryl's answer.

"You're the boss. You've been right so far."

"Well," added Darryl. "We will be armed with rifles in case a harvester comes around. Or we see our first Kraken."

Just over an hour later, every hook, line, and sinker Darryl and Jim put in the water off of the ferry dock netted a good sized fish. The two-man team soon had an example of almost every saltwater fish they had ever seen.

"Man, where did all these fish come from?" Asked Jim.

"No boat traffic, no other humans, they've been reclaiming some of the areas around the Port of Seattle as theirs," replied Darryl. "Next the seals and sea lions will come back."

"How about Orcas?"

"Good question, Jim. I wonder if they are a threat to the Tschaaa?"

"Good afternoon, humans." The loud slightly accented voice came from behind them. Darryl slowly turned around and saw his first robocop. How such a large being had snuck up on them was beyond his comprehension. It looked like a character from now-defunct Hollywood, with a helmet, and visor covered head. The jaw on the close to seven-foot cyborg looked a bit more massive than one on a Homo sapiens. Jim slowly reached for his pistol and Darryl motioned "No."

"Ah, good afternoon, Mister," Darryl said.

"You may call me Ismael. It is a pleasant sounding Earthling name. My ancestors came from Earth, but they were not Homo sapiens."

"That must have been a long time ago-Ismael." Darryl had learned how to talk with psychotic killers while in the Mafia. Those skills would serve him now.

"Yes. Millions of your years I believe."

"So, Ismael. I'm Darryl, this is Jim. I take it we are not on the menu,"Darryl stated.

"Menu? Oh. I understand," replied Ismael. "No, my Lords have their own source of cattle, of meat. Plus some have re-developed a taste for fish."

"Well then, Ismael. What can we do for you?"

The statuesque being stood rock still for a moment, as if deep in thought. Then Ismael answered.

"The Breeders and female Caretakers want me to inform you to stay away from that area you humans called the Seattle

Aquarium. It is a breeding Creche area for the Tschaaa young. If you harm them, even by accident, your existence will be terminated. Do you understand?"

Darryl knew he and his community were on a tightrope, and the answer he gave could lead to the collapse of everything. He swallowed and tried not to shake as he answered.

"Uh, I have not seen Breeders or Tschaaa young. I have only heard them described."

Darryl thought he heard some clicks, felt high-frequency vibrations. Again the robocop spoke."

"Turn and look where you fishing lines are placed."

Darryl and Jim turned slowly and looked down into the water. Staring up at them was a large cephalopod shape with huge eyes. As the two men stood in shock, much smaller versions of the creature appeared. Breeder female and young looked up the two humans, barely moving in the sea.

"Would they like some fish?" the Godfather finally croaked out.

"That may be an acceptable action."

Jim bent down, picked a large flounder they had just caught. He held it up for the being called Ismael to see.

"That will do," Ismael stated.

Jim tossed the fish near the Breeder. Five digit hands grabbed the offered fish. The Breeder held it out of the water, making some half-dozen young Tschaaa try to crawl up her to grab the prize. Then the creatures disappeared into the darkness below.

"I will go now," said the robocop. Jim finally found his voice.

"Will we see you again?" asked Jim.

"Perhaps, human. Please stay away from the Breeder area."

With that last comment, the cyborg turned on its heal and strode away. It was a good minute before Darryl found his voice.

"That was... special."

"Godfather."

"Yes, Jim."

"I think I crapped myself."

"I think I also did. We bring the dogs next time for early warning."

"Yes, Godfather."

Human renegades known as Krakens showed up a week later. They apparently had not gotten the word about the mutual non-aggression that Ishamel had talked about. The first hint there were nearby was a screaming girl. Men and women with weapons responded. Darryl found the half dozen Kraken men and women, tattoos and all, cornered in front of the former Federal Building on Second Avenue. They had young Emily.

"Stay back, or the picaninny gets it!" The supposed leader, face covered with a dark tattoo of some multi-limbed cephalopod, held a blade to her throat. He was used to getting his own way with little resistance.

"Why not let her go?" Darryl called out. "How important can one little black girl be to you?"

"She's Dark Meat. She gets harvested," was the shouted answer.

"How did this happen, Jane?" The Godfather asked.

"She wandered off, away from the dogs and us. You know how she likes to explore."

"Curiosity killed the cat," replied Darryl. He stepped closer to the Krakens.

"What will you take in trade?" The Godfather asked.

"Nothing, She's dark meat. Cattle."

"Well at least tell me your name, so I know—"

Darryl would often wonder how such a massive canine as Diana could sneak up and move so fast. So concentrated on Emily were the adults that Diana seemed to explode from behind some stone benches near the Federal Building entrance. She had her Mastiff sized jaws chomped on the head of the Kraken leader before anyone realized what was happening. Emily was knocked aside as the Godfathers people reacted swift and violent. Shots rang out with few returned as the Krakens were shot down like the rabid animals they were.

Diana, having crushed the unnamed Kraken leaders head like a ripe melon, limped over towards Emily as adults clustered around her.

"Hey!" Darryl called out. "Diana's hurt."

Immediately, people clustered around the canine heroine. Evelyn Johansen, a trained veterinarian, responded and examined the Mastiff Mix.

"A bullet went in and out of her leg," she told Darryl. "With some TLC, she'll be just fine."

"I know just the person to provide that," Darryl said.

He walked over to Emily. When the young girl saw the look on his face, she began to cry again.

"I'm sorry, Godfather. I didn't realize where I was until those,, those—"

The Godfather bent over and looked her in the face.

"Diana was hurt saving you. You realize that?" He asked.

Emily nodded 'yes' as she sobbed.

"So, you get to nurse her back to health. Sound fair? No more exploring."

Emily nodded yes, wiped her eyes with her hands, then hugged Darryl.

"I'm sorry, Godfather," she said.

"I know you are," the Godfather answered. " Doctor Johansen will tell you what needs to be done. Now, run along."

Darryl stood and watched as his people drug off the dead Krakens after stripping them of everything useful. He sighed. Now came the scary part.

The Sun was beginning to set as Darryl walked towards the entrance way to the former Seattle Aquarium. He held a pristine Sockeye Salmon filet high above him as he walked. He hoped who or whatever acted as security for this place saw the "I come in Peace" gesture, and understood it.

He was surprised as hell when a Tschaaa alien came rolling

out of the Aquarium on a six-wheel vehicle, similar to a harvester rob but without the turret. The Tschaaa alien stopped in front of Darryl, examining him with those oversized eyes of theirs. The Godfather noticed a sizeable box-shaped object was suspended by a thick strap around the bear-sized creature. To say he was surprised when English language sounds came from it was an understatement.

"We speak-again, human. More fish I see."

"You are the female I met before," Darryl replied.

"Yes. Now another offering of food. Why?"

The man called the Godfather took a deep breath and let it out. The Mafioso assholes he had dealt with in the past did not scare him as these Squids did.

"We killed some humans who work for you. Kraken, they are called. They—"

"So humans killed humans," interrupted the Tschaaa. "We think killing your own kind is a sickness. But you humans are quite good at it. How is that our... concern?"

"They said they work for—"

"It does not matter what they say. They have no connection with Breeders and Young. I thank you for the fish. Now please leave."

Darryl knew when to recognize and follow orders. He handed the fish to the Breeder, then turned to walk away. As he did, he mumbled to himself, "Universal Translator. What next?"

No more Krakens appeared. Darryl and company heard radio broadcasts about a man called The Director who had set up some form of government in Key West, Florida. This Director, Adam Lloyd, sounded like he was trying to thread the needle between surviving, helping others, and deal with beings who could kill you at the drop of a hate. To Darryl, it sounded like his career with Organized Crime. He heard some representatives of the Director nosed around, but none directly contacted him. Thus, life went on.

Darryl, as the Godfather of downtown Seattle, became the central authority figure, as well as an actual father figure. He officiated at christenings, weddings, funerals, graduations (they started a school for the increasing population) Quinceaneras, Proms, you name it. There was soon two thousand human survivors of all types imaginable. Plus, a couple hundred dogs to protect them. Rooftop gardens provided fresh food to supplement the fish and other seafood. The Tschaaa Breeders came around their fishing stations, and Darryl always paid them 'tribute' with the best of the fresh caught, for they were the true Dons of the area. Through salvaged solar panels, windmills and generators, downtown was electrified once more. The former Federal office building and surrounding high rises were turned into apartments for the residents. Life was as good as it could be under an occupying force that could eat you.

"Godfather, are you in there?" Angie's voice and knocking jerked him back to the present. *My God*, he thought. He'd been sitting here for at least a half hour behind his "Be Back in Fifteen" sign. *Early dementia?* He hoped not.

"Sorry, Angie. Just thinking." He went and unlocked the door. Angie had a hot plate piled high with food. She also had two mugs of coffee. Darryl pulled up a stool to the counter and attacked the plate. He looked at Angie sipping coffee between bites of his food.

"Coffee will stunt your growth, young lady."

"Yeah. Right." Angie added a derisive sigh to her reply. She set the coffee down and gazed at Darryl.

"Well, spit it out, Angie. I know that look."

"Two questions, Godfather. First, why did you not remarry? There are a bunch of women here that are interested in you."

Darryl laughed. He had heard veiled references to that in the past, but leave it to Angie, like a daughter to him, to be blunt.

"I tried it twice before, and it did not work out. Besides, power is sexy. I know people have allowed me power. So, would a woman at my age be interested in me or the power?"

"That is a fair answer," stated Angie. "Now, the next one." She pointed at his neon sign.

"Why Vile Smut? What is that all about? It seems like you were disrespecting what you were doing for a living."

From the mouth of babes, Darryl thought. Angie had grown up for the past going on seven years around various types of pornography most young ladies her age had never been exposed to in any fashion. He had carried legal adult toys that made even him blush.

"Started out as an inside joke. This store was the target of many a 'clean-up campaign' by the city fathers. At times I closed it down, then started it up under a new name to throw people off." He pointed at the sign, lit in all its glory.

"I put that together, Retro neon looks at all, myself. Since people claimed I dealt in vile smut, I figured I'd call it that. But my bosses would never let me put it up out front."

"And now they are dead," said Angie.

"That they are," the Godfather agreed. "But sex and fetish that does not hurt someone are not vile. Sex is part of life—and love."

"People say the Tschaaa think we are just nasty monkeys, don't understand how we want to have sex all the time," Angie added. " Or to kill each other all the time."

"Those are the great mysteries," Darryl agreed. "We humans want to make love, have babies. Then we kill the babies when they grow up. Sex and love changes to violence and hate. Why?"

The two humans sat silent for a few minutes, deep in their own thoughts. Darryl broke the silence.

"Well, tell your mother the food was excellent, as usual. Now, I have to get to work. Being the Godfather is not…"

The bell on the shops' front door, dinged as someone opened it. Darryl quickly stood up, his hand reaching for a concealed pistol under the counter. People around here did not ignore the "Be Back in Fifteen" sign. He saw an average sized

Asian man in a new business suit, something the Godfather had not seen in years. Everything in downtown was recycled. The man saw Darryl, bowed.

"Please excuse my rudeness. I am looking for Mister Darryl Largo."

"You got him. And you are?"

The man, whom Darryl now saw was Japanese, smiled and bowed again, a hair lower. Then he extended his hand to shake.

"Again my apologies for barging in," the man said in almost flawless English. "I was told you were the one to discuss... business with, here in Seattle." He glanced at Angie who stared back unafraid.

"Angie," said Darryl. "Please tell your mother how excellent a cook she is. See if she could brew some tea for my Japanese Friend and I."

Angie knew the drill. She would tell Joanne that a stranger was around, and somehow had slipped into the inner sanctum unannounced. Someone would get their ass reamed for that. Right now, Angie and Joanne would make sure Security showed up ASAP.

"Yes, Sir." Angie slid out the door past the man and was gone in a flash. The visitor watched Angie leave, then turned towards Darryl. He presented an ornate business card with his left hand. As Darryl took it, the Godfather saw the little finger was missing.

"My card, sir."

Darryl pulled his reading glasses from his shirt pocket, read the inscription.

"Akira Nagato. Import-export Free Japan," the Godfather read the card out loud.

"Yes, at your service, Godfather."

Darryl took off his reading glasses, looked hard at the Japanese man. "You know who I am, and somehow got through my people unannounced."

Nagato bowed again.

"Please. If I have offended you... "

Darryl Largo held up his hand to interrupt.

"Not to be rude on my part, but let's cut to the chase, shall we? Yakuza, yes?"

Akira Nagato smiled, nodded 'yes.'

"I should know that someone of your capabilities to survive here all these years could quickly assess who I am."

"Now the only question is, why are you here," stated Darryl.

"Why, to do what all of us...different people do. Discuss unique business arrangements."

Darryl examined the man in front of him Akira Nagato carried himself as the one used to command. He had people underneath him in the organization in which he belonged who would jump if he said "jump" and only ask how high. However, Darryl had no desire to have new bosses. So, things were about to get sticky.

"Well, Mister Nagato..."

"Please. Call me Akira. We are equals here. Or I am the one who may be in the inferior position. For this is your kingdom."

"You're not trying to bullshit me, are you, Akira?" the Godfather asked.

The Japanese man smiled.

"In moments, you will have loyal soldiers who could do me harm and dispose of my body in the sea. I have just myself. So, how could I have a superior position?"

Man, this guy is smooth, thought Darryl. He couldn't help himself. He liked this Yakuza gentleman.

He glanced over Akira's shoulder and saw Jim and his now seventeen-year-old son standing just outside the front door. Jim had the pistol he had shown up with years ago in his hand, and his son John had an assault rifle. Darryl gave them the "high" sign, and they backed off. Akira was right. He could just have him shot and feed to the fishes. Or the Tschaaa. Darryl chuckled.

"You like liquor, Akira? And call me Darryl."

"Why, yes-Darryl. I drink bourbon, scotch—"

"Ever had good old American moonshine?" rhe Godfather asked.

"I don't believe so. Is it flavorful?"

Darryl laughed. "I'll let you decide that."

An hour later, and several shots of downtown moonshine, Darryl and Akira were sipping the hot tea Joanne brought down. She smiled at Akira as she gave him the once-over. Joanne would let him know later if she saw something wrong. The Japanese Yakuza had loosened his tie and unbuttoned the top of his dress shirt. Darryl got a glimpse of the edge of the intricate body tattoos Yakuzas were noted for worldwide. The missing little finger told Darryl he had paid a severe debt of honor. Akira smiled at the former Mafia Soldier as he spoke.

"You have plied me with powerful drink and now will take advantage of me, my new friend."

"I? Take advantage of a Yakuza from Free Japan? How could I?"

"Through stealth and Western alcohol. How else?"

The two men laughed. Then Darryl set his tea down and leaned forward.

"So, despite you having a position in Free Japan, which was not Infested. In fact, your people came here to help the Unoccupied States fight the Squids, which has led to this alleged Great Compromise..."

"It is real, my new friend. Trust me on that. The broadcasts from President Paul, she with the Spine of Steel, are real. The Tschaaa Lords and we will live together."

"In harmony," said Darryl.

"In some form of co-existence. The Guardian Angels, former robocops, will see to that."

Darryl shook his head. "It's just so hard to believe. After living under the Sword of Damocles."

"That is the myth about the sword suspended by a hair. With

guardians on the Base One,　in orbit, the sword had been removed."

"So that is where the rock that took out the Smith Tower came from?" asked Darryl.

"Yes. And many more," Akira answered.

"So, you want to make a deal with little ole me. Why?" asked Darryl again.

Akira sipped his tea, set it down.

"In honesty, the Yakuza are the only organization similar to your Mafia in existence. Even the Russians were nearly wiped out. As were the Triads, the Albanians, the Czechneans, various radical Muslims." He leaned back in his chair, then continued.

"But we are relatively small in number. And are under extreme scrutiny by the New Samurai who help to rule Free Japan."

"Like Ichiro Yamamoto," added Darryl.

"Yes. Ichiro and his wife, Abigail, the Avenging Angel. They are legends in the flesh."

Now the Godfather leaned back.

"So, as I am here, not under scrutiny, you can use me to expand as well as market you... products."

"Yes, exactly," responded Akira.

"And the split is fifty-fifty," said Darryl.

"Hai. Yes," answered Akira.

Darryl sat thinking. He had a reasonably good set up. However, that was because he had expanded into a vacuum. With the old U.S. of A being reformed, with that would come more law enforcement, local government, rule, and regulations. They would use Darryl for a while. Then they would remember who he used to be and he would be frozen out. He picked up the DVD Akira had provided him.

"So you have real Squids helping you make this live... hentai. This tentacle sex."

"Yes," replied Akira." And as I explained, the market is for humans and Tschaaa. The Squids seem to become infected with some of our vices. To be honest, we have people working on certain substances that will affect them just as much as heroin and cocaine does humans."

Darryl stared at the DVD. Then he looked at Akira.

"No drugs to my people. The Squid, I hope they rot in hell. The local Breeders and I may have an understanding, but that's it. Some piece of shit Kraken or Squid ate my kids, my ex-wives. The ex-wives may have been pains in the ass. But no way did I want them eaten by some monster."

The Godfather of downtown Seattle dropped the DVD, stuck out his hand. Akira took it and shook it. Darryl held on to it a bit longer.

"Just one thing. All due respect, you fuck over my people here, I fuck over you. I expect, judging by a missing digit, you think the same about me. Right?"

Akira smiled.

"As they said in that classic movie so many years ago, I think this is the beginning of a beautiful friendship."

Two months later, Darryl Largo stood in the former Chase Bank on Second Avenue in downtown Seattle. It was renamed the First Bank of Downtown, with Daryle as the CEO. When the Unoccupied States kept "greenbacks" as a valuable currency, so did other human communities. Money is as much a state of mind as to what it represents than anything. So Darryl dealt both in cash and precious metals which were salvaged from all the abandoned areas. Of course, bartering for certain goods was still done, as with weapons and drugs.

Darryl was waiting for three significant representatives of the now reorganized United States of America. Two were legends he was looking forward to meeting. Colonel Ichiro Yamamoto and General Torbin Bender were both of the Key West Attack. Anyone who killed Squids with blades, as well as offed Krakens. The Godfather wanted to meet. The third person, Paul Miller, he was not so keen to know. For Commissioner

Miller was in charge of all Federal Civilian Law Enforcement Bureau activities. Darryl knew he had snooped around in the prior Mafiosos records.

The Godfather sighed. Well, he could not avoid it. Plus, he had been told that he was being held up as a shining example of how a community could survive under the heal of the Squids and do so without sacrificing fellow humans as meals for the Tschaaa. Thus, he thought he might just get through this day unscared, and without anyone the wiser about his new side job with the Yakuza. Unfortunately, an unannounced fourth member of the group threw him for a loop.

Darryl Largo had not expected to meet a Tschaaa Breeder. He and his people froze as the Squid used its cartilage supported limbs to walk almost crablike into the meeting. A security detail of the now legendary Banshees provided a protective ring around the alien, should someone not be able to control their anger. He saw the metal of all the humans, could tell they were tough customers. Darryl tried not to stare at the Breeder as the introductions were completed.

"And, Mr. Largo, the Tschaaa Breeder is known to us as Dorothy, her chosen human name. She is to be a pilot with the Banshees, flying a modified harvester Ark when it is ready. Part of the Great Compromise."

Well, Darryl thought, I dealt with murderers, I guess can deal with beings that used to eat my people.

"Pleased to meet you all," Darry said. "Jim here has been my most recent contact with the Tschaaa, although they have kept to themselves the last few months. He can take whoever you wish to the Seattle Aquarium area to meet the Breeders there."

"That sounds like a good idea," General Bender replied. "By the way, the President wants me to pass on her warmest regards for the job you did here. You helped save thousands from unfortunate circumstances and developed a working relationship with our new allies during a time of strife."

Darryl knew what Bender really wanted to say was he did

not have to kill any Squids nor feed any humans to them. The Godfather shrugged before answering.

"I just did what I had to, giving the situation."

"Well, you did an excellent job, and are an example going forward," replied Torbin Bender. "Dorothy, shall you go with Jim here?"

"Yes, of course." The translator gave the Tschaaa female a bit of a Midwestern accent. Wonders of technology thought Darryl.

The group split up a bit, with the two Heroes of Key West mingling with the crowd of well-wishers on the street outside. Everyone wanted to meet and greet the two men who came so close to killing the Tschaaa Lord responsible for millions of humans being turned into meat by an alien species. Jim went with Dorothy and the Banshees to connect with the Creche.

"I'd like to see your adult sex shop," Paul Miller had said. "The President is wanting to ensure the First Amendment we enjoyed before the Infestation is alive and kicking."

As the two men walked down towards First Avenue, Darryl felt out the Commissioner's general attitude. "So what do you think, Commissioner? Big Government presence in things to do with sex and adult entertainment, enjoyment?"

"You can call me Paul, as I think we'll be talking a bunch in the future. The formerly used name was Biggs, yes?"

"I knew you'd check on me," replied the Godfather. "So, any outstanding warrants?"

The Commissioner laughed.

"If there were, they'd be void. Madam President said that any people short of a serial killer, war criminals, sex offenders, and the such get a pass 'Go', get to start over again."

"Krakens also?" Darryl asked.

"Case by case basis. Like the Nazis, some were 'party members' in name to survive. She wants the country, the world to heal. No more fighting the War Between the States a hundred years later over grudges. However, no more recreating the

Mafia, whether you want to or not."

The two men arrived at Vile Smut. A Japanese clerk named Goro, supplied by his hidden partners, was manning the store. A lot of the sex toy merchandise was new, the result of 3D printer technology. Newer DVDs found in warehouses had been added to the stock along with brand new ones made recently. Sex was still a very sellable commodity in all its forms. Paul Miller looked the stock over then went to a rack of hentai. He picked up a 'live action' recording of tentacle sex involving a Tschaaa and a human.

"Why did I know you would take a look at that kind of DVD?" said Darryl.

"Because, Godfather as they call you, this is a very problematic activity no one foresaw. Who would have imagined intelligent alien octopi would show up and we would have to share the planet with them?"

"So, the President has a problem with it?" Asked Darryl.

"Sandra Paul does not care what two consenting adults do. And since the Tschaaa involves are sentient, consenting adults, as perverse as it seems, she will not interfere. However, she is not the problem."

"Who is?" Darryl asked.

"The Tschaaa Lords and Breeders," the Commissioner answered.

"Why? Why would that matter... wait a minute. They think we're nasty monkeys because we pork each other all the time as well as kill each other. So they think we are debasing them as a supposed superior species? "

Paul Miller smiled at Darryl.

"They had that come to Jesus moment with Andrew our cyborg friend and that unique mystical Breeder named Cassandra. They realized since coming to Earth for a new meat source, they were no longer the Tschaaa of old. Like killing each other, massacring the young of others for no reason, they knew a dark side was coming out. So, of course, they blamed coming in contact with us."

"This is ridiculous," Darryl interjected. "They came here to *eat* us. They kept us cattle, ate our infants as veal. Now they say we are corrupting and defiling their pristine culture. Give me a fucking break."

Darryl could not believe he was having this conversation. Who cared what a bunch of Squids who killed and ate millions of humans thought?

"Well, Darryl, as part of the Great Compromise so we would not go down the path of mutually assured destruction, humanity agreed to listen to Tschaaa concerns. We are going to have teams of Squids and Human Police working together very soon."

"So I'm going to have to start pulling stuff off the shelves?"

"Not yet, Darryl," replied the Commissioner. "Just be circumspect about selling it to Tschaaa."

The Godfather stood silent. He wondered what Paul Miller would say if he knew that Squids were already coming in, sans translators, a passing a note with a code on it to get the product.

"While I'm here," continued the Commissioner, "some wiseasses have developed a Squid version of meth, crack, and smack. I would appreciate it, with your previous experience in the human underworld, if you would pass on any information on these substances. They are beginning to play havoc in Creche culture. That havoc could destroy the Great Compromise in its infancy."

"What about Andrew and his new Guardian Angels? I thought, Paul, they were going to be this huge peacekeeper force?"

"They will try to keep us out of a Tschaaa/Human War, help with massive disasters, but they do not want to be our Caretakers. They will be a symbol of good, but won't be this force of superheroes who will appear at the drop of a hat."

"So I'll see cops walking the beat again?" asked Darryl.

"Glad you brought that up. Mister Largo, as the Godfather of Downtown Seattle, I see you already have a security force that keeps order. Until things are better organized in the expanded U.S.A. I would appreciate you maintaining order. Use force within reason. We are working at setting up a new court system."

Darryl laughed.

"I was rousted by beat cops in my younger years. Now I'm supposed to supervise them."

"Your President and country would be most appreciative," said Paul Miller. "Now, I think I need to get back with the others." He shook Darryl's hand. "I'll keep in touch."

"I figured you would," responded the Godfather.

After Paul Miller left. Darryl nodded at Gor. The clerk dialed on his cell phone, spoke a few phrases in Japanese, then disconnected the call. His nod told Darryl that Akira had been notified and would be in touch, soon. Business in both the porn and the new drugs was brisk. The Godfather did not care if it hurt the Squids. Fuck those human killers. He'd just as soon see them rot in hell.

Things went well with the meetings and immediately after. The Creche at the Aquarium was brought on board officially, and the Tschaaa were soon seen moving smoothly up and down Puget Sound. Of course, that made it easier for Darryl to conduct his business. With the population suddenly increasing to six thousand souls, the Godfather had more customers as well as citizens for whom to provide the necessities.

"We will keep things as they are for as long as possible," Akira had said during a recent visit. "When raids begin..."

"I don't think we need to worry anytime soon," answered Darryl. "The Federal Government is way too busy dealing with more serious matters."

Darryl would soon find he spoke too soon.

The Raid happened early one morning a month after the visit by the Commissioner. Darryl had converted the back of the shop into a lovely bachelor apartment, king-sized bed and all. So when the front door was smashed in before sunrise, Darryl was up with the original Over/Under 12 gauge he had from Day One as well as his .45 automatic. The former Mafia soldier came out yelling ready to kill. The shock was when he saw the perpetrators were all Tschaaa Breeders and young.

"What the hell are you doing?" The Godfather yelled out. One female Squid with a translator yelled back.

"You are corrupting our young!"

"You ate my kids!" Darryl yelled back.

It must have been something Paul Miller had said about getting along that kept him from blasting the Tschaaa. Jim and the Security Team made it there in record time after the shop alarm went off. A brawl ensued that trashed the shop but no shots were fired. The humans soon found out how strong even a young Squid was with their tentacle and arms.

The Tschaaa left after apparently making their point. The rest of the day was spent cleaning up and replacing damaged stock. Akira stopped by to survey the damage.

"So, my friend Darryl. What now?" The Yakuza asked.

"We clean up move on," replied Darryl. "Won't be the first time a place of mine was trashed. Usually, it's the Vice Squad making a point. Or a competitor trying to shut me down."

Darryl added to a pile of DVD that may be salvageable.

I'll need some replacement stock, Akira."

"Of course, my friend." Akira looked around at the damage, the Squid Tracks on the floor.

"Darryl, do you wish for me to bring someone else in for a while, to—"

"Fade the heat?" Interjected Darryl. "Hell, no. This is me, my life. Fuck those Squids."

He took a slug of Downtown Heat, his name for the moonshine they used for fuel and for a drink.

"I'm the Godfather of Downtown Seattle. And don't anyone

forget it! Now, someone hand me that mop—and get me another wife!"

The Vile Smut neon sign flickered. Then the light brightened, a beacon for the future of Seattle.

The Great Compromise, in all its ramifications for both the Tschaaa and humanity, continued. Only time would tell the outcome.

SEE YOU IN THE FUNNY PAPERS

BISMARCK, NORTH DAKOTA

"Where are the dailies on that new issue?"

Maxwell Marks was shoving pages and prints about as he impatiently searched for the new art he wanted to review. The barely twenty-one-year-old slender dark haired male was not noted for having a lot of patience. Then again, his drive had created a million dollar publishing comic and graphic novel company in the midst of a near genocidal war, in which Homo sapiens were kept alive as likely meat sources for cephalopodan aliens.

"Here they are," Maxwell said as he pulled several long sheets of art paper from under a couple of books.

Maxwell looked over the proposed colorful artwork as his senior Vice President Tadashi Nakajima, a Japanese American known as Tad to all his North Dakotan friends, walked in with more artwork. He completed a lot of the artwork these days, as Maxwell was more and more involved in the business and decision making part of the company known as Squidkiller Comics and Publication. The average sized Asian had kidded Maxwell when they first met in High School in Minot, North Dakota the gaijin had befriended him so he had a model for all the manga and anime Asian characters he drew. It took Maxwell many hours of art to master the epicanthic fold of the Asianic eye.

"Whaddya think?" asked Tad. Maxwell examined the colored pages, then answered.

"Aleks needs a bit more decolletage."

" That's the new General's wife, you know," said Tad. "Don't you want to tone it down a bit now that everyone is working on this Great Compromise with the Squids?"

"And that has what to do with former spy Aleksandra Smirnov's nice tatas?" Maxwell replied. "Yes, she is married to Squidkiller, now General Torbin Bender. But since we started this line over a year ago, it has been the flagship of this company. Hence our name."

Tad frowned, then picked up another draft page of what was a graphic novel more than a comic book.

"Well, you even have our Avenging Angel Abigail with her boobs about to burst out of her body armor in the last issue. She was married to Ichiro Yamamoto just a few months ago. I do not want to piss off *that* Samurai."

Maxwell laughed. "You think he would do any more damage to us than his wife? That last issue we did from those leaked reports of what she did to those Krakens and grays in Wyoming showed both blood and boobs to a new level. So far, it's selling like hotcakes."

Tad kept frowning as he looked at the strips of art.

I don't know," the Japanese American said. "We are both military brats, so I keep thinking about what if our Active Duty moms had been drawn and depicted like... this."

Maxwell guffawed.

"My mom has a nice chest. I think she would like to show

them off."

"Oh come on!" responded Tad, "You're not serious…"

The intercom buzzed and Miriam, the receptionist, and gatekeeper, spoke.

"There is a nice young Japanese lady out here asking for the owner," Miriam said. "She looks like she just came from cosplay. Is anyone expecting a model?"

Both of the men looked at the other.

"Expecting a long-lost relative. Tad?" asked Maxwell. His friend glared at him, then marched to the front of the of the office complex. Thanks to a substantial jump in sales, Squidkiller now occupied the entire two stories of the building. One large room was being outfitted for podcasts and filming of teasers for the company's projects.

Maxwell looked at all the storyboards. He would have to consider some modifications to the storylines if the Tschaaa aliens, known as Squids, were no longer being killed. Or, not harvesting humans for meat. The President and CEO—why stop at just one title—of Squidkiller Comics and Publications had heard some people on the west coast were producing Japanese hentai, pornographic comics, and DVDs of human/alien sex. Tentacle sex, to be exact. Not just animated, but with live performers. Maxwell had a fluid sense of morality, but even he had limits.

Maxwell jumped as Miriam's screech echoed through the offices. He had recently hired two body builder types to act as security after Maxwell and Tad had received some intoxicated visitors looking to score some free comics for resale. Now it sounded like they may earn their pay. Maxwell walked to his office door and peeked out. He looked just as one of the "security" personnel came flying into the hallway, bounced off the wall, then rolled to land near Maxwell's feet. The President and CEO let out a little girl scream, jumped back into his office and slammed the door. He bolted it, then scrambled for his desk telephone. Shaking fingers hit "9-1-1."

"Hello," Maxwell said, then realized the line was dead. His own cell phone had just died the other day, and he had no chance to buy a replacement. Loud yelling and smashing sounds reverberated through the office wall. Now he realized he should have bought a gun.

Maxwell looked around the room for a weapon. Then he saw the decorative katana someone had given him to dress up the office a bit. He grabbed it.

"Better than nothing," he said to himself.

There were more cries, crashing. Maxwell heard Tad's voice loudly complain. "I told you, I don't speak Japanese! I'm an American!"

This was followed by a loud and commanding voice spouting Japanese. Was that a female voice?

"Fool! You should know the language of your ancestors!" This was the same voice, now speaking English.

"Open the door, fool!"

"I can't," replied Tad. "He has the door bolted."

"Open the door!" the woman yelled.

"Go away! The cops are coming!" Maxwell yelled back.

"I have faced Krakens, Eaters, Beasts, and Tschaaa, and you think I fear the police?"

"You'd better, sister. We have laws here in Bismarck, new U. S. Capitol…"

A long and sharp blade sliced through the door. In a blur, two more cuts were made. A foot kicked a large hole in the door. A hand reached through and undid the deadbolt. The door was then kicked open as Maxwell screamed and ran behind his desk. He watched as a young Japanese woman of average build walk in. Maxwell saw and felt she exuded an aura of power and authority. On his knees behind her was Tad, shaking with fear.

"Stay back!" Maxwell tried to yell out, but his voice cracked. He attempted to hold the decorative katana menacingly. The

Japanese female looked at him and laughed.

"Are you really threatening me with that fake sword? It has no edge on it." The young woman's voice was from one who was used to command.

Maxwell looked at her, looked at his sword. Then he dropped his weapon.

"Please, don't hurt us." Maxwell's voice was almost a squeak.

"You are the owner of this business?" Asked the warrior woman.

" I... I'm the President and CEO, yes."

"So you are the one who draws the pictures and decides the content of each issue of these... comics."

"Yes, Miss..." Maxwell said.

"No Miss. I am Princess Akiko of the Free Japan Royal Family. And I am here to demand amends for the rude and crude depictions of my comrades and friends in these-scandal sheets I think is an American term for them."

Tad stopped shaking in the hallway and found his voice.

"You are Princess Akiko, the female Samurai, and hero of Hell Day on Malmstrom Joint Allied Military Base?"

"At your service," the Princess answered. "But I would not call me a hero, just a soldier doing her duty."

"Shit, lady," Maxwell blurted out. "You helped save all those infants, those patients in the Military Hospital from the Beasts and Eaters." He pulled a graphic novel from his desk drawer.

"We recorded it here, in this special Samurai issue of Squidkiller. We talk about you and Ichiro.."

"That is General Yamamoto to you, Mister..."

"Marks, Maxwell Marks. That guy in the hallway is Tad Nakajima. Hell, we are your biggest fans. Here!" Maxwell tried to hand the graphic novel to Princess Akiko. She strode forward and snatched it from his grasp with her left hand. The Princess stepped back out of retaliation range and glanced at the cover. A cloud passed over her face as she threw the publication back at him.

"Trash like that is why I am here. I look nothing like that, that, large breasted loose woman you portray,"Akiko began to seeth.

"Look it, Princess. I know our illustrations are a bit over the top, but, you know, this sells issues.."

"And you disrespected Abigail, the Avenging Angel. You realize he was a virgin on her wedding day? And you draw her like some street whore, clothes being ripped off?" The Princess' voice raised in anger as she stepped towards Maxwell. Just then, Miriam's voice echoed down the hallway.

"The police are here!"

Everything and every person froze in place.

Maxwell drummed his fingers on his desk in frustration. Things had not gone the way he assumed they would. The Police told him and Tad that there were three problems with them arresting the Princess.

First, she had Diplomatic Immunity, as an official representative of Free Japan.

Second, Maxwell's new security tried to lay hands on the Princess first, without any warning. Apparently, an average sized Japanese female was someone to shove around.

Third, and final, she was a Hero, who everyone in Bismarck seemed to know. The Police told Maxwell and Tad that it would be better for them to 'work it out,' rather than demand an official response.

Thus, Maxwell sat across from Princess Akiko as Tad tried to rustle up some refreshments. He finally came back with soft drinks, a bottle of scotch, Sake (from where?), rice cakes, cookies, and beef sticks. The Princess saw the bottle of scotch whiskey, raised an eyebrow.

"You have ice?" She asked.

"What? No Sake?" Maxwell replied. A demure smiled formed on the mouth of the young Japanese lady.

"General Bender has helped me to develop a taste for this liquor, out of sight of my royal handlers."

Tad hustled and found some ice. Soon all three were sitting around the desk sipping the booze.

Maxwell looked at his office door.

"So who pays for that large hole?" he asked.

Princess Akiko shrugged. "I guess I could. I let my impatience get the best of me," she said as she sipped her drink. "My father said my name should be the Impetuous One, as I act like a, like a..."

"Bull in a china shop," interjected Tad.

The Princess smiled and sipped her drink again. Maxwell looked at her and sipped his drink. Then, an idea hit him. Right between the eyes.

"Princess, you don't like how we portray your friends, your comrades," said Maxwell.

"That is an understatement. Your depictions offend my sensibilities," Akiko replied.

"Okay. Put your money where your mouth is. Do you want to be our official, and Royal, Advising Editor?"

The Royal Princess frowned. "How do you mean? What would I do?"

The President of Squidkiller Comics and Publications leaned over the desk. Now he was in his element. Wheeling and dealing.

"Look it. You know all of the characters-the people who we depict in our publications. You know the actual, inside story. We want to publish a good story, a good product that will sell. You may not like the overboard illustrations. But you have to admit our illustrators are excellent."

"I will admit to that," the Princess replied.

"So, you tell us the true stories. The inside stories of what happened. You were there!"

Maxwell took a slug of his drink. He was on a roll.

"Then, you pass judgment on the drawings of the main characters. You tell us if Abigail's tits, I mean breasts and rear are too big, You tell us how to depict how Abigail and the others look and really act both on and off the job. To include yourself."

"I will not violate any confidences," Akiko interjected. "That is dishonorable."

"Of course not. Just enough information to jazz up the storyline, make it more personal. After all, everyone wants to feel connected to our Heroes."

The Princess paused, and Tad refreshed her drink. She flashed him a smile in appreciation that made the Vice President of the company blush a bit. Akiko turned towards Maxwell and leaned across the table. She had allowed her kataginu top of her kamishimo to loosen, so when she leaned forward. Maxwell got a flash of some lovely shaped breasts as she spoke.

"And what do you two get from this-new arrangement. Other than my expert advice."

"Why, we also mention you in our credits and organization section." Maxwell held his hands out as he spoke as if to frame word written in the air.

"Special Technical Advisor Princess Akiko of the Free Japan Royal Family. She was there,"Maxwell added. "Then, maybe an official-looking Japanese seal, or coat of arms. You get the picture."

The Princess paused as if taking it all in. Then she leaned back into the padded chair as she spoke.

"I think we may have a deal. But of course, this must be in writing and notarized."

"Miriam!" Maxwell yelled. "We need you!"

Maxwell was in early the next morning, working on the changes Princess Akiro had outlined to the strips and storyboards. Actually, he was quite pleased with the suggestions. For the CEO of Squidkiller now realized they had been selling their talent short. He and Tad had been happy to push tits and ass to attract readers. Add to that the sensationalized killing styles of "Squidkiller Bender" and "Samurai Ichiro," and they had the equivalent of the old 'chopsaki' films of the 1970s and 80s. Long on blood, action, some nudity, and short on storyline and plot. Not to mention characterization. As he worked on the boards, he saw the superior product come together. More angst in the faces of the characters, more storylines around who the real heroes were, not just two-dimensional cutouts chopping the limbs off of Tschaaa aliens. Besides, with the Great Compromise, stories of constant warfare would not reflect the new reality. Reality would sell in the next phase of recovery.

As the morning wore on, the other employees came in with the new security guards. Now, off-duty Cops were in the building, as suggested by the responding officers (share the wealth Overtime, everyone's back gets scratched.) Maxwell looked at his watch. Man, Tad was unusually late. As he was about to borrow a cell phone to call him, a bleary-eyed Tad walked in. He went straight to the coffee station and filled his mug with black coffee.

"No cream and sugar this morning?" Maxwell asked him

"Gotta wake up," Tad mumbled, then sipped his coffee."

"Rough night?" Maxwell asked.

"Never offer to take a Princess home," Tad replied. "Nothing turns into a pumpkin at Midnight." He frowned. "Like a damned energizer bunny."

Maxwell's mouth dropped open a bit. Tad was not known for being a Lothario.

"So, you two—" Maxwell began to answer. Tad cut him off.

"A gentleman, nor a Samurai, ever tell. It is rude."

As Tad Nakajima tried to wake up, Princess Akiko was catching a ride in the back seat of a Free Japan F-15. Royalty had its perks. Pure oxygen in the cockpit helped to wipe away any morning fogginess from the night before. She smiled to herself. Once again, she could hear her Father scolding her about her impetuous behavior. Yet, she achieved her mission of protecting the honor of her friends and comrades. As General Bender would say, to hell with worrying. You may only live once.

However, the Royal Princess had one concern: how to break it to the Royal Family that the Royal Princess may appear in the funny papers.

PARTNERS

Special Agent David Jackson moved his tall and lanky body towards the Open Fisherman boat that was now his to use. He carried two large equipment bags up the dock, demonstrating his coiled strength on a rather slender frame. David took after his late father, Andrew "Andy" Jackson. Former Texas Ranger and bodyguard/driver for Madam President, he had died defending her on Hell Day not long before the Great Compromise put an end to the Tschaaa-Human War. David often wished that the Squids had not come, or that the War had ended just a bit earlier. Then, his father would still be alive. At the same time, had the Tschaaa *not* attacked with rocks from space, David would still be rotting in prison for a murder he had committed. Sometimes bad things created some good after all, even if limited.

David set down the two large bags on the dock and looked at the Open Fisherman. The boat had been found hidden in a private boathouse, up on blocks, and in near pristine condition. The owners were likely long since dead and possibly eaten by the Tschaaa Squids, and therefore the new Federal Government of the United States of North America had seized it for marine enforcement duties. The Special Agent grinned.

"Honey, you are one hell of a boat," he said to himself.

It was a high-end Catamaran design, with four large outboard motors capable of producing some 1600 horsepower. It had an increased fuel capacity of some eight hundred gallons so it could cruise all the way to Jamaica and back. David knew it could go about sixty miles an hour easily while having outstanding stability and maneuverability.

"You were either a rich man's toy or a drug smuggler's dream," the Agent mused. "Maybe both."

David Jackson loaded his two large bags on the boat and began to store his gear. The Open Fisherman design gave a deep hull with lots of room for the crew and passengers to move around. The high gunnels helped keep people from falling overboard. In the front shell was a small storage area that could add to the larger compartments in the center control console. The Special Agent also found spots where he could tie down miscellaneous items. He noticed there was still one bracket for a fishing pole. With a smile, he dug out an average-sized deepwater rig and made it sure it was secure in the bracket. If nothing else, it worked as protective coloration, made the large boat look like it was used for fishing. It was unmarked other than the Vessel Registration Number on the front hull port side. David had brought a low drag light bar to mount on the top of the center console frame. He had a cover for it so the boat could pass again as some rich guys toy. The new job he had to accomplish was as much about observation as it was about enforcement.

David shook his head and chuckled. If only his Dad could see him now. Former felon and murderer, now a Federal Agent working hand in hand with...a Squid. Some two months after the formal signing the Great Compromise, this was one of the first attempts at Tschaaa-Human cooperation. The Special Agent was to work with a selected Tschaaa male off the Florida Keys, now the Conch Republic, to put a stop to some illegal harvesting and smuggling operations. The Admiral, now Governor also, of the Conch Republic had suggested he could use help with some enforcement activities.

"No Director Lloyd, no Lord Neptune to control this area. The comings and goings of the Squids and humans are causing conflict. I was an Intelligence Officer, not a cop before the Squids arrived," stated the Admiral.

David knew how important it was, this "grand experiment" in interspecies cooperation. Soon, Squids would be working with units like the Banshees. He would not let his Boss—Commissioner Miller—down. Nor would he sully the memory of his father. He felt his father's Texas Ranger badge, that he wore on a chain around his neck. David had been made an Honorary Ranger by the surviving Texas Rangers and was allowed to keep his father's badge.

"Miss you, Dad," he said. Then he heard a familiar sound.

David clambered back up on the dock and looked at the advancing vehicle. It was a former harvester robot, the ball-shaped turret removed and replaced with a seat for a Tschaaa to ride in. The powerful electric motor emanated the signature whirring whine that had spread fear into humans not that long ago. Now instead of harvesting meat, it was used to transport the male Tschaaa who would be his partner. As the six-wheeled ATV shaped vehicle approached, David let out a light whistle. The Squid in the driver's seat was enormous, even for a bear-sized alien. Eight thick arms and the large body had trouble fitting on the former harvester. The male used his two Social Tentacles with the long-fingered five-digit hands to drive his mount. David had studied Tschaaa physiology enough to know that exobiologists believed the Squids fingers were much superior at manipulation than a human's. That made sense as they had as much to do with Squid reproduction as did their version of a penis.

The Squid slowed, then stopped the vehicle some ten yards away. David saw and felt the lunch plate sized eyes of the Tschaaa peruse him with an accuracy unattainable with normal human eyes. That fact seemed to explain why the Squids developed few electronic enhancement to their vision systems. A decent glass lens or two was all they needed to see for miles. Thus, the old Eye in the Sky. David saw the Squid had a translator box suspended on a strap hanging around the alien torso. The creature held up the translator device as he spoke.

"You are... the human... David Jackson?"

The Agent tried not to smile as a hint of a West Texas drawl flavored the words. David knew some human jokester had gotten ahold of the device before it was given to the Tschaaa male. There was no other reason for such an accent which David could imagine.

"Yes. I am Special Agent David Jackson," he replied. "And your name is...?" David had not been given a name as he could not pronounce the Tschaaa name and no human name had been selected by the Squid at the last notice.

"Yes. My given name is Wild Bill," the Squid replied, slight drawl and all. "The humans assigned to this... project said it is fitting. Is that true?"

"Let me guess, Sir. Hickock is the last part."

"Yes," the Tschaaa male replied. "That is the total name."

David tried not to laugh. He knew this was a joke played on the alien.

"Is it not a good name?" the Squid now known as Wild Bill asked.

"It is a very fine name. Wild Bill Hickok was a famous lawman and gunfighter in our Old West."

The Squid used his social tentacles to sign pleasure as he spoke, not having human facial muscles to display a smile or grin.

"A gunfighter was one who used firearms against other humans, yes? Even as a lawman?"

"Yessir. We humans are a complicated lot. One time on the side of the law, another time not. But the name you chose, Wild Bill, is an honorable name."

"Good," Wild Bill answered. "I am glad. Now, I have some equipment to take to your ocean craft, I was told you would have one."

"This Open Fisherman here. Come on, I'll help you stow your gear."

Some ten minutes later, David and Wild Bill—Bill for short— had all the equipment aboard. Bill parked the Squid ATV in the parking lot and disabled the starter. It would not be good if someone ran off with it. David watched the Squid use its 'crab walk' ability to approach their boat. The Agent knew that the Tschaaa could move for short distances with that form of locomotion. He also knew that the Tschaaa had adopted the word "Squid" as a perfectly honorable term, after encountering Earthly Giant Squids. At the thought of the Giant Deep Sea cephalopod and as the Squid set its bulk down by the Open Fisherman, David knew he had to ask one question.

"Bill, you are big even for a male Squid, aren't you?"

"Yes, I am," Bill answered. He signed with his social tentacles something that David thought meant embarrassment. The Agent's crash course on Tschaaa Non-Verbal Communication was not all-inclusive.

"I am bigger than most, even those born in Our New Mother. I was born shipboard, several years before our arrival in your solar system." Bill paused in his dissertation. A couple of his limbs darkened, which David had been told meant emotional upset, maybe even anger. The Agent started to wonder how to push the conversation onto another subject when Bill continued.

"I was accused of being too large, overeating our rapidly depleted stores of meat. However, since I was offspring of the one you know as Lord Neptune, I was given special dispensations."

At the mention of Lord Neptune, the Lord who had ruled North America, David tensed. That Tschaaa Lord had set into motion the Infestation and established the Protocol of Selective Survival which had turned human against human Wild Bill must have received briefings on human body language as he noticed the tensing in the Agent.

"I am sorry. I forgot what my Sire means to you. I will refrain..."

"Nope," interjected David. "If we are to work together, have each other's backs, there cannot be any off-limit subjects. So, we must tell our stories if we are to make this assignment work."

Bill signed with his tentacles understanding and agreement as he replied.

"Then you realize the importance of this...task we have been given."

"Of course. I volunteered for this. I don't want any more people like my father to die because we can't get this Great Compromise to work."

"You lost your...Sire?" The Tschaaa male asked.

"Yes. But to humans, not to Squids."

The two beings paused in their conversation. David was surprised how well the translator worked. Without it, he knew this arrangement would not be possible.

"That translator device works right well," he opined as a way to shift the conversation a bit.

"Yes. You humans helped to create this smaller and more efficient type," said Bill. "Your species is better at taking existing equipment and improving it. Once we Squids make something that works, we tend to become, I think the term is, hidebound to it."

"Except for your Sire," David said. He did not like having to shift the subject back to the matter of the Sire, Lord Neptune. However, it was the elephant in the room.

"True," Bill replied with positive tentacle signs. "I have been told I inherited some of this capability. Along with it from my Breeder mother, the one known as Elizabeth, strong empathy for all living things."

David's mouth dropped open.

"Your open mouth denotes surprise, yes, David?"

"You got that right, Bill. I guess you're close to a line of royalty among your kind. The two Tschaaa individuals behind the immense changes to human existence the past some seven years. One planned the Infestation, the harvesting, and the other stopped it."

The oversized male Tschaaa gave the equivalent of a shrug.

"I am not unique. I have thousands of siblings. I just decided to volunteer for something... unusual. Like you did."

"And I bet you volunteered to make a difference also," stated the Agent.

"You are correct, David. In that, we are very much alike."

Bill reached forward with his right social tentacle with a reach much longer than a human's.

"I believe males of your species 'shake hands' is the expression in greeting and respect. I think my hands can perform that function."

"You're right. It's a good time for it. Welcome aboard this boat. It's going to be a second home for us."

The two beings grasped each other's hands. David thought the long grasping fingers of the Tschaaa would feel a bit slimy. Instead, they felt dry and cool. As they moved their hands apart, David pointed at the port side of the bow.

"Our first combined task is to paint a name on this seacraft."

"A name?" asked Bill. "Why? It is a machine."

"Aw, how wrong you are, comrade. For all human seamen know that the boat, the ship they serve on have a spirit of a woman in it. And no lady wants to be called, 'hey you' when spoken to or about. So, a name we need. Any suggestions?"

The Tschaaa male manipulated some keys on the translator, which told David it also functioned as a computer tablet.

"Amphitrite," Bill stated. "It is the female mythological version of your Neptune or Poseidon. With who my relatives and creche mates are, I think it is appropriate."

The Special Agent chuckled.

"Good idea. Now, some waterproof paint and we are in business."

'AMPHITRITE' was painted on in record time. David had taken a chance on trying to paint the name on while the craft was in the water and subject to the fluid motion. However, something told the Agent that the Squid could handle it as a creature of the sea. Wild Bill demonstrated the excellent dexterity of his long digits. Not to mention that his superior vision gave him the ability to paint lines extraordinarily straight and exact. The paint was of a fast drying type, so the pair of new Law Enforcement Officers were ready to move in short order.

"Well, Bill. If you want another career, you will make an excellent artist."

The Tschaaa alien signed thanks and appreciation with its social tentacles.

"That is one subject in which you humans have an advantage. You have a more varied expression in the physical arts. Except for what you call 'music.' I would say our Ocean Songs we use to communicate with each other over distance are just as melodic as anything you humans can produce."

"How about musical instruments, Bill? Do you Tschaaa use many?"

"Few," the Squid answered. "We use our bodies to produce most of the out songs."

David turned on the blowers to clear out any gas fumes near the fuel tanks and engines.

"I know you Tschaaa have seacraft," he said.

"True, David. Though many are submersible, not surface craft."

"Once I get out into the channel. You want to take

AMPHITRITE for a spin?"

Wild Bill gestured affirmative pleasure as he answered "Yes!"

Five minutes later, David had the go-fast in a central channel leading out from the Port of Key West. He looked at his new boatmate.

"Want to take the helm?" he asked.

"You mean control? Why yes, David." Wild Bill slid over to the central control console.

The Agent started to give some advice on boat handling when the Tschaaa accelerated the AMPHITRITE with ease and confidence. The Tschaaa male had the craft up on a plane as he headed towards the deep water. Bill advanced the throttle until they were zipping along at sixty knots with few undulations. Five minutes out, Bill pulled back on the throttle and brought the boat to a smooth stop. David grinned at his new boatmate.

"Well, I know who'll be doing most of the boat driving. You make me look like a slug."

Bill gave the Tscahaaa equivalent of a shrug as he answered.

"We are creatures of the ocean, the sea. Of course, we are more attuned to traveling in water than are land dwellers as yourself."

"I was told you can both see and feel all the currents in a body of water," said David.

"True. We are born in Mother Ocean. Learn all her movements and moods from an early age." The Tschaaa alien motioned towards the ocean expanse.

"Your Mother Ocean is younger than our home world ocean, the original Mother. I have been told by Elders that thus this New Mother is so vibrant, so life-giving."

"Which is why so many of you decided to stay," replied David.

Wild Bill paused for a moment, then answered.

"Yes. Which led to more conflict between humankind and we Tschaaa. Thus we two beings, we lawmen, are here trying to ensure the Great Compromise prevents more death."

The two beings from different worlds, now living together on the home planet of one, stood quietly for a few minutes as the ocean gently rocked the boat. David broke the silence first.

"You brought us out here for a reason."

"Yes, David, I did. Please watch."

In a fluid motion for a being so large, the Tscahaaa now known as Wild Bill slid into the ocean. He slipped under the surface, descended some five feet below the boat. David thought he felt some light vibrations through the hull of the AMPHITRITE which meant that Bill was communicating with his own kind. Then the cephalopode was pulling himself back aboard the boat. His heavy weight did cause the craft to rock some, but his fluid motion reduced some of it.

"David, if you please, Bend over and place a hand in the ocean, just under the surface."

"Okay," the human answered. In just a couple of minutes, a dozen pairs of young Tschaaa eyes were just under the surface, staring at the boat. David heard some clicks and squeaks in sound frequencies he could listen to, which told him that was only a portion of the Squid communication. He held his hand still. Then, he felt the feathery touch of the social tentacle digits on his fingers and wrist. The Agent was sure, based on the many contacts on his hand, that all twelve young felt his skin. Then, one by one, the young disappeared below the surface, to be replaced by an adult caretaker.

"A Breeder, yes?" he asked Bill.

"Yes. Though it is doubtful, this Breeder will ever actually breed because of our caste system. But she will be a caretaker, a mother the young will know and remember."

Then the caretaker was also gone.

"So, Bill, correct me if I am wrong. But they will now remember me?"

"Yes," replied the Tschaaa. "And I told them that you are a

human they can come to for help. That you will protect them, as I would your young."

David felt this odd almost ethereal sensation. The thought of a Squid protecting human young that just a few months prior was "veal" for both adults and the young of the Tschaaa was plain weird. Not to mention him, a human, protecting that same alien young who had fed on human flesh? That was many times weirder.

"Well, Bill," David finally said. "That is what we are here for, I guess. To make sure all of our kids can grow up safe. No more War."

He turned and saw the plate-sized eyes of the Tschaaa staring at him. Then the being now called Wild Bill reached his social tentacle out and gently clasped David's right hand in a shake of greeting.

"I greet you in that task, my fellow lawman. May we always are successful." Bill then positioned himself behind the wheel of the Open Fisherman.

"Now, David Jackson. I will show you the extent of the Creche area and where the young are raised. Then you can show me the areas of your boat traffic and fishing. I see those as the areas of possible conflict."

"Lay on, MacDuff," David answered. This resulted in a sign of confusion from Bill's social tentacles.

"Sorry. Expression from a famous theater play."

"Ah, yes," answered Bill. "Those activities similar to the fables we tell our young."

David laughed.

"Man, old Willie Shakespeare will be rolling in his grave when he hears that." Seeing another Tschaaa sign of confusion with one set of digits, David hastily added. "I'll explain later. Let's go."

The next couple of days were spent by the new partners becoming familiar with the area. Actually, it was primarily David growing familiar as Bill had spent some time in the ocean before The Great Compromise. Discussing this led to David telling his history and how the Infestation affected him during the early days.

"If not for the fact your Lords invaded, I would still be rotting in prison."

The concept of imprisonment was an odd one to the Tschaaa. Bill expressed his confusion on the matter.

"So, your government literally locks you in a building for breaking a law of humankind?"

"Yes, Sir. For both punishment and supposed rehabilitation. Also to keep some people from preying on other people."

Wild Bill and David were sitting offshore letting the waves rock the AMPHITRITE, so the Squid's gestures of confusion with his social tentacles as he spoke did not affect his boat handling.

"I do not understand. Your Creche, your family, would not deal with your transgressions?"

"Not in these modern times, Bill," replied David. "In what we call olden times, families were allowed to handle the punishment as long as it met some basic standards and the victims of your crime, the people harmed by your actions, agreed."

"And that was not sufficient?" asked Wild Bill. "Humans had to change it?"

"We had things arise like blood feuds. That was when one clan, your Creche, decided that another group had injured one of the clan's members and had not received sufficient compensation. So they stole from, injured, maybe killed a member of the offending group. This led to a revenge action, and a blood feud resulted. Soon, half a country was feuding, causing death and destruction. Thus, governments and laws were formed to control all this violence and strife." As David finished his attempt at an explanation, he noticed a darkening of the Tschaaa's flesh.

"Bill, does this upset you?" he asked.

"I...I am trying to understand," replied the alien. "But until the Tschaaa traveled here, we had no history of wars nor anything like the strife you just reported for thousands upon thousands of your years. Extreme disagreements between Creche's over influence or resources were either arbitrated by Senior Lords, or through very limited and controlled duels, never to the death or severe injury. In fact, sometimes these duels were more verbal debates decided by a panel of Lords."

"When was the last time injury or death occurred due to a duel in your home world history?" David asked.

"It has been lost in legend," the Tschaaa male answered. "When the Lord was executed here on Earth for introducing Eaters to attack areas controlled by my Sire, it shook many of my people to the core. To use lies and secret acts to harm fellow Tschaaa? That is considered an abomination!"

David was concerned that Wild Bill would become too agitated because of the subject. But if the Squid was to help him keep order, it may involve physical force against Wild Bill's own kind. He needed to know just what his fellow Lawman was willing and able to do.

"So would you use physical force on another Tschaaa to stop them from doing something illegal?"

"Yes," was Bill's answer. "But deadly force? I will be truthful and say it would be tough. We kill to eat or to protect our species from other creatures. Especially our young. But to kill another Tschaaa?" Bill's limbs seemed to shudder.

"Was not a Creche dismantled on the home world as they were blamed for the White Plague?" David asked, knowing the possibility he was pushing the boundaries of understanding between two very different beings. It took a few moments for Wild Bill to regain his composure. The darker colors of the Tschaaa's flesh began to lighten back to normal.

"You have studied our records well, David. That happened over a thousand Earth years ago. We Tschaaa now say 'Never Again.' I believe a cultural group of you humans have much the same sentiment about a similar situation."

David paused in the conversation, He knew that he as a human had considerably pushed the "buttons" of Wild Bill. Maybe pushed a bit too far. However, people who worked together in a job where violence was a possibility, must know what the other person was capable or not capable of doing.

"Bill, I killed another human. He had hurt a female friend of mine. In my anger I killed him. That led to my prison sentence."

The Squid stood stock still as it examined him with his oversized eyes. Then, Bill spoke.

"So, you killed out of anger. Or was it revenge you mentioned, a blood feud?"

"Old style anger, Wild Bill. I paid the price for it. You Tschaaa gave me a second chance buy smashing the walls of the prison with a space rock. Although my freedom could not make up for the millions of dead."

The Squid once again paused before responding.

"Then I believe we must make sure that no more die due to conflict."

"You got that right. Now, if you wish, let's do a little patrol work to make sure there is no new conflict between the species."

The two Lawmen had there first taste of combined law enforcement the next day. It started out as a lovely sunny morning. Wild Bill was once again demonstrating his superior boat handling abilities when David saw a glass-bottom tourist boat near a Boston Whaler fishing craft. He tapped one Bill's "shoulders" and pointed towards the two seacrafts.

"Let's see why they are jawing at each other, Bill."

"Jawing?" Asked the Tschaaa male.

"Texan for talking," David replied.

With practiced ease, the Squid known as Wild Bill maneuvered the Open Fishman towards the two boats in question. David uncovered the light bar and activated the flashing red and blue emergency lights. The humans on the two seacrafts, now clearly arguing, did not notice the approach of the Open Fisherman until David activated the siren. Then all the occupants of the two boats looked up as Bill cut the throttle and slid the patrol craft in next to the tourist boat, port side to starboard.

"Who the fuck are you?" yelled out a darkly tanned male from the Boston Whaler. Then a second voice from that boat exclaimed, "Hey he has a fucking Squid with him!"

David quickly lashed the Open Fisherman to the glass-bottomed boat with a quick release knot as he answered.

"I am Federal Law Enforcement Agent David Jackson, and this fine specimen of a Tschaaa is Federal Law Enforcement Agent William Hickok. Now, why is everyone acting angry on this nice sunny day?"

A buxom but muscular lady called out.

"Heidi Faust here, certified tourist boat captain by the Admiral. I was trying to tell these nimrods…"

"We have fishing rights here!" A rather large man with high cheekbones and wearing a traditional round colorful brimless hat with a single feather as favored by local Seminoles loudly expressed his opinion.

"Well, be that as it may. I've been tasked to help keep the peace in waters that are now part Tschaaa and part human domain," replied David.

"Can you…," interjected the self-identified Heidi Faust, "Please tell them that there are prime Tschaaa Breeding Areas, a Creche around here? And that they are extremely protective of their young."

David looked at the comely brunette. She seemed oddly familiar.

"Well, Ma'am, that we will do. But you need to show me something that says your tourist boat is allowed out here to observe flora and fauna. That may also disturb the Tschaaa Breeders and their young."

"Fucking Squids," a third voice from a scraggly male in the Boston Whaler opined. At that moment, Wild Bill found his voice.

"I find it fascinating you humans keep referring to us Tschaaa as Fucking Squids as if it is an insult. May I explain as a Tschaaa male that your Deep Giant Squids are a source of awe and wonder to us. So calling us Squids who wish to procreate? All that does is to state reality, and ignorance on your part."

Heidi Faust began to laugh as she handed some documentation to David.

"Shut up, bitch!" The insult came from one of the four crew on the fishing boat. Heidi's face flushed with anger.

"Come over here and say that, you pieces of shit," she snapped back.

Suddenly, the four from the Boston Whaler scrambled and leaped onto the now immobilized glass bottom boat.

"Halt, goddamnit!" yelled David. But it was too late. The fight was on.

The first male boarding was caught by a front kick from Heidi as the tourists huddled in the back of the boat. The man was knocked over the gunnel and into the ocean.

The second one was the dark tanned original speaker, with a nasty looking fishing knife in his hand. He was focused on Heidi Faust, so he did not notice David leaping to body slam him on his left side. A lead sap David had inherited from his father flattened the man onto the bottom of the tourist boat.

The Seminole tribal member came up with a twelve gauge pump shotgun from under a fishing net. As he raised it, Wild Bill demonstrated the long reach of his social tentacles by grabbing the barrel of the firearm with one grasping Squid hand and shoving it skyward. The Squid's other hand wrapped extra long digits around the man's throat. Bill yanked the Seminole in reach of his thick limbs and wrapped him up like a constrictor snake.

The fourth Boston Whaler crewman froze in the bow of the tourist boat.

"Hands up, cabron!" ordered David. The slightly built man jammed his hands up as if he was reaching for heaven. David had him down and handcuffed in record time.

"David," called out Bill. "The human who went overboard has not come to the surface."

"Aw, shit!' As David started to shuck his equipment belt, Bill shoved his prisoner towards the lawman. David was forced to grab the Seminole, noticing his face was a bit blue from the constriction of the large Tschaaa limbs. Then the cephalopod was over the gunnels and into the ocean. Of course, he was the logical pick for ocean rescue. He was a true amphibian. In short order, Wild Bill was shoving the unconscious man back onto the boat.

"He does not breath," Bill said.

"I got it," said the woman called Heidi. In moments she was performing CPR on her former enemy. A couple of tourists moved to help. With that, David turned his attention to the other three crewmen. With Bill's help, all three were in the bow of the Lawman's boat with zip-tied hands.

"My ribs are broken," complained the Seminole. David snickered.

"Never wrestle with a Squid," said David. "Especially a big fellow like Wild Bill here. I'll put money on him wrestling one of your 'gators."

"He's breathing!" Heidi called out.

"Good," said David. "Less paperwork."

The nearly drowned man joined the other three in the Open Fisherman. The three conscious men glared at David and Bill, the 'sapped' one was still out for the count.

"You'll be going into the local lockup provided by the Admiral," explained David. "Next time, don't try attacking women or Lawmen."

He noticed Bill was holding his translator/computer up as if using a camera to film the occupants of the tourist boat. The sizeable Tschaaa male then put the device back hanging on his body. Bill then raised his social tentacles in a gesture of great respect.

"What's up, Bill?" David asked.

"It is She. The Breeder of the Tears."

"What?" asked David. Just then, Heidi came to the connected gunnels.

"Sorry if I caused a ruckus, Agent," the young lady said.

"You are She. The one who met Cassandra before she became Cassandra," stated the Tschaaa. With the comment, Heidi began to blush and fidget as she spoke.

"Man, I wish people would forget about that. It was by sheer chance..."

"I remember now," interjected David. "First kindly contact between females from both species. Cassandra was part of the Great Compromise meeting which happened years later, yet mentioned the contact it as a prime reason to ask for peace." The Lawman frowned.

"Too bad it couldn't have happened sooner. My Dad would still be alive."

Heidi gave him a bit of a hard look.

"I was also the bodyguard for Director Lloyd. So I guess that cancels things out."

"No," argued David. "I know that story direct from the horse's mouth. Abigail, the Avenging Angel. She is the cousin of the Agent who broke me in. Brynhilde Jorgensen. They were both at the Meeting of the Females, which led to the Great Compromise." He paused.

"Then to Director Lloyd stopping a specific Lord from sending more Space Rocks down on us, for which he died."

A tear started to run down Heidi's cheek, but she stopped it with a swipe of her hand.

"It will all soon be ancient history," the former Coastie stated.

"No, honored lady, it will not." The Squid translator seemed to give the Tschaaa's voice more gravitas.

"It is a history that helped my species to find its way again. We are again creatures of Mother Ocean, not eaters of monkey meat."

"May I touch your face, Heidi?" asked Bill.

"Aw, hell. Sure." Another tear started down her cheek, and Wild Bill captured it. He transferred the moisture to his hidden mouth.

"I have tasted your salt from Mother Ocean. I am honored."

Heidi turned away. "I need to get my passengers back to land."

"Sure," said David. "I'll find you later for a report."

He watched as the former Coast Guard member calmed her passengers down then ran the boat to shore. Wild Bill, one large eye on the prisoners and the other on David, another Squid trick, spoke.

"Is she an attractive Breeder?"

"Right now, she is a very sad one," answered David. "Bad memories do that."

David turned towards Bill.

"Thanks for handling the nimrod with the shotgun. And saving the drowning guy."

"That is what we do David, Yes? As fellow lawmen?"

The Ranger's aon grinned at the great bear of a creature. Funny, he thought, he was already thinking of Bill as a "he", not as a Squid, an It.

"And now, Wild Bill, we get to do what lawmen dislike but spend a lot of time finishing."

"What is that, David?"

"Paperwork."

The next day Heidi Faust found them as they prepared their boat for another patrol. Wild Bill with his great sight saw her coming a half mile away.

"The Breeder of the Tears approaches, David."

"Where, Bill?"

"There, David," the Squid answered as he pointed with his long social tentacle. David strained his eyes to see and only saw a blurred figure.

"Damn I wish I had your eyesight, Wild Bill."

"And I have always wondered how it would be to walk so easily upright, on just two legs So David, we are even in unfulfilled desires."

David chuckled. Bill was becoming quite the philosopher. He sat down and waited until Heidi was closer, then the Lawman up onto the dock and walked to greet her.

"Well, Ma'am, what brings you here?"

"To give you a statement, as you asked," Heidi said that with a warm smile and eyes that twinkled in the sunlight. "And to apologize for being so short with you."

"Water under the bridge," replied David. "I have some statement forms here. You have some time right now?"

"Yessiree. Day off. The Admiral told me to have some fun, that I was getting grumpy."

Heidi sat on the dock and quickly wrote a statement. As she did, David kept glancing at her. The Tschaaa male noticed this.

"So, David is she a Breeder of great potential?" Wild Bill asked. "Is that not what the large mammaries signify?"

The face of the Ranger's son turned a bright red as he began to stutter. Heidi's mouth fell open. Then she started to laugh. Then it turned into a tearful belly laugh as she saw David's stuttering attempts at answering.

"Did I say something-odd?" Asked Bill. "I thought I understood Human Mating activities and strategies."

"Dammit, Bill! There are just somethings you don't say to a lady," David finally sputtered out. Heidi wiped her eyes as she controlled her laughing. She grinned at the two Lawmen.

"David, no worries. That is not the first time some Squid made similar comments due to my nice rack." At Heidi's comment, David began to blush again.

"Oh, come on! Oh, that's right. You're an old-fashioned

Texas Boy, right? I recognized that drawl. So your Mom never said 'rack' in front of you."

"No Ma'am. At least not talking about her own breasts."

"Please, quit with the 'Ma'am.'. It makes me feel ancient."

"Okay-Heidi."

Heidi paused and examined him. Then she spoke.

"Agent, can this former Coastie buy you dinner tonight? Or is that too forward?"

"After working with Brynhildr, nothing is too forward or blunt, "said David.

"So. What's the answer?" Prodded Heidi.

"Yes, Ma-I mean Heidi. But we won't be back until about 6:00pm."

"Fine. I'm a night owl anyways. Meet you back here at the dock."

"Hey, I'll need to take a shower..." David began to protest.

"No, you won't. We're going to a little Dive that has the best raw oysters. Nothing fancy." Heidi winked at him, and David tried not to blush again.

As the former Coastie walked off, with a slight extra sashay of her hips, David could not help but watch. Once she was out of earshot.

"That, Bill, is a fine figure of a woman."

"So, I was correct, David?" Asked the Squid. "She is a Breeder of great potential."

"Bill, friend, please quit while you are ahead."

The rest of the day was reasonably regular. The two Lawmen chased a could of Human fishing boats away from the reefs of the Tschaaa Creche and the Young, and Bill told a couple of young Warrior Squids to quit trying to scare the few pleasure craft around.

The Conche Republicans were quickly rediscovering the 'tourist life,' which meant snorkeling and a Skidoo or two zipping around. The equivalent of Tschaaa Teenagers, discovering their warrior roots, loved to harass the Republicans.

"Kids, they are all alike," opined David.

"The young are unruly at times."Said Bill.

"By the way, Wild Bill, just how old are you?"

The Squid paused in thought. Then he answered.

"I believe I am about eighteen in Earth years. Tschaaa mature faster in the Ocean so that by sixteen Earth years we are adult."

"So, Bill, you will be looking for a Breeder?"

As the Tschaaa known as Wild Bill began to turn the Open Fisherman towards their berth slowly, he answered.

"If I can prove my superior abilities as a male, I should be allowed to mate by my Sire and the Creche." Bill then paused before continuing.

"But things are... changing. Many of the younger males like myself look at you Humans and the sexual freedom you have and they... wonder."

"Well," said David. "As they say, the grass is always greener on the other side of the fence. Different or new is not always better. We humans, at least we males, are horny, want to mate for many hours of every day. It can cause problems."

As David finished his statement, Wild Bill began to accelerate the patrol craft.

"Then I guess, David, we must get you to shore so you can explore 'problems' with the Breeder Heidi."

David snorted, then spoke.

"Are you developing a human sense of humor?"

"David, that is a possibility. Your species seems to be having much more of an effect on our culture than ours has on yours."

"Great. Ten limbed comedians," said David. "That is all we need."

"Comedian?" asked the Tschaaa.

"I'll explain later."

Heidi met David and Bill at the dock, helped them clean the boat and stow the gear.

"Hey, Heidi. We can do this," protested David. "No need for you to get wet and sweaty."

Heidi had laughed and grinned at the lawmen.

"That is my natural state these days. Wet and sweaty. Boat work is not like in all those old television commercials, where the bikini models never had a hair out of place."

Wild Bill had gestured with his tentacles to signify some confusion.

"Commercials?" the Squid verbalized.

"Short videos used to sell items to us which we did not really need," answered David. Bill gestured, relating a bit of surprise.

"I still do not understand how you humans traded goods, bought and sold I believe are your terms. Within Creches, everyone shares everything, with the young getting the best food and shelter."

"How about between Creches, Wild Bill?" asked Heidi.

"We trade food, tools, beautiful gemstones, and seashells that are especially desired by the young. We also swap for tools and weapons, at least any excess we have. Creches work together to produce the machinery we need in Mother Ocean."

"Then how did you build all your starships, Wild Bill?"

"Heidi, we cooperated in the early days of our space travel. When the Meat Sickness, the White Plague, all Tschaaa were forced into a frenzy of effort to build the ships needed to transport over half of our population to where we knew was plentiful Meat. Earth," the Tschaaa quickly signed and gestured with his tentacles sorrow and concern.

"I hope I do not cause you both unpleasant thoughts about the past," Bill added.

"Water under the bridge," replied David. "Today is a new day. Now, please excuse us, Bill, but I believe Heidi here still wants a date, which means sharing food, drink, and conversation."

"Part of the mating ritual?" Wild Bill asked, David began to blush, and Heidi laughed. She linked her arm through Davids.

"Come on, David. If you blush anymore, you are bound to have broken blood vessels." She turned towards Wild Bill and added, "I promise David will be back in one piece."

"There is a concern?" asked Bill. Even David laughed as he walked away with Heidi.

David soon noticed that Charlie's Tacos was a "dive" in the purest sense. It was in the basement of an older hotel so as a customer walked from the sunlight into the establishment, it took quite a few moments for the eyes to adjust. The clientele were all rough-looking residents of the shore and sea, and so for a few seconds, David wondered if he would have to fight his way out. However, everyone seemed to know Heidi as there was a round of greetings and a table was explicitly moved for her. She was definitely a regular. Ice cold mugs of beer appeared without any verbal request, followed by a large platter of fresh oysters. Crackers, cocktail sauce, hot sauce, and recently baked bread followed. As Heidi took a large drink from her beer, following it with a shucked oyster, David chuckled.

"You don't stand on ceremony, do you, Heidi?"

Heidi smiled with twinkling eyes. "Life's too short and violent these days. I like to go with the gusto. Now, try this hot sauce on an oyster. Homemade locally and hot."

"We'll see about that, my lady," replied David. "You forget I come from a land of hot Mexican chiles."

Heidi soon discovered that David had told the truth. She could see he was used to the hottest of food on the Scoville heat scale. He sweat a bit, which she thought was a healthy reactions, but neither did he start gulping beer, nor did his eyes bug out.

"This sauce is right tasty. Adds some kick to the oysters," David opined.

"You are not a big raw oyster fan, are you?" asked Heidi.

"They are okay. But I have to admit, I like cooked food,

including fish. Ichiro Yamamoto tried to make me a fan of sushi and sashimi. I did not take to it."

Heidi laughed, then turned and waved at the bar staff. As if by magic, two plates of fries, onion rings, and corn tacos appeared, all cooked of course. David grinned and dug in.

"This is more like it. American staples."

"Yeah, David. I figured a Texan would like more fried stuff. However, raw oysters and I are a fixture here. I've been a regular since I showed up in the Keys, about a year after the Tschaaa came."

"So, Heidi, then I have to ask something," said David. "I hope it won't piss you off."

The former Coastie shrugged. "Not much bothers me these days. Other than idiots who poke the bear by bothering Tchaaa young."

"So, how did you come to like Squids?" David asked. "Not just tolerate, but *like* them?"

Heidi paused in thought for a moment, and then answered. "Well, because I worked for Director Lloyd here in the Keys, I had a lot of contact with them. They were all around the channels and cuts, especially the teenagers', the young males were trying to act like warriors. None wanted to eat me until Torbin Bender and company attempted to kill Lord Neptune." She sighed. "I had more grief from my fellow humans than from the Squids. Cassandra showed me more empathy than all those Kraken assholes."

Heidi fixed her eyes on David. "I lost just about everything after the Rocks hit. But it was a human that killed a young boy that was like a son to me. The only person I loved who died thanks recently to a Squid was Adam Lloyd." She chugged the rest for her beer, then waved at the bartender.

"Shot Time," she called out.

"Hey, Heidi," David said. "I did not mean to ruin the mood."

"Nothing some whiskey can't solve," she replied. "Now, my turn."

"Yeah?"

"So, Rangers Son, how do you like working with a member of the species who got your father killed?"

Now it was David's time to pause. Which he shouldn't have had to, as he had been thinking about this the past week.

"It's... complicated," he replied.

"How so?" asked Heidi.

"You know I did prison time, right?"

"I heard rumors that a lawman who had been a convict was coming. But since half the Florida Keys supported smugglers at one time or another, what people did in the past macht nichts."

"The Tschaaa space rocks broke me out. I was serving twenty to life for murder. So I owe them for that."

"But Squid Minions killed your father, Ranger Jackson," stated Heidi.

"Yes. There is that." After answering, David threw the shot into the back of his throat and down to his stomach.

"Whiskey helps dull things," said Heidi.

"Yes, it does. But I did not want to dull things." David looked into the empty glass.

"I took the job of working with Wild Bill in my Dad's memory. The President wants this Great Compromise to work, and he supported Madam President. So, I want it to work."

The bar staff brought another round of whiskey and beer. The man and woman sat drinking, lost in thought. Heidi broke the morose mood and shocked David all at the same time. She stood up, stepped to David's side of the table and put a legendary liplock on the young Agent. He surprised himself by kissing back with passion. Heidi sat on his lap.

"Your place or mind, Tex," she whispered.

"Ma'am, I... am not a one night stand kind of guy. My Mom and Dad raised me differently."

Heidi looked into his eyes and searched his face to see his true mettle. Then she sighed

"Wouldn't you know it," she said. "Find this big hunk of

Texan who turns me on, and he is one of the Last Gentlemen."

Heidi started to rise off his lap, and David stopped her. They looked into each other's eyes. Then David spoke.

"I just don't want you to think I'm going to use you as just a quick lay to relieve stress."

"You killed over a woman you loved, didn't you?" Asked Heidi.

"Yes, Heidi, I did. She didn't love me. The guy she thought she loved hurt her bad. So I killed him."

"Not out of passion. You killed the guy with ice-cold blood after the fact. Which got you the twenty to life."

"Yes, Ma'am."

"So that makes you no good, right? And now you have something to prove."

David sat silently. For the former Coastie had hit it on the head. He was no good and was trying to prove to himself otherwise. So, he had taken the assignment with a Squid, connected to beings who killed or helped to kill family and friends. Heidi slowly stood up.

"Come on. You can walk me home. I have a suite the Admiral set me up in a few blocks away. The night air will sober us up. Then you can walk home."

Heidi paid the tab, ("Hey, I asked you out!") and they left Charlie's. Like opposite magnets, their hands found each other. A silent minute later and they stopped, turned and kissed. Then Again. Then one more time. Heidi looked up into the tall and lanky Texan's eyes.

"This does not feel like a one night stand to me, Tex," said Heidi.

"We hardly know each other, Heidi," David answered.

"Wrong. We know each other because we have suffered much the same. And we still try to do what is right, despite our pain."

David's mouth displayed a small smile in the night.

"You have this all figured out, Heidi. You must be smarter

than I am."

"Could be. So if that is the case, my Texan, kiss me you fool. Before the mood escapes us."

David tried to sneak out of Heidi's place and was tackled by this muscled and voluptuous woman. She had him down on the carpet and wrapped up in some arcane martial arts hold in seconds flat.

" I warned you I grew up in a Dojo," Heidi growled in his ear, then nibbled on it. "You can't get away that easy, Tex."

Somehow David moved his hands enough to caress some of Heidi's sensitive areas. She almost purred with pleasure.

"Someone taught you nice things, Tex."

"Why must everyone from Texas be called Tex by everyone else?" David asked.

"Because it's easier to remember, David, Especially in a fit of passion."

In a mutual movement, David was then on top with Heidi's legs wrapped around him.

"You mean like this, lady?"

"Why yes, Harvey. Just like... that. God." Heidi stopped talking as she kissed him deeply. As their mouths parted, David spoke.

"Yer right purty, Murien."

Heidi began to laugh, and David joined with her, in more ways than one.

David had a large cup of coffee in hand as he neared the berth for the AMPHITRITE. He saw water motion and some bubbles which told him that Wild Bill was already checking the hull of the Open Fisherman. The human wondered to himself if Tschaaa had a drink like coffee to help them after a long night. Hell, did they have "long nights' like humans? David kept walking and let out a loud whistle that he knew would be heard underwater by a sensitive Tschaaa. In a moment the need and eyes of the giant cephalopod popped above the surface. With a quickness that still surprised David Wild Bill had slithered up onto the dock and greeted him.

"Good Morning, fellow Lawman. How are you this fine morning?" The Tschaaa Translator still had a West Texas Drawl.

"Fine, Wild Bill," answered David. "Have you had a morning meal?"

"Why yes, David. I found some tasty mollusks and small fish that were unable to escape me when I first entered the water."

"So you have an additional benefit while you check out hull?"

"Yes. I believe you have an expression, kill two flying creatures with one rock. That is what I do."

David chuckled. Well, that answered what the Squids thought was a way to break their fast. Fresh sea creatures from Mother Ocean.

"So, I guess you are waiting on me, Wild Bill."

"True. But we are not late, so there is no hurry."

David climbed into the boat and stowed his gear. As he did, he thought about the conversations he and Heidi had the previous night and the current morning. David glanced at Wild Bill. The Agent had come to realize he now looked at the Squid as a fellow "person," not some Bug-Eyed Monster trying to eat them. Maybe it was like that moment when Early Man came to realize that a wolf could be a dog. The Tschaaa must have sensed David was contemplating about something.

"You are deep in thought, David. May I ask if it has anything to do with your Breeder, Heidi?"

David laughed.

"She is definitely not my 'breeder'. Or anyone's for that matter. She is very independent."

"But you did breed with her last night. At least had physical mating rituals."

"Hey, Wild Bill. A new social rule with humans to learn. Gentlemen don't tell. Shall we hit the road?"

The Tschaaa male gestured some confusion.

"Road? We are on the ocean."

"Never mind. I'll explain the expression later. Shall we depart?"

With natural ease, Wild Bill piloted the AMPHITRITE out into the open sea. The male denizen of the sea brought it to a smooth halt as the two surveyed the expanse of salt water. The Tschaaa slid into the ocean to see if he sensed any communications in the nearby Creche. No sooner had Bill slipped into the water, that he was pulling himself out at speed with his eight arms.

"Something is wrong, bad, David," the translator seemed to boom out. "Secure yourself. We must go."

Wild Bill had the seacraft almost flying across the open sea. He was so concentrated he explained nothing. But David by this time had come to know that the Tschaaa did not exaggerate.

David had to use the high powered binoculars to figure out where Wild Bill was headed. He finally picked out a large Sports Fisherman stopped near the official edge of the Creche Breeding Area. As the image cleared, David swore. There was human blood everywhere. Wild Bill cut the boat's outboards at just the right moment and slid its port side to the starboard of the other seacraft with barely a bump. David lashed the two craft together in record speed. Then with pistol drawn, David scrambled onto the Sports Fisherman.

"Police! Federal Agents. Is anyone hurt?" No one answered his hail. The boat deck was awash with red blood, making it slicker than usual. David performed a tactical search, with Wild Bill behind him armed with a Tschaaa two shot spear gun. Other than the blood, they found nothing.

"What did you hear in the ocean, Bill?" Asked David.

"A Breeder screaming."

David knew that for a Breeder to scream meant that young was in danger. But only red human blood was evident.

"I'll call this in, Bill…"

Something began to beat on the hull of the Sports Fisherman. Both David and Bill looked into the water and saw the frantic Breeder. David felt the high-frequency communications between the Breeder and Wild Bill. But he knew enough of the visual language to tell that the Breeder, waving and jerking her tentacles around, was on the verge of the catatonic breakdown which leads to Death with the Tschaaa. Somehow, Wild Bill seemed to calm her down a bit. He turned to David.

"Two armed Tschaaa and two tattooed humans in a small craft came up on this boat. There were five occupants in this seacraft. The Breeder said all were attacked and taken. She surfaced and told Tschaaa what they were doing was a threat to the Young. They threatened to kill her." As Wild Bill spoke, his arms and body began to darken to almost black. David knew this was the shade of killing rage. This was not a reaction Tschaaa were supposed to have towards each other.

"She is the Breeder you met the other day, David."

"I'll call for back up," David said.

"No time nor need. Another Tschaaa has tracked them up to an islet in Key Largo. We go to capture or kill these Kraken and Tschaaa."

"Kill fellow Tschaaa?" David asked.

"They and the Kraken with them are monsters. They should die. We go."

David called the situation in on the radio as Wild Bill once again made the AMPHITRITE fly across the Atlantic Ocean. The Tschaaa seemed to be able to pinpoint the destination based on the information from the Breeder. The Agent knew this was a horrible situation. Tschaaa and human Krakens 'harvesting' innocent people? Threatening to kill Breeders? Was the Great Compromise about to collapse? Not on his watch, David said to himself.

Wild Bill piloted the Open Fisherman into the channel on the north end of Key Largo. A lot of the mangroves had grown back during the Infestation due to reduced human activity. Thus the channel was partially overgrown. This was a good thing as newly broken branches marked the very recent passage of a boat. The Tshaaa Lawman throttle back and the Open Fisherman crept around a bend.

"There," David pointed to a shadowed area created by some dense brush. Human voices were heard cursing as David noticed a large bulk floating and twitching in the center of the channel. "The bastards hit a manatee, smashed their boat..."

Wild Bill slammed the engine throttles full forward as the AMPHITRITE took off like a raped ape. As he did, David saw two things. Bills color was turning black, and two Tschaaa males were halfway in the water, trying to free the boat.

The two men's heads jerked up at the sound of the racing outboards. One seemed to be reaching for a weapon as Wild Bill Hickock spun the wheel and cut the engines at the same time. A wave from the decelerating speedboat hit the trapped craft first, then the starboard side slammed into the Kraken's seacraft. David managed to brace himself enough to keep from being thrown overboard. Where the renegade Tschaaa were was anybody's guess. The two Kraken's were thrown onto the branches of the mangrove trees. David jumped on to the Crisscraft boat and unholstered his father's former Texas Ranger .357 pistol as he confronted the Krakens hung up in the mangrove trees. The one on his right sporting a full face tattoo pointed some type of handgun at the Agent and received a killing round through the chest.

"You want some?" David yelled at the other. He then noticed the Kraken had a broken branch impaling his right arm. He wasn't going anywhere.

The loud sound of an overstressed Translator jerked his attention back to his own watercraft. He looked to see Wild Bill grappling with two adults Tschaaa. As he raised his pistol to shoot, the three Squids toppled over into the water.

"Fuck!" David yelled as he scrambled back to his boat. He shucked his gun belt, grabbed his massive bladed Texas bowie knife and dove overboard into the murky water.

"He's coming around." The voice seemed to David to come out of thin air. Then his eyes focused on a man in an EMT uniform.

"How many fingers am I holding up?" The EMT asked.

"Three."

"Good. Agent Jackson, you had a whole bunch of people worried," the EMT stated. "You have a large and varied fan club."

"Yeah?" David said.

"Yeah, asshole. Like me." Heidi's face came into view. "You know, I have had a lot of men try to ditch me in my lifetime, but this is the first time someone tried to drown themselves. All you had to do was say something, and I'd leave you alone, you hard-headed…"

For all her joking, Davis saw tears on her cheeks. He reached up a finger, captured one, and fed it into his mouth.

"Heidi, I have tasted your salt from Mother Ocean. I am honored."

Heidi's chin began to quiver, and she buried her face into his neck.

"Damn you, damn you, damn you," she muffled into his throat. "You are not supposed to make me care for you. Not this soon."

"Heidi, where is Wild Bill?" He asked as he stroked her hair.

"I am here, David." The translator's voice sounded as before, Texas drawl and all. "But you must remember. I am the one who is the amphibian, can breathe underwater. Knowing this, why did you jump in to help me fight?"

It took a few moments for David to form the answer he wanted to convey.

"Because you are my pardner. My pard. Texan for partner. You may be ugly, with too many limbs, and the weirdest sexual practices, but you are my pardner. Never forget that."

The Tschaaa male gestured his social tentacles to signify honor.

"You pay me an honor I will work to deserve."

"You already deserve it, Pardner. You just saved my ass. That is enough work."

A voice cut through the commotion on the dock where the EMT vehicle was parked.

"Somewhere I have a Special Agent... oh, there you are."

Federal Law Enforcement Commissioner Paul Miller pushed his beefy form through a group of people.

"Agent Wild Bill. Glad to see you pulled David's chestnuts out of the fire."

The Tschaaa gestured confusion.

"Just an expression. But you did save this young man from drowning, yet still, managed to arrest those two Tschaaa miscreants."

"To be fair," responded Wild Bill, "David cut the two evil ones with that large blade of his, which I recovered. That seemed to shock them and make them easier to restrain."

"Well," continued the Commissioner, "That just showed excellent teamwork. So, Madam President and I want to express our gratitude for a job well done. Take tomorrow off, you two. The paperwork can wait."

"Sir, what happened to the people..." David tried to ask.

"Dead and butchered," Paul Miller responded. "Thanks to the new drug trade, some of the surviving Krakens and Squids have formed a new unholy alliance."

"What? I don't understand," David said.

"Some Tschaaa and some human scum have developed a new form of drug, a chemical substance we are still trying to figure out. It not only makes the Tschaaa feel great in an addictive manner, but humans get a craving for human blood. Right now the street slang for it is Dracula. For the first time, an equal opportunity abuser between two species. I came down here to check on you and to coordinate response to this crap. It seems it appeared here first."

"So, I'll have even more work to do," said David.

"No rest for the wicked." Paul Miller looked at Heidi. "Miss Faust, can I place this man in your capable hands so you may ensure he rests tomorrow? And checks with the medical staff at the Key West Operations Base before he goes back to work?"

"Yes. Sir," Heidi said with a grin.

"Good. Carry on. See you later." Paul Miller walked off as Heidi grinned at David.

"Hear that? You are in my charge, David Jackson."

"Well, it could be worse, Heidi. I could be dead."

Heidi gently squeezed his arm. Wild Bill noticed the action with his highly accurate eyes.

"So David, does this mean Heidi is your Breeder?"

Heidi began to laugh as David blushed.

"Pardner, do me a favor. Shut up."

PEST CONTROL

WYOMING, UNITED STATES OF NORTH AMERICA

Bobby Parsons walked back into the campsite with fresh meat for the pot. The twenty-one year old, who was tall and slender, with broad shoulders had managed to snare a rabbit and a squirrel with his Alabama hunting skills. His dad had taught him well. Then the Tschaaa had come, and his father was killed. Since then, he had done what was necessary to keep his sister and mother alive.

This led him to this camp with two other men. Despite the fact he had helped save the Voice of the Free States—Alesha Taylor—years ago, he had served as a guard in Cattle Country, where the aliens had kept their dark meat. Thus, he was a Squid lover, who few wanted to employ. Now, he was out bounty hunting for Eaters, the nasty six-limbed creature brought by the Tschaaa.

He walked over to the older one everyone called Pops McCracken. No one knew if that was his actual name, but he was gray, grizzled, and looked older than dirt when he woke up in the morning. He was also a drunk, a fact Bobby and the other member of the small group had found out late in this adventure.

"More fresh game, Bobby?" asked the third member of this official Pest Control Team. Brian Ramsey, the source of funds for the team, was one of the fortunate humans during the alien Tschaaa Infestation. His immediate family, mother, father, and sister, were helping him settle in as a freshman at the University of Wyoming Laramie on a sports scholarship when the first space rocks hit. As everything fell apart, his family was able to use some wealth and social standing to find permanent lodging in Laramie. His mother was a nurse, so she had a marketable skill in the survival society that arose as the cephalopod Tschaaa took control of all the coastal areas. Their spacious home outside the Bay Area in California was gone. Brian's father was a Light Colonel in the Reserves, so he was immediately re-activated into what was to become the armed forces of the Free States of America. Thus, Brian and his sister Susan were never in any danger of starving or being harvested.

Bobby walked over to Pops and dumped the game at his feet. The older man already had a buzz on. The fact he drank to excess was terrible enough. What made it worse was that the money he was to use to buy supplies for the foray into forests and mountains of Wyoming had mostly been spent on rotgut booze and locally brewed beer. Bobby dropped the gutted kills at the drunk's feet. His beagle, Jobber, sniffed at the fresh meat.

"Here, Pops. Something to cook up," stated Bobby.

"Who said I was the cook?" growled Pops.

"Well, you sure as hell are not a guide. Where is a that Eater sign you claimed you saw?"

Pops, before he was in his cups, had bragged far and wide that he knew where all the Eaters were in Wyoming just as soon as the new post-Great Compromise United States of North America had posted a bounty. That was why Bobby Parsons had left his mother and sister at Malmstrom Armed Forces Base in Montana so he could make some money. No one wanted to hire a Squid lover near the base.

At Bobby's less than respectful comment, Pops somehow

scrambled to his feet.

"Keep with that smart mouth, boy, and you're going to get a bruisin'." Pops tried to sound as menacing as possible.

"From you? Or is Jobber going to do it for you?" Bobby had put up with too much crap just surviving to be cowered by a loudmouthed braggart.

"Hey you two, knock it off," Brian called out. "We need to make the best of a bad situation if we are going to break even."

Brian looked directly at Pops. "Since you drank up most of our food budget, yes, you get to cook. I don't see any great guide capabilities coming from you."

Pops glared at Brian. Then he picked up the two dead animals and went to create a spit for each.

"See any eater sign out there?" Brian asked Bobby.

"Nope, I did see some deer sign, but it was a few hours old." Bobby paused in thought for a few minutes, then continued. "If there were Eaters around, any deer would have been long gone or eaten days ago. Damn things can swallow animals whole, like a snake, and digest even the bones."

"Bobby, did you see an Eater close up before the two we killed?"

" A couple of dead ones near Cattle... near the Alabama border. They tried to get through a border fence and were electrified."

Brian shook his head.

"I think we may head out tomorrow. We've wasted a week here, ate up the little food Pops bought, and have just two pairs of Eater claws to show for it. A hundred dollars per pair bounty won't go far."

"Well, Brian, it's your SUV. I go where you want to go."

Bobby walked over to where he had his pack stashed. He made sure Pops had not disturbed it as when the man was drunk, he forgot where he was half the time. Bobby shook his head as he thought once again how he could miss all the signs of an alcoholic about the old man. Brian had not noticed either.

"Talk about the blind leading the blind," he mumbled to himself. He took out his gun cleaning kit and gave his two weapons a quick once over. They weren't much, but they worked. Beggars could not be choosers, and as many wanted nothing to do with Squid lovers, Bobby was cursed to be a perpetual beggar. The Great Compromise signed with the Squids to prevent mutually assured destruction did not mean that human attitudes would change overnight.

Bobby ran a patch down the ancient 8mm Lebel bolt action rifle. The damn thing was well over a century old, with World War I technology limiting it to three round clips that inserted through the top of the weapon. At least the bullet was large and nasty, his one shot in the body of the first Eater they had seen dropped it like a sack of rocks. Its barrel had been cut back by someone which made it into a usable "bush gun" that handled well in the thick forest. His second weapon was a .22 semi-auto Colt pistol, almost as old as the Lebel. The elderly woman he had bought them from had just lost her husband and wanted to get rid of them. She did not check to see who is buying them. Bobby had a box of old but in good condition ammunition for each. Those two weapons would have to do until he could obtain others.

Brian carried a heavy compound hunting bow with a quiver of broadhead arrows, plus a few target arrows. He had shot the second Eater through an eyeball and into its brain. The man had done it with such ease that Bobby knew he must have thousands of hours of practice under his belt. Pops had a long barreled pump shotgun, but both the younger men thought his drinking would prevent him from being a very accurate shot. Pops had bragged about his hunting and guiding skills. He also had Jobber, who seemed to have a good nose. It helped, of course, that all dogs hated Eaters. Yet, even the canine's nose could not locate any other of the "pests" the group was hunting for bounty.

Eventually, Pops growled that dinner was ready and the

three dug out their mess kits. At least Pops was a passable cook and had also cooked up the rest of the ramen noodles with some tasty seasoning of his own concoction. After the meal and cleanup, Brian mentioned his plan.

"Tomorrow morning, zero dark thirty, we head out to another area. South, closer to Evanston, the site of the first pack level infestation."

"Hell, that area was hunted out last year by the military!" protested Pops. "I tell you, I'll find…"

"You'll tell me nothing, old fool." Brian's generally cordial tone turned to ice, something Bobby had not heard before. Pops' face flushed with anger and his hand went to a hunting knife on his belt. Bobby started to reach for his pistol, but from a hidden pocket, Brian magically produced a snub nose revolver and pointed it at Pops' face.

"For a drunk, you are full of yourself. Try anything, and you will be buried out here."

"I didn't…" Pops began to sputter as the barrel of the pistol seemed to sober him up.

"And you won't," replied Brian. "I financed and organized this little foray as a means to do something different for the new U.S.A. and make some money at the same time. Now, how much of that so-called 'liquid bread' do you have, since that is about the only type of food supply we have left."

"Two cases, over yonder," answered a much more subdued Pops.

"Bobby, please move the beer to the SUV and lock it up. Pops here has had enough," stated Brian. "Pops, I want that rotgut bottle of yours given to Bobby. Or you can walk home."

As Bobby complied with Brian's instructions, he noticed Jobber sat and watched.

"You're probably the smartest one here, pup," Bobby said with a smile. "We humans are a contentious lot, as Alesha says on her newscasts.

There being nothing much else to do, and with the night

approaching, the three men readied their bedrolls. Bobby laid down and looked at the bright, star-filled sky. After the Long Winter caused by the rocks and with significantly reduced human industrial activity, the night sky had cleared up in many parts of the world. Bobby knew that surviving amateur astronomers were having a blast.

"Well. I'm glad someone is enjoying this," the former Cattle Country guard said to himself. He soon drifted off into sleep.

Bobby woke up just as the sun was poking up over the mountains. He liked the quiet of late at night and early in the morning hours. As he rolled out of his bedroll, a rifle shot echoed through the forest and foothills. Bobby was up on his feet just as another far-off shot sounded. Then a series of reports from what seemed like a rifle of substantial caliber.

"What's happening?" Brian's voice came from behind him.

"Series of shots, from over there." Bobby pointed towards a small ravine about a mile or so distant from the camp.

"Bobby, take the electric moped. It's quiet and will get you there faster," said Brian. "We need to know if we have some competition."

"Will do." Bobby began grabbing his gear.

"What's going on?" A bleary-eyed Pops asked.

"Start breaking camp," ordered Brian. "We're leaving."

Bobby grabbed the moped from alongside the SUV, mounted it and turned it on. The electric motor purred into operation, and Bobby accelerated down an old trail that was still open enough to allow decent passage. Thanks to Tschaaa solar energy development, a small moped like the one Booby used was quickly charged and could zip along at about fifty miles an hour on good pavement for an hour or so. The trail was a bit rough, so Bobby kept the speed to below twenty-five. His rifle was slung across his back, necessitating he watch out for branches along the trail which could hang him up. Bobby still made good time. About fifteen minutes into his journey, he heard loud voices arguing ahead. Bobby stopped the moped, leaned it up against a small tree, and continued on foot with his now unslung rifle at the ready.

Bobby Parsons soon found the source of all the noise and commotion. The trail opened out into a clearing where a couple of large SUVs were parked. Bobby saw the owner of one of the loud voices. A bronze-haired young woman with an athletic build and bumps in all the right places was giving hell to three good-sized bearded males outfitted in hunters camouflage. As Bobby stepped a bit closer, he realized the three men where the Smithers Brothers, all members of the semi-formal scavenger community out of Great Falls, Montana, near the Base. Once a significant source of scavenged goods for the Free States, the new Federal Government had stamped down on their activities after they had acted as if they were a law unto themselves. The men were not triplets, but the family resemblance was close. The redhead was showing a stereotypical ginger temper towards the brothers.

"I told you not to shoot them in the head. I need undamaged brain samples for the official research. Later on, you will need to kill them with headshots, as I will need whole bodies. Can you understand the difference? Are you deaf, or just stupid?"

The four humans were standing among the corpses of four large Eaters and a stack of rifles. The alien creatures looked more massive than most based on Bobby's experience. Two of the Smithers looked towards the third brother.

"You gonna let her talk to us like that, JoJo?" one of them asked.

Bobby figured by the question that JoJo was the eldest and in charge.

"No, Willy, I'm not," replied JoJo. He stepped towards the ginger woman.

"Professor MacDuff, I suggest you watch your mouth. We do not take kindly to insults."

"May I remind you who is paying you for this trip?" MacDuff shot back. "You're receiving substantial pay in addition to the Eater bounties provided by the Government.

"How about just do your jobs?" the woman added.

JoJo looked at his brothers. "Willy, Jay, whattya think? Too much shit?"

"Yeah," the two brothers answered in unison.

With their answer, JoJo turned towards the Professor and swung a flat hand slap at her. She ducked and kicked him in the family jewels. As she scrambled backward, she reached for a holstered pistol. Willy came and wrapped his thick arms around her, stopping her attempt to grab the handgun. JoJo, holding his groin, limped up to the woman.

"Now the real fun begins," growled JoJo.

Bobby stepped out from behind a tree, rifle pointed at the tableau.

"Stop right there!" Bobby bellowed. The brothers looked at him as if he had three heads.

"Who the hell are you?" JoJo asked.

"Someone who doesn't like to see women beaten up, no matter how much they piss you off."

"Look at the old piece of shit rifle he has," called out the brother Jay. "He's lucky it don't blow up when he shoots it."

"Want to try me?" Bobby shot back. "I killed an Eater with it a couple of days ago."

"Now, boy, let's not do anything rash here," Jojo said. "We're all just trying to make a living."

"Then do your goddamned jobs!" yelled the Professor. Willy squeezed her tighter, which resulted in the woman stomping on his foot, then putting a heel into his shin. Willy lifted her off her feet, twisted and threw her to the ground. He reached for a long-bladed knife in his belt as Bobby prepared to shoot him.

An Eater burst from the underbrush, heading straight for the four figures in the center of the clearing. It hit Jay first as he was the closest. Jay man screamed as the Eater opened its expandable jaws and latched them around his entire chest. Man and monster collapsed in a heap, as JoJo pulled a Bowie knife from his belt and scrambled to help his brother. Another Eater came running from the treeline on all six limbs, lather dripping from its oversized maw. Willy screamed as it went for him. The Eater leapt at him as Willy swung his blade, slicing the bug-eyed monster's eye open. The creature let out an unforgettable scream and began to spin around in a circle as a third of its kind dashed from the vegetation. Bobby shot it as he yelled, "Make for the vehicles! Get inside!"

The Professor was up and running as a fourth beast made its appearance. Bobby shot it between the eyes as it beelined toward the woman. He worked the bolt and ran towards the SUV the Professor was jumping into. She held the door open for him as he saw a fifth and then a sixth Eater explode from the underbrush.

JoJo had gutted the Eater which had latched onto Jay, but not before it had chewed on the Smithers brother and gotten some of its highly corrosive digestive juices on him. Jojo lifted his brother up onto his shoulder and tried to run for the vehicles as Willy made it to the rifle stack and grabbed an AK-47. He fired a burst of bullets at the fifth and sixth Eaters, taking them down.

As Willy raised the rifle to shoot the Eater the man had cut, the Smithers brother did not notice the seventh Eater until it had latched onto him. He tumbled to the ground screaming. The cut Eater now joined the other in doing what it lived for—eating prey. Willy was cut off in mid-scream as his head was consumed whole by the mouth of the monster. Jojo was a few yards from the open door of the SUV when an eighth eater seemed to appear from nowhere. It slammed into him, impaling him with some of the quills that grew on its forearms. The front limbs ended in clawed hands which were used to grasp and rend prey—in this case, JoJo. Bobby stepped out of the SUV, jammed the Lebel's barrel into the Eater's face and fired. Brains and gore splattered about the clearing. He grabbed JoJo and dragged him into the SUV's backseat as the Professor took the front. They shut and locked the doors. Bobby had been told Eaters would enter open windows but generally would not try to force or dig their way into structures or vehicles. They would usually wait for prey to come out into the open, then they would run it down.

Inside the SUV, the wounded JoJo tried to open the doors.

"My brothers…"

"Gone, stay here," Bobby said calmly. "We can save you. Not them."

JoJo slumped forward as the information sank in. Booby turned towards the ginger woman. "What's your name?"

"MacDuff, Erin MacDuff."

"Well, Erin, we need to find a first aid kit without moving around a lot and make noise. And we need to keep an eye on those Eaters."

"You keep an eye out," Erin said. "There should be a first aid kit in the back."

As the woman crawled to the back of the SUV, Bobby reloaded his Lebel with a three round clip. Erin found the kit and stopped JoJo's moaning with a syringe of morphine and bandaged him up.

"I do not know why I am doing this for you, JoJo," Erin said. "I guess I'm a nicer person than you are, and your brothers were."

.The two remaining Eater had gorged themselves on Willy, then took a few bites from Jay. After that, satiated, they crawled out into the brush to digest.

"They will now digest, and begin to bud in about a day," explained Erin.

"Bud? You mean to make more Eaters?" asked Bobby.

"Yes. When Eaters have sufficient food, the monsters breed like our rabbits."

"Well, our rabbits don't try to eat us," opined Bobby.

"No, they do not. By the way, what is your name?" asked Erin.

"Bobby. Bobby Parsons."

"Are you with a Pest Control Group?"

"Yes. The other two folks should be along any time now. If not, we find some spare vehicle keys, or I hotwire the SUV, and we leave."

"I can't do that, Bobby," stated Erin.

"Why not?" Bobby inquired.

"I have to have samples—Eater brains as well as Eater bodies to dissect. Something is going on with these damn aliens. Maybe a mutation."

Bobby frowned. What was she saying? He repeated his thoughts aloud. "What are you talking about, Erin?"

"I'm working for Colonel and Doctor Bettie Bardun, the President's Exobiologist. The Eaters seem to be getting larger, and their psychology and thinking patterns are changing. Some say they are becoming more like a social insect, like ants. Ants can make war. Can you imagine if Eaters conducted warfare activities like ants? We need to find out why."

"Think it's the Squids screwing around with genetics again?" asked Bobby.

"That, or some sick bastard humans."

"So, that may be why so many came at us?" Bobby pondered.

"That, and the combination Eater vomit and human blood scent we developed to draw them in worked too damn well."

Bobby laughed, then replied. "You scientists need to ask some of us Alabama farm boys about the animal scent. It's hard to figure out what is needed to make animals do what you want them to do. Less is always best."

Things were quiet for a few minutes. Then they heard an SUV approach.

"Hope that's Brian," said Bobby. "If I hadn't left my radio in the camp, I could have led him to us."

The SUV that approached was Brian, with Pops and Jobber. The dog went nuts with all of the Eater smell, barking and dashing around. Bobby stepped out of the vehicle to warn Brian and Pops about the Eaters still roaming around.

"You say the Eaters are in the brush over there?" asked Brian.

"Yes. Two at least. Sleeping off their meal," replied Bobby.

Brian looked at both Pops and Jobber, then spoke. "You get to earn your keep. Jobber should be able to track them. Get your 12-gauge shotgun."

"Why in the hell?" Pops protested. "Look at all these Eater carcasses. Cut the hands off for bounty..."

"Because most belong to the young lady and her crew. Those two Eaters will soon bud, and make more eaters. Now, get to it or walk home."

Pops swore and cursed under his breath, but he did what he was told. Bobby walked over to Brian, telling him, "This could get Pops killed. I'll go along..."

"Then you can walk home. My father said that in the new world order, weak and worthless drunks like Pops have to pull their own weight or die. Think about what would have happened if all these Eaters had hit our camp."

Bobby didn't reply. He was in no mood for an argument. Besides, he did not want to be killed because of Pops either. Empathy was one thing. He still had to think about his mother and sister.

As Pops slowly entered the bush, Brian was able to raise some authorities on his cell phone, telling them that they had a wounded man and two dead. The military related they would send a helicopter out to get the injured and to survey the situation. Erin MacDuff then asked to be patched through to Colonel Bardun. Bobby recovered the Smithers brothers' weapons and reloaded the AK-47. He wanted more firepower than his bolt-action Lebel. After Erin was off the telephone, she had an odd look on her face. She walked up to Bobby.

"I did not realize you were *that* Bobby Parsons."

"Yeah. I'm the Squid lover," Bobby growled.

"Hey, the Colonel said you were a good person, that the Voice of the Free States Alesha said you were was a close friend of hers. She wanted to make sure you were okay."

"Well, Erin, tell that to the rest of people who won't hire me because I spent time as a guard in Cattle Country. I did it so my family could survive."

"A lot of us did crap to survive, Bobby," replied the Professor. "I was a student in Key West, and saw the Director close up. So I guess I'm guilty of supporting the Occupied Areas also."

Bobby didn't reply. He just wanted to collect what bounty he could on the Eaters, and feel like he was contributed something for his family.

"Tell you what," Erin continued. "I'll need to take some more field trips. I need people I can trust. Want to help me hunt and harvest Eaters?"

Bobby contemplated the offer. Erin did seem tough, smart, and was pleasant to look at during a long day. He shrugged as he answered. "Sure, why not. Maybe Brian will come along. But not Pops. He's a drunk."

At the mention of Pops, there was a rapid string of shotgun blasts up in the brush. Then silence. Bobby moved over to where Pops had entered the woods. A few minutes later, Jobber came tearing back into the camp, then hid under the SUV, shaking. Bobby raised the AK-47 to where the dog had exited the brush. He heard something stumbling through the vegetation. A bloody Eater stumbled out, and Bobby immediately shot it through the head. Brian walked over with a machete.

"Want the hands?" Brian asked.

"Of course—it's money. But I think Pops has had his last drink."

About an hour later, JoJo was medevaced out by the military helicopter. The crew brought a sealed envelope for Erin MacDuff. Bobby watched as she read it. Then continued to watch as she began to laugh. A lot. He walked over to her as she wiped her eyes from laughing so hard.

"That must be some joke," said Bobby.

"Yes, Bobby. A huge cosmic joke." Erin held up the report she had just read.

"Turns out Eater protein may be the ultimate diet food. It fills you up, passes through your system, but our body only absorbs about five percent of the calories. It's like celery. You chew it, eat it, use up almost as many calories in the eating as it provides the human body, and then it passes through your body. But not like those other foods, like those horrible potato chips that gave everyone the 'runs.'"

"So, will you still need me for field trips?" Bobby asked.

"Oh, hell yes! Some wisenheimer will try to figure out a way to breed them in captivity, and make them less dangerous rather than wipe them out. This report says Eaters taste like a cross between lobster and crab. And they breed like rabbits. So all the diet food in the world in some five to ten years when we are all fat, dumb and happy."

Bobby contemplated her statement, and then responded. "Yeah, Erin, they breed like rabbits, and are like celery in calorie count. But then again, people forget certain facts."

"What's that?" asked Erin.

"Celery and rabbits have never tried to kill and eat us. Maybe this is how we will get our revenge."

CHOICES

GREAT FALLS, MONTANA

The young girl, not yet eighteen stood outside of the office building and shivered. She looked at the sign one more time: REPRODUCTIVE SERVICES INC.

How she had had the nerve to get this far, she still did not know. All she did know is she could not handle the expanding abdomen and what it signified. She blinked back tears as she stood on an indecisive spot on the sidewalk.

"Can I help you?" The voice from behind her made he jump.

"I'm sorry, dear. I didn't mean to startle you."

The slender brunette turned around to see thirty-something dishwater blonde woman smiling at her. The young woman tried to speak, but nothing seemed to want to come out. The older woman looked at the brunette's protruding stomach and knew the reason for her visit.

"Come on into the office, dear. I have some hot tea, and we can discuss options…"

Just then another figure approached. A somewhat muscular dark-skinned woman marched up to the two women and stood blocking the path into the clinic. The dishwater blonde frowned as she spoke to the intruder.

"Look, Sergeant Power. I told you this is none of your concern. You need to go back to your Unit, the Banshees..."

"So you can convince another woman to do what the Squids did? Kill babies?"

"This is different. No one is forcing her to give up what is in her body. It's her choice."

"The results are the same," Sergeant Power answered. "What's your name, young lady?"

"Mary..."

"You don't have to talk to the Sergeant. Mary," the other woman said. "Now, please get out of our way, Sergeant, unless you want a report to your Commanding Officer this time."

"Why, June? So you can kill another baby?" The Sergeant spat back.

"Come on, Mary. We'll go inside," June said. She tried to push past Sergeant Power.

A second later, the woman called June was on her back, looked up with blood streaming from her nose. Mary screamed and stepped back, holding her abdomen protectively. A man and a woman in white lab coats came running from the building, the man yelling into a cell phone.

"We need the police. Now! One of our staff has been attacked."

Sergeant Power stood with balled fists, ready to fight more.

"Don't nobody touches me," she growled. "Ever again!"

A siren echoed a few blocks away. The sound grew closer to the clinic as Mary sobbed.

General John Reed, Allied Forces Commander, sat behind his desk in the headquarters building of Malmstrom Armed Forces Base. He looked at the four individuals arrayed around his office. Despite the size of the room, the four persons and the subject which had brought them together this day seemed to make the office feel small and oppressive. General Reed glanced at the police report one last time, then tossed it on his desk.

"We need crap like this about as much as we need more reports of Eaters." He glanced at the only other male in the room as he continued. "Commissioner Miller, what does Law Enforcement say?"

Paul Miller, the Commissioner of Federal Law Enforcement, shifted his beefy but sturdy frame in the padded chair. The older man was a fast friend of the General, but he had a job to do. Thus, he never minced words.

"I can't keep making excuses to the locals about PTSD—cut the troops a sprout because of the Squids, making the Great Compromise work, etcetera, etcetera. Somebody needs to pay the piper. Soon."

General Reed a had noticed a few more gray hairs in the mirror that morning even before the police report was plopped on his desk. He knew he would have more before this was all over. He shot a hard look at the young black haired Colonel, and the mother of his Godchildren, Aleksandra Bender.

"Well, Colonel. You're the miscreant's Commander. What do you suggest we do with this Banshee of yours."

Aleks sat up straight in her chair as she answered.

"Sir, in my former position in the Russian Army, Sergeant Power could be flogged. But I understand that is not part of the Code of Military Justice in the new United States of North America."

"So, what do you suggest?" the General asked.

"If I may interject, Sir." The new voice was from blonde Abigail Yamamoto, the legendary Avenging Angel, and the Banshee's Banshee. As she was also an adopted daughter of the General, her opinion carried additional weight.

"Go ahead. Major. You have an idea?" asked General Reed.

"In ancient times, specialized units of warriors handled their own 'off the record' punishment for those who brought dishonor to their comrades. I think Colonel Bender and I could come up with a unique sentence to help with these anger control issues of Sergeant Power."

General Reed shook his head. "Sorry. It is the same problem as before. We can't make a habit of treating Banshees different than anyone else."

The General then looked at the third woman in the room.

"Well, Agent Jorgensen, I know as head of the Security for Madam President that you were sent here with a message from her. Correct?"

The tallest human in the room, a true Shield Maiden in the classical sense, smiled slightly.

"Yes, General," Brynhildr Jorgensen replied. "She wishes me to remind all that she was serious about preserving the rights people here in the U.S. had before the Tschaaa appeared. Thus, *Roe v. Wade* still applies. No matter anyone's personal opinion."

General Reed surveyed all the participants in the room one more time before he spoke.

"Okay. I don't want to regret the day I allowed an all-female unit to be created. Thus, the Officers in Charge of the 101st Special Attack Unit, the Banshees, will ensure said Sergeant Power will be remanded to the civilian authorities for judicial action. After that, the Armed Forces will have its pound of flesh. Any questions? Good. Let me know when this is accomplished."

The back of the clinic building was a mass of flames. However, the Fire Department was standing back some distance from the burning structure. In their response path were two figures, one with a nasty blade held to the throat of the other.

"Stay back, or I slit her throat!" Sergeant Power yelled. She emphasized her warning by tightening her grip on the clinic worker named June.

"Keep choking her like that, and you won't need that knife to off her," an EMT responded.

The local Police Sergeant was about to call on the radio for the SWAT to hurry up when a black SUV with wig-wag lights in the grill came to a screeching halt nearby. Three women, two in military combat fatigues, jumped out. The tallest one showed Federal Law Enforcement badge and ID to the Sergeant.

"Special Agent Jorgensen with the two Commanders from that woman's unit. We'll take it from here."

"Good luck with that," answered the local police official. "That one over there seems bent on being shot by SWAT."

Abigail and Aleks moved towards Sergeant Power.

"Banshee! Put down that blade. You are dishonoring it and your Sisters," Abigail called out in her best Avenging Angel command voice. Aleks was the Senior Commander, but she knew Abigail had a special connection with all the troops. It was because of her that the Sisters of Steel and the Banshees were created.

"Stay back, Major," ordered Power. "This is more important than the Sisters."

"More important than the oath you took, Sergeant?" Aleks interjected.

"My oath to life is, Colonel," came the response. "Now stay back."

"Sergeant, we all have suffered..." Abigail began, but the dark-skinned Banshee cut her off.

"Did you have a baby ripped from your womb, Major? Huh? Did you see it taken to feed some Squid?*Did you?*" Sergeant Power's rant ended in a screeching yell. The SWAT vehicle arrived at that moment. The tactical geared personnel began to deploy as Aleks cursed and stepped forward.

"Look. I carried two children who could have come out as monsters thanks to Squid chicanery with my womb," stated Aleks. "I chose to take that chance. Some women are unable to handle that. It is their right to chose..."

"No!" Sergeant Power screamed. "How is killing the baby in your womb because of fear, any different than killing it for veal?" Tears began to run down the Banshee's face. "It is human life. The Squids took too many of our babies in Cattle Country, in Atlanta. *You weren't there!*"

"No, we were not," answered Aleks. "We were putting out asses on the line to try and stop it. Which we finally did."

"Too late," snarled Power. "You were too late. I made a promise to all those who did not make it that I would never let another baby be killed in the womb, cut out like mine was before I could escape."

The Sergeant shivered. "It was a little girl. The bastards did not even care. They said there were enough human Breeders."

Abigail stepped closer to Power and her hostage. She thought that her enhanced physical abilities from some similar Tschaaa tampering similar to that done with women's wombs might enable her to disarm the Banshee.

"Please. I do not want this to end badly. I've seen enough killing," explained Abigail as she moved extremely slowly towards the Sergeant. "You took an oath to Madam President. You are one of the President's Own. Do not sully that fact."

Sergeant Power locked eyes with her.

"I have no President if she condones the murder of innocents," Power said. Then she slit June's throat. Abigail screamed and was a blur as she dashed towards the Banshee. A SWAT bullet beat her, splashing Power's brains and blood over Abigail, June, and the street pavement.

Somehow they saved June. Her vocal chords would need some Tschaaa nannite reconstruction, but she was alive. Whether her psyche could be repaired was another matter. A somber service was held for the fallen Banshee. Despite what had happened, it was the War and the Infestation that had killed her, not the SWAT bullet.

Madam President attended, despite some political grumblings by some of the politicos. President Sandra Paul had responded in her typically blunt manner.

"She was one of my many daughters, who sacrificed all. She did not ask for this life, the Infestation. She served until she broke. Like many of us have."

As the service ended in the new private Banshee Cemetary overlooking Malmstrom Armed Forces Base, Aleks walked up to the President.

"Madam President. I must offer my apologies for my failings as a commander. If you wish to replace..."

"Please, Aleks. Don't. It is not your fault. People break. I almost did. I was lucky."

The two women stood for quietly for a moment. Abigail walked up.

"She is with God now," stated the Avenging Angel.

"How can you be so sure, Abigail?" Madam President asked. "She tried to kill someone."

"She thought she was saving a life. God is merciful, Ma'am. Trust me. I have known God's mercy."

Sandra Paul grasped a hand of each of the Banshees.

"Remember this. I am always there for you, whatever that means. We are Sisters, who take care of our own, no matter the mistakes, the problems."

The President paused for a moment, then continued. "But we have a higher calling to ensuring the United States of North America and the Great Compromise succeed. That success is what matters."

Sandra Paul looked at her watch.

"Time to go. Hugs, please." The President was not one for military decorum. As she left, Aleks and Abigail stood together and watched her.

"She is the greatest woman I have known," proclaimed Aleks.

"Yes, she is," answered Abigail. "There is one sad thing."

"What is that, my little sister?"

"Thanks to the Tschaaa, Sergeant Power and her daughter will never have the chance to be that great."

The two Sisters of Steel walked away as clouds overhead obscured the sun.

MEMORIES

GREAT FALLS, MONTANA

"Hey, Dad! What's this?" twin voices asked in loud unison from further up the sidewalk. A casually dressed Torbin Bender kept walking at a relaxed gait as he looked at his twin sons, Gage and Tristan. They pointed through a display window of a book and periodical store in downtown Great Falls, Montana. The two boys, although only a bit over two years old, acted at least twice their age. Torbin silently cursed the genetic tampering their former enemies—the cephalopod aliens called the Tschaaa—had done to the human species. Raising kids was hard enough without having to deal with accelerated development, both mental and physical.

Yet he loved them to death. Strange though they might be in some ways, they were still his and his beloved wife's children.

"Wait up, guys!" General Torbin Bender called out to his sons. "Remember what I said about running ahead?"

"Yes, dad," they answered in perfect unison. Torbin had heard that identical twins often did that, even without any genetic tampering by the Tschaaa. But it still made him feel a bit... uncomfortable.

As the two black-haired (from their Russian-Ukrainian mother, Aleksandra Smirnov) children turned and looked at their father with their piercing blue eyes (from the Bender side of the family), he smiled to himself. Just before the Tschaaa Invasion and Infestation began, now over eight years past, Torbin had no idea he would ever have a real family with kids. Then again, he had also thought that his military active duty days were past. The first huge rock launched from Earth orbit by the Tschaaa changed all that.

His sons both pointed at the window of the local bookstore with intense interest.

"What's up, guys?" he asked.

"Dad, come look!" Gage—the elder by a minute or two—answered excitedly.

"Yeah, Dad," added Tristen. "It's a comic about you and Mom!"

Tobin walked up and looked through the large glass display window.

"Shit," Torbin swore under his breath.

He thought that an arrangement had been made with various comic and graphic novels to find some other subject than the alleged adventures of Torbin "Squid Killer" Bender, and his wife Aleks "Killer Spy" Smirnov. It was true that he had killed many a Squid, including one using his K-Bar fighting blade. And Aleks had been a trained Russian intelligence operative, a spy. They had been in the thick of things for what seemed like forever, even before they met. Now, his actions to shield his sons from some of the crasser parts of their parents' history were in vain.

The current "work of art" displayed on its cover an over-muscled Torbin with a knife that looked more like a Roman gladius, a short sword. Back to back with him was a stylized version of Aleks, with an overly endowed chest, blasting away with a machine pistol in each hand. They were surrounded by dead and dying, drooling Tschaaa cephalopods, Kraken tattooed human traitors, the mutated beast creatures created by sick people, and of course the alien life form known as Eaters, named for what they did.

"Is that what you did, Dad?" asked Gage. "Is that what Mom did?"

"It's exaggerated. Remember, you learned that word. It means..."

"Made up a lot," answered Tristen. "It's a big made up story."

Torbin sighed. Now, how to explain to young boys wise beyond their year?

"Your mother and I did fight. We just were not the superheroes these comics make us out to be. We were warriors, doing what we had to do so you two could be born, and not eaten."

"Were you and Mom friends before the Squids came?" Tristan inquired.

Torbin tried not to laugh. Friends. Yeah, right. The U.S. and Russia were going through a rough time in their relationship, thanks to accusations of election tampering, funding proxy wars, and screwing with each other's economies. He sighed at the memories. At least he could thank the Tschaaa for bringing him together with Aleks. Without their attack, their Infestation and subsequent harvesting of humanity, he never would have met his love.

"No, sons. Mom and I had not met yet. You can thank the Squids for that. It was one good thing that came out of the war."

Torbin felt the two pairs of eyes boring into him, and knew their genetically enhanced mental capabilities were working overtime to figure out this new question of Mom and Dad's timeline.

"So, that's a reason the Squids, and we are friends now?" Gage asked. Torbin had to chuckle.

"Hey, guys. You are important, but not that important.

Remember what Mom and I taught you before you started school?"

"Yes, Dad." Again, in perfect unison. "The Squids came to eat us."

Torbin sighed. No use beating around the bush with these two.

"Yes, they did. Your Mom and I were fighting them when we met."

"You met Mom, and fell in love?" Gage asked.

"That about sizes it up, son."

"Now, the Tschaaa— the Squids—are our friends?" Now it was Tristan's turn to ask a question.

"Kind of. Sort of." Torbin sighed. "I'll let your mother explain all the details."

Torbin was about to take over as the Chief of Staff and the Commanding General for the United States of North America and its allies—Free Japan and Free Russia, forces in the western hemisphere. Thanks to the Great Compromise, he would not be locked in a deathmatch with the Tschaaa. They came to harvest and eat humans. Some people like Torbin fought, some tried to hide, and many had just died. Now as the Marine stood on the street in downtown Great Falls, Montana, he was one of the principal people responsible for making the new cooperative relationship with the Tschaaa work. Damn, Torbin thought. All he had wanted was to be left alone.

But fate or karma had decided that he was to be in the thick of things from day one. Then again, without all of that, he never would have met Aleks, his one true love. Nor would he have two handsome sons. He glanced at his reflection in a store window. He laughed to himself as he saw a person with Hollywood good looks and some gray mixed in with his dark brown hair. A lot of good his physical attractiveness did these days.

Both of his sons nodded in unison at the mention of their mother. As he contemplated whether he should try and explain more to two children advanced well beyond usual standards, he felt someone watching him. His old combat instincts, what he often referred to as his "Spidey sense"—what Aleks attributed to cockroaches—made him look up. Standing a storefront and a half down was a slender young girl about eight or nine years, tall for her age. She had long dark brown hair, braided and hanging down past her shoulders. She was examining Torbin and his sons with an intensity that matched how his sons often studied something new or unusual. Torbin thought her mother must be tall also. Then he saw Her.

The tall and slender former pilot stepped from the doorway of a shop, started to say something to her daughter, and then noticed who she was watching. The dark-haired woman, whom Torbin had known as Lori White, looked up and froze. She grabbed her daughter.

"Let's go, Adrianna," she said as she tried to pull the young girl along with her. The girl tugged back.

"That's him, Mom. That's the General, the hero."

"Come on, move!" The former pilot tried to grab her daughter's arm, but the young girl stepped away.

"I want to say hi!" Adrianna protested. Lori made a successful second attempt, and grabbing her daughter's arm, started to turn away.

"Wait, Lori!" he called out. "Dammit, *stop!*"

"He knows you, Mom," Adrianna declared as Torbin strode up, his sons automatically following him. Lori looked at Torbin; her eyes widened as if in panic. He noticed a scar on her right jaw that showed through her light tan.

"Hey, Lori. You know me. I don't bite,"Torbin said as he stopped a couple of steps away, Tristan and Gage behind him.

"I'm just not ready..." Lori stammered.

"I thought you were dead." Lori avoided his gaze.

"We saw you on TV," Adrianna interjected. "You helped save us all."

"Torbin," Lori began to say. Tears welled up in her eyes.

Just then, a voice sounded from behind Torbin.

"Husband, are you bothering someone again?" It was Aleks. "Sons, what are you doing?"

The well-built and fit shorter woman walked up with a shopping bag in each of her hands, jet black hair tied back in a ponytail.

"The woman knows Dad," volunteered Tristan.

"You are a friend of Torbin?" inquired the former Russian spy.

"Lori helped save us all in Yuma," replied Torbin. Then the memories of that night began to flood in. Human bodies, including children, hung like slabs of beef in the harvester ark alien spacecraft. Screams of injured soldiers, a memory of a young Lieutenant dying on his first mission, followed by a short night of passion with Lori. Over eight years past, yet now it seemed like yesterday. He began to shake. Aleks noticed, and grabbed her husband's hand to reassure him.

"Dearest, that was then. This is now," she offered in a subdued voice.

"My name is Adrianna White," the young girl stated as she presented her hand for a handshake. "I just wanted to meet the General. My Mom said he knew him years ago. I know him as a hero."

"Pleased to meet you, young lady," responded Aleks. "From what Torbin has told me, your mother is a hero as well." She let go of Adrianna's hand and looked at Lori White, who tried to control her tears.

"You're a hero to me too," added Lori's daughter. "I want to be a Banshee someday, a Sister of Steel, like you, Colonel Smirnov."

"Torbin told you about... us?" Lori finally managed to choke out.

"Of course. We have no secrets," replied the spy turned wife and mother.

"He also said you had lost your family, and your... husband."

"Yes, I did. A Squid rock hit my home." Lori straightened her stance as she sought to control her emotions. She then continued.

"After Yuma, I did what I could to fight the Squids. Then I tried to survive." Lori motioned towards her face. "I got this scar. Next had Adrianna."

"Mom took care of me," the daughter explained as she grabbed her mother's hand and squeezed. "My Dad was killed."

Lori jerked a look at her daughter as she heard the comment. Her bottom lip began to quiver a bit as she spoke.

"Lots of people... died. Come on, Adrianna. We have to go."

"Mom..."

"No need to rush off, Lori," Aleks said. "We can have coffee or lunch. A friend of Torbin's..."

"No!" Lori snapped. "Too many memories... and too many dead."

"Why..." Aleks stopped in mid-comment. She looked at Torbin, then back at Adrianna, then at Lori. Then once more at the young girl, examining her before she spoke.

"Dearest husband. Lori. You need to introduce your daughter to her two brothers, Gage and Tristan."

"What?" exclaimed Torbin.

"She has your eyes, your chin," responded Aleks. "I am trained in detailed observation. You have a daughter."

Lori White let out a sob.

"Mom?" questioned Adrianna. "Is that true? You just said you thought my father was dead."

"I didn't know!" Lori blurted. "Then I saw him on the broadcasts after the nuke attack attempt on the Tschaaa Lordship in Key West. I thought it was too late. I saw he had a whole other life, with a wife..." The former USAF Pilot began to cry, and her daughter's eyes began to fill with tears. Out of the blue, Gage and Tristan stepped past their parents and grabbed the hands of the two former strangers.

"Please don't cry," pleaded Gage. "My Mom and Dad will fix it. They fix everything!"

"From the mouth of babes…" began Aleks. Then she stepped forward and hugged Lori as she cried. This was not the first time Aleks had held a fellow human in the throes of grief. Sometimes she had been the one on the receiving end of comfort.

Adrianna looked at Torbin as she spoke. "Dad?"

"I… guess so," answered Torbin. He reached out and took her hand.

"We have some catching up to do."

"Yeah, I guess we do… Dad," Lori replied. Then she hugged him.

"I always wanted to hug my Dad."

The Marine tried not to cry but failed.

The three adults and three children sat at a back table in the *European Café and American Eats* restaurant and cocktail lounge, the same location where the Russian Orthodox christening of Gage and Tristan celebration had occurred years prior. Adrianna sat next to the father she never known, with her two new half-brothers on her other side. Gage and Tristan were smiling as if this was all their doing, this sudden appearance of a sister. Tristan had opined that this was the best way to have a sister, as Mom did not have to carry her in her tummy like they did with him and his brother. No more complaints about another troll. The advanced development and intellect of the two young brothers kept catching their parents off guard. Aleks forgot that they seemed to hear and remember everything.

"After we finish this fine repast, we will have to arrange for you to come with us to our home," stated Aleks.

"No, I can't impose like that," protested Lori. "I'll find a place, a job…"

"You are family; it is no imposition," answered the Russian spy.

"But, how? We are not related," began Lori. "Besides, I have my baggage and troubles that come with me."

"In this new age, post-Great Compromise, family is who we claim as family. I claim you and your daughter as family. Thus, you are. No arguments."

The former USAF pilot looked at Torbin as if to implore support for her position. The now General held up his hands.

"Don't look at me! Once Aleks makes up her mind, I find it best to comply."

"Smart, my husband," agreed Aleks. "Besides, I have a selfish reason, if you agree with it, Lori White. With both Torbin and I having the extreme new responsibilities in running this 'new' military, you can help with my two trolls—I mean sons."

"Please say yes," interrupted Adrianna. "I like the idea of having more family." She looked at Torbin. "And a Dad."

Lori White looked at her daughter, her eyes damp. Gage, nearest to her, patted her arm.

"Please, Mom Two. Come with us. It will all be okay."

Lori hugged Gage, and kissed his forehead. "With that logic, how can I refuse?"

"Good!" exclaimed Aleks. "Now, you and your daughter go freshen up, pick up your vehicle, and meet us back here. Don't change your mind. I am trained in tracking people down."

They all laughed and then Lori and Adrianna went to get their things. Torbin looked at his wife.

"I don't know how you can adjust to this, dearest," stated Torbin. "Your husband suddenly has a long-lost lover and child show up, and you deal with it, organize everyone and everything."

Aleks reached over and kissed him deeply.

"Dearest Torbin, I love you with all my heart. And you love me. Thanks to the Tschaaa harvesting activities, we are short men in the world, with a ratio of women to men at some three to two in most places. Worse in others."

"Jealousy exists..."

"Not here, Torbin. If a certain Russian Senior Training Instructor we know can deal with three wives, and a bunch of children, this Russian-Ukrainian can do the same." She kissed her husband again and then continued.

"We do what we must for family. You have a daughter. I can accept another sister, even a sister wife. Life and our children must go on."

Aleks stood up.

"Time to go. We have a war dog at home to let out."

"Yes, Ma'am," agreed Torbin. "The woman rules the roost."

"Now *three* women," stated the Russian Spy. "And don't you forget it."

Made in the USA
Columbia, SC
15 August 2021